Blood I
Book Two in tl

By Nicola Claire

ISBN-13: 978-1482536836
ISBN-10: 1482536838

nicolaclairebooks.com

Cover Art by LA LA
Image credit: 123RF Stock Photo
Image #12942160 & #24460505

More books by Nicola Claire:

Kindred Series

Kindred
Blood Life Seeker
Forbidden Drink
Giver of Light
Dancing Dragon
Shadow's Light
Entwined With The Dark
Kiss Of The Dragon
Dreaming Of A Blood Red Christmas (Novella)

Mixed Blessing Mystery Series

Mixed Blessing
Dark Shadow (Coming Soon)

Sweet Seduction Series

Sweet Seduction Sacrifice
Sweet Seduction Serenade
Sweet Seduction Shadow
Sweet Seduction Surrender
Sweet Seduction Shield
Sweet Seduction Sabotage
Sweet Seduction Stripped
Sweet Seduction Secrets (Coming Soon)

Elemental Awakening Series

The Tempting Touch Of Fire
The Soothing Scent Of Earth
The Chilling Change Of Air
The Tantalising Taste Of Water (Coming Soon)

H.E.A.T. Series

A Flare Of Heat
A Touch Of Heat
A Twist Of Heat (Novella)
A Lick Of Heat (Coming Soon)

Citizen Saga

Elite
Cardinal
Citizen

Scarlet Suffragette

Fearless
Breathless (Coming Soon)

For my boys:

Thanks for sharing mummy with her vampires.
(And you can't read this until you're a lot older!)

Definitions

Accord – A blood binding agreement, often between two parties of equal power; cannot be broken.

Alliance – A word of honour agreement; has varying degrees of binding, some alliances cannot be broken.

Blood Bond – A binding connection between master and servant, requiring the exchange of blood to seal. It can only be broken by someone more powerful than the master who created it. A blood bond establishes a close relationship between the blood bonded. The master provides safety and protection, the servant offers obedience and loyalty.

Bond – The connection between joined kindred Nosferatu and Nosferatin; reflects the emotional and psychological relationship. Enables both parties to find each other over distance; to perform whatever is required to get to that person, overcoming any obstacle; to direct thoughts to each other; to feed off the life force of each other. It is always an equal exchange.

Command – A directive given by a Master Vampire to one of his line. It requires *Sanguis Vitam* in order to enforce obedience. It cannot be ignored.

Dream Walk – A Nosferatin power, enabling the Nosferatin to appear in a different location. The Dream Walker is invisible, cannot be sensed or smelled, and only heard if they talk when in this realm. They can, however, interact and be harmed. The only exception to a Dream Walker's invisibility is another Nosferatin. Two Dream Walks in a 24 hour period results in prolonged unconsciousness once the Dream Walker returns to their body. A very rare power.

Final death – The true death of a Nosferatu. There can be no survival from the final death.

Glaze – The ability to influence another. It requires direct eye contact and *Sanguis Vitam* to insert the influence. Usually a Nosferatu skill, allowing a vampire to influence a human.

Hapū – (Maori) Tribe; sub-tribe – e.g. the Westside Hapū of Taniwha is the local Auckland sub-tribe of New Zealand Taniwha.

Herald – The Nosferatin who recognises the Prophesy. It is the Herald's responsibility to acknowledge the *Sanguis Vitam Cupitor* and thereby initiate the Prophesy.

Iunctio – (Latin). The Nosferatu connection and governing power. All vampires are connected to one another via this supernatural information exchange highway; enabling sharing of rules, locations of safe havens and hot spots to avoid. It is powered by both Nosferatu and Nosferatin *Sanguis Vitam*, but is operated by the Nosferatu in Paris. There are twelve members of the *Iunctio* council, headed by the Champion. The *Iunctio* is tasked with policing all supernaturals throughout the world.

Joining – The marriage of a kindred Nosferatu with a kindred Nosferatin. Upon joining the Nosferatu will double their *Sanguis Vitam* and the Nosferatin will come into their powers, but for the Nosferatin, their powers will only manifest after reaching maturity; the age of 25. The joining will also make the Nosferatin immortal. A symbiotic relationship, should one member of the joining die, the other will too. Without a joining, the Nosferatin would die one month past their 25th birthday. The joining also increases the power of the *Iunctio* and Nosferatu as a whole.

Kaitiaki – (Maori) New Zealand shape shifter (Taniwha) name for Nosferatin. Meaning protective guardian of people and places.

Kindred – A Nosferatu or Nosferatin sacred match, a suitable partner for a joining. To be a kindred there must exist a connection between the Nosferatu and Nosferatin; only those suitably compatible will be kindred to the other.

Line – The family of a Master Vampire, all members of which have been turned by the master, or accepted via blood bond into the fold.

Master – A Nosferatu with the highest level of *Sanguis Vitam.* There are five levels of Master, from level five – the lowest on the *Sanguis Vitam* scale, to level one – the highest on the *Sanguis Vitam* scale. Only level one Masters can head a line of their own. Some Nosferatu may never become Masters.

Master of the City – A level one Master in control of a territory; a city.

Norm – A human unaware of the supernaturals who walk the Earth. They also do not have any supernatural abilities themselves.

Nosferatin – *(Nosferat–een)* - A vampire hunter by birth. Nosferatin were once of the same ilk as Nosferatu, descendants from the same ancestors, or a God. The Nosferatin broke off and turned towards the Light. Their sole purpose is to bring the Nosferatu back from the Dark, this can include dispatching them, bringing them the final death, when they cannot be saved. They are now a mix of human and Nosferatin genetics.

Nosferatu – A vampire. The Nosferatu turned towards

the Dark, when their kin, the Nosferatin turned towards the Light. They require blood to survive and can be harmed by UV exposure and silver. They do not need to breathe or have a heartbeat. They are considered the undead.

Pull – The Nosferatin sense of evil. Guides a hunter to a Dark vampire; sometimes, but not always a rogue, who is about to feed off an innocent.

Rākaunui – (Maori) Full Moon.

Rogue – A vampire no longer controlled by a master, full of evil and Darkness, feeding indiscriminately and uncontrolled.

Sanguis Vitam – (Latin) The Blood Life or life force of a Nosferatu. It represents the power they possess. There are varying degrees of *Sanguis Vitam.*

Sanguis Vitam Cupitor – (Latin) The Blood Life Seeker. The first part of the Prophesy. The *Sanguis Vitam Cupitor* can sense and find all Dark vampires throughout the world.

Sigillum – (Latin) A permanent mark of possession.

Taniwha – (Maori) New Zealand shape shifter. Dangerous, predatory beings. The Taniwha have an alliance with the Nosferatins.

Turned – The action of changing a human into a vampire.

Vampyre – Old term for vampire; used rarely in modern language.

I am the Light to the Dark.
You call to me as I call to you.
I will always hold you dear.
Prophesy Mantra

Chapter 1
Rome

I could hear the lambs bleating in the fields even before I saw them. Michel knew I liked to hear them. Even if we weren't sharing a bed, he had lately taken great lengths to make sure my dreams were as realistic as possible. Usually, if I was alone in my apartment in my own bed and he was elsewhere when he entered my dreams, the sounds and colours wouldn't have been as bright. But since we joined two weeks ago and then Bonded not long after, it's been easier for him to go for technicolour, surround sound, excellence.

I didn't mind. I loved being back on my parents' farm.

Of course, I hadn't always accepted Michel's presence in my dreams quite so easily. I had resented his hold over me, rebelled against it even. But it's not always easy to fight a Master Vampire and especially the Master of the City. And Michel Durand had been nothing if not persistent in his pursuit of me.

Sometimes, I wonder if what I feel for him is actually real. It feels real, but so much has happened in the past five weeks, I just can't be sure any more.

The breeze was playing with the long pale lilac skirt of my dress, making it flap delicately around my bare ankles, tickling the sensitive skin in the groove below the bone. Another thing Michel liked in my dreams was long dresses, something I don't normally go for. My usual attire is more black mini skirt, tight fitting black Tee and matching black denim jacket to hide the stakes. But Michel for some reason, liked me to appear a little more dainty, I suppose. Not so Gothic. It was an on-going argument, but I wasn't budging. It's hard to stake the evil undead if you're battling wads of material at your feet.

I could feel the soft grass of the paddock I always stood in, in these dreams, beneath my bare feet. I wriggled my toes into the soft earth, getting them dirty, but I didn't care. If I couldn't actually get through to see my folks as often as I would have liked these days and recharge my batteries on the farm like I used to, then these dreams had to suffice. Dirt in my toes just felt like home. Home is where I charged my batteries.

Michel hadn't yet appeared, probably giving me a few moments to soak it all up before he stole my attention. He knew what sort of effect he had on me in these dreams. When he turned up I practically forgot about everything else and would fall into his arms. I'm sure he found it amusing as hell, but he hid it well.

I sat myself down on the grass, smoothing the skirt under me to avoid creases. Habit, it's a dream, the dress is not real, my upbringing however is. The sun felt good against my bare arms and my face and neck. The dress had a low scooped neckline, baring my shoulders and neck to the heat from the sky. I'm sure that was entirely intentional too. Michel loved to smell the sun on my skin. I guess if you have to avoid it as much as possible like he does, you'd tend to miss it too. Often I felt he was living vicariously through me, but I could hardly blame him. Five hundred years of being undead allowed you a few privileges.

I took a deep breath in, trying to smell all the freshness, the farmland around me. I could smell the trees and the paddocks and the sweet smell of silage from further fields. It's an acquired taste, but you get used to it. I think I could almost smell the sun, like Michel does, but I'm not sure. I could however smell the sea. There is no sea where my parents' farm is, it's just south of Hamilton, inland in a small farming community called Cambridge. No sea for miles. So, I knew what or who it was. I turned my head and looked over my shoulder to where the fresh salt sea spray was coming from.

Michel stood a few feet away with his hands in his tight black casual trousers. I didn't know how long he had been standing there, probably a few minutes, just watching. He could have easily hidden his fresh and clean smell from me and only allowed it to enter my mind when he was ready. He controlled these dreams, they were all him.

The sun sparkled against his bare arms, where his black shirt had been rolled up to reveal well toned forearms. The golden cream of his skin glowing under the rays. He's tall, 6'2" and all long lithe legs and beautiful sculptured muscles. Broad in the shoulders, something I have to admit I love, with his dark brown, almost black hair lying free around his handsome and strong lined face, just scraping the tops of his shoulders. He usually wore it clipped back at the base of his neck, but he knew I liked it free, so it was always loose here.

I'd taken my time looking him over, it was always a feast for the eyes when he appeared in my dreams. It's not that he was different as such here, just more. More brilliant. More beautiful. More captivating. More him. He kept his persona well contained in the real world, wore a mask, behaved a certain way. Only those closest to him knew the real Michel. I was just lucky enough to be one of them and even then, sometimes, I think he acted with me. Call me a sceptic, but years of hunting evil undead vampires has not entirely been wiped out by the enthralling presence of Michel in my life.

He gave me one of his most dazzling smiles, his eyes lighting up with their hypnotic blue-with-violet flecks that seemed to pull me in to the deepest part of him. Trapping me, wrapping me up in warmth and light. It's been a long time since Michel could glaze me, I mean really hold me with a vampire glaze, but his eyes still pulled me in, just in a different way now.

"Are you going to join me?" I'd long learned that offence was the best defence as far as vampires were concerned. Never let them see fear, even if it's just fear of falling in love.

"It would be my pleasure, *ma douce*."

Ma douce is his pet name for me, French of course, that's where he's originally from. Although aside from his name, you'd never know it normally, he sounds very English. But here in the dreams I hear it, that slight French lilt, that wonderfully seductive curve to his words.

He sat down next to me in a fluid movement that only the supernatural can perfect, all grace and elegance and something entirely otherworldly. It used to unsettle me, until I found out I'm a little otherworldly too. It kind of changes your perception of the bad guys when you realise you're part of their team.

His hand felt warm when he picked mine up, stroking the back of it in gentle swirls, sending tingles up my arm and down my spine. I sighed, I couldn't help it. Michel just has this effect over me, one that I have little control over and I'm sure one he attempts to manipulate at every opportunity. He raised my hand to his lips and kissed the back lingeringly, his eyes locked with mine. The deep blues fighting for light amongst the mauves and violets creeping in.

We looked at each other for a moment and I swear I could see right inside his soul. A topic I have long been debating, do vampires even have souls? But when I'm with him, it seems so natural that they do, or at least Michel sometimes does to me any way.

He smiled and opened his mouth to say something, but I never heard what delightful thing it might have been, because suddenly I felt my body lurch sideways and then up and away through blackness and the dark nothingness of my mind. I floated for a moment, suspended in that void and then felt my stomach leave me, like on a particularly aggressive roller coaster and then plummeted down towards the unseen ground below.

I opened my eyes to a night time scene. Paved cobblestones at my feet, old stone buildings lit up with strategically placed artificial lighting to show off the striking architecture in a courtyard. The sound of trickling water in amongst murmurs and the laughter of many people. It was warm, but the warmth only made me more aware of what I was, or better said, was *not*, wearing. I was dressed in my slinky deep red satin night dress, a gift from Michel and the one I had been wearing to bed tonight. I had a sudden sinking feeling and it had nothing to do with the roller coaster ride to get here. I was Dream Walking and I hadn't even realised I was doing it.

Dream Walking was a relatively new Nosferatin power I had come into, but since acquiring it four weeks ago I had been in complete control. Sure, the first time I Dream Walked I hadn't realised what I was doing, but since then I had been firmly in the driver's seat. But not tonight it would seem.

I ran my hands down the thin material of my outfit self conscientiously, then realised if I was Dream Walking the people around me couldn't even see me. I was a phantom to them. I could move and touch and hear and smell and even talk to them, but they couldn't see me, nor could any vamp sense me either. It was one of my most useful powers, but certainly not the most impressive. Still, I liked it, but I wasn't so sure about it tonight.

Why had I Dream Walked here? Why here? I looked around to try to get my bearings. There was a large fountain off to the side, lit up with lights, displaying the intricate carved stone statues and building façade behind, all in a pale cream stone. It wasn't just large, it was huge. The statues of people all over the carved rock base were larger than life-size, God sized. The building façade behind, two storeys high. People were sitting around the edges, leaning over backwards and throwing coins over their shoulders into the large pool at the base of the fountain.

I still had no idea where I was.

Until I heard someone talking. A group of young teens walked passed, jabbering away in a foreign language. They didn't look like the tourists that dotted this obviously famous landmark. These looked more like locals, unaffected by the gigantic water feature, not even sparing it a glance. I may not speak Italian, but I can understand the odd phrase. Especially as one of the girls in the group, who had her arm draped over the arm of a boy looking lovingly into his eyes, said *mio caro*. *Mio caro* is not a phrase I warm to lightly.

Italy then, so this mammoth water feature must be the *Trevi Fountain*. I'm not a well travelled person, I'm only 25 and live on a bank teller's salary, but I watch the *Discovery Channel* and love the travel shows. So, even if I didn't recognise the landmark immediately, I could fish it out of the depths of my armchair traveller mind.

So I knew where I was, I just didn't know why.

I really had no idea what to do. I looked around for anything familiar, half expecting Alessandra to pop out from behind a statue in some slinky slutty outfit, but nothing, no one. Alessandra is an Italian vampire, a Master Vampire aligned to Michel. More than that, they have an accord, which basically means they will fight for each other and help each other out whenever required. Unfortunately, I think Alessandra made the accord for different reasons than that. Anything she could do to get her claws into Michel, her *mio caro*, she tried. The woman was determined.

That's why she was the first person I thought of when I realised I was in Italy. And yes, I call vampires people, I've come a long way since I arrived in the city two years ago.

But, no Alessandra, no one I recognised at all, but there was a vampire signature in the air. As soon as I homed in on the *Sanguis Vitam*, or blood life power of that vampire, I felt it. The pull. I call it the evil-lurks-in-my-city pull, but this wasn't my city. So why was I feeling the pull?

I started heading in the direction of that magnetic force like a fish being reeled in on a line. It was instinct, it was what made me a Nosferatin, or vampire hunter by birth. It was part of who I was and undeniable. I could no further have fought that pull than turned into a bat. It called to me like sweet music on the air. A lover's embrace waiting for my body, but there'd be no loving embrace when I got there tonight, it would all be deathly real.

And that's when I realised I didn't have a stake. Not even a silver knife. I don't sleep fully armed, it's just not safe, you could get a knick or two and besides extremely uncomfortable. When I Dream Walk normally, I lay down in my hunter gear, fully armed and ready to go and that's what I appear as in the Dream Walking state. But tonight, I'd been asleep, in my sexy slinky shortie nightie with nothing but my wits to protect me from harm. Crap.

It didn't stop me from running towards the evil stench of vampire on the hunt though, did it? It wouldn't be able to see me, they can't when I Dream Walk and I'd think of something when I got there. I'm clever, I can do this. Besides, if I was feeling the pull, then an innocent was in trouble and I simply could not ignore that even to protect myself from possible pain.

I ran past the tourists milling around that beautiful fountain and on down the cobbled street, barely recognising the sharp stab of loose pebbles on my bare feet. I rounded a corner and felt the humming of *Sanguis Vitam* in my mind reach a crescendo. This was no baby vamp, maybe 300, maybe older. He was pissed off and not hiding it. I doubled over briefly, trying to catch my breath after the onslaught of that powerful signature, staggered slightly, but managed to stay upright. I took a slow deep breath in and centred myself, concentrating on my frantic heart beat. I didn't try to slow it, I just used it as a focus to centre my mind and calm my nerves. It's what I use when I enter the Dream Walking state usually. Of course tonight, nothing was as usual. Still, the heartbeat meditation worked and I felt I could move against that terrible anger-filled power.

Just what was going to appear behind door number three?

I walked steadily towards the pull, the power and the crescendo of noise, all of which were sending little prickles of pain down my skin, like red fire ants on a march. I worked hard on not trying to scratch myself to pieces, but I still failed miserably. I could feel blood under my nails where my skin on my bare arms had been scratched raw, but still I wanted to keep doing it. This vamp meant business and I was unarmed. The first tendrils of fear started to creep in.

I swallowed as I approached the corner of an old slightly dirty brick building, which was on a lean towards the centre of the cobblestoned road. I knew what was behind that corner, I knew I wasn't going to like it and I knew without a doubt that I couldn't walk away. Go the big bad hunter, me.

One last breath to centre myself and I stepped out into the weak glow of a nearby lamplight. I felt the soft spray of its light bathe me as I stood stock still in the centre of its circle. The vampire wouldn't be able to see me, the human wouldn't either, the light was all for me. There's just something about facing your worst fears, light makes it easier, there's just no denying it.

Down the alleyway - it's always an alleyway, somehow they just seem to be drawn to creepy dark dead end places - about three metres away stood a tall man dressed in a long black cloak. It was summer here in Italy, I could tell, because even though it's dark, it was still really warm. So, the cloak alone gave me a hint. Not to mention the ooze of *Sanguis Vitam* pouring all over the alley. His hood was down, so I could see his long black hair, tied back at the nape of his neck. It shone slightly in the residual glow of the street lamp. His head was bent over a smaller figure; male, about 5'8" I should think. Making the vampire well over six feet, he was having to bend significantly to get fang to neck.

I was late, usually I can get there before they bite, but this was not a usual hunt. I wasn't even in my own city for crying out loud. This was so far from usual it wasn't funny. The man being served up for dinner was dark skinned, although I only knew this from his arms, desperately tying to pry the vampire's grip from around his shoulders and chest. His face, in comparison, was deathly pale. The human wasn't succeeding and by the look on his face, he'd been trying for a few minutes. Michel only feeds for about 30 seconds, no longer, but then again, he is a mega Master Vampire. This vamp although powerful, wasn't quite at Michel's league. Still several minutes can mean a death sentence and is not necessary if you're just satisfying hunger. I was guessing this vampire was satisfying a hell of a lot more than just hunger.

What to do? I'm unarmed, but I am strong. Stronger than your average bear, that's me. Just another freaky perk from Nosferatin ancestors and joining with a kindred vampire. But even if I get him off the man, what then? Frighten him off with a growl. Well, it was worth a chance, wasn't it?

I started walking toward the horror scene at the end of the alley. I can't be heard, unless I talk, in this realm, so I wasn't trying to sneak. That's why when I accidentally kicked a pebble into the brick siding of one of the buildings bordering on the alley and it made a loud clattering noise, I didn't jump. But then, why did the human? And why was he now staring at me with big brown, almost black, eyes showing way too much white?

Shit. He was a Nosferatin and I hadn't even noticed. His eyes flicked from me to the vampire and then back again. *Yeah, I got it dude, hang tight I'm coming.*

I jumped at the vampire and tore his grip from the man. Somehow he managed to withdraw his fangs without taking half the guy's neck with him. This vampire was old and had centuries to practice. He spun to face his attacker and stopped. No one there, whoopee for me. I grabbed his arm, which had been hanging out in front of him ready to grab his assailant's neck and threw him against the wall of the alley. The Nosferatin had slumped to the ground with his hand to his throat to try to staunch the blood flow. Blood continues to flow from a vampire bite unless they lick it, something in their saliva coagulates the blood. But this vamp hadn't had the time nor the desire to be so kind, so the blood flow was still pretty impressive.

The vamp's head pounded into the brick wall causing a dent. Bricks don't normally dent, but then neither do vampire heads unless you use something sharp, preferably silver coated. In the world of physics I'd just discovered a new substance stronger than concrete, yippee. He didn't stay still for long but rounded on me in a flash. I'm not a novice, I've been hunting for two years now and picked up a few tricks along the way, especially play fighting with my best friend Rick's shaper shifter Hapū, so when he turned I had already moved up beside him. My knee hit his groin and when he doubled over I gripped both my fists together and brought them down hard on his neck. He stumbled to the ground landing flat on his stomach.

I didn't waste time, I jumped on his back, with my legs around his arms and chest and gripped his long hair in one hand twisting his head to the side and grinding his face into the cobble-stoned ground as hard as I could. He tried to buck and nearly succeeded in dismounting me. I'm not heavy, I'm a little person. Only 5'4" and trim and fit. I'm a box of tissues to a vampire, they wouldn't bust a gut lifting me one-handed that's for sure. But my grip on his head was enough to keep him down for now. That wouldn't last too long though.

"Where's your stake?" I asked the Nosferatin without shifting my gaze from the vampire beneath me.

"*Che*?"

"Your stake?" I mimed stabbing with my free hand, you know, the Norman Bates look: ee ee ee!

"Oh, *Vampiro gioco*. It is gone, he throw it away." His English was not perfect, but I got the gist of it.

"Spare? Do you carry an extra one?" I always carry two stakes when I hunt, plus a silver knife as back up, you can never be too careful.

"No. No spare. Nothing."

You have got to be joking. Maybe European Nosferatin had it easier than the antipodes, but still, no spare? What an idiot. And now what? I'm sitting on 110 kilos of super strong and buff vampire arse, without a stake. We're just dinner waiting to be served.

"You are unarmed, Hunter. What now?"

The vampire's voice was low and even, smooth like a hot chocolate drink, dripping in sweetness and marshmallows. Something you just wanted to devour but knew you shouldn't. He had a hint of an English accent, laced with something else, something older, but I couldn't tell what. Not many vamps can capture me with their voices any more, nor their gaze, just the powerful ones. They *can* still glaze me if I'm not careful or I'm injured and by the judge of my increased heart rate, this vamp wasn't having any trouble coating me with his voice right now. Damn.

"What's an old chap like you doing slumming it for your meal? A bit *Bela Lugosi* isn't it?" I asked between clenched teeth.

He laughed at that, actually laughed. Here he is with his face in the dirt, an invisible entity sitting on his back managing to hold his arms against his sides and he laughed. Comfortable bastard wasn't he?

"Your accent is unmistakable, Hunter. You are a long way from home. And as I cannot see you or sense you, I am picking you are Dream Walking. Not a common Nosferatin trait. The *Iunctio* will enjoy this piece of information."

Shit. The *Iunctio* was the vampire equivalent of the Net, but all telepathic and supernatural. All vampires could connect to it, download the latest information; where it's safe and where it's hot, or find out what the rules are for any given city. It's the power that keeps the vampires in line, protects the humans from mass hunting and genocide, and offers a great gossip network when required. It's run on both Nosferatu and Nosferatin power, but controlled by the Nosferatu, somewhere in Paris I think. Basically, it's the eyes, ears and head honcho of the vampire world. Michel and I had been trying to keep my new powers from the *Iunctio* since the get go. This vamp wasn't the first to threaten my exposure. The others are no longer alive.

"Shame you wont be around to tell them then, isn't it?" I replied coolly.

His responding laugh was warm and comforting, it wrapped around me like a familiar coat, snuggled in against my cheek and neck and ran it's fingers down my spine.

"Cut that out!" I said as I banged his head against the ground.

He stopped laughing, but his chest was still moving, little rumbles rolling across his shoulders. It was doing nothing for my equilibrium, let alone my pulse. What was with this guy?

Suddenly I was airborne, the vampire had jumped to his feet in a smooth glide, like he had been lifted up by puppet strings. He spun around before my feet even touched the ground and thrust his hand out towards my neck. I don't know how he managed it, he couldn't see me, he couldn't sense me, but somehow he managed to grasp my neck.

And he had no intention of letting go.

Chapter 2
Deal

"You know, I think I can smell you." The vampire's face was against my neck, under my hair, his nose resting on my skin. My hair is straight and shoulder length and I don't normally wear it tied back, but as I was in my nightwear it was a bit bed head messy.

He ran his free hand through my hair, softly, gently, a complete contrast to his firm grip at my throat. My heart was hammering like a jack rabbit, I could hear my pulse thumping in my head. I couldn't swallow and could hardly breathe. I'd been in tighter situations before, but somehow they all seemed to pale to this.

"You smell of sunshine and candied apples, spring and honey. I can almost taste you."

And then he did just that. His tongue lapped at my ear, the soft skin behind my lobe. His hot breath making my body shiver where it touched the wet trail of his mouth.

"You are a delight. I shall enjoy meeting you in person. Michel has done well for himself."

Whoa. Back up the trolley. "You know Michel?" I croaked.

His grip lessened slightly, as though he had no intention of hurting me, killing me, feeding from me. As though he hadn't realised he was hurting me at all.

"An old friend, you could say." His face hadn't left my neck when he spoke. I guess if he couldn't make eye contact with me, there was no point. He seemed to be enjoying himself snuggling up against my side though, smelling me, breathing on me. A shiver ran down my spine.

"Do I affect you, Hunter? Do I send shivers down your

spine? Would you like the feel of me against you, flesh on flesh? I can smell your fear, but I can also smell your desire. You are a quandary, aren't you?"

"I'm cold, that's all." I knew he couldn't really smell me, I was Dream Walking, vampires couldn't sense me in this realm. Or at least I hoped that was the case with this one. He seemed so sure of himself.

His hand ran down my sides, feeling the satin material of my nightdress, running it through his fingers until he found the very short hem. He then traced his hand up over my stomach, past my breasts, found my thin straps, one of which had fallen off my shoulder, half way down my arm, exposing way too much flesh. His hand lingered over the exposed skin, not touching but so close I could feel his warmth.

"I feel your heat, Hunter, I smell you. I have never wanted to see something which is not there so much before. Do you always hunt in lingerie? Tell me, what colour is it?" His voice had lowered to a husky whisper on that last question.

"Go to hell!"

"I'm already there." He chuckled then, as though it was a private joke and pulled back from me, allowing himself to really get going with the laugh. It rocked through his body and down his arm to my neck, shaking me against the brick wall.

I could see him clearly for the first time. His black hair had come loose at the base and now framed his face, hanging loosely over the black cape. Underneath the cloak he wore a tux; modern, elegant, expensive. This was no run of your mill vampire, this was a Master with some class.

What the hell was he doing in an alley with a Nosferatin by the fang?

He opened his eyes finally and I was blinded by the most brilliant shades of grey. Silver streaked with platinum, hints of deep granite in the mix. They weren't a flat colour either, but bright and clear and shining, undulating and swirling. Hypnotic. The eyes were why I had not noticed his scar at first, but now I could see it. A ragged cut from his right eyebrow down his temple and cheek, maybe 8-10 centimetres in length. Something had nearly taken his eye when he was still human, before he had been turned.

I reached up and traced it. I don't know why, it just seemed to call to me. He stilled, vampire still, that preternatural calm; no breathing, no heartbeat, nothing, but didn't pull away.

"How did you get it?" I asked quietly.

He had an odd look on his face, puzzled, as though he couldn't quite figure me out. I didn't blame him, I should have been a blubbering mess, but somehow I knew that this vampire did not want to kill me. The evil that I had felt before was gone. How he could turn it off like a faucet I didn't know. I'd felt the evil when I entered the alley, but now it was simply no longer there.

"A gift from an admirer." His voice was low, soft, it ran along my arms and curled around my shoulders, pulling me closer. I could feel myself actually leaning in to him, against his grasp. He weakened his hold slightly, bending his elbow a little more, allowing me to come closer. He would have been able to feel my breath against his skin, his mouth. I studied his face, he eyes, his smooth cream coloured skin, his scar. He was beautiful, but aren't they all?

“You're stunning. Your eyes are amazing,” I said, with a little awe, chiding myself immediately for the telling tone.

He pulled back and shook his head, a small smile edging his full lips.

“What are you, Hunter? A temptress, I have no doubt, but there is more to you, is there not?”

“I'm a kindred Nosferatin joined to the Master of Auckland City. Isn't that my official title? The one you guys always want to hear?”

His smile hadn't wavered, he couldn't see me, so focusing on me was difficult, but I think I had killed the moment for him and he no longer wanted to go in for a sniff. He glanced over his shoulder at the Nosferatin man, still on the ground, hand to throat, eyes now shut. He was pale, but I could still see his chest rising and falling. He was still alive.

“I am afraid I got carried away, Hunter. Nosferatin blood calls to me. I find it difficult to stop when I lower my guard. I had not meant to hurt him so.”

Huh? Confessions of a blood addict. Who would have thought.

“You know the rules, vampire, no feeding on the unwilling.” I crossed my arms over my chest. He wouldn't have seen it, the move was lost on him, but it made me feel better.

“The name is Gregor and he was willing. At least at first.”

He released my neck then, which was more of a surprise than the sudden pain of swallowing without hindrance. I've felt *that* before. It's not the first time I've had my throat almost crushed by a vampire. Hell it's not the second or third either, they seem to have a fixation with necks. I wonder why? However, it was the first time a vampire had let me go that I had been intending to kill. But then, there's the thing, I had no intention of killing him now. Which was strange, he had broken the law, the rules set by the *Iunctio.* Even if the Nosferatin had been willing, Gregor had taken it too far. He should have stopped.

I rubbed at my neck while I studied him. He stood still, looking at the fallen Nosferatin with a slight sadness to his eyes.

"You know I should still kill you for this," I said softly.

He turned towards the sound of my voice and smiled a slightly wicked smile. Somehow vampires can master that look so well.

"But you won't tonight will you, Hunter?"

"No."

There was no point denying it, I was still unarmed. And he was, I realised now, a very powerful Master Vampire. He had been containing his *Sanguis Vitam* well, but I could feel it now, he was way older than the 300 years I had at first thought. But by how much I couldn't be sure and besides, something was telling me this bad boy wasn't all bad. And if there is one thing I have noticed from my recent discovery of Nosferatin skills, bringing the vampires towards the Light is the most prevalent of our desires. It's what rules us, what makes us tick. If the vampire can be saved, we just want to do it. I didn't want to kill this man.

"Maybe, I shall be careful what I tell the *Iunctio* after all, Little Hunter."

"Deal," I replied instantly.

He hadn't actually offered me one, but if I could let him go without a rap across the knuckles, he could keep my secret a little longer. Fair was only fair after all.

He smiled and took a step backwards, his cape swirling about his long legs. He gave a little bow, similar to those I had seen Michel give to other vampires of equal standing, hand fisted across chest and said, "Until we meet in person, Little Hunter. It has been....intriguing."

With that he shot up in the sky and simply disappeared. I couldn't see where he had gone, or if he had just vanished into thin air.

I let the breath I had been holding out slowly and then turned towards the Nosferatin on the ground. He was still conscious, but had lost a lot of blood. I grabbed the edge of his T-Shirt and ripped a strip of cloth off, then padded it into a ball to press against his neck. His eyes flicked open and he looked at me.

"You like angel come save me. How you know to come?"

I smiled at him, I wasn't going to let him know I hadn't controlled this Dream Walk. I certainly wasn't going to let him know I had the ability to home in on any Nosferatu throughout the world. That little secret was still all mine, but I did say, "Female intuition, I guess."

He smiled blankly at me.

"What's your name, soldier?" I asked.

"Marco."

"Hi Marco, I'm Luce. Have you joined yet?"

"No, not yet. I not found a kindred. I think maybe this vampire tonight be right."

I laughed, it sounded harsh even to my ears, as if I'd seen too much of the world already, way too much for my 25 years.

“I don't think Gregor is the joining type. How long have you got?”

“I am just 24, one year left.” *One year left*, yeah it sounds pretty fatal doesn't it and it is. A death sentence hanging over your head unless you join with the creatures of the night, those creatures you are born to hunt.

“Have you found the website?” I asked him.

He looked at me blankly and shook his head. The website is the site that saved my sanity. It's run by Nero, an Egyptian Nosferatin who is close to 500 years old and my trainer. I found the website by surfing and searching the net and then getting a friend of mine from the our local shape shifter Hapū to hack it. It's a place my kind can go to get answers, to find kin like us. It led me to Nero and I don't know where I would be now if not for him.

I told Marco the website address and latest password. “Try it out, the guys will be able to help you. What about now, how are we going to get you home?”

The bleeding had stopped on his neck, so he didn't need two hands any more to staunch the flow. He reached into his pocket and pulled out a cellphone, flipped it open and pressed a button. A few short words in Italian into the mouthpiece when it was answered and it was set. His friends would come for him.

“I'll wait with you,” I said as I sat down on the ground next to him.

He had propped himself up against the brick wall of the alley, a little colour had begun to come back into his face.

He'd be all right. I just hoped he didn't throw himself at too many stranger fangers in the near future. You should always try to get to know your date first. Of course, with vampires, that can be a little tricky. They are a secretive lot.

"Where you come from? And why you dressed in night wear?" Marco's gaze had lowered from my face and was brushing the length of me slowly, as only an Italian can do. Somehow managing to undress you with a glance. Not that it would have taken much tonight, I was practically naked in this thing.

I sighed and leaned my head back on the wall behind me, keeping my eyes on the leering Nosferatin. "I can Dream Walk, it's one of my talents. *This*, is what I was asleep in when I heard the call."

Marco looked suitably impressed and then just as quickly puzzled. "You don't think a stake be good idea when Dream Walk?" he asked.

I laughed. "Yeah a stake would be a bloody good idea, Marco, a bloody good idea indeed." Just how was I to take a stake with me when my Dream Walks happened unexpectedly like tonight, I didn't know. Sleeping with a very sharp weapon in my bed was a little unnerving. I guess I was going to have to divulge my little dark secret to Michel and Nero to get some answers.

When I turned 25 I came into some of my powers, or more accurately some more of my powers. I had already come into several before I joined, which was well before my birthday. But on the day of my 25th birthday and at the exact time of day that I had been born, I came into a woozy of a power. I could sense all the Nosferatu in the world. Like I was drawn to their *Sanguis Vitam*, like it called to me. This latest Dream Walk could only have been the product of this new power. But, and here's the clincher, I haven't told any one about the power yet. It kind of scared me. And to be honest, when I saw the look on Michel's face when all that power came pouring into me, I wasn't quite sure what he would do with the knowledge of my newest talent, so I hid it. I said I had only received the increased strength and speed, heightened senses and such on my birthday. It's not unheard of, most Nosferatin powers come to them over the course of a couple of months after their 25th birthday, so I think he believed me. I think.

But now, I was going to have to 'fess up and I could just imagine how that conversation was going to play out. Michel did not like being left in the dark. Metaphorically speaking of course.

"How are you feeling now?" I turned my troubled thoughts back to the young guy in front of me.

"Better, Luce. Thank you for coming. I think he would not stopped."

"No. I don't think so either. Did you really go willingly with him, or did he glaze you?"

He looked a little embarrassed then. I couldn't blame him, things had gone so *not* how he had imagined. I would have been embarrassed too. Letting a vampire bite you willingly is not something to be proud of in Nosferatin circles. Unless they are your kindred. I still had trouble letting Michel bite me and we were joined and Bonded, practically married in the vampire world.

"He well known in city. He *Iunctio* here. I did no think he would lost control so."

"What? He is the *Iunctio.* What does that mean,

Marco?" I suddenly had that sinking feeling in the pit of my stomach. The one that tells you you've been duped and you're about to pay for your naivety.

Marco looked at me innocently, all open faced and young looking suddenly. He didn't understand the tone of my voice, the feeling of fear that had crept into my words.

"He on *Iunctio*. He one of the Masters who run it. On their Council. He is the word of law in Europe. You not heard of him?"

No. I hadn't. But I was sure I knew someone who did.

Before I could ask another question a couple of youths entered the alleyway and ran towards us. I stiffened, but Marco called out hello, so he knew them. This was his ride.

They couldn't see me, not Nosferatin. So I quietly said good bye to Marco, squeezed his hand and let myself drift off to that nothingness, that space that allowed me to Walk back to my body.

The first thing I registered, was arms around me, cradling me, rocking me and soft words in my ear.

"*Je suis ici, ma douce cherie. Venez à moi.*"

Chapter 3
Secrets

"I'm here, Michel."

Michel's arms pulled me closer, almost crushing me to his chest. He kissed my head through my messy bed-head hair and left his mouth against my skin, breathing me in. He didn't say anything, which in itself was a bit unnerving. Michel when he's shouting can be frightful, but when he's quiet and angry, which I was betting he really was right now, he is downright spooky.

I cleared my throat. Me nervous? Nah. "Why are you here?"

We had agreed to let me have some nights to myself, last night was one of them. If Michel had his way, I would be living with him at his quarters beneath his club *Sensations*, but I needed to have *me* time. My apartment was my sanctuary. Michel visited here, of course, but he rarely stayed and even if he did, he was gone before dawn. My place is not light-tight like his chamber at *Sensations*, it doesn't suit his needs. Well, his light-sensitive needs anyway.

"You disappeared on me, my dear. Left me stranded in your dream. I naturally wished to make sure you were OK."

Oh boy. We'd already made it to *my dear*. Michel had a tendency to call me *ma douce,* which means *my sweet one* in French, when he was happy, or sometimes even *ma belle* or *ma petite lumière.* But in public or when he was angry it was *my dear* and then finally, when he was really getting going, *Lucinda*. I could always gauge how things were heating up by what name he called me by.

"It wasn't on purpose," I answered a little sullenly.

He tensed. "What do you mean?"

I pushed away from him, so I could get a look at his eyes. Another indication of how Michel's mood was going were his eyes. If they were still deep blue with indigo swirls, I was OK. But if any violet or amethyst had crept in, then things weren't looking good. And if there was magenta hiding in their midst, then hold on tight we're in for a rough ride.

Still blue. Still good.

I took a deep breath in, I guess it's now or never. "I got pulled into a Dream Walk."

Michel's head cocked to the side, his eyebrow delicately raised. He could make looking puzzled an art form.

"Is there something you have not been telling me, Lucinda?"

And there you have it. *Lucinda*. Crap. Things were going down hill fast.

"Why would you say that?" I'm not stupid, he was fishing, but to be fishing he must have thought there was a chance of catching something. Just how much had he suspected I had kept from him on my birthday?

He ran a hand through his hair. A movement that most people would never see Michel Durand do. He just never lost control like that, but with me? Let's just say, I've seen that gesture a lot over the past few weeks.

"*Ma douce*. You are my kindred Nosferatin. Do you really believe I would not know when you are being secretive?"

I held my breath, he just looked a little sad.

"I had hoped you would feel comfortable to come to me in time, tell me what you had chosen to hide, when you were ready. But this," - he indicated my dishevelled self and scratched up forearms with the sweep of his Armani suit clad arm - "is not something you should hide from me. Tell me *ma douce*, what has got you so scared you cannot share?"

How is it that Michel could read me so well? Oh, that's right, he can sense my emotions. A perk from our joining. You don't realise how many emotions you feel during the course of a day. Michel had forgotten, vampires don't have the plethora of emotions humans do and he'd been a member of that undead club for over 500 years, so when he first started sensing my emotions, he had suffered. I manage to keep them in check most of the time, but I am human, well mostly, emotions are what makes us what we are. Nero had once told me, my emotions, or the fact that Michel could sense them, was what would make him turn towards the Light. I was doubtful sometimes, but hopeful. Always hopeful.

I bit my lower lip. How to tell him? The thing is, I *was* scared. I had seen it in Michel's eyes when the power came flooding into me. A greed. A sense of triumph. It was not a look I had been prepared for. What would he do with all this power we now shared? He had more than doubled his in the joining, something that had been unheard of in the past, but there was just something not quite normal about Michel and me. And for the life of me, I couldn't stop being fearful of what that might mean.

But, if my powers were taking me on Dream Walks in my sleep and I was not prepared for where they were going, then this was dangerous, even by my standards. I'm a vampire hunter, I court danger on a regular basis, but I'm usually armed. I needed help with this and Michel, as much as I feared what power would mean to him, did care for me, maybe even loved me, I'm not sure. He is a consummate actor.

He reached over and took my hand in his, rubbing the back of it softly with his thumb. Encouraging me. Comforting me. Well, it was now or never.

"I can sense all the Nosferatu throughout the world. If I concentrate, I can feel their *Sanguis Vitam*, the level of evil or Dark within each. Where they are, what they are doing. It's like a glowing map inside my head, beacons of light flashing, fighting for my attention. I try to block it out and mostly that works, but when I sleep..." I stopped there, he could make out the rest and besides, I'd kind of lost my voice by then.

I didn't move, I couldn't bring myself to look into those eyes. Would there be something I didn't want to see? I think I had seen enough - for one lifetime - emotions in that face that weren't what I wanted to see, I just couldn't bring myself to look any more.

He pulled me towards him and wrapped me in an embrace, kissed my forehead and put his hand on my head, in my hair, pushing my cheek against his chest. Warmth surrounded me. The beating of his heart, the rise and fall of his chest. It was all so steady, so normal. He seemed relaxed.

"I will not ask why you did not tell me this sooner, *ma douce*. You have your reasons. I will ask this though, what has Nero advised?"

What it must have taken for Michel to ask me that. He did not trust Nero, he saw him as competition for my affections. He did have a point. Nero was one of a kind and I readily admit, I struggled to remain in control of myself when in his presence. But, he has only ever been a gentleman. Sure, the odd look, the odd flirtatious remark, but nothing more. And since we helped him and his kindred vampire Nafrini against some rather nasty vampires hell bent on stealing one of their immature Nosferatins recently, he has been my Nosferatin trainer. Nothing more.

I kind of fell into this lifestyle. I didn't know what I was when I came to Auckland two years ago. My first encounter with a vampire had been a shock and a near miss. And after that, I had to make my own way with the bizarre vampire hunter skills that had suddenly developed. I researched on line and found the website, the one Nero runs, but I never found out what I was, what my heritage was, until just recently, when Michel was forced to divulge.

I don't think he would have told me quite so soon, he probably would have continued to try to woo me into his bed and into a joining without ever letting me know what I was. But an evil vampire by the name of Max came calling and spilled the beans. Michel didn't have much choice then, he had to tell me, he had to open up. Nero had only ever given me glimpses of my life, he was too concerned with keeping us hidden from prying eyes, safe from those vampires who wanted us dead. It wasn't until he and Nafrini needed our help, that he started filling in the gaps too. Now, he's progressed to my teacher, helping me hone my skills and come to terms with what I am.

Michel is jealous of that relationship. He would rather I

had nothing to do with Nero at all. I understand, but I won't stop seeing him. I don't have any Nosferatin family here in New Zealand. My parents are actually my Aunt and Uncle, not of Nosferatin blood. My father, who was of Nosferatin blood, died in a car accident with my mother when I was just a baby. I don't know my father's extended family. Nero is my Nosferatin family now.

"I haven't told him," I finally answered.

He tried to hide it, but I could feel Michel's body relax, just slightly, just a fraction. If I hadn't have been wrapped in his arms I don't think I would have noticed.

"Do you think it may happen again, *ma douce*?"

I sighed. "This was the first time it has made me Dream Walk when asleep. Usually, it just wakes me up and I'm aware of evil somewhere on the planet doing something not so nice and I can do nothing about it." I shuddered involuntarily then.

Michel stroked my back. "I am sorry, *ma douce*. I had not noticed, you have hidden it well."

I hadn't hidden it for him, I'd hidden it for me. I was scared that he'd find a way to use this power, this talent. I was scared he'd find a way to use me. I really wasn't giving this relationship the attention it deserved. I'd practically signed it's death warrant before it had even begun. Why? Because he's a vampire. Why else?

I pulled away then and looked at him. "What could you have done? What can anyone do? I don't know what to do with this knowledge, Michel. I don't know how to stop being sucked into the evil that invades this world. I thought I had enough right here in Auckland to contend with, but now it seems I have to take on the world too. I don't know if I can do this. It's picked the wrong Nosferatin. I'm not strong enough for this." My voice had got quieter and quieter, until it was just a hushed whisper, barely heard.

"You are the strongest, most capable human I have ever met. Do not ever forget that, *ma douce*. Do not."

His hand touched my cheek, rested at my jaw, his thumb stroking slowly over my skin. When I chanced a look into his eyes I noticed a swirl of amethyst in the blue. Did it scare me? No. It made my breath catch, my heart beat faster, but not out of fear. He looked at me with such tenderness. I will admit, there are times when I forget he's a vampire. When I forget that I should be careful, should not trust. There are times when I simply don't care. All that matters is him and me. Nothing else.

He brushed his lips against my mouth softly, almost chastely. He paused, ran a hand through my hair, rested it at the back of my neck, so warm, so soft, then bent his head again and kissed me more deeply.

It never seemed to take long for Michel and I to get close, to melt into the heat of each other. If only my body would be as cautious as my head, I'd be OK. But it isn't, not by a long shot, where Michel is concerned.

He smelt divine. A beautiful fresh smell of wild flowers and freshly cut grass in the meadow at home on the farm, laced with a soft scent of the sea. The two would not normally exist together, but with Michel they just seemed right. Comforting. Clean. Home.

I pulled back reluctantly, he needed to know everything. The fact that I had Dream Walked unintentionally was only part of the problem. Gregor was a concern

He looked at me with slight surprise. I don't often pull away from his embrace any more. I may have, in the beginning, but not now. My body called for him on so many levels. I was truly undone by this man. But, he needed to know.

"I ended up in Rome just now, near the *Trevi Fountain*. My pull had taken me to a Nosferatin about to be killed by a vampire."

Michel's eyebrows rose. He was intrigued.

"His name was Gregor." I went to say something else, but Michel had stilled, so still, vampire still. Uh-oh.

I took a deep breath in, it might be the last I get for a while, by the looks of the deep amethyst and violet now swirling around in his eyes.

"He has silver or grey eyes and a scar on the right side of his face, from his eye down his cheek." I showed where the scar was on me. Michel had practically turned to stone.

"The Nosferatin said he was the *Iunctio* in their area. Their law. The vampire knew who I was and what I was and that I was your kindred Nosferatin."

I stopped there, his stillness was beginning to creep me out. I mean, he did it from time to time and I am kind of used to it, but when it went on like this and you were talking to him, you couldn't help feeling he was somewhere else, not listening, not here. And you were just talking to a statue. It was spooky and unnerving and just not right.

"Did you stake him?" Even, low, nothing else.

But whew, he was breathing again. Still though, very still.

"No. I didn't have any of my stakes and the Nosferatin had lost his."

Whoa. And there was the magenta, full blown, like a strobe light from his eyes. It bathed the room in its glow, bouncing off the bed, the desk with my laptop on it in the corner, my bedside table and me. The room was a friggin' purple puddle.

"What's wrong, Michel?" My voice was tiny, thin, his *Sanguis Vitam* had all but filled the room, there was no air to breathe. His power didn't normally have any effect over me, since we had joined. Well only if I have my shields up that is. I checked them now, they were up, so what he must have been expending was unfathomable. Why was he so scared?

Because, that's what I was feeling right now, not anger, not even frustration, but outright fear. Huh.

"He said he was a old friend of yours. Michel, what's wrong?"

"He is no longer a friend. He is the Enforcer for the *Iunctio*. He is their *guillotine*."

Chapter 4
The *Iunctio*

He stood abruptly then and began to pace. Yes, vampires pace, but only when they are *really* having a bad day. I think I've seen Michel pace only once. This was a new enough movement to make me blink in shock.

"First things first, *ma douce*. Where was your stake?"

"I don't sleep with a stake. When I Dream Walk, I lie down in my hunter gear and that's how I appear in my Dream Walk. This time I was asleep, in this." I indicated my slinky nightdress.

He glanced at me, took in what I was wearing, then let out a long breath and a soft, but firm cuss.

"You will have to sleep with a stake from now on."

"I can't sleep with a stake, it'll be uncomfortable, I'll scratch myself."

"Find a way! Is it not better to be uncomfortable or would you prefer dead? This is not a game, Lucinda. You need to be able to protect yourself. I do not know what is going on here, but I do not like it. Your first non-controlled Dream Walk and you happen to meet the Enforcer. This is no mere coincidence."

Oh shit. And now I was scared too. I hadn't even considered that this had anything to do with Gregor directly, other than the fact that he was about to kill a Nosferatin. What if he had engineered it? What if somehow my loss of control of Dream Walking was due to manipulation? Shit.

Michel sensed my fear, he came to me and sat down on the bed at my side, reaching up to pull me to him.

"I am sorry, *ma douce*. I do not mean to frighten you,

but I am frightened."

Oh my God. Michel was never frightened. Not really. Sure he has worried over me getting hurt when I hunt, when I Dream Walk and he can't help me. I put it down to just his need to protect me, nothing more. Annoying, but not unbelievable. But, to say he was frightened. I didn't quite know how to handle that.

He sighed against me, his breath warm on my neck. "Gregor *was* a good friend. We were inseparable. We did everything together." His voice was low, soft, almost too quiet. "He is a complicated man, he has such... anger in him. Regret for a life lost, disgust at what he has become. When I met him, he was a hedonist, I did not recognise the anger for what it was. He was fun to be with, life to him was one big party, as they say. I am not proud of all I did when with Gregor, but it was intoxicating. To a vampyre there can be no greater love than the pursuit of our own desires." He took another breath in, as if telling me this about himself, could be his undoing. Could be the one thing that makes me turn away.

I didn't comfort him. What could I say? I knew he had a life before me, before New Zealand, but I also wasn't sure I wanted to know about it.

"When I chose to leave Paris and come here, we fell out. Gregor could not understand why I would move to such a place, why I would give up what we had."

I knew Michel had lived in Paris before he came to New Zealand, Nero's Nafrini had hinted at that, but I did not know what he had done there, what he had been. Somehow I thought it might be important now.

"What were you in Paris? What did you do?"

I could feel his smile against my skin, his lips were still resting on my neck, his head on my shoulder. I was betting it was a rueful smile, not a happy one.

"You can read me well, *ma douce*, can you not? I worked for the *Iunctio*, I was the Creator. I set the rules."

"So, one of the good guys?"

He pulled away and looked at me, a look of sadness on the edges of his eyes.

"There are no *good guys* on the *Iunctio, ma douce*. They are law. And law is never nice."

He stood again and started pacing. I got the feeling he didn't want to touch me right then. I tried not to be hurt by that, I think it was more because he believed I would not want to touch him.

"When I left for New Zealand Gregor cut off all contact. I have not heard from him since." He sighed and turned to look at me. "Just because he was once a friend, do not underestimate him, *ma douce*. He is ruthless, especially when he sets his sights on something. I fear he may have set his sights on you."

"Why? Because of you? Could it not just be a coincidence he appeared in my Dream Walk? Does it have to be something to fear? This is my power after all, maybe it is the power trying to tell me something."

Michel smiled, it wasn't unpleasant, just a bit condescending I think. "You always look for the Light, Lucinda, when there is often only Dark."

I got up off the bed then and went to him. He didn't take me in his arms, just stood there, his hands fisted slightly at his sides, his eyes edged with sadness. He may think the world is full of Darkness, but I know otherwise. I know better. I am the Light, that's what my name means and somehow, I don't think my father chose that name just for how it sounds. I never knew my father, but part of me believes he knew what I was to become.

I reached up and touched his face, my palm against his cheek. He hesitated, then leaned his head into me, closing his eyes, rubbing against my hand like a cat, smelling my scent at my wrist. Sometimes, he was more wolf than a werewolf was.

"There may be Darkness out there, Michel, but I only know how to spread Light. Look at me when the Darkness comes and I will light your way."

His eyes opened and he stared at me, the deep dark pools of blue pulling me in.

"You are more than you appear, *ma douce*. Every day I see it, yet I cannot believe it. I could not bear to lose you."

I smiled. "If I'm lost, you'll be lost too." In this case, lost was a euphemism for dead. If either Michel dies or I die, the other of our joining will too. The joining is symbiotic in nature. We will always be together, only death will part us now.

He sighed, again, he seemed to be doing a lot of that lately, and said, "There are more ways to be lost than simply death, *ma belle*."

I didn't think I liked the sound of that.

He kissed me lightly on the lips, the cheek, the forehead, pulled me close and held me for a moment. Then bent down to my ear and said, "*Je t'aime, ma petite lumière*. Dawn approaches, I must go."

Before I could even voice an argument to that, he was gone. No blur, no flicker, simply gone and the room was left smelling of a sea breeze on a late summer evening. The light of the sun could be felt, but not quite seen, as it breached the horizon.

I rubbed my bare arms, suddenly feeling cold. I didn't think the temperature had dropped, it was more an internal thing, this cold. I looked at my bed. I couldn't go back to sleep. I couldn't risk being sucked into another Dream Walk. If I Dream Walk twice in one night, I'm out for the count for a week. Well, maybe less now that I have turned 25, but it would be several days and I just couldn't risk that.

It was early, just after half past six according to my bedside clock. Might as well get up and embrace the day. I took a quick shower and changed and was just switching the coffee machine on when the phone rang. No one usually rings at this hour. Hmm.

I picked it up while the smell of freshly ground coffee beans permeated the air. I was going for an Arabica bean this morning, something with a bit of zing.

"Hello."

"Luce, it's Celeste." Celeste is a Taniwha, one of Rick's Hapū and his fiancée to boot. I like Celeste, we've always got on and much more so since she and Rick became an item. Before then she was friendly, but distant. I had put it down to the fact that I was an outsider, not one of the Hapū, but now I realise she had just been jealous of my friendship with Rick. She's got him now, so I'm no longer competition. Besides, Rick and I haven't been seeing as much of each other as we used to. I no longer monopolise his time.

"Hey you, what's up?" I asked.

I could hear her taking a deep breath in on the other

end of the line. Fortifying herself it would seem. "It's Rick, Luce. I need your help."

My stomach felt like it had just dropped to my feet. I may not be seeing that much of Rick right now, but he has been my best friend since I came to Auckland. I would hate for him to be in trouble, or worse, hurt.

"What's happened, Celeste? Tell me."

I realised then she was crying, I could hear it in the catch of her breath, the roughness of the whisper. She was trying to hold it in, smother it, but it was there, raw, waiting to be released.

"Celeste? You're worrying me. What's wrong?"

"He's been so angry lately. So not my Rick. I didn't know who to turn to, Luce. I didn't know what else to do. He'll listen to you"

"It's all right, Celeste, you've come to me now, we'll sort it out together. Why's he angry? What's happened?"

Rick may be a shape shifter, and shape shifters have mighty fine tempers, but he's more of a hugable Taniwha than most. He's big and athletic and strong, built like a pro wrestler, well a pro-kick boxer any way, but he's all gentle kindness and heartfelt caring usually. Anger is not something you see too often on Rick. But, in saying that, I had seen a fair bit more of it than usual recently.

"Ever since the battle and losing Rocky he's been different," she replied.

Rocky was a young member of the Hapū who died fighting Max, the evil vampire who came to steal me away. I had always felt Rocky's death had been my fault. It didn't help that I had witnessed it and not done anything to help him.

"He's determined to get revenge. He's consumed by it," Celeste continued.

"Max is dead, Celeste. Michel killed him. There is no one else to get revenge from."

She laughed, a slightly bitter bark of a laugh, something so unlike Celeste's dainty, feminine titter. "He's not satisfied with just one vampire death, Luce. He wants them all dead."

I felt the world fall away briefly and slumped down onto the floor by the phone, my back against the wall the base unit was attached to. I closed my eyes and took a deep breath in. "He can't mean that." My voice sounded wrong, not mine, a little restricted, strangled even. Rick wouldn't be this foolish. Wouldn't be this unkind. I may be the official vampire hunter in this city, but even I don't want them *all* dead. There is good in some of them, there is Light. Surely Rick can see that too?

"He's fixated on it, Luce. It's all he thinks about, all he talks about. He's started to get a few of the younger Taniwhas on his side. He's talking them 'round. It's almost like he wants a little posse, so they can all go out hunting vampires in a group. I've never seen him like this Luce, he's a man possessed."

"What does Jerome say?" Jerome is the Westside Hapū's leader, he's big and gruff and rough around the edges, but he's got a heart of gold in there too.

"He doesn't know yet. Rick has managed to keep this very quiet. They meet in secret, at night and off Hapū land. I only know because he talks in his sleep."

That little bit of information I didn't need to know, but I pushed it aside. None of my business. And anyway, how could I possibly talk? I slept with one of the undead.

"What do you suggest I do, Celeste? You know how he feels about my current domestic situation. I can't help thinking he wouldn't hear me out on this one. Have you confronted him?"

"He'll listen to you, Luce. You've been his best friend for so long. He looks up to you, he adores you. He'll listen to you, I know it."

I wasn't so sure any more. Maybe once upon a time, but lately Rick had been growing more distant, unable to comprehend why I would be in Michel's, the Master Vampire of the City's, arms.

"I don't think I have that kind of sway any more, Celeste. I'm sorry."

"Please, Luce." She was really crying now, I could hear the sobs between the words, the hitch in the breath, the whimper as she let it out. Crap.

"OK. OK. I'll talk to him."

"Oh thank you, Luce. I know you'll make him see sense. I know you will."

I wasn't so convinced, but I didn't say it.

"Look, I've got to get ready for work now, but I'll try to swing by the gym on my way home, OK?"

"Yes, yes, that'll be great. Thanks, Luce. Thank you."

She hung up before I could say good bye. She'd accomplished what she rang for, she obviously didn't want to risk me changing my mind by hanging around for a girlie chat.

Damn. A rogue pack of shape shifters in my city. Could my life be any more complicated?

Chapter 5
Lynch Mob

Work was busy. Sale season. There's always a good sale on when winter winds down. Spring was just around the corner, but not yet fully blossomed. The days were getting slowly longer, the nights shorter. I always loved the onset of summer. Vampires did not.

I'd had a steady flow of customers all morning. Sales mean money, shops don't want to hang on to that kind of cash, so they high tail it to the bank. I'm the business banking teller for Queen Street's BNZ branch. The others do everything else, I just deal with the big deposits.

Counting coins is my day job, but it's the one thing that keeps me sane the most. There's just something so comforting about counting coins. Hunting vampires at night can be unpredictable, counting coins is not. I know what my day will bring from the moment I step in the door. It's cathartic, relaxing, reliable. Michel wanted me to give up my day job, he didn't feel being a bank teller was an appropriate job for the kindred Nosferatin of the Master of the City.

Needless to say, he didn't win that argument.

By the time the big clock on the wall behind our counters read 5pm, I was centred and calm and felt well and truly ready to face the night. Whatever it would bring. Even my fear of what would happen when I slept next didn't sway my good mood. Would I Dream Walk again? Would Gregor be there? All of it had faded away to just a soft shushing in the back of my mind.

I wasn't trying to ignore it. I was trying to control the fear. You never stop being afraid when faced with so much personal danger, I had just got good at breathing through that fear.

I changed into my jogging gear and headed out the door. Luckily for me, *Tony's Gym* is on the way home. I run past it on the way to and from work daily. It's handy, that's why I joined up as soon as I came to Auckland. I'm a gym junky and always have been. Sure, I've done the martial arts thing, a little Karate, a little Judo, but Kick-Boxing is where my heart is right now. That's how I met Rick. He's the kick-boxing instructor at *Tony's*. I met him three days after I arrived in the city and we've been friends ever since.

It didn't take long for us to share all our dirty secrets. Me being the vampire hunter extraordinaire, him the Taniwha shape shifter. I know Rick and he knows me. That's why I was having so much trouble getting my head around him starting a vampire hunting posse up right now. It just wasn't his style.

He was sitting in the corner of the kick-boxing area with a couple of guys. I recognised them immediately. One was Josh, a brainiac member of the Hapū. Josh was the Taniwha who hacked Nero's website for me. He's young, about 22 and built as big and as tough as Rick is, but he's got a naughty side. He's a teaser, a joker and a major flirt. I couldn't help liking Josh. The other two were also members of Rick's Hapū. The testosterone from that one little corner outweighed the entire gym right now, I should think.

The other two Taniwhas were Mikey and Joe. Mikey was a little on the tubby side - even shape shifters have a penchant for fast food - but an OK kind of guy. I'd not really had that much to do with him. He's about 27, so older than me, but about Rick's age and has long shaggy hair. I've never seen him in his Taniwha form, I wondered if his teeth were as sharp as Rick's or blunted from too much good eating. Joe was Rocky's twin brother. Just as boisterous, just as lovable, but alive. How must it be to lose your twin? I could not imagine.

The first time I saw Joe after the battle was the hardest of my life. I made a special trip out to Whenuapai to see Jerome and thank him and the Hapū for their help in the battle against Max. Also, to pay my respects. Joe had been there and at first I was mortified to have to face the brother of the boy who had died because of me, but afterwards I realised it was for the best. Facing him had been hard, not facing him would have ended up being worse in the long run.

I looked at the group huddled in the corner and I saw it. Anger, frustration and hurt. This was the posse then. I hadn't expected to have to face them all, no time like the present though.

Rick noticed me first as I crossed the mat towards them. His chocolate brown eyes didn't give anything away, there was no smile, but I didn't sense any unease either. Just neutral. Nothing.

"Hey guys. How's it going?" I asked the group at large.

The others spun around a little too quickly for normal humans, but they weren't normal were they? I kept reminding myself that right now as I felt the prickles of all those negative emotions running over my skin. It's not like I can read or receive emotions like Michel can mine, it's just you get used to the otherness of supernaturals and their mood or aura has an effect on me. I think with strong emotions that effect is sometimes more intense. Their auras practically try to smother me.

"Hey Luce." That was Rick. Nothing more, just a greeting. It used to be we'd fall into a conversation with ease. Why was I getting the feeling that was no longer the case?

The others all nodded, Josh winked.

There was a moment of awkward silence and then I thought *to hell with this* and said, "So, what's this I hear about you wanting to hunt vampires?"

I've not always been this forward, usually I have a little more tact. I'm no diplomat, that's Michel's area not mine, but I can usually curb my thoughts before they reach my mouth. Recently however, life has just become too precious to beat around the bush.

Josh laughed, Rick stiffened and looked angrier and the others just stared at the floor.

It was Rick who spoke first.

"You been checking up on me, Luce? I didn't think you cared."

Now that was a bit low, wasn't it? I was still his mate. Wasn't I?

"Celeste is worried about you, Rick. She phoned me."

I'm not sure if Celeste wanted me to divulge that little bit of information, but she was going to have to face him sooner or later about this, I was just speeding it along a little. It's not that I was trying to cause trouble, but Celeste needed to toughen up over this. She's the one about to marry him, not me.

Rick's face clouded over briefly then he stood abruptly and took a step towards me. That placed him well within my personal space. Not something I normally have a problem with, as far as Rick is concerned, but right now he was not looking like a controlled kick-boxing instructor, just a very angry shifter.

"Well, if you're not prepared to do your job, someone has to, haven't they?" His voice was actually quite even, low and rough, but well controlled. At least something in him was. That anger rolling off him was causing my palms to sweat and a small increase in my heart rate.

"I do my job quite well thanks. I don't need your help," I replied with forced calm.

"How many have you killed this week? Huh?" His face had come closer to mine, he was leaning in, I could see the muscles in his neck twitch. I would not take a step back. Years of coming up against the evil creatures of the night had taught me one thing. Never show fear. I just had never thought Rick might fall into that same category as the vampires.

"None. They've been well behaved," I answered.

He laughed out loud at that and took a step back. I let my breath out but did not release the tension in my shoulders.

"Well behaved. Huh." He turned to the others now, who all wore varying degrees of unease on their faces. "Do you see now? She doesn't care any more about the safety of humans. She won't kill the evil any more. She's too busy fucking them."

"Now hang on a minute, Rick. That is totally out of line." I'd taken a step forward and touched his arm in order to turn him back towards me. He threw my hand off and snarled. A real Taniwha snarl, all teeth and fierce grimace. I held my breath and my place. I would not show fear in front of Rick.

"What's got into you? This is not you talking, Rick. This is insane."

"What's got into me? What's got into me! Rocky dying has got into me, Luce. Or did you conveniently forget that little bit of news, sweep it nicely under the rug out of sight, so you can look into the eyes of your lover without guilt?"

I chanced a glance at Joe. He was staring at Rick with a look of shock on his face. I didn't think Joe was quite on the same page as Rick yet, despite it being *his* brother who had died.

"Michel didn't kill him, Rick. Neither did I." I didn't say I could have stopped it, I was right there and did nothing as Max drained the blood and life from the Taniwha in front of me. That was something I held close to my chest. Something I thought about every day of my life. Something I had to live with alone. It was a guilt, no two ways about it. But it was a private one.

"He died because of you though, didn't he? He died because a vampire wanted you and came to this city to fight Michel. For you. He died because your people trapped us in an alliance, one that we" - he pointed at himself then - "had no say in. He died because of you."

What could I say? He was right. Oh dear God, what could I say?

"You disgust me, Lucinda. I don't ever want to see you again."

He turned away from me then, shoulders rigid, back straight. I could feel the tears welling up in the corners of my eyes, the sting they created as they burned unshed. I noticed Josh stand and take a step towards me, but even he stilled when he received a low, long growl from Rick.

I've never been good at playing the victim. I don't usually cry. I'm capable of it, but I can normally control the urge. Rick had hurt me right now, really hurt me. I felt a small piece of my heart break away at the look of him so angry, so full of hate for me. But, I would not let it rule me.

I wrapped that hurt up and pushed it to the furthest corner of my soul, then gripped my fists and pulled my own anger around me as a shield.

"Whatever you think of me, Rick, you cannot go up against the vampires. You must see this won't work. There's too many of them and they are not all evil, despite what you think. It would be tantamount to murder, Rick, do you want to murder Shane Smith? Has he done anything to you?"

Shane Smith is one of Michel's flunkies. He's a bit of a weakling on the *Sanguis Vitam* scale, he's just not got an evil vampire bone in his entire body. He's strong and fast and can glaze if Michel commands him to, but he'd rather get you a cup of coffee and push your chair in for you at the club. He's a gentleman, a nobody on the Durand line power ladder. He's also someone I call a friend. Rick knows him and has had decent conversations with him in the past. Rick's always liked him too.

"They're all evil, Luce. Just to varying degrees. Isn't that what you used to tell me?"

Hell, he had me there. It's exactly what I used to say. Before I got to know Michel really well and before I came into my Nosferatin powers. When that switch was flipped however, they changed for me. Sure, they are all still capable of bad, Dark things, but there is also Light. I see the Light. I can't help it any more.

"I was wrong, Rick. There is good in them too. How can you contemplate killing that good?"

He let a breath out in a harsh burst, grimaced at me and shook his head. "He's really got you, hasn't he? Spelled you into thinking they are good. Into thinking you can save them. You can't. And I don't even think you can be saved any more either. You've chosen your path, Lucinda, let me choose mine."

"I can't let you go around killing them, Rick. I just can't. There are rules the vampires must adhere to. I follow them too. So do you. All supernaturals are subject to the rules Michel sets in this city and therefore the rules the *Iunctio* has made. Will you go against the *Iunctio*?"

Even though the *Iunctio* is the vampire network of rules, it sets the basis for all supernatural behaviour. They don't police the shape shifters, ghouls or magical community, but they won't stand back and watch mass slaughter outside of their own guidelines either. Rick would be biting off more than his Taniwha teeth could chew.

"All of them, Luce. Bring it on! I don't scare that easily. They are wrong, they should not exist. They don't deserve to breath the air we do."

I wasn't going to correct him on the breathing part, vampires don't need to breathe to survive, but it was just semantics. I knew he hadn't intended that to be literal. But, I wasn't going to leave this right here either.

"I'm part of the race that vampires descended from, Rick. Does that make me something that doesn't deserve to breathe your air too?"

Nosferatin and Nosferatu come from the same kin,

apparently. No one's actually super sure on that, but it's been said we were once one of a kind. But centuries ago split into those of us who went towards the Light and those that went towards the Dark. You pick which one I am.

He looked at me then, a good hard look, as though he could see more of me than what was standing there in front of his face. His eyes burned brightly and I did not like what I saw there. So much anger. So much hate. What the hell had happened to my Rick?

"Maybe you don't, Lucinda. Maybe you should be afraid of me when I come too." His voice was soft, low, almost too low to hear. "You should go now."

"I'm not leaving it like this, Rick. We need to talk about this. You need to see this is not right, at all." I am nothing if not persistent.

He took three long strides towards me, making his broad chest butt up against mine. I could feel the heat coming from him. He was hot, so hot, and it wasn't even nearly *Rākaunui* yet. His breath against my face scalded, I tried not to pull away and blink, but it stung my eyes and I could feel it almost blistering my cheeks. I didn't step back, but I did lean back, just a bit.

"Consider this your warning, Lucinda Monk, Vampire Hunter, Nosferatin," he practically spat the last in my face. "I will hunt the vampires to extinction in this city and if you get in my way, I will hunt you too."

I stared up into those deep brown eyes, which had been so familiar for so long, and didn't see a trace of anything I recognised there. He was gone. Rick was gone. My Rick was gone forever.

I swallowed and tried desperately to think of something

to say. He leaned in and pressed his mouth to my ear and whispered, "Run."

"What?"

He pulled back and gripped my shoulders tightly, I could feel his nails digging into the flesh there.

"I said RUN!" And then he growled, a real honest to goodness Taniwha growl. His face began to elongate, his jaw jutting out at the base, his forehead falling back, his lips peeling away to show long fangs. Taniwha fangs, with drips of saliva dangling off the end. He raised an already clawed hand in front of my face. I couldn't stop staring at the two inch sharp nails, no claws, protruding through the flesh of his fingers. There was a smattering of scales on the back of his hands. Shiny, grey, slick.

I've seen Rick shift before, but he made it seem so elegant, swift and surreal. This was something altogether different. He was using his shifting ability to scare me. It was working. I couldn't move. He said run, but for the life of me my legs would not obey. I wanted to run, I wanted to hide, hell, I wanted to curl into a little ball and whimper, but I couldn't get past the fact that this was my friend. Threatening me, scaring me and he meant every word, every action as it was intended to be received.

Before I could pull myself together, his hand pulled back, the claws flexing in the light of the room and he slashed out towards my face.

Several things happened at once. Josh and Joe jumped on the back of Rick, trying to pull him away. Mikey stumbled over whilst trying to get his big bulk up off his chair and ended up in a heap of snarling fury. I fell over backwards with my heart in my throat and the breath stolen from my lungs. And then I also heard Michel's voice shouting out in dismay in my mind.

Lucinda!

Chapter 6
Cease Fire

I scrabbled backwards from the melee of arms and legs and bodies flying around on the mat in front of me. I could hear yaps and snarls, growls and curses, a combination of animal sounds and human swearing. Rick, Joe and Josh were a furious ball of energy, blurring in front of me, tumbling over each other.

I've seen Taniwhas play fighting before, I've even been involved in the odd one. They are rough and play for keeps, but I had never seen this before. This depth of destruction. They weren't play fighting here, they were out for the kill. And I was still too close to that action to be safe.

Mikey came to stand by my side, where I had backed up against the rails of the kick-boxing ring. He squatted down in front of me, trying to get me to look at him. I was staring at the mess of fury where I had almost been slashed to pieces, I couldn't move or think. Everything else had just faded away to nothing.

Mikey reached out to touch my shoulders and I nearly jumped out of my skin in fear. He looked concerned, but was also thrumming with energy, not anger, but fear. I finally pulled my gaze away from the fight and looked him in the eyes. He'd been saying something to me, maybe even yelling it, trying to get my attention over the loud noises coming from the Taniwhas.

"You've got to go, Luce!" He glanced over his shoulder at the battle. "They can't hold him for long, he's too strong. He's an alpha. They will hold him as long as they can, but you have to run now. Run, Luce! RUN!"

It finally sunk in and I found myself struggling to my

feet, staggering a few paces, before getting my balance and then I was off. I didn't care that there were humans in the hallway, come to see the show. I didn't care that they were in danger, as I was. I didn't care that they could see I was faster than any person on this Earth could possibly be. I dug deep into the part of me that is Nosferatin and ran like the wind.

There was a time when Rick could have beaten me in a race. Easily. But with my new speed that was impossible. Even if the others couldn't hold him long, I would be gone, faster than they could even blink.

I came out into the late afternoon, early evening sunshine and was momentarily blinded. I stopped in my tracks for fear of running in front of a vehicle and getting squashed by a bus.

Come to me, ma douce. You will only be safe here.

Shit. Michel's voice in my head was right. Rick would follow me home. I saw it in his eyes. I didn't want to believe it, but it was there. He had issued a challenge, a warning and by Hapū law he was honour bound to carry it out. My friend, my one-time best friend, had signed a death warrant on my head.

I ran. I don't think the humans would have recognised what they saw. A blur, a streak of colour, a figment of their imaginations. It took me mere minutes to make it to *Sensations*. The door stood ajar as I raced towards it and shut immediately on my entry.

The room was full of vampires.

They didn't waste time securing the front of the building behind me. They seemed to know exactly what they were doing, what needed to be done. How many battles had they faced in their lives that made this moment so natural to them?

I collapsed onto my knees in the middle of the club floor. Michel was beside me in an instant.

"What happened, *ma douce*? Tell me."

I whimpered slightly against his chest, my breath was coming too quickly, I couldn't see properly, everything was blurry. I realised it was tears, filling my eyes to overflowing, spilling down my cheek, hot and wet and so very much unwanted. He stroked my head and waited for me to calm. I couldn't stop seeing Rick's face as he changed, still holding on to me, still within centimetres of my nose. His claws, how they burst out from the edge of his flesh, so red and raw around them, how long they were, how they looked as they came towards my face. How close they came to marking me.

I let a loud sob out, somewhere between a cry of anguish and a moan. It wasn't very attractive, it was gut wrenching and unrefined. Natural but so alien to my ears. I couldn't calm myself, I couldn't stop my heart bounding in my chest, it ached against my ribs, it pounded in my skull. I was going to pass out if I didn't slow my breathing down, but I had no idea how to stop this. This naked and raw fear, hurt, surprise and anguish.

Michel pulled my face around to look at him. His eyes blazed a deep amethyst and blue, the colour didn't move me, but the look in them did. He was feeling everything I was. Every emotion, every thought. My mind was crashing against his and he was taking it all in. The only evidence a slight creasing around his eyes, an intensity to his stare.

"Let me help you, *ma douce*. Lower your shields."

I wasn't sure if I could concentrate enough to lower them, everything seemed to be getting more distant, harder to see or control. Like I was swimming through thick sludge, barely able to keep my head above it. It took three efforts, but finally I felt my shields fall away and a cool, calm sea breeze flooded through me, chasing away the fear and anguish and hurt and pain. Replacing it with a fresh smell of sunshine, candied apples, honey and spring. It was my scent he was returning to me, trying to centre me, bringing me home.

I relaxed against him and felt his arms curve around me a little tighter, his head on top of mine, his chest rising and falling a little too quickly.

There was a thrumming energy in the room, the vampires were all on high alert, waiting for instructions from Michel, but eager for a battle. It's in their natures, they can't help it. It's what makes them what they are. Vampires thrive on conflict, on confrontation, on dominance. This was a chance to prove their dominion over those who came against them. They could not ignore that part of them even if they tried.

Michel recognised my breathing and heart rate had returned to nearly normal. He stroked my face, but didn't move me from the curve of his arms or the warmth of his chest.

"Tell me, *ma douce*. Why are we at war with the Taniwhas?"

I pulled away to look at him then. "The Taniwhas? You mean all of them?"

"Yes. We have just received an ultimatum from the Hapū. Hand you over or they will attack tonight."

What the fuck? Rick was mad at me, Rick had issued a challenge, a call to fight, but all of the Taniwhas?

"Did it come from Jerome?" I couldn't imagine that Jerome would go for this. Not that level headed, down to earth man. Not a chance.

"No. From their Beta. Jerome is out of the country on business."

What business did Jerome have out of the country I didn't know, but Beta? I didn't even know who that was. Some Hapū groupie I was.

"Who is their Beta, Michel?" I think I already knew the answer.

He sighed. "I thought you already knew, *ma douce*. He has always been an alpha in training, one day he will lead the Hapū. Rick."

Holy crap. I just shook my head. "This is all so wrong. This isn't happening."

"It is and you need to tell me why."

He hadn't said it firmly, but it was definitely more of a command than a request.

I let my breath out in a huff and told Michel about Celeste's phone call that morning and my visit to the gym. I even managed to keep my voice level, not a crack in sight.

"So, he plans to usurp your position as hunter then? I can imagine how you feel about that," Michel said dryly.

"Are you smiling, Michel? Do you think this is funny?"

"Not at all, *ma douce*. I just know you." He looked at me innocently, all wide eyed and beautiful curves to his lips.

I rolled my eyes, even in a crisis Michel could make

light of things, try to pull a smile out from behind my mask.

"How do we stop this?" I asked, to get him back on track.

"Let me make a phone call. It may not be as bad as we feared. There is still an hour before dusk and I am sure they would not attack until well dark. They risk too much exposure, even for Rick."

He stood up then and offered me his hand, pulling me lightly off the floor and then flashing me a wicked grin and pulling a little firmer until I slapped against his chest. His arms encircled my waist, trapping me, his lips brushed mine. In my ear he whispered, "I think you should stay here tonight, do you not agree?"

"You mean right here in your arms?" I gave him a scolding look, how could he even think of things like this right now?

"Of course. Where else would I want you?" He flashed that wicked smile again and spun away, walking in a languid glide towards his office. Leaving me slightly bemused and then belatedly realising I had a smile on my face. He'd done it. He'd made me smile despite all the fear and heartache I was feeling. He'd made me, for an instant, forget and he hadn't even used his powers to do it.

I gathered he wanted privacy for the phone call, if he had wanted me there, he would have taken me with him. I turned to look at all the vampires gathered in the bar. Michel's line had recently almost doubled. So, there were a lot of vampires I didn't immediately recognise around me right then, as they were part of the new influx, but there was one I did.

I walked over to Bruno as he sat at the bar. More like, propped against the bar. Bruno is Michel's second. He's big and strong and like most vampires, striking to look at, but that's not what you notice when you look at Bruno. It's his eyes. They scream evil. Before I got to know Bruno better, I really did think he was better kept at arms length, hell at a barge pole or longer length if possible. But it's all for show. Bruno used to bounce at the front of the many bars and clubs that Michel owns, he took great delight in scaring the Norms. He doesn't scare me quite so much any more.

Bruno is also one of only two vampires I have ever glazed. Another Nosferatin power, one I don't think had emerged before me. I feel rather protective of him now, like I have violated him somehow and I need to make it up to him. Vampires glaze as a standard, it's their way of controlling the Norms and keeping themselves hidden. I don't approve of it. I never have. So, when I realised I could glaze a vampire, it was a mixed blessing. It's got me out of a tight situation before and helped me get to Michel when he needed me. But, it's not something I'm proud of and I refuse to use it unless it's a last resort. Me or them kind of deal. If my life is on the line then I'll use it, but otherwise, I'm on my own.

It's just the kind of girl I am. I have standards. Someone's got to.

"Hey, Luce." Bruno's voice is always gruff and low, a bit gravelly.

"Hey." I slid into the seat next to him and Doug, the barman, came over to pour me a drink.

"It's a bit early, isn't it Doug?" The sun hadn't set after all.

"I think you could do with one, Luce. You look a little pale." He poured me my usual, a *Bacardi and Coke*, pushed it across the bar and went down the other end. Doug's a man, or vamp, of few words. You'd think being a bartender he'd have better communication skills, but he doesn't. I don't mind, I didn't really feel like talking anyway.

Bruno was nursing his own drink, swirling the ice around the bottom.

"It's always entertaining to be around you, Luce. Never go a week without someone after your arse. The Master's got his hands full with you, that's for sure."

"I don't think he truly realised what he was getting himself into, do you?"

He laughed. "Hell no. But it's fun. Michel always did like to have a bit of fun."

That was a bit too tempting to pass up.

"How long have you been with him, Bruno?"

"He turned me, I thought you knew that."

So, that would be over 200 years, a long time for a vampire of Bruno's *Sanguis Vitam* to remain under another. I'd always thought there was more to Michel and Bruno's relationship than met the eye. I've never asked. I'll wait for the right opportunity, but first things first.

"What kind of fun has Michel had in the past?"

Bruno stilled slightly, but smiled at me, giving me the full force of his evil eyes. I have to be careful around Bruno, he's glazed me twice before, under Michel's instructions. I'm not usually that easy to glaze, but he caught me at a bad moment. The thing is, once you've been glazed by a vampire, it's easier for them to get a hold of you again. Like they've travelled the road and no longer need a map.

"Five hundred years is a long time to live, Luce. A long time. You get to experience everything. Nothing seems all shiny and new again. You have to find ways to keep you enthused, alive. Michel is a master at finding new ways to satisfy his hungers."

I felt a little chill go down my spine. "Are you trying to scare me or warn me, Bruno?"

"Neither. It's just a simple fact."

I stared at him, but all I could see was self assured knowledge. He wasn't pulling my chain, he was simply stating a fact, just like he said.

"Better I don't know the details then," I said almost to myself.

"Luce. He has never, in all the time I have known him, ever felt for someone the way he feels for you. He may be experienced in many things, but when it comes to you, the Master ain't got it all sussed. Sometimes I wonder just which of you is the one in control."

I didn't know what to say to that. I certainly did not want Michel to think he was in control of me, but then, did I want to be in control of him? I opened my mouth to come back with a retort, but was beaten to it.

"Are you giving away all my secrets, Bruno? Or just the ones close to my heart?"

Bruno stood and spun to face Michel, a blur of preternatural speed. "Master."

They didn't usually go for all this *Master* crap, not Bruno and Michel, but with so many new vamps in the family line all of a sudden, they had upped the ante a bit on the dominant master of the line crap. It got the message across to the newbies, if Bruno showed that level of respect, they sure as hell could too.

Another blur and Bruno was gone, across the room and out a side door. Michel just stood there staring at me with a look on his face I couldn't quite place. Resignation with a hint of humour? He slowly walked towards me, hands in his pockets, all debonair ease. He was dressed in his more casual attire of black trousers and black shirt, sleeves rolled up to show off his muscled forearms, neck loose displaying his smooth cream skin. He knows how I love black. Usually, on a business night he'd be dressed in an Armani suit, just off black, with white shirt and some shade of blue tie. He was always so well turned out. But I love black on a man and he knows it. He also wears it well.

I swallowed, he didn't miss the movement, just grinned, flashing me a sparkle of violet and blue from his eyes.

"So, how did the phone call go?" I asked, returning my attention to my drink.

He came and slid into a seat next to me. There was already a glass of red wine, probably Merlot, sitting waiting, Doug back down the other end of the bar. I hadn't even seen him pour it, I'd been too busy gawking elsewhere. Idiot.

"We have a reprieve. Jerome has issued a directive." When he saw the look of slight confusion on my face, he added, "A command. No Taniwha is to act against us until his return. He will not offer more until he can ascertain in person from his Hapū what has happened."

"Will it be enough? Rick seemed pretty determined."

"Yes. His directives are as binding as my commands to

those in my line. The Hapū will not be able to disobey. However, I do think it best you not exercise at the Gym for a while, *ma douce*. Crossing paths with the Taniwha would be unwise."

I noticed how Rick had been relegated to the Taniwha. I was not surprised, I was kind of thinking along those lines right now too. What had happened to my Rick? How could it have got this messy, this quickly? How could he have turned on me, his friend, so easily?

I was shaking my head slowly from side to side, looking down at the floor of the bar, unaware of what I was doing. Michel's hand came up and brushed against my cheek, the backs of his fingers tracing down to my jaw, his thumb rubbing along the edge there.

"I am sorry, *ma douce*. I know how much he meant to you."

Already we were talking in the past tense, was there no going back from this? How do you rebuild a friendship when one of you has tried to physically harm the other and when war has been declared? I wasn't sure it was possible, but I also wasn't prepared to give up on him just yet. I'm loyal, it's just who I am. When you become my friend, it's forever. I don't roll over that easily.

Michel sipped his wine and watched me, he could probably feel the emotions playing through my body. He couldn't read my mind though, only those thoughts I chose to throw his way. He was trying to decipher my thoughts from my emotions though. I could tell, he did it every now and then. It was kind of like a game. Eventually he gave up. I wasn't going to help him. He got free rein on my emotions, but not my thoughts, they were all mine.

"Well, it seems my luck is holding and I get to see you earlier than planned this evening, *ma douce*." He lifted my hand up to his mouth and lay a lingering kiss there, keeping his eyes on mine. I knew what that look meant, it had a tendency to distract me, to lure me in. I bit my lip, then noticed a flickering off to the side, in the centre of the bar.

Nero appeared and slowly looked around the room in casual interest, raising his dark eyebrows at the clientèle. His short, thick black hair shined in the light of the room, making his fine Egyptian features stand out in stunning relief against the backdrop of the room. He was dressed in black. Not his usual style, normally it's off white linen trousers and long linen shirt, rolled halfway up his arms. The white shows off his dark skin to perfection. But, he also knows I like black. Am I that readable? He made eye contact with me and just stood there, a small smile playing on the corners of his mouth. The cinnamon and bronze flecks in his eyes mixing with the darker coffee colours within and sparkling in the artificial lights around the room.

"*Ma douce*?"

I turned back to Michel, his eyebrows raised, a slight look of amusement on his face. I was sure it wouldn't be there for long.

"Um, can you hold that thought for a while?"

"Hold that thought for a while?" The amusement was slowly leaving, best to land the hammer blow.

"Nero's here."

He didn't move, still holding my hand. He didn't bother to look around the room either, he knew he wouldn't be able to see him. Nero was Dream Walking.

"In my bar?" Each word, however, was annunciated

slowly.

"Well, it would have been my apartment, but I'm here. He's homed in on me, so he goes where I go." I bit my lip and held my breath. This should be fun.

Michel blinked slowly. "There are several things I could say to that." He stopped as if considering which phrase on the tip of his tongue to use.

"We had planned to practice some moves tonight. He is my trainer," I added.

"So you have declared." He paused, then looked sternly at me. "Moves? In your apartment?"

Oh boy. I knew Michel wouldn't have approved, that's exactly why I hadn't told him. I chanced a glance at Nero. He was still standing in the same spot, relaxed, watching the scene play out before him, with a slightly amused smile on his lips. He was enjoying the entertainment.

"Can we discuss this later? I need to talk to Nero any way, about the Dream Walk last night."

That seemed to do it, Michel straightened, looked resigned, and just sighed.

"Be sure to train in the basement, *ma douce*. I would not be amused if you chose our chamber."

I hadn't missed his use of *our* for the chamber. He knew Nero would be listening. It was his final dig. He stood up from his seat and pulled me to him, wrapping one arm around my waist and pulling me close, the other he ran through my hair and rested at the back of my neck tilting my head back slightly. His kiss was deep and full of meaning. Michel could take no prisoners when he wanted. Sometimes it was like he kissed as though the world would end and there was only so much time to show me he was mine. I always felt a little weak at the knees when he did that. Hell, not just weak, totally jelly-like.

He finally pulled away and smiled, that knowing smile he so often wore. "*That, ma douce*, was the final dig." And then he was gone.

Leaving me catching my breath and gripping the bar to stay upright and frantically wondering if I had actually flung that thought out at him or not.

Chapter 7
Connected

I managed to pull myself together eventually and walked towards the door to the basement. Nero would follow, I didn't have to ask and right now, I wasn't sure I could look him in the eyes anyway.

The basement has a series of storerooms and day-time sleeping quarters for Michel's vampires. The room we would use is the largest storeroom, it's partially full but there's still heaps of room to move. Plus, recently, Michel's vamps had put in a sofa and table and chairs, almost a private day-time retreat for the sunshine challenged.

I slumped myself down on the couch, still avoiding Nero's eyes. I was going to have to get over this. Damn it! I'm a big girl, I shouldn't be embarrassed.

When I lifted my head to look at him, Nero was taking in the room, glancing around the stored liquor bottles at one end, taking in the table and small mini-bar off to the side, the remnants of a poker match still evident on the table top. Finally his eyes found mine.

He just looked at me for a moment, his eyes an intense golden brown. Nero's always quite intense, it's just the way he is. He's been around a long time, almost as long as Michel, he tends to take things rather seriously. But, I have seen a lighter side to him, occasionally he lets it shine.

"Kiwi. You always manage to surprise." His voice was soft, low and luxurious, the Egyptian accent unmistakable.

"Change of plans Nero. My apartment is not safe right now."

That got a response. He raised his eyebrows and cocked his head, then proceeded to come forward and sit on the couch next to me. There was room for him to have sat further away, but Nero was a touchy feely kind of man, he liked a closer proximity.

"Do tell, Kiwi. What have you been up to now?"

Why is it that everyone thinks I get myself into trouble? I know I attract a certain amount of otherworldly attention, but it's not always my fault. Somehow, when someone asks me *what have you been up to now*, I get the feeling it's all because of me. All my fault and no one else's, as though contemplating that I was a mere innocent bystander in the wrong place at the wrong time, is impossible.

Then come to think of it, they're probably right.

I sighed and told him all about my adventures with homicidal Taniwhas.

"I thought you had an alliance with the shape shifters," Nero asked.

"I do, or at least I did. Maybe that was forfeited when they fought alongside me against Max. Maybe the alliance no longer stands."

"From what you have told me, Kiwi, this should not be so. The Beta has made an error. His Alpha will put this right."

"I wish I could be as optimistic as you, Nero. But, I saw the look in Rick's eyes." I shuddered from the visual memory, Nero's hand came to rest on my shoulder, the warmth spreading through my body and chasing away the chill. "Jerome has issued a directive, so for now, I should be safe, but I can't get my head around why Rick would do this, how he could be so cruel. He is my friend Nero, friends don't do this to each other."

“You value friendship.” It was a statement, but I answered any way.

“Yes. Once someone is my friend, they are for life. I don't take it back when it's been given.”

“Am I your friend?”

I turned to look at him then, really look at him. What was he asking? Of course he was my friend. He was my trainer, my link to the Nosferatin side of me. I relied on him, I counted on him to teach me what I needed to know, I enjoyed being with him. He was definitely my friend.

“Yes.”

An emotion fluttered across his fine features, I couldn't quite make out what it was. Relief? Happiness? Confusion? It didn't make sense, but then often Nero didn't quite make sense.

He reached up, as if to stroke my cheek, but his hand stilled mere centimetres from my face. I fought the urge to bring my face closer to his hand, to rub it against his warm skin. I would have done it, but the look of anguish that briefly touched his eyes was enough to stop me in my tracks. I shook my head, unsure what to do. His hand fell back into his lap and he flashed me one of his trademark dazzling smiles. He uses them sometimes, I think it's a ploy to distract.

“So, we train here tonight, Kiwi?”

“Actually, I need your help, your advice on a different matter, Nero. It's a little more pressing than training tonight.”

“I am all yours, Kiwi. Use me as you feel fit.”

I shot him a look, but his face was serious, no hint of flirtation within. Nero could flirt when he wanted to, but lately that had taken more of a back seat. The more serious and intense Nero had been on display recently. I kind of missed the flirt.

"I Dream Walked last night in my sleep. I didn't have any control, I just got sucked into it and ended up on a street in Rome."

Nero had stiffened slightly, his forehead was creased. "No control at all?"

"None."

"Were you aware you were about to Dream Walk, or did you just wake up standing in the street?"

"It happened suddenly, I was in a dream and fell away to that nothingness before Dream Walking, but it was a stronger pull than I usually get. I felt like my body was being yanked around on the path to the Dream Walk.

"You were in a dream, or having a dream?"

Trust Nero to pick up on that. "Michel visits me in my Dreams, I was with him." Even though nothing sexual had happened in the dream, even though it was merely me standing on my parents' farm and Michel being there too, I couldn't stop the blush that rose up my cheeks at talking about it. My dreams with Michel haven't always been so chaste.

Nero noticed, he didn't say anything, he didn't need to, his eyes lingered on my cheeks where the warmth of the blush still sat and he just watched. Sometimes the weight of Nero's gaze can almost be too much to bear.

He cleared his throat softly and went on. "The pull was stronger than usual? Can you describe it?"

"Well, when I usually fall into a Dream Walk I have to seek the nothingness before I emerge in the Dream. This time, the nothingness just enveloped me, and then I felt a tug in one direction and pull in another, whilst still in the nothingness. It was abrupt and fast and I couldn't do a thing to stop it."

"This is most unusual, Kiwi. As you know, we control our Dream Walk, we initiate it. I have never heard of a Dream Walker involuntarily entering that state. Certainly not whilst asleep. A novice Dream Walker may accidentally cause a shift to Dream Walking, due to heightened emotions, but you are experienced now. I would not have thought this was an accident at all."

Yeah, Michel had the same thought.

"There's more. I ended up in an alley with a Nosferatin and a vampire already draining him."

"A Nosferatin in Rome? I have not met this Nosferatin."

"I gave him your website, he'll be in touch."

"Good, then you were successful in dispatching the vampire."

I squirmed slightly in my seat, I hated having to admit my failure to Nero. Nero was my idol, he was wickedly good at being a vampire hunter. He was fast, he was brilliant, he was perfect. I hated letting him down.

"Well, no."

He smiled slightly at me, his eyes dancing in the light of the room, he knew exactly what I was feeling. I rubbed my face.

"I didn't have a stake and the Nosferatin had lost his."

Nero paused for a second, digesting that information. "Where do you store your stake when you sleep?"

"Either in my chest under my bed, or in my bag."

"You don't have one under your pillow or under the mattress?"

"No. Should I?"

"When we Dream Walk, Kiwi, we appear in what we are wearing, but we are also able to take with us, those things nearby that we may need. They must be very close, a stake under the pillow is best. Your Dream Walk will automatically acknowledge it's presence and take the stake with you. That aside however, a vampire entering your bedroom would be hard to tackle if your stake is in a chest under your bed. Time is always of the essence after all."

"Vampires can't come in unless invited."

"Not all vampires arc subject to that rule. Some of the more powerful are able to override the need for an invitation."

Huh. I'd always wondered how Michel had entered my apartment, to this day I have never actually invited him in.

"Well, that sucks. Where's our protection?" We rely on the invitation required for a vampire to cross the threshold of our home to keep us safe. It's just one of the rules. They can't keep changing the rules on us. It's not fair.

"There are very few vampires strong enough to achieve this, but they do exist."

"Yeah. They bloody well do."

Nero looked at me intently. "You have had experience of this." Again, not a question, just a statement. This time I didn't bother to answer.

"So, a stake under my pillow then. Beats having to have it down my night dress I guess."

That received a wicked grin flashing across Nero's face. He recovered himself and said, "Back to the uncontrolled Dream Walk." It almost sounded reluctant. Almost. "How did you save the Nosferatin?"

"I guess a little bit of luck and the fact that the vampire didn't want to kill me. I don't think he even wanted to kill the Nosferatin, I think he just lost control. I felt his evil when I landed in the Dream Walk, but it vanished as soon as I confronted him in the alley."

"Vanished. That is unusual. Do you know who this vampire was?"

"Yes, Michel knows him, you may too. Gregor. He's on the *Iunctio*. Michel called him the Enforcer."

Nero let a breath of air out in a long rush and sat back on the couch looking at me. "He let you go? Just like that? The Enforcer let you go after you had him cornered, draining a Nosferatin against the *Iunctio's* rules? Did he at least threaten you?"

I thought about that for a moment. He had said he would look forward to when we actually met in person, that wasn't really a threat, was it? No.

"No, he didn't. We kind of came to an agreement. Although in retrospect, I was a little naïve. I didn't realise who he was and thought he meant it when he said he would be careful what he told the *Iunctio* about my skills as a Dream Walker. At the time he seemed genuine, I let him go. Besides, I didn't have a stake and *Sanguis Vitam* rolled off him in waves"

Nero nodded. "There was nothing else you could have done, Kiwi. He is very powerful, but" - he paused shaking his head - "I do not like that he appeared in your Dream Walk. In *this* Dream Walk. It is too coincidental."

And there you have it. Both Michel and Nero were on

the same page. *Too coincidental that the Enforcer appeared in my Dream Walk.* Crap.

"What does it mean then, Nero? Does he have some control over me, to make me Dream Walk to him?" Saying it aloud actually brought goose bumps out on my skin, I could feel the coolness of sweat on my palms, raised hairs along my arms.

Nero sighed. "It is never straight forward with you, is it Kiwi?" He paused then, in his own little world, then added, "Is there anything else you have not yet told me?"

Huh. I'd totally forgotten about my newest power. I'd been so wrapped up in telling the story of Gregor, that I had forgotten how thc Dream Walk had initially felt, like homing in on the evil of his signature, like that had been the reason for the Dream Walk. I had been sidetracked by the idea that Gregor could have control over my Dream Walking ability, when in fact it may not be the case at all.

I felt a slight weight lift off my shoulders at that thought.

"Well, there is one more thing and I admit it's what I first thought this uncontrolled Dream Walk was all about. It just felt like a pull towards evil." I took a deep breath in. "I have another power I hadn't yet told you about."

Nero smiled, it was a joyous smile. He wasn't angry that I hadn't told him, he wasn't upset to have been left out of the loop, he was happy, maybe even excited. It was a look I hadn't seen on his intense face ever before.

"Tell me, Kiwi. What treasures have you in store for us now?"

"I can sense all the vampires throughout the world. It's like I'm pulled towards their evil, their Darkness. I see it all laid out in my mind. Where they are, how many there are. And it's what I felt when I started the Dream Walk, well, when I appeared in it, any way. So, it's controlling my Dream Walking, isn't it? This new power. It's taking me to evil so I can deal with it."

Nero's smile dimmed slightly, he reached and out and took my hand, stroking the back like Michel does. Nero's fingers aren't as soft as Michel's, they're warrior hardened, but they are as warm.

"It is not the new power that controls your Dream Walk, my Kiwi. It does not work like that. I am afraid it *is,* it *must* be, the Enforcer who controlled that Walk."

How can you go from being hopeful, even excited at the thought of something, to only have it dashed by the naked harsh truth? I didn't want to believe it was Gregor who controlled my Dream Walking. If he controlled my Dream Walking, he controlled me.

"There is some good news though, Kiwi."

I looked up into Nero's coffee coloured eyes, his hand still on mine, his other coming up to stroke my cheek, as he had intended to before. He looked slightly amazed, in awe even, like what he saw before him was something divine, special, worthy of worship. I didn't feel like any of those things, sitting here in my gym gear, slightly messed up from my confrontation with Rick. I felt so far removed from that look in Nero's eyes that I could meet his gaze without embarrassment or discomfort. He was surely looking at someone else.

His voice reached me down that long narrow tunnel of remoteness, pulling me back into his world. "The *Sanguis Vitam Cupitor* has returned to us. The Prophesy is true."

Now why was I thinking that I wasn't going to like hearing about this?

Chapter 8
Sanguis Vitam Cupitor

"The *Sanguis Vitam* what?"

I knew what *Sanguis Vitam* was of course: the blood life, or power force of a vampire. But, what the hell was *Cupitor*?

"*Sanguis Vitam Cupitor.* You are the Blood Life Seeker. This is brilliant news, Kiwi, it could not be better. If the *Sanguis Vitam Cupitor* has been returned to us, then our powers are building again."

He seemed very excited, very excited indeed. His eyes were dancing, wicked shades of brown; chocolate and chestnut, bronze and burnt umber, copper and mahogany. They shone in the lights of the room, sparkling like diamonds, lighting up his face. It was almost like he was a vampire. I have never seen another human, even a part human like we are, have eyes that can change with emotion like this.

I could understand what he was saying though, I guess, why he was so happy. He's almost 500 years old and for most of that time he has had to live in seclusion, hidden from the world, unable to be what he actually is. The Nosferatin had decided to go into hiding several centuries ago, to pull away from the Nosferatu, thereby denying them the power they craved. Most took this undertaking seriously, literally, they hid and rejected all creatures of the night. It meant that their first borns, those with the Nosferatin, vampire hunter, gene like me, were unable to join with a kindred vampire and avoid death. It meant that they had consciously chosen to allow their first borns to die.

Because of that choice both the Nosferatu and the Nosferatin had been losing their powers. Together is how we are meant to be, apart we lose strength, we slowly die as a race. It also meant that there were far fewer Nosferatin today than there used to be and therefore for more Nosferatu.

"I understand why you're all happy and such, but what does this actually mean for me? What does being the *Sanguis Vitam Cupitor* entail?"

Nero practically rubbed his hands together in glee, he was just so damn happy about this, wasn't he? I'd never seen Nero like this before, he was like a whole different person, so full of delight, almost exuberant in his euphoria. I couldn't help laughing at him, it was just so strange.

He realised he was acting a little weirdly then, he looked quite abashed, it was kind of cute. "I am sorry, Kiwi. I am already happy to be in your company, this is too much for even my self control to contain. We have been waiting a long time for the return of one of prophesied, it has become a dream, a non-reality we did not dare to expect. When I met you, I had begun to hope again, you shine the brightest of all Nosferatin I have ever seen. Even my family could see it. Even they began to hope."

"I know I glow with the Bond I have with Michel and all, but what made you think I shined?"

He smiled and touched my cheek. "One of my powers is to recognise auras for what they represent. I am, you might say, a Herald for our kind. It is my calling to perceive what might become. As to what you may expect as the *Sanguis Vitam Cupitor*, you are merely one of several who will be. Now that you have arrived among us, there will be other Nosferatin who will fulfil various parts of the Prophesy. Together you will help us take back the night, only together do we stand a chance against the Darkness which has threatened to overtake us all."

OK. So, I've got to hang around for some more of my kind to get on the band wagon, then together we kick the evil undeads' butts. What do I do in the meantime?

"So, how long until these other Nosferatin turn up with the special dose of powers needed?" I asked.

"It could be soon, or many years, but the power that makes us what we are will determine when they are needed."

"And in the meantime, what do I do with this knowledge, because I'm telling you now, Nero, it's not much fun. It keeps me awake at night and threatens to consume me at odd times during the day. I sense when they will strike, I know where they are and that they intend someone harm, but I can't get to them all, can I? Or is that what I am meant to do? Is that why I can Dream Walk too?"

Aside from Nero and myself, there is apparently only one other Nosferatin who can currently Dream Walk. It is a powerful tool in our belt, but also a rare one.

"When the others arrive, it will be easier. You will be drawn to each other and then you will work together. You will not necessarily need to go to the evil, it may come to you. But alone, it would be unwise to face that amount of Darkness, alone it may consume you."

"So, how do I ignore it? I know without a doubt that someone, somewhere, is getting hurt, maybe killed. How can I not do something to help?"

Nero brushed my hair back behind my ears, it's shoulder length and straight and sometimes can fall forward and get in the way. I hate tying it back. You'd think I would, fighting vampires, it's too much of a temptation to grab, but I'm a girlie girl through and through, despite my birthright and being an evil undead slayer, I just have to have girlie hair.

"If you give in to it, you will place yourself in too much danger. Alone you cannot face what is out there. You are too precious now to risk. Your survival is paramount in our fight against the Dark. Without you the rest of the Prophesy will not succeed."

He saw the haunted and tormented look in my eyes. I didn't think I could ignore this. I didn't think I could stand idly by and watch the world be consumed by so much Darkness, watch the innocent die because of my inaction. I knew what he was saying made sense. I understood that I was needed when the others arrived to direct them to where the evil was, but I couldn't just do nothing, I wouldn't do nothing. I'm just not that kind of person.

It's not that I'm a hero, or wish to be a martyr, far from it. I fear death, but I cannot watch others die when I could help. I did that once and it eats me up inside daily. It has taken a part of my soul from me, that I will never be able to reclaim. If I do nothing in the face of so much death and evil now, I will lose all of myself. I will cease to exist. Then how much help would I be to the others?

He nodded, he understood. Sometimes it was like he could read my mind, or maybe he was just better at gauging my feelings, from the emotions playing across my face, than Michel is. But, sometimes, I felt more in tune with

Nero than I could ever be with Michel. It frightened me. Nero was not my kindred Nosferatu. Nero and I did not share a particularly strong Bond. But Nero was the one I felt I could trust, implicitly, completely, without reservations. If only I could combine the two men, my life would be so much easier.

"I will work on a spell that will bind me to you when you Dream Walk, then you shall not be alone. When you feel the need to be somewhere, when you feel that pull, I will know and I will come to where you are if I am able. But - and this you must promise me, Kiwi - do not Dream Walk intentionally right now. Should you Dream Walk twice in a night you will be vulnerable. If the Enforcer pulls you under and you have already Dream Walked once that day, you will be unable to rise. Your kindred vampyre may be able to protect your body while you rest, but then again, he may not. The Enforcer may be waiting for such an opportunity, he would be difficult to repel."

I nodded, he was right. Dream Walking was a nifty little talent, but it came with a caveat. More than one Dream Walk per day/night and you were taxed out, unable to wake from that nothingness. The first time I did it took a whole week for me to wake. Now apparently, as I have passed my 25th birthday, meaning I have matured as a Nosferatin, it would be more like three days. But, three days is enough for Gregor to get here. Three days is too long.

"So, what are we going to do about Gregor?" I asked.

"As soon as I have the spell, I can come to your aid. In the meantime, make sure you have your stake nearby and perhaps your vampyre too."

"My vampire? You mean Michel?"

Nero looked a little pained at what he was about to say. "If your Dream Walk is potentially a threat to your safety, such as Dream Walking to the Enforcer would be, then it will take along what it sees is best for your well being in that realm. If Michel is by your side when you sleep, he will be pulled into your Dream Walk too. At least for now, until I can master the spell, it would mean you are not alone."

Well, wasn't Michel just going to love this? If he had his way, I would be by his side 24/7. Luckily, it only seems to be when I sleep that Gregor can call me to him, but as soon as Nero gets that spell perfected, I swear I'll be back to my apartment. I will not give Michel more control over me than he already has.

"I will also do some research, we have old tomes that provide for more detail on the Prophesy. I have read them all over time, but much has been forgotten and buried under too much clutter now, I need to revise. I will see if there is something of importance I have missed."

"What *is* the Prophesy exactly, Nero?"

He's talked about the Prophesy before, even before I knew what we were, he mentioned it in a conversation we had, a teleconference with other Nosferatin. He said it had been foretold that we would face Darkness again. At the time he was unable to elaborate and afterwards I clear forgot to ask.

"I have told you what our people call us, have I not?"

"Yes. *The Children of Nut.*" He had told me the Legend of Thoth, the God of Knowledge and Wisdom. Thoth once prophesied a child would be born to Nut who would become Pharaoh after Ra. It was told that she had five children, Osiris was the first born and it was proclaimed to the heavens on his birth, 'The Lord of All comes forth into the Light!' We are the Children of the Light, apparently. We force out evil and banish the dark. To Nero's people we are *The Children of Nut*.

He smiled, pleased that I remembered.

"It is an Egyptian legend, but it is merely an Egyptian version of something that exists in many cultures, if not all. Dark versus Light, Good versus Evil. It is a battle that rages in all human history. It is not just singular to ours. We are the descendants of Nut, her son Osiris is our ancestor, he was the first of the Lords of the Light. It was foretold that his children would battle evil and bring forth Light. You have it in you stronger than most. The Light you used in Egypt to destroy so many vampyres is evidence of that. I have never witnessed such power before, such Light. It is part of the Ancients' sovereignty. It is a power of the Gods, it is divine."

Well hell. I knew what I did in Cairo a few weeks ago, when we were aiding Nero and Nafrini and trying to get their stolen immature Nosferatin back, was unprecedented. I knew it was pretty darn big. I mean I managed to burst into light and dust about thirty vampires, but I have no idea how I did it and it scared the bejeebers out of me. I sincerely hope I never have to do it again, because it's doubtful I could repeat it on request and I sure as hell don't want to either. But, to say it is divine, god-like, is just too much. This could not all be true.

"This is just some elaborate way to put into words the supernatural abilities of our kind, isn't it? That's what people do, they make up stories to fit the unreal, to make it seem more logical than it is. None of this makes sense, Nero, none of it could be true."

He smiled at me then, a sad smile laced with pity. As though he was sorry for me that I could not see it, could not understand it, could not believe it. I guess that's what faith is all about. I was raised a Christian, we don't have any stories of Lords of the Light. It's just not in my psyche, it's just not ever been placed there.

"You do not have to believe, my Kiwi, you just have to live it. You are what you are and there is no denying that you are a *Child of Nut*."

Well, I wasn't so sure, but what could I say? I can force the Light out of my body, I am drawn to the Dark if only to bring it Light, and my name, Lucinda, means *Giver of Light*. What could I say?

We sat there for a while, just looking at each other. Nero was no longer touching me, but it felt like there was a line between us, a string suspended in the air connecting us to each other. I wondered briefly, if that was what people felt when they were with their kin. That connection on such a basic level, unseen to the human eye, but felt within the deepest part of our souls.

I don't know how long we sat there, saying nothing, just looking into the eyes of the other. There were no words for what I was feeling. I may not fully believe in what Nero had said, I could not comprehend that we were descendant from some ancient god, but I knew without a doubt, that we were of the same ilk. We were of the Light and the vampires were of the Dark. That alone connected me to him more than anything else, but there was something more. I hadn't wanted to acknowledge it, I put it down to the mere fact that we had been through quite a lot together. Life and death situations tend to bind people to one another, they create heightened emotions, providing for a false sense of intimacy. It wasn't real, but it felt real and right then it was taking all of my self control not to give in to it. Not to move that foot or so closer to be in his arms.

I could tell he was feeling it too, all it would have taken would have been for him to shift, just slightly towards me and my hard won control would have been lost. He was fighting it, as I was fighting it, but we both knew that it was a losing battle. I could see it in his eyes, in how they devoured me, begged me, to make that first move. I have never been asked such an intimate question from just the look in a man's eyes before. It stole my breath away, it stilled my beating heart. Right at that moment nothing else existed but Nero.

There was a soft cough from the corner of the room. A clearing of someone's throat. The spell, or whatever the hell it had been, was broken and we both turned swiftly to the source of that sound.

Michel stood there with his hands in his pockets, relaxed and at ease, but his eyes shone a deep magenta, softly, he was controlling it, but it was there. Magenta is the big bad no-no, I never liked witnessing it in those beautiful deep blue eyes. He may not have been able to see Nero, but he had seen me. I couldn't have fought the blush that suddenly rose to my face even if my life had depended on it. At one stage I would have said that right now it did. The only saving grace was that if Michel killed me right now, he'd only be killing himself. It kind of limits the options for revenge, doesn't it?

"Your training seems to be progressing rather swiftly." His voice was even and low. At any other time I would have wrapped it around me, I would have let it draw me to him, right now however, I blanched.

Nero stood slowly, a stake appeared in his hands like magic. First it was just a closed fist, then poof, a silver stake shone in his grip.

I sighed. "Put it away, Nero. What are going to do, stake him and kill me?"

He didn't move, didn't look at me, but kept his gaze on Michel. "I will protect you at all cost, Kiwi."

"You do not need to protect her, Nosferatin, she is not yours to protect."

"Am I yours, Michel?"

"*Oui.*"

Always a bad sign when he reverts to French in everyday conversation. This, however, was not an everyday conversation, was it?

"So, what now? Do we just stand here all night, a stalemate? Draw pistols at dawn?" I could have said, it's not what it looks like, I could have denied that anything was going on, it wasn't really, but even that would have been a lie.

"There has been news on the *Iunctio*." I didn't think Michel could have surprised me any more than he did with that statement. It was so unexpected. I had been bracing for a fight, for some form of confrontation, that would only have ended in bloodshed and tears.

"What news?" I asked.

"Your secrets are no longer safe. They know what you

are capable of. They know you can Dream Walk to them, that you can destroy them without them even knowing you are there. They also know you can *seek* them."

"How is that possible? Gregor only knew I could Dream Walk, how have they heard that I can *seek*?"

"I do not know, my dear, but they know it."

"So, what does this mean, Michel?"

"It means, that they are prepared. It means, that they will be on the lookout for you. It means, they will no longer hunt alone."

Suddenly, what could have been an easy task had become so much more harder. Alone I can battle a vampire, just, but in groups it was damn near impossible. The odds were no longer in my favour.

I had stood when Nero had, but now I sank back down into the couch. This changes things. If I thought I could just go to the aid of innocents being hunted by the evil out there when I sensed it, then I was wrong. I couldn't battle groups of vampires, it would be suicide. Vampires as a rule don't hunt in groups, they are territorial, they don't want to share, but it wasn't unheard of, so therefore quite possible.

At least I'd sense if there was more than one of them on a hunt, but what good would that do?

"Has the *Iunctio* given a ruling?" This was Nero, the first time he had said anything since Michel had dropped that little bombshell.

"They have advised for us to use all methods possible to avoid Lucinda's abilities," Michel replied, his eyes still firmly on me.

"Why would they do that? If vampires are hunting indiscriminately, breaking their rules, why would they encourage them to avoid my abilities?" I asked dumbfounded and not in just a little shock.

This didn't make sense, I was practically their pet policeman. I am the one that punishes those that have broken their rules. They have always accepted my part in their world, the need for my kind. I'm the Nosferatin equivalent of their Enforcer. That little thought did not sit well.

"They have recognised the shift in power to your kind. We all felt it just now. As though a switch had been flicked and suddenly the Light is more dangerous than the Dark. They are scared, they do not relinquish power well. What has just happened, *ma douce*, to have made that sudden tip of the scale? What have you been doing?"

His stare was intense, not at all friendly. I didn't know what answer he expected for me to give, but from the looks of him right now, I was sure he did not want to hear it, not really. The anger was there now, it rolled around the room like a caged tiger, it brushed against my sides, pinning me to my seat. Michel didn't usually have this effect over me any more, his powers can not influence me now we are joined. I had no idea how he was doing this, but I did not like it. Not one little bit.

"What the hell, Michel? How are you doing that?"

"Doing what?" he asked calmly.

"I can feel your power, it's crushing me. You shouldn't be able to do that." My voice was weaker than it should have been, my breath was coming in short gasps. Nero had knelt down beside me, he obviously wasn't feeling it, Dream Walking can have its benefits sometimes, but he could see the strain on me as I pushed back against that

Sanguis Vitam and all its force.

"Stop it," he said. "You are hurting her."

Michel just laughed, a short sharp harsh sound that filled the room with stabs of pain. "The *Iunctio* has sent us all power, power to combat the Light. It appears it has negated our joining."

"Is this what you want, Michel? To hurt me?" I was on my side now, curled in on myself like a ball, my words just a whisper, each one a strain between clenched teeth and small breaths of air.

I couldn't see Michel, I couldn't even sense the Bond, it was as though he was just another vampire out to kill, as though my Michel had ceased to exist.

Abruptly the *Sanguis Vitam* retreated. I took a deep shaky breath in and almost whimpered in relief. Nero was rubbing my back.

I sat up slowly, Nero helping me with his arm around my shoulder. I looked at Michel, there wasn't a shadow of regret on his face, just blank, his mask. I couldn't tell what he was thinking, what he was feeling. The Bond was back, in the background, I could sense that, but nothing else. The mask he wore made it hard to think, it shattered my confidence and squashed my strength. I couldn't have summoned the energy to read his aura if I had tried.

"Leave us, Nero." Michel almost spat his name out. "I wish to talk alone with my kindred Nosferatin."

I looked at Nero, begging him to not leave with my eyes. He shook his head and whispered, "I am sorry, Kiwi, I cannot Dream Walk with you if he does not allow it. It is a fail safe of the joining and Bond. If your kindred vampyre wishes privacy, my Dream Walk must obey."

He bent and kissed my forehead, his lips just above my skin as he said, "You have a strength in you, Lucinda, a brightness of Light that cannot be destroyed. Trust it. Trust yourself."

And with that he was gone.

And even though Michel stood there in that room with me, I felt so alone, so very, very alone.

Chapter 9
Alone

"You can be a bastard, you know that?" I shot a look of hatred at Michel. He really had pissed me off.

"I have been more than patient with the infatuation you have for this Nosferatin."

"He is my trainer. My teacher. Nothing more." I said each word slowly, clearly, trying to convey the meaning of what I was telling him.

He laughed, not quite as short and sharp as before, but not Michel's usual dripping-with-sex laugh either. It had an edge to it I didn't much like.

"If that is how you look at a teacher, my dear, you would have been an impossible temptation at school."

I glared at him.

"Tell me. What happened just now?"

It was a command, I could feel it, wrapped up in *Sanguis Vitam* pushing against my mind. I almost succumbed, but even before we joined I could fight Michel's hold over me, the effect of his power. The knowledge of that warmed me inside and helped to push away the cold his power had brought. It was clumsy and not altogether successful, but he felt it's backlash and that only made me more determined to push out the rest.

His power left me in a snap, like a twig had broken, or the mast of a yacht under full sail. I almost fell back against the couch with the recoil it produced.

He nodded his head slowly, a sign of defeat. He even smiled a little, just a hint, not too much. His eyes were still full of magenta, but his fists were no longer clenched.

"Please, *ma douce*, it is important."

He always could get me when he was polite. Michel was so used to demanding what he wanted, hearing him say please was always a slight shock. Even when I was mad at him, like now, it somehow managed to break down a carefully constructed wall.

I let a breath out in a long huff and ran a hand through my hair. "Nothing happened, Michel, we were just talking about Gregor and my new power."

"Not when I came in the room."

"Nothing happened. What else do you want me to say?" I was getting angry again, my voice had risen slightly, my back had gone stiff.

He hadn't moved from his position against the closed door throughout all of this, but he took a step forward now. He stopped though, as if coming closer would cause him pain. My heart ached at that.

"Did you..." He paused, swallowed thickly. "Did you feel a connection between you?"

Huh? How did he know?

He sighed, he'd seen the look on my face, felt the emotions rolling off me. I don't think I have ever seen Michel look so defeated before. I wanted to crawl to him, to wrap my arms around him, to beg his forgiveness. Then a little part of me rebelled, *nothing happened, you do not need to feel guilt.*

He looked up at me then. I knew that thought had reached him. I hadn't meant it to be thrown out, it just had.

He nodded. As though he finally accepted my explanation, my defence. He came the rest of the way towards me and sat down on the couch.

"A connection between you and Nero." He rubbed his

forehead, ran a hand through his beautiful shiny dark hair. "The *Iunctio* has announced that you are the *Sanguis Vitam Cupitor*, is that true, *ma douce*?"

"Yes."

"This is the power you told me of before? I had not recognised it. If you have a connection with Nero, then he would be your Herald. True?"

"Yes." I hadn't taken my eyes off him, nor moved from where I sat, still rigid, still waiting for him to pounce. How is it that I could love this man yet be so scared of him too?

He didn't say anything for a while, just sat there thinking.

"The connection you felt to Nero activated the Prophesy."

"You know about the Prophesy?"

He laughed a bitter laugh. "We were there when it was uncovered." He sat back against the couch, almost relaxed, I knew better.

"The Prophesy can only be fulfilled if the Herald recognises the *Sanguis Vitam Cupitor.* If he does not, then no further part of the Prophesy can come true. You are both, in point of fact, the keys to the whole thing. Without Nero, it does not come into existence, without you, it does not get fulfilled."

"How is it you know so much about this, you personally can't have been there when it was written?"

"I was not, no. But I was on the *Iunctio*. Remember, *ma douce*?"

Yeah I remembered, buddy-buddy with old Gregor.

"The *Iunctio* will do everything in its power to stop the Prophesy. They may have tolerated your powers, your abilities to hunt those of us that breach the law, but the Prophesy they cannot ignore. It represents the end of their position of dominance. It is prophesied that *the Light will capture the Dark, and will hold it dear*. Vampyres do not like to be held captive, *ma douce*. No matter the beauty of the creature who captures us."

"How do you feel about all of this?"

He turned to look at me, he had a strange combination of emotions playing across his face; tenderness, anguish, fear, longing, regret, disbelief. I couldn't keep up with the progression of it all. For a being that does not feel too many emotions naturally, he was doing a mighty fine job of displaying them all.

"The power the *Iunctio* is projecting right now is designed to turn all vampyre against you, including me." His voice was low, rough, as though he was forcing the words from between his lips. "I can fight it, *ma douce*, but not when I have such raw emotion to battle too. The sight of you as I entered this room was too much to bear." He closed his eyes slowly and took a deep breath. "Tonight, it would be better if you stayed in your apartment. The wards there will protect you from my kind. I cannot be near you, I am sorry. Not until I get this under control. It would not be safe."

My hand was covering my mouth trying to hold the cry I wanted to release in, to stop from making any sound that would tip me over the edge. My eyes were stinging with tears I refused to shed. My chest was tight, my head hurt, my body ached with an emptiness that appalled me. My heart was shattering with such raw pain.

"Please, *ma douce*, try to rein it in. I am so close to the edge, I do not want to hurt you."

Too late, I thought numbly as I stood and took a couple of steps away, keeping my front to him, placing my back against the wall.

Michel looked awful, in such pain. His body was rigid with the effort it was taking to maintain control, his face was twisted in agony, his fists clenched at his sides. I hadn't noticed until now that he held handfuls of the seat cushion bunched in his grasp. He was shaking in a fine tremor, right across his body. I could see sweat gleaming on his forehead and upper lip. Oh my God. Oh my God.

Bruno burst through the door then and stood looking at me, he slowly turned to Michel. I held my breath. Bruno was big, hell he was enormous compared to me, I did not want to know if he was under the same spell as Michel, a spell the *Iunctio* had set in motion.

He took a small step towards me, when I yelped and jumped back against the wall, he held both hands up in a placating manner, trying to tell me he meant me no harm. I wonder why I didn't believe him?

"Luce. Michel has commanded me to protect you. To get you home. He has commanded all of his vampires to give you safe passage. We can fight the *Iunctio*'s power for a while, but not long. You need to glaze me to reconfirm Michel's command. With your glaze, I can resist the power indefinitely."

Shit. Did this qualify as a life or death situation? Hell yes.

I nodded. He walked towards me slowly, hands still out in a pacifying stance, trying not to scare the skittish Nosferatin. I could feel my heart in my throat, a huge lump that was hard to swallow passed. My breathing was rapid, my palms were sweating. This sucked big time.

He stood a foot in front of me, looming over me. He couldn't help it, even if he bent over and scrunched his shoulders he would tower above me.

"What do I say?" My voice was tiny, barely a whisper.

"Make it a command. Not a request. Command me to protect you and get you home safely."

I swallowed and nearly choked on my fear. I had to do this and I had to mean it. I'd only glazed a couple of times, but both times I was full of heightened emotion, desperate, kind of like I was now. I took the step closer needed in order to place my hands on Bruno's shoulders. It was quite a reach from my height, but I managed. I'd had my hands on Bruno's shoulders the last time I glazed him, so it just felt right.

I looked into his eyes and felt a door opening, wide, before it had a chance to slam in my face I commanded, "Bruno, get me home safely and protect me at all cost!"

There was a brief moment when his dark brown eyes flashed golden yellow, then he just nodded. In an instant he had me in his thick muscled arms and we were out the door. I didn't even get a backward glance at Michel. We moved with such speed, the interior of the club was a blur. I didn't feel any elevated *Sanguis Vitam* as we passed. Bruno mumbled against my ear, "The line has been ordered to leave town for a few hours, even if they can't fight the *Iunctio's* power, we will be at your home before they can return."

Michel had thought of everything. Despite being in the grip of the *Iunctio*, he had ensured the best possible chance for my survival. Of course, it was only self preservation at its best.

It took mere seconds to reach my apartment, vampires can move faster than even me. Bruno placed me down in front of my door then turned to scan the area outside the building. The wind made the nearby bushes rustle, giving me a shiver down my back. I fumbled with my key and finally managed to get the door open, stepping across the threshold. By the time I turned to tell Bruno to stay outside, he had pushed me back and closed the door behind him. He quickly did a circuit of my flat. It took three seconds. It's a small apartment. He came back and stood in front of me.

How had Bruno got in my home? I had no idea, but also no desire to rescind any invitation I may have made. Weird. I did know however, that I didn't want him indoors with me.

"You can't stay in here."

He looked at me oddly, his head slightly tilted to one side.

"Are you rescinding my invitation?"

Huh. I must have invited him in at one time, funny, I didn't remember it.

I found myself saying no, even before I had thought of it. He just smiled.

"I shall step outside, but I will not leave your front door until dawn. Good night, Lucinda. Safe sleep."

He flashed in a blur as he exited, door clicking softly behind him. I could see his bulk on just the other side of the glass in the door, a shadow against the night.

I closed the curtains and checked all the locks. Not that I didn't trust Bruno, or that any vampire could really get in.

Michel had placed a protection ward on my property for some time now, he recently used some of my powers to enhance it even more. I knew I was safe from the average vampire. It was Michel I was worried about though tonight.

I turned and glanced around my tiny apartment. It's cream on cream, simple, small, but all me. It's home. I have always felt so safe in my home. Not tonight.

I went and sat on the three seater sofa, staring at nothing, feeling a little numb. The only emotion I could identify was fear. It was strong and constant and determined to stay. I don't know how long I sat there, unfeeling, unmoving, barely breathing. The lights were off, it was dark, I didn't have the energy to get up and switch them on, despite the fact that a little illumination would have been nice right now. My mind was a riot of thoughts, so messy, all tumbled together, I couldn't decipher one from the other. It would have been nice to have a friend with me right now, but who is there? Rick no longer fills that role. Celeste couldn't even if she wanted to.

I have acquaintances, work colleagues, people I rely on for information, contacts and the like. I wouldn't want any of them to be in the middle of this. It would have been nice to have Nero here, but he's Dream Walked once tonight, he couldn't risk another, I may need him again soon. There would be no point Dream Walking to him, it would be like burying my head in the sand, leaving my body out unprotected for anyone to harm.

I reached for my bag and pulled out my stake. The feel of it's weight in my hands as I held it loosely in my lap was reassuring. I ran my fingers over the smoothness of the silver, every stroke a comfort, a balm to my ragged nerves.

I'm not quite sure when I lay down on the couch, when I let myself drift off to sleep. I hadn't meant to. I'd actually had no intention of sleeping at all, wanting to stay awake all night. Not that it would have helped. Gregor was somewhere in Europe, if it's night here, it's day there. I knew he wouldn't be asleep, he's a master vampire, he only needs to be indoors, protected from the light. But somehow, the thought of making it to our daylight was appealing. If I could last until then, then I could stay awake all day. Michel would get himself under control, he would find a solution to this mad, mad problem. He would save me. He had to.

But sleep did come, despite my protests. It wrapped me in its soft cocoon, comforted me with its embrace. It made the stiffness in my back and neck ease, the tension down my spine evaporate, the thumping of my heart quiet, my breathing deepen and lengthen. I was free of all that had happened that day, free of the nightmare of my life.

Only to fall into another.

Chapter 10
Dreams

I woke to a soft light. I struggled against it, I knew I had been in the dark. I hadn't switched a light on. Then who had?

I opened my eyes and found myself standing in a room. It was not overly large, but as big as my lounge, dining and kitchen put together. There was an antique four poster bed to one side, thick dark red, almost burgundy covers flowed over the sides, copious amounts of rich dark red pillows were scattered on top. The lights were low, coming from two bedside lamps on tables either side of the bed. They matched the dark antique wood of the four poster.

Curtains hung in swaths of heavy fabric at two floor length windows to the side, they were drawn, not an ounce of light penetrated from behind, they matched the bedspread. There was a painting on the wall. It was beautiful. Soft brush strokes of an old English scene. A horse drawn cart stuck in water, an old farmhouse to the left, a King Charles spaniel in the front. My eyesight is good, so I could read the signature from where I was standing, a metre or more away, even in the low light: Constable. I was betting it was an original.

I knew I was Dream Walking, this wasn't a dream like Michel creates. It was too real. As soon as I acknowledged that thought, a thick, strong arm came around me from behind, a warm breath against my neck, pushing my hair aside.

"You smell just as I remember, little Hunter. Candied apples and sunshine, honey and spring. I can't decide if it's the spring I prefer or the sunshine. Or maybe just the softness of your neck."

His face buried deep against my skin, his lips brushing lightly against the pulse of my neck, the graze of his teeth causing a shiver down my spine. He laughed, low and throaty.

"Your body betrays you."

"Stop using your power, Gregor and then see how I react." I was surprised my voice was even, strong and level in fact. Bully for me.

I felt his shoulders and chest move with his unheard chuckle. "Where would the fun be in that, little Hunter?"

His free arm, the one not wrapped around me, holding me trapped against his chest, came down the side of my body, deftly finding it's way to my hand and plucking my stake, which I hadn't even realised was there, out from my grasp and throwing it across the room behind the bed. Some hunter I am. The flash from the silver caught by the light briefly blinded me and then it was out of sight. Just like my hope.

He didn't stop caressing though. His hand trailed down my leg, feeling my leggings, the ones I usually wear to the gym. I hadn't had a chance to change since after work. At least I hadn't had a workout in them, they were still pretty much newly laundered. His fingers found the bottom of my skin-tight T-Shirt. I always wear pretty tight fitting clothes when I work out, not out of vanity, clothing is so easily used against you when you spar with an opponent, even in kick-boxing gloves. The more skin tight, the safer, no purchase. My entire outfit was designed to provide the least amount of leverage in a fight, unfortunately it pretty much failed to hide my figure. Not that he could see me, but his hands were painting their own picture right now.

"Hmm. No lingerie, but perhaps this is even better. I can't wait to see what beauty is hidden, so poorly, by these close fitting garments."

I didn't answer, what was the point? He was playing with me, like a cat would with a mouse. Not for mutual pleasure, but for his own sadistic needs. Besides, I was too busy trying to figure out how to get out of this little dilemma.

"I must admit..." His breath was hot against my neck, it trailed down my skin leaving a tingling behind that sent a shot of pure desire right through me. I was sure he was using his power to give me that effect, but I couldn't sense it. Oh dear God. "I am enjoying being able to call you to me. I had thought perhaps the first time was a just a mistake, a one off as they say, never to be repeated. But here I am, in my boudoir thinking of you, and what should happen? Your scent permeates the room. Bliss."

I realised with growing mortification, that this had to be his chamber, his day resting place. And he had been resting, because all he was wearing was a robe, satin or silk, but very fine, very thin. I could feel this body through the material, his hard chest, flat stomach, strong thighs. All pressed against me now. God I hoped he didn't sleep in the buff and actually had something on under there.

"What to do with you, little Hunter? I find myself reluctant to turn you over to the *Iunctio*. I rather like the thought of keeping you all to myself."

"You've already put a death warrant on my head, why stop now?"

He laughed, a couple of short throaty chuckles. "Did

Michel behave himself? Were you able to get away? You must have, because here you are, in my arms, uninjured and whole. You must have even fallen asleep, for me to have been able to call you so easily I think. No concern for your kindred's disdain? Perhaps life is not so rosy in the joining as reported? Perhaps you seek the comfort of another's embrace?"

"You're really enjoying this aren't you?"

He shifted slightly against me, so I could get the full effect of just how much he actually was enjoying me right now. There was no missing it, not when he pressed his full hard length against me. I laughed, I don't think he expected that. He stilled ever so slightly.

"Do you challenge me, Hunter? Do you choose to test my resolve?"

"And if I did?" Fight fire with fire they say.

I felt his lips spread in a wide smile against my skin. "It has been a long time since I have had a worthy opponent. There are rules to be obeyed."

"Such as?" Maybe if I just kept him talking long enough I'd think of something to get me out of this mess. Maybe he'd lower his guard and I could reach my stake. Because despite the fact that I felt nothing of the evil that poured off him last night now, I was sure, damn sure, that I could stake him just the same and not lose a moment's sleep over it.

"Well for starters, one must be able to see one's opponent for a fair fight. It would mean I could not attempt to seduce you here. Now."

That sounded good to me, but... "What's the catch?"

He laughed, again with that low manly chuckle which

sent shock waves of desire down my body to places it had no right to be. He stiffened slightly, I felt, more than heard, him inhale. I suppressed a whimper.

"You don't make it easy, do you?" His voice was soft, so smooth, so tender. It surprised me enough to make me catch my breath. "What are you?" It wasn't angry, it wasn't outraged, it was intrigued, surprised, amused. "You have no idea how much I want to see you, to see if that face matches the beautiful shape of your body, to look into your eyes, to see *you*. What are you doing to me?"

He spun me around then to face him, so quickly it threw me off balance, long enough for him to frame my face with his hands, run his fingers over my chin, find my mouth and then claim me with his. His lips were warm and soft, his tongue as it darted confidently between my teeth, so wet and strong. I had been so shocked by the move my mouth had been slightly open in surprise, he hadn't wasted the opportunity. He pressed his body against me and forced me to take a step back. Two. Three. Four. Then I felt the bed at the back of my knees and was unable to stop the fall backwards onto my back. I was trapped under his weight, his firm long body holding me still, moulding to mine.

I hadn't tried to stop him, I was momentarily numbed into inaction, but the fall onto the bed and the feel of his hard body against mine, had woken my bedazzled brain up from it's sleep. *One step closer to my stake.*

He stilled. Then pulled his mouth away from me and laughed. "Oh you are good. You think you can reach it from here?"

Huh? Okey dokey, just how much could he read of my mind? You're an idiot. Nope, no reaction. You weigh a tonne. Nada. You smell like cherry trees in the spring and chocolate coated ice cream. Oops. I didn't think that one would have had the desired effect I was going for. Still, no response and I was betting he would have had a good one if he'd heard that. *Get off me!*

"No."

Well, well, well. He could read my thoughts if I threw them. But I hadn't thrown that first one, I had shouted it in my head though.

"So, now what?" I asked to fill the silence that had bloomed between us.

"Do you accept the challenge, my little Hunter?"

"I'm not quite sure what the challenge is?" I couldn't lie, he'd lost me somewhere between lying on top of me and chocolate coated ice cream. Damn!

"The game is simple. I release you now, let you return to your body unharmed, with the invitation to court you in person in due course."

"Not good enough."

He smiled, it had the ability to light up those amazing silver and platinum eyes. I resisted the urge to moan.

"What would you accept as a satisfactory exchange?"

"Release me now and I promise not to stake you. Today."

He laughed then, a full body laugh that made the length of him shift against me, his chest against my upper body, his thigh over my leg, pressing between mine. I failed to stifle the moan this time.

He stilled. "You know, I don't believe you would mind my seduction, at all. I think you crave it." His voice was barely a whisper, so intimate, so private, just for me.

"Quit using your powers and we'll see."

"I'm not using my powers, Lucinda."

Bugger.

"What? No witty retort? Have I finally stilled that sweet voice of yours? Are you giving up so easily?"

I pushed against him. I may be super strong for a part human, but no match for a vampire of his level of *Sanguis Vitam*. He hadn't been using his powers before, but as soon as I attempted to shift him, it came flooding in, crashing against me and taking my breath away.

"Now, now. Don't force me to resort to such easy, such barbaric, methods to hold you. Where's the challenge in that?"

I gave up on physical assault and tried for mental. I don't give up entirely that easily though. *Give it your best shot then!*

"You accept?"

"Let me go, call off the hit squads and it's a deal."

"Are you so sure, Hunter?"

I swallowed, maybe I was missing something here. I wasn't even sure what a challenge like this entailed. I was getting a little creepy feeling between my shoulder blades though, never a good sign.

"What, what are the rules again?

He laughed. "Oh I do wish I could see your face. Simple. A challenge has been made, exchange of acceptable desires given, the game is on."

That didn't sound too bad did it? I mean I'd get to go home, he'd call the *Iunctio* off and would just *try* to court me, whatever courting means. I'd be home free.

Just one clarification. "You will call the *Iunctio* off?"

"Yes. I will tell them you are mine to deal with. That will suffice."

"You carry that sort of clout?"

He smiled. "Does it surprise you?"

"No, I guess not. I had heard you were called the Enforcer."

"Indeed. You have been doing your homework too, it seems."

"Just what does the Enforcer do exactly?" Best to be prepared.

He lowered his head slowly to the side of my neck, then traced a line from my ear down past my pulse point to my clavicle with his tongue. Against my skin he whispered, "I take what I want and carve it to my will. No one has stood against me and won."

Oh Fuck.

"Will you accept the challenge, little Hunter? Or shall I demonstrate now how I can bend you to my will?"

I swallowed, I hadn't meant to, not with his lips against my neck, so close to my throat. He felt the movement and groaned.

"Say it. Say you accept and I'll let you go. Say it."

My mind was reeling, there had to be another way. This didn't feel safe, this didn't feel right. I knew he was withholding something, I knew there would be more to this than what he had divulged. He was a vampire for God's sake, they are treacherous and devious and out for only themselves. But, what choice did I have? I couldn't reach my stake, he wasn't giving me a moment's grace, his hold so firm, so sure. He could lay here with me trapped beneath him for hours. I did have powers. I couldn't glaze him though, not without him seeing my eyes. I could try to use my Light, like I did to kill those vampires in Cairo, but I knew without even trying that it wouldn't work. He meant me no harm, physically, he had not an ounce of evil flowing from him, I could only sense Darkness laced with Light. If he already had some Light in him, I could not force mine too. Somehow, I intrinsically knew, that my talent wouldn't allow for that. When I had used it those two times at the Coptic Museum in Cairo, I had been surrounded by evil and a Darkness so complete that it called to my Light. It was as if that calling brought the power forward and nothing else would.

"Will you answer the challenge, *ma petite chasseuse*?" Huh. French. I hadn't picked that.

No matter which way I looked at it, I couldn't think of an out. But, if I did this I would have Michel back. The *Iunctio* would have to remove the power boost and influence they were currently exerting. Michel would know what to do.

"Yes." It was a whisper, hardly a sound.

"The challenge has been accepted, now to exchange marks."

"What?" I finally found my voice.

He chuckled. "I said there were rules, I didn't say I would play fair."

You bastard!

"No. My parents were married before I was born." He couldn't stop laughing.

"So, so what type of mark?" I tried to interrupt his delightful chuckles.

"Nothing too predatory. Well, maybe just a little." His

fangs came out in a slow, silent glide, sliding down to glint brightly in the room. I was so relieved he didn't pull his lips back in a nasty grimace, like so many of the vamps do when about to feed, that I didn't even have time to register what was happening next.

His lips met my skin, moving smoothly, quickly, until they found the right spot and his fangs pierced through to the blood vessel below. I pushed against his chest with all my might, but as soon as the sharp sting of his bite was replaced with a sense of total bliss, unadulterated joy and a quick shot of heat and desire, I forgot to push and simply rested my hands against his chest.

His voice floated inside my head, so soft, like a caress, a wave gently lapping at the shore. *Mark me, my little Hunter. Mark me now.*

I didn't know what to do. I'd never had a challenge like this before. It all seemed so permanent, so frighteningly permanent. I didn't like this. I didn't like this at all. I had no idea what to do, but despite the lust he was filling my body with, the fear of what I had done was overriding it, slapping it away. What had I done? What had I done? I felt the anger and desperation rise up inside me, consume me from within, it pushed against his shields, it felt around the edges, it pried against the wall of his defences and the only thing I could think of was Light. Bright, beautiful, Light.

It's what I am made of. It is what I am. It shines within me with such intensity it blinds. As soon as I caught that thought I felt it, like a tangible energy, something I could grasp. I reached out with my mind and wrapped a mental hand around it, gripped it tight within my fist. It felt warm and safe and filled with love, goodness and everything that made this world so beautiful, unique and precious. I gripped it tight and thrust it against Gregor's shield, I wrapped it around the wall he had built and pushed with all my strength. I felt them give, I felt the Light pour in, I felt him still, stop breathing, stop drinking me in. I felt that Light fill him up and bathe him in its glory. I felt him accept it.

His fangs retracted from me slowly. He licked the bite marks, stopping the flow of blood. He hovered over me for a moment, not saying anything, still not breathing.

"That, my little Hunter, was unexpected." His voice was low, husky, sexy.

You're telling me? I felt like I'd just made love for hours, I hadn't orgasmed, but my body thought that was just a mere technicality. I was basking in a glow that had nothing to do with my inner Light.

"You could become quite addictive. What have I got myself into?" Gregor murmured.

I thought that was my line, but I was too sated to make a comment right then.

"You can go. I will let you. The challenge has been made, the exchange of marks given. It is set."

He raised off me and fell to the side, collapsing back on the bed. His hand was still touching me, subconsciously I think, as though he couldn't break that contact just yet. I noticed he was breathing again, rapidly, but he was trying to get it back under control.

I almost wanted to say *was it as good for you as it was for me?*

"Yes."

Shit! I was going to have to be more careful around

this man.

"Why have you not left?" he asked quietly.

"Um," I was having difficulty finding my voice. "I don't think I can move just yet, um, concentrate on Walking, I mean."

He laughed and it warmed my soul. So beautiful and deep, and wrapped me up and held me tight.

"What have we begun, Lucinda? I asked for a challenge, I think I may have just met my match."

I was beginning to come down from that impossible high, the world had begun to focus again, my breathing was back under control. I could feel my heartbeat, settling, still too fast, but I could focus on it again, force myself to calm with the help of its rhythm and return to my body.

Just before I left the warmth of his hand in mine and embraced that nothingness that begged, I whispered, "Don't underestimate me, Gregor. I belong to no one."

The last thing I heard before the world faded to blissful black was, "And I always get what I want, Lucinda, always."

Oh crap.

Chapter 11
Light to the Dark

I woke up on my couch, it was still dark, no light filtered past the closed curtains in my lounge. I could still see Bruno's bulk outside the door, silhouetted against the moonlight. I rolled into a sitting position and reached up to trace the marks left by Gregor. They were slightly raised, I was betting if I looked in a mirror right now, they would be pink, precise dots, but still slightly pink.

I ran my hand around the other side of my neck and felt the familiar raised marks of Michel's. His were no longer pink, they had faded long ago, you couldn't even see them with the naked eye. Well, at least humans couldn't, every vampire I met always flicked a glance over them. It's like a signature, they recognise the mark and who it belongs to. It definitely makes me feel like a possession, but I guess that's the point. I may not have been able to see them in the mirror any more, but I could still feel them with my finger tips. Michel could find them without even trying, like honey to a bee. Damn. I did not like being a pin cushion.

When a vampire feeds, he does leave marks, but if it's just a normal feed, they vanish and heal relatively quickly. Again something to do with their saliva, it not only coagulates the blood but heals the marks. Can't leave too many obvious fang scars on the Norms, it would out the vamps way too quickly. But, if they mark you, like Michel did the night of our joining, it stays, forever. I hadn't realised Michel was going to do that when we joined, he hadn't warned me, omitted that little piece of news. I don't think I have ever forgiven him.

There are different ways to be marked and the

permanency can vary. As a Nosferatin, we obviously can do it too. I'd never tried, this was the first time for me and I'd had no idea how it was accomplished. Instinct had just taken over, but I have been marked by a Nosferatin before. Nero marked me with a false vampire scent once. I don't think he really had meant to, he'd got carried away, at least I have chosen to believe his explanation. Sucker, who me? But, his mark had been temporary, a brief marking that ended when Michel confronted me, as though it was designed to only stay until the intended recipient had witnessed it. Michel and Nero have been having little pissing contests ever since.

But, this mark by Gregor felt different. I couldn't be sure, but it felt extremely close to how Michel's had done. How is it possible to be marked by two vampires at the same time? The whole idea of a mark was to claim possession. I fought that notion every day, I belong to no one, but it still remains the root cause of marking. It seemed I had a mark from Michel and a mark from Gregor now, but what would it mean?

I guess I was about to find out, because I felt him approach. Michel's *Sanguis Vitam* flowed passed Bruno through the door and wrapped around me, gently touching, tentatively sweeping over my arms and body, as though it was checking to see if it was all right to come in. Michel didn't need an invite, but I did kind of acknowledge that at least he was trying.

I got up and switched the light on, then returned to my seat. Standing around looking nervous was not going to help my cause.

The door opened and I noticed Bruno had gone, no

longer blocking the moonlight, Michel however, was. He stood there a moment and looked at me, his eyes on mine. I thanked my lucky stars that his were no longer magenta, just a deep blue and indigo, pools of brightness. His gaze swept over me and didn't miss a thing. He took a long shaky breath in, closing his eyes and only opening them again when he had released the air from his lungs. They were still blue, a trace of violet, but no amethyst. Amazing.

When Nero had marked me that last time, Michel had lost all control, almost choking me to death. If I hadn't have had a stake on me, I don't think he would have stopped. How was he controlling himself now?

He stepped across the threshold and the door swung closed softly behind him, all on its own. He walked - well maybe more like glided towards me - and stood a metre away, looking down. His face hid all emotion. I didn't know if he was actually feeling anything at all, or just hiding it. It was so blank, so bare, so nothing. I hated that mask he so often wore.

"What have you done?"

His voice was empty, not harsh, not soft, not sad, not angry. Just nothing. Simply words spilling from his mouth. I had a sudden shiver go through me, as though I was looking at a shell. As though whatever it was that had animated Michel in the past, was gone. He was still there, but he also wasn't.

"Gregor," was all I could manage. I really didn't think words could have saved me right now.

"I can see that. Why?" And now a brief emotion flashed across his face. Betrayal. He felt betrayed. Oh God.

It vanished swiftly, to be replaced by that empty,

horrible mask.

"I didn't realise." An argument that would not help matters. It is irrelevant to a vampire if the intent was not there, ignorance is not a defence in vampire circles, the end result is the punishable offence. And here I was sitting in front of my kindred Nosferatu with someone else's mark. I was guessing this was not a good thing.

He hadn't moved. He was still breathing, albeit a little unevenly. I could see his heartbeat in the pulse on his neck, the one I wanted to reach up and brush my finger tips across so desperately right now, to help slow it's slightly elevated speed. The blank look on his face stilled my hand, even if my brain had already shouted, *don't.*

I might as well get this over with, there was no point delaying the inevitable. "I really believed I didn't have a choice, Michel. I couldn't fight him off, he would have handed me over to the *Iunctio*, or worse, for himself. He offered me a deal, an exchange, I took it. Now I'm back here and the *Iunctio* has called its power back, hasn't it?"

He didn't confirm it, he didn't nod, he didn't need to. He wouldn't have been here unless it had been removed.

"What challenge did you agree to?" His voice was so even, so controlled. There was no hint of warmth, no hint of its usual light tone, just a hollow echo of nothing.

"He let me go unharmed, he called the *Iunctio* off and I agreed he could try to court me."

Michel suddenly fell to his knees onto my carpeted floor. A look of anguish crossing his face, a small desperate cry escaping his lips. He pulled himself together quickly, returning to that mask, but there was a hint of haunting to his eyes now that hadn't been there before. He didn't, however, get up from the floor. I didn't think his legs would have held him.

"There is no *try* to it, *ma douce*. He will succeed." Now, just wait a damn minute! I am not a foregone conclusion. He could try all he liked, but that didn't make it a *fait accompli,* did it? "And you do not want Gregor to succeed. Seduction to him is a game. A cruel, vicious game."

I swallowed at that last comment, but chose to ignore it for now. One problem at a time. "What makes you so sure he will succeed?"

He laughed, it wasn't bitter, as I would have expected it to be, but heavily laden with resignation. "He has never failed in acquiring what he wants and now you have set a challenge in motion, it is impossible for any other outcome. He has marked you as well, as his own. The mark is permanent, *ma douce*. It will never leave you for as long as you live. The mark binds you to him and makes his task that much easier."

"How can he mark me, when you already have?"

"The choice of number of *Sigillum,* permanent marks, is up to the marked. It is *you* who have invited him in. Had you refused to accept his *Sigillum*, he would not have been able to mark you."

Oh dear. How had I let this happen? I didn't know I was accepting something, I just thought it was happening and I had no choice. Just like when Michel marked me.

"Did I have to accept your mark too?"

"Yes.

"I don't remember being asked?"

He smiled, the first hint of Michel on that mask since

he arrived. "I could not have marked you unless you wanted me to. That is why I did not ask."

"It would have been nice to know, Michel."

"Perhaps. Would it really have changed things though, *ma douce*?"

"At the time, yes."

"And now? Would you be without my *Sigillum*?"

I couldn't answer that straight away. His mark, or *Sigillum*, or whatever the fuck he called it, was a sign of his possession of me. I would never agree to that. But, and yes there is a but, it also felt like he was mine. By having that connection to him it didn't feel all one way, it felt like it was my mark on him too. But, that's not altogether true, is it? Still, I couldn't give him an honest answer right now, I just didn't know.

"Have I marked you?" I asked for want of something better to say.

"You would know if you had. But no, you have not." He did look sad then. Slowly, little by little, Michel was returning and with it emotions decorating his face. "I gather Gregor wears your *Sigillum*?"

He had voiced that statement as a question, a slight inflection at the end of the sentence, but with an obvious layer of hurt unsaid in his tone.

"Yep. I think he does." A thought occurred to me. "Did Gregor trick me into this exchange of marks? He said it was part of the challenge."

Michel's smile was bitter this time. "He never did play fair." The pain in those few words was heart breaking. As though this had torn his heart in two.

"He wears your mark." Michel sighed, a sound so

mournful it rocked my soul. "I have long wondered what your *Sigillum* would be. What form it would take. I have ached for it." When I opened my mouth to tell him what had happened, what I thought had happened when I marked Gregor, he raised his hand to stop me and closed his eyes, as though in pain. His voice when he spoke was strained, low and slightly uneven. "Do not tell me, *ma douce*. I do not think I could bear to know right now. I will know before too much longer, Gregor will come calling, but not tonight. Please, not tonight."

In all my 25 years I have never felt so rotten. It was as though a fist had entered my chest, grabbed hold of my heart and squeezed it with unrelenting force. I ached from inside out; sharp, stabbing, deep, penetrating pain. I let the tears fall freely, I couldn't have stopped them if I had tried, they ran down my face and dripped softly onto the carpet. I didn't know when I had slid off the couch to my knees, but I vaguely acknowledged that's where I was now. I didn't make a sound, it was as though the pain did not want to leave me, wanted to stay trapped in my heart for eternity, rolling around my body without release.

I numbly realised that Michel was at my side, brushing my hair out of my eyes, smoothing it down my head, stroking my neck. He pulled me to him and whispered something in French I didn't understand, just soft soothing words without meaning that tried to chase away the pain, but it was too late. It had grabbed a hold of me, of my heart and was not letting go. I'm not sure I wanted it to. I deserved this, I had caused this mess. Michel had suffered because of me. What was I becoming? I had always thought that I was the good guy, that the creatures of the night were the baddies. Why is it then, that I felt more evil right now than they had ever appeared to me before? That I felt suffocated in the Darkness and I could not feel my Light.

I heard the phone ringing in the background, like a buzzing you can't quite place. Michel let it ring for a while, but it was persistent, then reluctantly he let me go, murmuring something angrily under his breath, to answer it. I felt myself curl up into a ball, protecting my chest from attack. It wouldn't do any good, the attack was on the inside, but it was a natural reaction to the pain. I couldn't help it.

I heard Michel talking, but I couldn't pick up the words. He sounded frustrated and annoyed though, I could pick up the tone, it then turned to sarcastic. Michel was always good a sarcasm. I think he was arguing with whoever was on the line. I blocked it out and concentrated on the Dark that was smoothing against my skin. Enticing me down to the blackness below, encouraging me to sink further in, cover my body, my head, with black. It promised to take the pain away, to make it all better, if I just acknowledged the Dark.

Michel touched my shoulder, when I didn't respond he shook me. I ignored him, I didn't want to face him again. To see the hurt and pain and sense of betrayal there. Not that. Not ever again. I turned away and buried my face in my hands. He tried to pick me up. I noticed the cordless phone sitting on the floor beside him, the green light on to show it was active, a call in progress. The green glow made me think of Light and the Darkness sprang, slapping me, grabbing me and pulling me closer. I pushed against

Michel's hold and collapsed on the floor.

I saw him pick the phone up and say something harshly into the mouthpiece, he then dropped it and tried shaking me again. I felt his *Sanguis Vitam* fill the room, felt it pushing against my shields, trying to find a way in, but my shields weren't mine any more, they were big and black and reached farther and higher than I could see or sense. They were impenetrable. I marvelled at their magnificence, at the sheer enormity of their scale. I had never been able to make shields like this. Never.

I noticed a flickering in the room, a lightness that burnt my eyes. The Darkness inside screamed in pain, lashed out at that flickering Light, but couldn't connect with it, so lashed out at me. It was my fault there was Light in the room, it was my fault the Darkness felt threatened, I needed to make it go away.

Michel moved to the other side of me so the bright flickering Light could come to where he had been. I felt a hand touch my shoulder, heard words trying to sooth, but I screamed and shoved and clawed at that Light. I had to get away from the Light, I had to destroy whatever it was that had come to bathe me in it. I did not want the Light, I wanted Dark. Dark had promised me an end to the pain, an end to the guilt, it would take it all away. With Light everything is so visible, I didn't want to see any more.

I felt someone's rough arms lift me up to face them, there was a Light to their features I couldn't open my eyes to, but I felt the Light behind my closed eyelids any way. I blanched and tried to turn away. The Light in front of me moved their hands to either side of my face, I felt Michel's hands hold me from behind, not allowing me to pull back. I tried to turn my head, but the Light's grip was too firm. And it hurt, oh dear God it hurt. Why did it hurt so much? Was this my punishment? Was this the end?

Suddenly, I felt warm lips meet mine, harsh and firm, desperate in their need for me to acknowledge them. I pushed back against Michel's hold, trying to get away, but those lips kept finding me, kept pursuing, kept hunting. I opened my mouth to scream at them, but then a tongue slipped between my teeth. I wanted to bite that tongue, to sever it from the Light, to stop it invading me. I wanted to cause pain so badly I ached.

Then I felt a warmth, just a small tiny speck of it, seep inside. It swirled around my body and settled next to my heart, like a dog at your feet in the evening, content and happy and at home. After the warmth came a glimmer of Light, just a flash, then another. The Darkness recoiled, only slightly, but the Light was determined, it was so strong. I couldn't fight it. The Darkness couldn't fight it. And then I realised, I didn't want to fight it. I recognised it. That shocked me. I didn't want to recognise it, I wanted to wrap the Dark around me and cry, but I knew this Light, I couldn't deny it and all of a sudden, I wanted it.

I felt my arms go up around the person in front of me, I felt myself mould against the strong broad chest, I began to devour that Light, I craved it, I wanted all of it. A need so strong it rocked me and made me moan out in frustration that it wasn't giving me all of it. It was my Light, damn it! Give it back!

And then I could hear whimpers that sounded strange, but vaguely like me, a man's half suppressed moan. Then I felt things around me, the touch of his hands on my face, my neck, behind my head, the way he caressed there, pulling me closer, the firmness of his body against mine, the heat of his breath against my mouth, the feel of his skin under my finger tips, the warmth of him.

I opened my eyes and stared into deep pools of cinnamon and coffee. I cried out in alarm and pushed away, my back against the sofa, my breath panting in and out. I doubled over as though I was going to be sick, I even dry retched, but nothing came up. I felt cold and clammy, my hair was plastered to my face, my palms itched with the wetness there.

I looked around me trying to take it all in. Michel sat back against the couch, his mouth in a thin grim line, a look of anguish washing his face. He was breathing hard, as though he had run a marathon, his gaze was intense, his eyes not leaving mine. I could hardly look away, but I knew I had to. I knew I had to face the man in front of me.

I turned my head slowly and looked Nero in the face. I bit my bottom lip then, frowned at him, but he still just sat there serenely, with a slight smile on his lips. A look of chagrin on his features.

"What are you doing here?" My voice was small, quiet, shaky. I was not surprised at that at all. I was surprised that Nero was in my apartment, was here Dream Walking for the second time tonight.

He cleared his throat softly, as though he was having difficulty finding his voice too.

"I am the Light to the Dark, Kiwi. Your need called to me. I came."

He paused then, and shook his head, trying to dislodge a thought I think. He smiled, that dazzling, light-up-your-world, Nero smile.

"When you call, you *really* call, don't you?" he said softly.

"What do you mean?" My voice was getting stronger, thankfully. But it was Michel who answered my question.

"He means, that your need required something more than just a conventional intervention. I do believe he is pleased with the method required to reach you, my dear. I believe... he rather enjoyed it."

The sarcasm was not lost on me. I felt my cheeks flame bright red and there was nothing I could do to stop it.

Bugger.

Chapter 12
Revenge is Sweet

"What was all of that?" I was still sitting on the floor between the two men, no one had moved. No one had said anything else, just leaving it up to me to start the ball rolling. Gee, thanks.

"All of what?" Nero answered, his smile had toned down a bit, but I could still see he was enjoying himself. Quite relaxed sitting on the floor of my lounge, taking in every inch of me. He knew Michel couldn't see him, so he didn't try to hide his appraisal of me. I gave him a glare. He got the message and reschooled his features into the more intense look he usually wore.

"All of that...Darkness. It felt like it was eating me up. Consuming me. What was all of *that?*"

Nero sighed and frowned slightly, his forehead furrowing in concentration. "It would seem your new skills as the *Sanguis Vitam Cupitor* has made you more susceptible to the Dark. It recognised your....pain, whereas normally it would not have had the courage to attack so boldly, one of the Light, now it sees it as a necessity. You frighten it, you are more a threat to the Dark than you have ever been before."

"You talk about it as though it is a sentient being. I always thought of the Light and Dark as being metaphors for what we represent: Good versus Evil," I said.

"Yes, they are that too, but they are a power from the gods and as such, they are more than just that."

I sighed and ran a hand through my still sweat soaked hair. I so did not want to think about *gods* and how they fitted into this mess.

“I know you do not believe that we are descended from a god, Kiwi, but just because you do not believe, does not mean it is not true.”

I shot him another you're-not-being-helpful look, then turned to Michel. “What do you believe?”

Michel had managed to get himself well under control again. He was not exactly wearing his blank mask, but he was protecting himself. He showed mild interest, but a relaxed demeanour, as though what had just happened hadn't scared him half to death. I knew better though.

“My kind have long given up the notion that any of us are descended from gods, but we are more capable of open-mindedness than most. What animates us, is not of this world, so what else does it leave?”

That didn't help me one little bit.

“Will it happen again?” I'd turned back to Nero, he seemed to be the one with all the answers.

“It could. You are closer to your Dark side than you have ever been in the past. You have been brushed with Darkness. Your Light must now battle it. It is a war that only *you* can win or lose.”

“Have you ever had to battle it?”

Nero looked suddenly embarrassed, as though I had asked the most intimate of questions. His face had gone a deep red, his eyes were looking at the floor unable to make contact with mine, his shoulders even hunched slightly. Whoa. I reached out and placed a hand on his shoulder, he blanched slightly, but didn't pull away.

“Nero?”

His voice was soft when he did answer. “Sometimes I battle it daily, Kiwi.”

What could make Nero fight Darkness on such a regular basis? Nero was the most brightly lit person I had ever met. I wanted so badly to ask him, but I felt it was not something he would willingly share with me in front of Michel, if at all. I pulled my hand away slowly from his shoulder and just sat there looking at him. He didn't raise his face to mine at all.

Michel had kept very quiet throughout all of this, he hadn't moved at all, but I felt his gaze on me now, intent, interested in what I would say next. I didn't spare him a glance. If he had something to say, he could just pipe up and say it.

The silence stretched out for a while, taking on a calmness that I hadn't felt before. Despite what had just happened, I did feel safe with these two men. Sometimes for completely different reasons, but both of them had the ability to settle my nerves.

So, I had just had my first introduction to the Dark. The Dark that lurks inside every vampire. It didn't surprise me, as I thought it would. We are of the same ilk, vampires and Nosferatins. If they suffer Darkness, then we should be capable of it too. But, what did surprise me was how easily I had accepted it, almost completely allowed it in. If Nero had not come along, what would have happened?

"How did you make it go away, Nero?"

He knew what I was asking about, *how did I make the Darkness go away?* He also knew I wasn't asking about the physical aspect of the task. We all knew he had kissed me. What I wanted to know, was why him, why not Michel?

He glanced at Michel quickly, then back to me. "Like I said, Kiwi. I am the Light to the Dark. I am your Herald. It is within me to call your Light forward. That is all I did."

"Who calls your Light forward when the Darkness comes calling?" My voice was soft, quiet, scared of frightening him away.

He smiled, it lit up his dark brown eyes, making the copper flecks which had started blazing there, dance around the pupil. I couldn't take my eyes off them, they were so beautiful.

"Nafrini, sometimes. My family. Myself. You." The last was a whisper.

I didn't know what to say to that. Part of me had expected him to say Nafrini, his family of Nosferatin in Cairo, even himself. Nero is strong, so strong on so many levels, being able to fight the Darkness himself just seemed so natural. But, I had not expected him to say me. What had I ever done to help him?

I paused, then decided it was best to get back on track. "OK. So, I'm going to have to battle this Darkness from time to time. Any suggestions on how to do that? Any tips?"

"You need only remember that you are Light, Kiwi. The brightest Light I have ever met. Do not hide it, let it out. The Light will always prevail over the Dark."

"Always?"

"Always. It is only our self doubt that would make it stumble, the Light itself is strong enough. We need only believe that, for it to be true."

And there you go with the belief system again. I can't believe we are descended from gods, but I can believe we have Light in us. How much harder would it be to believe the Light always wins? Yeah, right.

I finally turned back to Michel. I wanted to say I was sorry, so very sorry for hurting him. I wanted to say I'd make it better, I'd correct my mistakes, but I had absolutely no idea how to do that. No idea at all. He must have read something in my face, because his softened and his hand reached up and stroked my cheek, his thumb running along the edge of my jaw. We stared at each other for a moment, then I sighed. Why was my life so complicated?

"What is it, *ma douce*? What is wrong?"

I smiled at him, a little sarcastically, I'll admit. "I have Dark inside me, that I can't control on my own and I also have a master vampire, member of the *Iunctio*, tricking me into marking him and being marked by him *and* trying to seduce me as his own. What could possibly be wrong, Michel?" My voice hadn't risen at all, it was just tired, almost resigned. Where had my fight gone?

"This is not like you, *ma douce*. You would not normally accept this fate so quietly. Gregor has wronged you. He *has* tricked you and now threatens your safety, your life as you know it. Will you not fight back?" Michel's eyes had not left mine, they were asking something of me themselves, more than his question actually did. I didn't have the strength right now to work it out.

"I need a shower," I said abruptly and stood, walking towards the bathroom, but stopped just in the doorway and looked at Nero. "Will you be here when I get out?"

"Yes, if you so desire it."

I just nodded and shut the door behind me. They could have it out in privacy for all I cared, I just wanted to get clean.

I turned the shower on, got undressed and when the

water came up to temperature, slipped in. I let it fall against me, hard and fast, almost stinging my bare back. I thought I might cry. I thought perhaps, I would break down at the injustice of it all. But I didn't. Gregor *had* tricked me, he *had* taken away something very personal, very mine. Something that I may or may not have chosen to give to someone else in due course. He had made me mark him. I realised now just how personal, how special that was. Vampires don't give their marks, their *Sigillum* easily. It is an honour and an intimate thing to share. Michel had alluded to that. I hadn't thought of marks as being like that before, but I knew better now. And Gregor had made me give mine away without even realising it. I hated him for that, but I also couldn't understand him either. Why had he given me his?

I sighed and let the water run freely through my hair, grabbed some shampoo and began washing the metaphorical sweat and dirt of being tricked by Gregor away. I numbly watched the soap suds disappear down the plug hole and decided one thing. I was not going to be a victim here. So, Gregor had used trickery to gain my mark against my will. He had violated my trust. I would not lower my guard again. I realised then, that I wanted him dead. Dead-dead. The final death. I had never wanted someone so dead before in my life.

That thought calmed me. It made me feel strong. Not a victim, not a helpless thing waiting for the hammer blow to strike. Gregor thought he had all the answers, that he held all the cards. But, I am the *Sanguis Vitam Cupitor*, I can find him when he least expects it and I can kill him. I will take the battle to him, on my terms, at a time that suits me.

I got out of the shower feeling invigorated, dried myself off and grabbed some clean clothes out of my laundry cupboard. My usual hunting garb, black short mini-skirt, tight fitting black Tee and a new black jacket with custom made pockets for my two stakes and a spare silver knife. I slipped on some tights and came out of the bathroom.

Michel and Nero were both sitting on my couch, as far apart as possible. If they had been having it out, I couldn't tell. Michel looked relaxed, almost sleepy. Nero was sitting in his usual stance, legs crossed at the ankles and stretched out in front of him, hands clasped behind his head. Both sets of eyes took me in. I walked passed them into my bedroom. Grabbed a couple of stakes from the chest under my bed, my silver knife from under my pillow and slipped them into their pockets. They were balanced perfectly, not hindering the line of the jacket at all. You wouldn't have been able to tell they were there, unless you knew to look for them. I slipped into my black leather knee length boots and took a quick look at myself in the mirror.

My hair was hanging damp around my shoulders, I flicked a comb through it, but didn't bother with anything else, it would dry pretty much straight. A natural curse. My face was pale, not its usual lightly tanned glow. I admitted to myself then, that the events of the past few hours must have had an effect on me after all, but I didn't bother with make-up. Who was going to see me anyway?

I came back out of the bedroom and noticed that both Nero and Michel were sitting up straighter in their seats, no longer faking casual disinterest. It was Nero who spoke first.

"Why are you dressed for hunting, Kiwi? The night is almost over and I do not sense the Pull." The Pull he was referring to was the evil-lurks-in-my-city pull, all Nosferatin feel it. There wasn't a pull here, in Auckland, but for me there was most definitely a pull elsewhere. Before I answered him, I let myself sink into the blackness ever so slightly. The blackness that allowed me to Dream Walk, but also allowed me to *seek* other Nosferatu around the world and *sought* Gregor. I found him alone, right where I wanted him. I smiled and could tell it wasn't at all friendly.

"I *am* on a hunt, Nero, just not here." Michel cocked his head at me, but didn't say anything. Nero stood up, his full height making him tower over me, not hard to accomplish, but still, I think he was doing it on purpose. It was a waste of time, I've been short all my life, I've long ago learned to ignore height when used as a tool of power or sway.

"You have Dream Walked once this evening already, Lucinda, you would risk yourself to Dream Walk again?" He'd hit the nail on the head, he'd worked out my plan. If I wasn't hunting here, then I was hunting in that other realm. And, because it would be my second Dream Walk of the night, like his, it would lay me up for three days when, *if*, I returned. Something we Dream Walkers try to avoid at all costs.

"Look, Nero. I'm grateful for you coming again tonight, for a second time, for placing yourself at risk to save me. Really I am. But, it was your decision to do that, just as this is my decision now."

"You are angry, Kiwi, I understand, but you are letting

your anger cloud your judgement. And, what is it you plan to do when you face him? What exactly is your goal with this?"

And there you have it, the crux of the matter. I could deny my intentions, but he'd see through me. He knows me well enough by now. And what would be the point? I'd already decided, I knew what I was going to do, nothing he or anyone else said was going to change that now.

"I'm going to end this. I'm going to kill him. He has broken the *Iunctio's* law already and forced me into something that I did not know was happening. He deserves to die." My voice was even, no hint of emotion, so cold. I'd never heard myself talk like that before. A small part of me cringed, but a bigger part just smiled.

"He means you no evil, Lucinda. You said this yourself. How can you kill him, when there is Light within?"

"I'm not you, Nero, this is me. And this is what I have decided to do. I will not be a victim. I will not wait for him to come to me."

"I understand your need to take back control, but there are other ways. You not only endanger yourself by Dream Walking twice in one night, but you assume you can take him on alone, without support. I cannot come to your aid again for three days. I cannot help you even if I desired to."

"Then it's just as well you don't *desire* to then, isn't it?"

We stared at each other for a heartbeat. I thought he'd give up then, but of course, this was Nero, he never gives up that easily.

"This is not who you are, Lucinda. This is not the Light talking, but the Dark. You will regret this. You will not be able to live with this decision; to take someone's life when they did not truly deserve it. Do not do this. I am begging you."

I almost froze at the look on Nero's face. He was so concerned, so anguished at what I had chosen to do. He didn't understand. He is so full of Light, he would never understand, but I had to do this. I had to do this for me. I turned to Michel.

"What do you think?"

He smiled, his knowing smile, that for some reason didn't have the same effect on me that it usually did. It didn't make me frustrated or annoyed, it settled my nerves and left me feeling vindicated.

"I support whatever my Nosferatin chooses to do."

Of course he did, this would mean an end to Gregor's claim on me. This is exactly what Michel would want.

"Then you get to come with me." If he was near me when I Dream Walked, then he would also appear in the Dream Walk too according to Nero. A more perfect back-up I couldn't possibly have. He nodded his head in agreement, the smile turning a little wicked then.

Nero sighed and glared at Michel. It was wasted on him of course, but it didn't stop the Egyptian from doing it. "You would willingly encourage this madness? Have you no concern for the Light that resides in your kindred? Do you wish to crush all that she is?"

His words were bitter, accusatory, he threw them at Michel as though they were a weapon. Michel didn't even blanch, but suddenly appeared in front of Nero with his hand closed around his throat. Like Gregor had managed to do to me in my first Dream Walk to him. Somehow Michel knew exactly where Nero had been, despite not seeing him at all. Vampires could obviously home in on the the voice and various other indicators, to form enough of a picture to make that move. It wasn't a fluke, but skill. I'd have to remember that for future Dream Walking reference.

"Do not underestimate my feelings for my kindred Nosferatin, Nero. You would not understand the depth of connection we share, so do not even try."

His voice was low, a growl. He wasn't squeezing Nero's throat, merely holding him still, threatening him. Nero didn't even try to remove the fingers, he simply moved his eyes to me and said, "Please do not do this, Kiwi. Please."

I shook my head at him, I'd made my mind up and if there is one thing to be said about me, I don't go back on my word.

We looked at each other for a moment, no one said anything, just the stillness of silence wrapping around our bodies like a shroud. Nero was the first to break it.

"Good luck, my Kiwi. May the Light call you back from the Dark." And he simply faded into a flickering light and was gone, leaving Michel with a closed fist in mid air and me with another hole in my heart the size of Australia.

Chapter 13
Missed

We decided that it would be better to Dream Walk from Michel's chamber at *Sensations*, as the night was drawing to a close and it would endanger Michel if we weren't in a light-tight environment.

The bar was quiet when we entered, the last of the late night clubbers long gone home to either finish their party there or get some much needed sleep. Michel's day crew wouldn't arrive until dawn and his vampires were out doing whatever creatures of the night do in the last few moments of true darkness.

It had been a few days since I had been in Michel's chamber, since I had stayed overnight. We'd been trying for a little separation; my idea not his. To allow me to have a hint of a normal life again. When I joined with Michel and then Bonded shortly after, my life had been turned upside down. The need to be near him so overwhelming. Part of me resented it for the mere fact that it infringed on my independence and another part of me resented it, because I really wasn't sure if what I was feeling for him was genuine. Or just a by-product of a tightly bound joining to my kindred Nosferatu. I was determined we'd take things slowly for a while and just see if what we felt was deeper than convenience and ancient magical rights.

So far I wasn't sure. I'd craved him when apart and savoured every moment together, but I could not tell, for the life of me, if that was me talking or the Bond.

I felt a frisson of excitement go through me as I entered his day resting place. Michel liked luxurious surroundings, his chamber was not excluded from his tastes for the extravagant. The giant sized bed was adorned with richly dark fabrics, in bronze and gold, deep brown and cream. The carpet felt plush beneath my boots, making me feel like I was sinking into soft grass back home on the farm. The walls were cream with a delicately embossed pattern to them, one I hadn't noticed before. Had he redecorated recently? I took a step closer to see what the image was. It was of a dancing dragon, barely visible from a distance, but noticeable up close. I had seen this dragon once before, on Michel's private jet. It obviously held some significance, but I'd never asked. I turned to ask him now, but he wasn't there. I thought he'd followed me into the chamber, but the room was empty and the door stood ajar.

I shrugged and turned back to the bed. I suddenly felt a little nervous. I shouldn't have. Despite it only being less than four weeks since we had joined, I'd known Michel for over two years now, all of that time he had tried to woo me, tempt me into his arms. He'd failed, but then he was also quite patient when the need arose. His patience had eventually been rewarded when we joined and since then, just over three weeks ago, I'd got to know Michel a hell of a lot better. Even that thought made me slightly blush.

I shook my head to clear the thought. You'd think I was an innocent the way my hormones were behaving. Just because it's been a couple of nights since I last fell into his arms. Jeez.

Michel's scent filled the air around me, a beautiful heady mixture of salty sea spray and freshly cut green grass. It washed over my arms managing to raise goose bumps even under the material of my jacket. I felt a tingle go down my spine. Michel may not be able to affect me with his power any more, since we joined, but his mere presence was always enough to get a reaction. He came up behind me and bent his head to the curve of my neck, taking the smell of me in, barely touching my skin, but leaving a hot trail down my flesh, making me shudder ever so slightly.

"You are nervous, *ma douce*. I can not tell if it is because of me or because of what we are about to attempt." His hands took hold of my shoulders from behind and his lips found that sensitive part of my skin, just at the base and side of my neck, above my clavicle.

I leaned back into him involuntarily, my body seemed to have a will of its own, I lacked any self-control over it when Michel was near. His tongue lay a wet circle just above the bone making my body tighten and my heartbeat increase. His lips began caressing my neck, slowly, tantalizingly, up towards my ear lobe, where he sucked the lobe into his mouth and gently nibbled. I closed my eyes and sighed. I had missed him.

"I have missed you too, *ma douce*." He continued to lay kisses all over my neck, turning me slowly to face him and carrying on with more kisses around my throat, up to my jaw, across my cheek. Then two kisses on each closed eyelid. I felt my hands go around his neck and found myself on tip-toe to get closer to those lips. He was bent over me slightly, meeting me half way. I hadn't opened my eyes again, but I knew when he was about to kiss me. I felt his warmth against my face, his breath against my lips and then his soft mouth against my own.

I moaned, I couldn't help it, he felt so damn good. His mouth became firmer, his hold tighter around my back and neck, pulling me against his hard chest and taking my breath away. His tongue pushed inside, between my teeth and then I was lost. Lost in a wave of desire and heat and a need to get closer to this man, closer than I now was. My leg wrapped around his thigh, I started to climb up his body seeking his mouth, his touch, his warmth. I felt his hands move to my rear, lifting me off my feet, pulling me against his waist. My other leg went around the side of him and I settled into position devouring every inch of his face, his neck, his chest.

He held me against him as we explored each other's face and neck and mouths. Tasting, seeking, trying to get closer and closer. I felt him shudder against me, then take a step closer to the bed. I lost a few seconds then, because the next thing I registered was Michel on top of me, both of us lying on the bed, his hand frantically reaching up under my short skirt, grabbing my tights and pulling them down. The cold air on my skin woke me up from the blissful dream we were having and I pulled away from his mouth.

"We're getting distracted." It came out all breathy and completely not how I normally sound.

"I disagree." He didn't stop removing my tights. Somehow managing to get them, my boots and then my skirt off without me even realising he had moved in order to it. He had vampire speed on his side and sometimes, just sometimes, it came in very handy indeed.

"Michel"

"Mm-hmm" He wasn't listening, he was too busy removing my jacket and T-Shirt in a movement that took my breath away and also impressed the hell out of me.

"We don't have time for this." My voice was husky and

less than convincing.

“We could make it, how do you say? A quickie.” His hands were still moving with assured practice over my body, finding every spot he knew would make me melt, destroy my will. I had to swallow twice before I could get the next sentence out.

“You're not capable of a quickie.”

He laughed against my skin sending another wave of heat through my body. “I could make an exception, if it would ease your mind, *ma douce*.” And then he did something that completely stole my resolve and made me forget what we were talking about for a few minutes.

“You were saying?” His voice was soft, just a murmur against my skin. Like velvet it caressed me, wrapping me up and enfolding me in its embrace.

“Um.”

He smiled, a little of that knowing smile he so often wore and a whole lot of just sheer male. The look they get in their eyes when they know something is a foregone conclusion, when they know they've won and about to get their just reward. It's all hunger and need and desire and hot, hot fire. If I hadn't already melted into a puddle of wanton sexual desire, it would have undone me for sure. As it was, I was already lost.

My answer was to rip his shirt off, making the buttons pop and the material tear. I didn't manage to get the front undone in one movement, but Michel came to my rescue and slipped the shirt off over his head, baring his broad chest and delicious deep cream skin to me. I ran my fingers over that chest, relishing the feel of his hard body and taught nipples. The darker skin surrounding them making them stand out in sharp relief against his pale chest. They fascinated me and called to me. I lifted my head, glancing up into Michel's eyes - which had turned a beautiful shade of amethyst - and licked around the edge of each nipple.

He groaned and threw his head back, closing his eyes and pushing against my mouth, trying to get closer to me. I ran my hands up his back, digging in my nails and scraping down his sides. His mouth found mine again in rough possession, his tongue lavishing attention to my own. His hands finding my breasts and thumbs stroking my nipples. I arched against him and wrapped my legs tighter around his waist, grinding against his hard length through his trousers.

"I think a quickie would be good," he said breathlessly against my chest as his head came down towards my nipples and his waist pulled away from my grasp. I didn't want him to pull away, so tried to follow, climbing my body up his thighs with my legs, kind of like a koala climbing a tree.

"Oh no," he purred, pushing gently against me and undoing his trousers at the same time. "Patience, *ma douce*."

"Not one of my better qualities," I managed as I watched him strip in front of me. He noticed my attention and slowed down his actions, drawing them out, teasing, tempting, frustrating me. My eyes flicked up to his and we locked gazes, his a deep amethyst with violet flecks and with such a look of utter desire and need that it stilled my breath.

Finally, he stood naked in front of me and just watched as I took him all in. Every inch of that masculine body, lithe shape, strong physique. He was literally magnificent, beautiful, like a painting by an renowned artist, perfect in every way. I licked my lips, he always did manage to make me have these involuntary movements, but they also were quite useful from time to time, because he crumpled and was upon me in an instant.

He kissed his way back up to my mouth, his hands stroking my skin along the length of me. I arched up trying to bring us closer, but he managed to keep a small distance between us, making me crave to close that gap and bring my body against his, feel his weight on me, his hardness between my legs. He held himself there for a full minute, just kissing me, keeping me captive under the spell of his tongue, his lips. Then finally he lowered himself gently against my entrance, just inside, no further, just a hint of what could come.

After a few seconds of this torture I thought to hell with this and rose up to wrap him with my body, making him sink that final few inches inside. He called out in surprise and then thrust hard against me. I could feel him deep, to places I didn't even know he could reach. He felt so big, so long and full within me. He slowly pulled out, but my patience had well and truly left me and I moved in against him in a fast rhythm that he couldn't fight.

We began to find a pattern that worked for both of us, in tune with each other. Floating higher and higher on a need to climb closer, to practically climb inside one another. His thrusts became hard and fast, a pounding against me that was close to pain, but just this side of ecstasy. Before I even realised what was happening I crested a wave of delight and sailed away on a spray of bliss, floating there while Michel found his point of release and then finally falling down together in a crash of euphoria.

Michel collapsed against the bed beside me, breathless. I could feel his heart pounding in time with mine. His arm and leg draped over me, clinging to me, holding me tight. I didn't complain, there was no where else I wanted to be.

It took a few minutes for my breath to even out, my heart still pacing a quick beat across my chest. It was Michel who spoke first, his voice quiet, soft, barely recognisable.

"Whenever you feel the need for a quickie, *ma douce*, I am more than happy to oblige."

I smiled, but couldn't think of a decent reply. He was right, of course, I could never refuse him again. Right now, as far as I was concerned, he was always right. I'm just glad I didn't say that out loud.

We did manage to shower and dress again relatively quickly. It might have been because I insisted on separate showers, despite Michel's protestations. But we were dressed and ready for battle without any further undue delays, so things were looking up. Or not, depending on what way you looked at it.

I was already resting on the bed, relaxing in the afterglow that still bathed me in it's light, when Michel came out of the dressing room. He was wearing his tight fitting black casual dress trousers, the ones that hugged his thighs and hips, and a simple black shirt, sleeves rolled up to bare his muscled forearms. This was his usual fighting garb. Normally, he'd be in an expensive Armani suit, just off black, white shirt and blue tie of some description, but recently with all the battles we had had to face, he had lowered his dress standard to encompass something a little less formal. For me, it wasn't too much of a disappointment. I loved him in black.

He climbed on to the bed in a sensual glide, something akin to a big sleek cat, predatory but smooth. His eyes never leaving mine. If he was intending to distract me again I would have to seriously put him in his place. But something must have registered in my face, because he just smiled, a teasing sort of smile, one that said *just kidding*. Humph.

His arm curled around the back of me, pulling me closer, his lips brushed my neck and cheek. I settled into his side, completely wrapped up in him as though he couldn't bear the thought of letting me go.

"Are you ready for this, *ma douce*?"

I took a breath in to settle my nerves. Whatever way I looked at this, I was going on a hunt to kill something, something that really didn't deserve to die. Yeah, Gregor had wronged me, but that doesn't mean I have the right to kill him, just because I'm pissed off. There are rules to be obeyed when you're a vampire hunter and I was pushing them to the absolute limit. Not that I thought for a moment that the *Iunctio* would accept his death easily. I knew I was opening up a can of worms and I knew Michel knew it too. Yet, he backed me completely, unfailingly. This could mean war on a massive scale for us, yet he wasn't tempering my mood or desire for revenge one little bit. That thought alone really did scare me a little right then.

"All right. Let's do this." I wasn't sure what Michel was meant to do. Try to sleep, try to think of a black nothingness like I do? I settled on, "Just relax and close your eyes, hopefully I'll do the rest."

"Hopefully?" came his sardonic reply.

"Yeah, well, I haven't exactly taken someone along on a Dream Walk before, but Nero said you should just appear in it if you are nearby and the Dream Walk thinks it's necessary for my protection. So, let's see." I shrugged as I said the last. What else was there to say really, this would either work or it wouldn't. I didn't want to dwell too long on the negative. So I concentrated on my heartbeat, letting myself fall towards the black nothingness that called to the Nosferatin within me and allowing me to *seek* out Gregor and Dream Walk to him.

I became aware of noise around me at first. Music, softly playing. Bellini perhaps? My Dad had an extensive opera collection back on the farm, I vaguely recognised the *Bel-Canto*. The room came into focus around me, just as I had expected. Gregor's chamber in Rome, where I had visited before. I turned around slowly getting my bearings and released two things at once.

One, Gregor was not here.

And two, neither was Michel.

Damn. The Dream Walk couldn't have thought it necessary to bring Michel along for the ride. Or he needed to be asleep, fully relaxed in order to do so. We'd have to practice that one, but now what?

I settled back into that nothingness again briefly and *sought* them both out. Michel was back at *Sensations,* agitated. No wonder. And Gregor was down the hall in a room with several vampires. Shit, shit, shit, shit. Now what? I could just abort the mission, as it were, allow myself to simply drift back to Michel. That would be the sane thing, the safe thing to do. Or....or I could wait to ambush Gregor here or on the way back here.

I glanced at the windows to his chamber. The curtains had been pulled back and wooden shutters were open on either side. His chamber wasn't underground like Michel's, but with the shutters in place it would be light-tight during the day. Now there was an expanse of glass illuminated by the street lights outside which clearly showed a dark and clear Italian night.

Shit again.

OK. So, it's night time, that would mean he probably wouldn't come back to his chamber. That would mean, if I was to do anything, it would have to involve me going after him and avoiding all other vampires. My spidey sense told me there were quite a few in the area, but not all of them were with Gregor now. Just three.

Would they stay or go? I started pacing, trying to think things through. This was not good. I should just return to Michel and try again at another time, but - and I know I shouldn't be thinking of a but - Gregor wouldn't be expecting me now. He wouldn't think I had it in me to come after him at all, let alone in his night. A second Dream Walk in quick succession. This would be the element of surprise I was going for. All I had to do was wait until he was alone.

I sat down tentatively on the end of his bed and allowed my mind and senses to wander. Most of the vampires were heading out into the dark, hungry, seeking their dinners. There wasn't too much evil floating off them, they had intent to feed, but only in so much as it would allow them to sate their thirst. These guys weren't breaking any rules. I moved away from them and back to those still inside the building.

Gregor was down to just one vampire with him in the room down the hall. I couldn't tell what they were doing, I can't sense quite that level of accuracy. There was no evil, that's about all my powers of *seeking* will allow me to judge. They could have been dancing a Tango for all I knew. So, do I make a move now or not?

If I wait, Gregor may go out into the night as well, then I really would be hunting, but hunting in unfamiliar territory. Never a good thing. If I head in the general direction of the room he was in, I could be ready if the chance arose. If not, then simply Dream Walk back to Michel and try again another day.

Part of me did not want to waste this opportunity. I was going to be out for three days after this second Dream Walk. I had to make this count.

Right, I knew what I wanted to do. I hadn't come this far to turn around at the first hurdle. I grabbed a stake out of my pocket and headed out the door.

The corridor was empty as suspected and I made my way Dream Walk quietly towards the room where I could still feel Gregor within. The door was slightly ajar, a bonus, but I couldn't see enough inside to get a visual on where Gregor was, or where the mystery companion vampire was either. I'd have to bide my time, but at least I could listen to their conversation.

It was in Italian, surprisingly. Somehow I had forgotten that Gregor was based here, not in Paris with the *Iunctio* and as such he would speak Italian on a regular basis with his vampires. I'm not so good with Italian. I understand a smattering of French, a hint of Maori and a little of German. Italian, not so much.

What I do understand, or more appropriately recognise, is a particular phrase. An endearment I had heard once before in Michel's office at *Sensations*. An endearment I *really* did not like. So, you can understand my reaction was justified, if a little unfortunate, when I firstly recognised the voice and secondly recognised the phrase.

Alessandra's dulcet tones drifted out of the room Gregor was in as she said, "*É sempre un piacere, **mio caro***".

And I gasped out loud.

Chapter 14
Alessandra

The door swung open immediately and there she stood in all her slutty grandeur. She had poured herself into yet another slinky short-short dress, barely covering her arse and not nearly covering her décolletage. It was red. Blood red. Her favourite colour and matched her lipstick and nails to perfection. Oh, and her three inch high stiletto heels.

I took her all in, every inch of her tall-tall frame, you can't not be mesmerised by Alessandra. Her blonde curls hung down to her waist, covering more of her body from behind than her outfit did. Her face was made up to exquisite perfection making her pale blue eyes stand out and her high cheek bones cut a fine line across her face. Her mouth was set in an accomplished pout. I'd no doubt she practised it in front of the mirror.

All of this had taken me a mere second to comprehend, a mere second too long. Her slender, but very strong, hand came out and clasped around my throat and she dragged me back into the room.

Mother fucker! What is it with these vamps being able to find my throat so unerringly whilst I'm Dream Walking and supposedly invisible! It's just not fair.

The door slammed shut behind me, but I couldn't turn to see if it had happened on its own or if there was someone else there. I couldn't concentrate enough to use my senses, Alessandra's hold was too firm, painfully so.

Alessandra. What on earth was she doing here? She had an accord with Michel, an agreement that was binding, it could not be broken. Their accord was to come to the aid of each other when asked and also because Michel is so much more powerful than her, she has pledged her undying allegiance to the Durand line. Hell, she even pledged her undying allegiance to his kindred Nosferatin. That would be me. But, I'm sure it grated on her nerves to do so. So, she was either unaware of who I was, or treading a very fine line between pleasure and pain, because to break the accord, would be to call down the wrath of Michel. Not a pleasant thing at all. Plus, he would have the full backing of the *Iunctio*. He'd probably be able to enlist Gregor's talents as the Enforcer to track her down and be done with her too.

That was of course, if Gregor could be bothered. Somehow I thought perhaps not.

"So Gregor, you are courting danger with New Zealand's finest Nosferatin? Whatever have you done to deserve this?" Her thick Italian accent curled around the room but didn't settle against my skin. I'm guessing it's target wasn't me.

But, I hadn't missed the *New Zealand* reference. She knew who I was. So, treading that fine line between pleasure and pain then. At least I knew where I stood. I just couldn't fathom why.

Sure, Alessandra had tried to use every female wile she had to seduce Michel into her bed, right in front of me, in plain sight. But I had never thought she would be this stupid. To break an accord would not get Michel on her side. Stupid. *Blonde and stupid. Go figure.*

Gregor laughed out loud, a short chuckle that had more of an affect on me than Alessandra's voice could ever have. I was puzzled briefly by his response to her and then realised he had picked up on my thoughts. For some reason that didn't frighten me as much as it should have.

"You would be surprised what dangers I court, Alessandra."

I glanced at him then and realised he looked a little different. Not that I had really studied him the last time we met. But, I did notice a shine to his eyes now. No, that wasn't quite right either, it was a shine *around* his eyes. Not overtly obvious, but definitely not there before. It made his beautiful platinum and silver eyes stand out even more than usual. The shine or *sparkle* around his eyes seemed to complement them and enhance their otherworldliness, it was hard to look away. I felt an undeniable pull towards that beautiful light around his eyes and then I realised what I was seeing. My mark, my *Sigillum*, he wore it on his face. Other than wearing sunglasses, something a creature of the night did not normally do, my *Sigillum* would always be obvious. He could never hide it. I laughed out loud at that.

"You find something amusing, *bambina*?" Somehow Alessandra's use of a pet name for me did not sound endearing. She knew I felt like a child in her presence. She seemed to always have a way of making me feel small, *bambina* did not sit well with me, but it did make me realise I could do something about it, but would I?

I fingered my stake cautiously. Could I stake Alessandra? She had me in a threatening hold, was that enough to slice through her heart and end her life forever? Let's see.

My stake slipped through her thin blood red slinky dress just above her heart and bit into her flesh ever so slightly. Just a hint, a threat, a little like her firm grip around my throat. Her eyes opened wide, her breath caught.

I could feel her heartbeat racing beneath the silver tip of the stake.

"I don't know, *bambina*, what do you think?" My voice was low and steady, just like my hold on my stake. I didn't tremble, I didn't shake. This was what I was made to do, slide my stake home and end the evil.

That thought was enough to make me realise I wouldn't stake Alessandra here, right now, not unless she really intended me harm. I may have come here to stake Gregor, but collateral damage was not something I could readily accept. There had to be a line drawn in the sand somewhere.

"Let me go!" I demanded.

"Remove the stake," came her cool reply.

"You first, bitch."

Gregor did laugh out loud at that. "This is most entertaining. I see you two have both met. No need for me to introduce you then."

"Oh, I don't know Gregor," I said dryly. "I *am* interested in why Alessandra is here."

She bared her fangs at me. It doesn't work, she should have known better. "That is none of your business, *piccola*"

"I'm sure Michel would find it very much part of his business."

She glared at me then, her breath becoming rapid. Then she smiled, a truly unpleasant grimace that looked completely out of place on her beautifully fine features. "I could just break your neck. It wouldn't take much." Her grip tightened, making it difficult to swallow. "Your throat would crush in on itself, your larynx squeezed through my fingers, your breath unable to flow. It would hurt, *cucciola*, very much I think."

Alessandra always had a penchant for the dramatic and for over using pet names. I didn't really go for it myself, wasted too much time, too much effort, that could be used in far better pursuits. Like slicing her face open with silver.

She hadn't even felt my other arm shift, she couldn't see it reach inside my jacket and she most definitely missed the slim slender silver knife I pulled out. Her attention was completely on the silver stake protruding from her chest. I had no intention, for now, to stake her; hurt her maybe, make her bleed, that was another thing altogether.

The knife arced through the small space in between us and slit a sleek line down her left cheek, over those impossibly high cheekbones, right down to muscle. The blood began to flow immediately followed instantly by her shriek. She released her grip on my throat pushing me away from her hard and used both hands to stem the blood flow on her face.

"You shall pay for that!" she spat at me.

I moved silently away from where she had thrust me and calmly said, "That's what they all say." Moving again as soon as I uttered the words. I wasn't letting anyone *guess* where I was standing. Fool me once, shame on you and all that.

"Ladies, ladies. Please. Is it really necessary to resort to such tactics over me?"

I laughed, I couldn't help it, Gregor was just so damn cocky. Then I moved again to a new position.

"You have learned well, my little Hunter. You seem to be everywhere and nowhere. Not so blonde, I am guessing." His lips quirked in a small smile at that last comment, but he reschooled his features as he reached out and handed Alessandra a handkerchief to stem the flow of blood. It had slowed and was already beginning to reknit itself. Silver could hurt, but it takes more than a slender knife to inflict permanent damage on a vampire.

"So, what do I owe this unscheduled visit to, Lucinda? It is, if you remember, outside of the rules."

Rules, schmules. "So I gather is exchanging *Sigillum*." I moved again to the other side of the room.

He smiled, it just made the sparkle of my mark shine even more vividly.

Alessandra found her voice. "The *Sigillum* is hers!" I gathered then, that this was not the first time she had questioned him on it. Was Alessandra jealous? "You said I would not know them. You never mentioned it was *hers*!"

"I never knew you were acquainted with one another. What have *you* been up to, my dear?" He said *my dear* just like Michel did, it was so similar, it made me blink.

"I have known Michel for centuries, this is no secret," she replied haughtily.

"Yet I do not believe it is the whole truth." I felt his *Sanguis Vitam* as it rolled towards Alessandra, it brushed passed me in a solid wave of sharp spikes, leaving me gasping for breath and doubling over.

I have no idea how Alessandra was able to stay standing once it finally found her, but the effort required looked tremendous. I couldn't take my eyes off her, my chest felt tight at the elevated power circling the room. I was fighting to still my breathing, fearful it would lead to hyperventilation. That was probably why I hadn't noticed that Gregor had moved. And I hadn't. Alessandra was taking up all of my concentration, so much so that it was only as his hand tightened on my arm that I actually sensed him.

He pulled me against his chest, my back to him, my sight still on Alessandra. Then he brushed my hair from my neck, leaning in and running his nose along the length of me, inhaling deeply, like a drug addict getting his daily fix. I didn't stay frozen in shock for long, but turned out of his grasp and placed my stake against his chest in a move so quick it would have been a blur, had he been able to see me. I pushed a little harder than I had intended, the adrenaline rush from being caught still pumping through my veins. The tip of the stake slid in a centimetre or so, it must have hurt like hell. He simply took a step back, trying to dislodge the stake, but instinct took over and I paced after him. Step for step. Not letting the stake slide out, but remain where it sat.

He didn't try to reach up and grab me or the stake. He didn't try to dislodge it at all. Just kept taking one step back after the other until finally his back was to a solid wall and I actually made the stake go a little further in by mistake, my momentum still carrying me forward. Oops.

He cringed slightly, a small shine of sweat appearing above his lips and across his forehead. He licked his lips and closed his eyes, shifted slightly beneath the stake as though trying to get comfortable, but only succeeding in grinding the stake further in. He let a gasp out then and stilled. We stood like that for a minute, maybe more. Alessandra was still battling his *Sanguis Vitam.* How he could continue to expend that kind of energy and concentration on her and be faced with near death and excruciating pain of silver in his chest, was beyond me.

"Are you going to slide it home, Hunter?" His voice was strained, but even.

"Would you let me?" Mine was slightly surprised. He had kind of shocked me, this was way too easy.

"Would you prefer a battle? Is that what turns you on?"

Huh. I frowned at him, it did no good. He couldn't see me and his eyes were still closed. He was laying himself so bare, so open for attack, all it would take would be for me to push a little harder and he couldn't do a thing to stop me. My goal for the evening would be met. I felt myself leaning in ever so slightly, the stake sliding a millimetre more towards his heart. He didn't move, just caught his breath and held it.

This was not how it was meant to be. I had expected a fight, resistance, a reason to justify what I was doing, but not this. Not this inaction, this blatant call for his own death.

"Do you wish to die so much, Enforcer?" This time my voice was soft, a whisper against his skin.

"I am already dead, Hunter, there is nothing in this *life* for me." He spat the word *life* out as though it tasted foul, something bitter on his tongue.

Well, I'll be. He wanted to die. He wanted out of this life, this existence as a creature of the night. Is that why he was chasing me? Is that why he set the challenge, hoping I would do just that, end it for him? Suicide by Hunter. Huh.

Now what? I couldn't stake him. Nero was right. This was not me. I may have been able to finish the job had he resisted, had he threatened my safety or life, but we'd never know now, would we? And now, could I kill him? Not a chance. I am not a murderer, even if I kill for a hobby. All my kills have been deserved. This, despite whatever reason he seemed to have, was not deserved. Not by me.

I felt the stake slide out even before I had finished that thought, but I didn't step away. He would have been able to smell me this close, he would have been able to feel my warmth. Somehow Gregor was able to do those things despite me Dream Walking. It didn't scare me. Gregor was not going to kill me. Hurt me maybe, but not physically, not now. His eyes opened and he looked right at me, as though he *could* see me. I raised my eyebrows at him and he smiled. Shit.

"You can see me?"

"No. I can sense you. I can feel you. It's almost like I can see you. You shine so bright, I see the light, the silhouette of your face, your body. It calls to me." His hand reached up and stroked my skin on my cheek. I jumped. Yikes. This was too weird. Michel could sense me and feel me in a Dream Walk, it was a by-product of the Bond, but Gregor should not.

"How?" was all I could manage.

"The *Sigillum*, we both share a connection to each other. It binds us together."

"Oh no. That is so not happening. Stop it."

He laughed. "I cannot, *ma petite chasseuse*. It is permanent. Neither of us can change what has come to be."

"Damn you, Gregor. I did not want this. You forced it on me." And just like that, my anger was back and with it my stake against his chest. Just resting, not entering, not yet.

His hand came up and wrapped around my wrist, the

wrist on the arm holding the stake. He raised it effortlessly up from his chest - or maybe I just wasn't trying too hard any more - and brushed his lips across the back of my hand. So close to the stake, but somehow missing it. His lips were so soft, warm and wonderful. I felt my grip on the stake loosen and then the stake simply fall away to land on the carpeted floor.

He pulled me towards him and claimed my mouth with his. I tried to push back against his hold, but it wasn't really a concerted effort. His body called to me in a way I couldn't explain. I didn't wrap myself around him, pull him closer, or any of those other stupidly romantic things, I just didn't stop him from kissing me. And then his mouth left mine and his hand at the back of my head tilted me gently, carefully over, exposing my neck. And before I could register what was happening - although in hindsight I think I kind of knew but chose to ignore it - his mouth found my pulse at the base of my neck and his fangs slid effortlessly in through my skin to find my blood below. The sharp sting of his bite replaced with the warmth of his desire and the pull of my blood making my heart race and breath quicken and other parts of my body tighten in response.

His voice in my mind, so familiar, so natural, *mark me with your Light, ma petite chasseuse, mark me again.*

No. I couldn't possibly consider marking him again, I'd done that once and look where it had got me.

It is only a sharing, do not fear, it is not permanent.

Sure. So you say.

He ramped up the desire then. His *Sanguis Vitam* flowing through me unhindered. I had no way of fighting it, it called to me, it enticed me, it lured me in and told me all would be right, to trust, to let go. To fall that last forbidden step and allow this to happen. So I did.

I let the Light build inside me, let it fill me up and when I could hold it no longer, I released it. I pushed it hard against his shields, against his wall and mind, and felt it slip effortlessly in, bathing him, cuddling him, holding him dear.

He groaned out loud and we both slid down the wall, me landing in his lap, cradled by his arms. The Light flowing through us both, circling us, touching us, enveloping us, until there was nothing left but pure bliss. And the rapid beating of our hearts.

His fangs withdrew slowly, I felt his tongue against the marks, his breath against my neck and I let myself collapse against him, moulding to him, almost clinging to him.

What the...?

Neither of us spoke for a minute, just basked in that after glow, that was so not sexual, but oh so much more intimate than that.

Thoughts tumbled restlessly against my mind. Why had I let this happen, again? How had he tricked me, again? Did it matter? He had said to me that I could become additive, I wasn't so sure that applied to just me any more.

He kissed my cheek, so softly, so intimately, it was wrong, he wasn't Michel. But for the life of me, right then, I didn't care.

There was a low whistle from the other side of the room. I think we had both forgotten Alessandra. I had assumed she was still held captive by his *Sanguis Vitam*, but then it occurred to me, Gregor had lost all control whilst basking in my Light. To do that, he had stopped his attack on Alessandra. She had stood unhindered and watched it all unfold in front of her eyes.

"*That, mia cara*, was entertaining. And I am sure Michel will find *this* very much part of his business."

My words, back at me. And I didn't, for a second, think she was bluffing.

Damn.

Chapter 15
Master

I stiffened in Gregor's arms. He gently stroked my back, the side of my neck, but I didn't relax. I couldn't move, not yet, so I couldn't defend myself should Alessandra choose that moment to attack. I was guessing, but I'm not sure, that Gregor couldn't move yet either. We were both at her mercy and I did not like that at all.

I felt Gregor's *Sanguis Vitam* before he spoke. It was hot and harsh, but laced with a power that I recognised, Michel used that type of power when he commanded vampires in his line to do his bidding. It was the power that made the request or demand, a command, something they could not ignore, even to save their own lives. But why would Gregor use it on Alessandra? She was a master vampire in charge of her own line, she was definitely no one's flunky.

"Alessandra." Just one word, but behind it a wealth of threats and unsaid challenges.

"Master."

Whoa. What the hell was she saying? How could she be subject to another master, just like a level two or lower master vampire or vampire servant. Either Alessandra was acting above her station when with us. Acting the role of a level one *Sanguis Vitam* master, which is impossible I would have thought, or there was something going on here I did not comprehend.

"Leave us. I will call for you when I am ready."

"Yes, Master." She turned towards the door taking a few steps, but Gregor had not finished. "You will speak of this to no one."

She paused, as though she really was trying to battle that command, but Gregor's hold was obviously too strong and she simply continued, after a moment, on out the door. Closing it softly behind her.

To say I was confused, was an understatement. Alessandra was one of the strongest vampires I had ever met. No where near as strong as Michel was now. But she had managed to hold off an extremely strong master vampire once, Max, all on her own, until Michel could recover enough to come to her aid. She had been phenomenal. I have yet to witness another female vampire as strong. So what was with all of this?

I turned back towards Gregor, who was watching me closely. That in itself was unnerving, he shouldn't have been able to see me to watch me that intensely. He smiled when our eyes met. It lit up his silvery eyes and made my mark shine back at me, coating me in light.

"You knew I was powerful, Hunter. Why is it such a surprise that Alessandra is one of my own?"

"She's a level one master, in charge of her own line. I didn't realise it was possible." There was no point denying what I felt, I was puzzled, I wanted to know. Did Michel know? Was this something that could threaten him?

"I made her. She is mine and I have never fully released her. I give her some leeway, enough to strike out on her own, but she is mine to call when I require it."

A thought occurred to me then. "Did you make her come to Michel's aid when he asked recently?"

Michel had called for aid from those vampires closely aligned with him when Max came to New Zealand to capture me. Alessandra, along with two other vampires called Enrique and Jock, had honoured their alliances with Michel and come to his aid. I wondered now if Alessandra had been sent as a mole.

Gregor's face didn't betray him, but through that damn connection we now shared, his feelings, or more accurately, his aura did. I've never been very good at reading auras, but when connected to someone, it was a little easier to accomplish it would seem. Gregor's aura fluctuated slightly, the striking lights that had started glowing more and more brightly over the past 24 hours, shimmered and waned, just enough to let me know he wasn't about to tell the truth. Master vampires can smell lies, I can't, but it would seem when I have a connection to a vampire, such as mine to Gregor, then I have truth seeking abilities too. Handy to know.

Not that I wanted to connect to another vampire in the same way any time soon.

“I have not seen Alessandra for over a year, she has been following her own path for some time. I had no need of her until tonight.”

“Liar.”

OK, so I could have been more diplomatic, but no one likes being told porkies. They just don't.

He cocked his head at me, looking hard at whatever it was he saw in this Dream Walking realm. Maybe he could sense my aura too. After a moment he seemed satisfied with what he saw and said, “Interesting. I guess I shall have to be more careful around you in the future, my little Hunter.”

“Who says there'll be a future.”

He smiled. “There is still the challenge, it cannot be

left unanswered for long. I have already set in motion my planned visit to your country. I believe it is an entertaining destination. I look forward to my...holiday."

"You're taking a break from the *Iunctio*?"

"One never takes a break from the *Iunctio* Lucinda, but a change is as good as a holiday, or so they say."

Yeah, right. But, it hadn't been lost on me that he had changed the topic of conversation easily, deflected my question without even trying too hard. He didn't know me well enough yet, to realise I don't give up that easily.

"So, did you send Alessandra to Michel?"

He sighed. "You will not give up, will you?"

"No. I guess that's something else you should remember for the future. If there is one."

He laughed, that warm chuckle that made his body move and sent warmth through to my soul. The movement reminding me I was still sitting in his lap, his arms around me, his hands stroking my side. I hadn't even noticed that he hadn't stopped touching me after Alessandra had left. I was losing my edge, I had to get my game back on.

I made an effort to stand up, to get away from him, but he growled, low and long, and gripped me even tighter.

"I am not ready to relinquish you so soon. You have called unexpectedly, unannounced, after a challenge has been set. You have attempted to harm me, outside of the rules. And you will be unavailable to me for three days, I do believe, as this is your second Dream Walk within 24 hours." He raised his eyebrows in a challenge when he sensed the surprise in my aura. I had not expected him to know that little secret. Dream Walking is rare, even Michel had not been familiar with that little titbit of news, prior to my first Dream Walk where I had been out for a week afterwards. “I will not let you go so easily, so soon, my dear. You are my prize for the inconvenience of your visit.”

I laughed, I couldn't help it. This guy just had a tendency to make me smile.

“Inconvenience? I didn't see you complaining,” I managed to get out between chuckles.

“Just because I enjoy your company does not mean you have not inconvenienced me. I had business to attend with Alessandra this night and you have delayed that for me. I will seek compensation.”

Oh dear. I didn't like the sound of that one little bit.

“What kind of compensation?” My voice was slightly breathy, anticipation I guess, I cringed inside though. Damn, I did not want him to know the effect he had on me.

His smile broadened. “I have not yet decided, but I'm sure I can think of something that will fit the bill.”

I'm sure he could, but I wasn't planning on being around to find out. I began to seek the blackness of that void, that space where nothingness enveloped me and allowed me to Dream Walk back to my body. I knew a lost cause when I saw one. I'd stuffed up big time tonight, I wasn't hanging around to see how much worse things could get. As much as I would have liked to have left with the upper hand, I knew my advantage, whatever surprise my unexpected visit had had, was well and truly over. Gregor held all the cards and I just needed to be big enough to realise it and let myself walk away. Not an easy thing for a vampire hunter, let me tell you.

I felt his soft, warm lips meet mine, his tongue force its way in through my teeth, his hand reach up and cup my breast, kneading, stroking, tweaking. His other hand run up under my skirt and flick the top of my tights, my underwear, ever so slightly, then run a finger along the inside, just a bit, not too much. And I realised I had fallen away from the black nothingness right back into his arms.

Once he sensed I was back, he pulled away and smiled. "Oh, I don't think so, little Hunter. You cannot leave until I say so."

Oh dear God.

I took a deep steadying breath in. I don't usually let the bad guys see that they have had that much of an affect on me, but I needed that breath, I needed it like a lifeline to the drowning. Once I had myself more or less under control, I hardened my resolve and prepared for battle. Not physical, but mental, emotional. I would not let him see fear and I would come out guns blazing. I called on every trick, every small thing I had learnt over the past two years and in particular over the past few weeks with Nero, and I met his gaze.

"Either exact your compensation or let me the fuck go."

"Tsk, tsk. Such language, Lucinda. I understand the antipodes are a little unrefined, unsettled as it were by those of us with far greater standing, but you do yourself no justice by resorting to such foul language."

"I don't give a shit what you think. You don't like it? Go fuck yourself."

He laughed, a full bodied laugh, that sent goose bumps down my arm. Damn him.

"You are simply too easy to rile, *ma petite chasseuse*. You wear your heart on your sleeve, I can see your thoughts, your desires, you are like an open book to me."

Open book this. "Why do you want to die, Gregor?"

That had the desired effect I was looking for. He stilled, vampire still, that preternatural calm they do when they feel threatened, or wish to conceal their feelings from a particularly difficult opponent, or when they get surprised. I was betting this was a result of the last. He hadn't expected me to ask, to be so bold, so blunt. It had caught him by surprise all right and he didn't like it. Oh goody.

"What makes you say that?" Even, low, threatening. But, I hadn't come this far to back down now, besides, what other options were open to me. Give up? I don't think so buddy.

"It's obvious. It's written all over your face." It wasn't, but he didn't know that, I was going for unsettling, so far it was working. "You want out of this life, this existence and you want me to help you achieve it. I won't. You have to know that. Not unless you threaten me, try to kill me. Not unless you deserve it."

His smile was bitter, but it didn't match his next words. Somehow I thought he had been about to say something else, then in the last minute changed his mind.

"You are simply a challenge, my little Hunter. Nothing more. And a challenge I intend to win."

"Not if I can help it, Gregor. I may have changed my mind about killing you tonight, but don't take it as consent to march forth and battle for my affections. I am not yours, nor will I ever be. I will do what is necessary to protect myself. You don't want to back me into a corner"

"Oh, but I think I do." His hand had come up to stroke

my cheek, his soft smooth thumb running along the edge of my jaw, his eyes scanning whatever it is that he sees while I Dream Walk. "I most definitely do."

I hadn't realised I'd been holding my breath. Damn, why was it he had such an effect on me? Why did my life have to be so complicated?

"Find another Hunter, Gregor. I'm not yours."

"You were mine the moment you first Walked to me. You just have not realised it yet, Lucinda."

I stared at him. I didn't want to agree, I didn't want to acknowledge what he had just said, but a part of me, a very small part, just nodded. I felt a pull to this man like no other, not even Michel, not even Nero. Michel I loved, I craved his body, his company, him. Nero was my Nosferatin idol, someone I respected, I admired, I strove to impress. But Gregor? What was Gregor to me? A challenge too? Or was he someone I could save? A fallen Nosferatu that called to my Nosferatin side. The Dark calls to the Light and vice versa.

And with that, I knew without a doubt, that I would not kill this man. Not now, not ever. For whatever reason he called to me, the thought that I could save him, could lead him to the Light was too big, too strong, too compelling. I fought almost daily to draw Michel towards the Light. I think I was even winning, but it would no doubt be a constant battle, one I would be committed to for the rest of my life. But I loved Michel, I was joined to him, Bonded to him, it was not too far from reason to see that I would accept that responsibility.

Gregor held no sway over me emotionally, well not in that regard. Clearly I was attracted to him, but I wasn't sure that was all simple physical attraction. The attraction could have been because I longed to bring him towards the Light. I sighed. I could tell myself that, but could I really believe it? Still, committing myself to bringing Gregor to the Light could very well be a lifetime chore. If I battle Michel's Dark daily, then surely Gregor's would require that amount of attention too. Could I do that? Would I do that?

And then what? More vampires call to me? More make me long to lead them to the Light?

My life was only so big, my abilities only so strong. I am only one person, I can't do this alone. Nero helps, but I really needed those other Nosferatin to show up and fulfil this prophesy. Where the hell were they?

Gregor hadn't said another thing while I was battling this little problem inside of me. He had simply sat there, holding on to me, stroking me and watching me. His patience was a surprise.

"I am not yours, Gregor." OK, so it wasn't much, but when faced with the daunting sometimes repetition had it's benefits. A girl could try.

He smiled, I was getting used to the way it lit up his eyes and made my *Sigillum* shine and glow. I was even getting good at not allowing it to have an effect on me. Well, sort of.

"We'll see, *ma petite*, we'll see. But for now, I think I would like my compensation."

The look in his eyes then was pure hunger. He didn't try to hide it, he let the full force of his desire show. I wasn't sure if he would truly try to take me by force. Somehow it didn't sit with the new Gregor I had come to know. It did sit, however, with the Gregor Michel had warned me of. So perhaps it was that thought, or perhaps I really am a hunter through and through, but before I even knew what I was doing, my spare stake was in my hand and it had entered his chest, right up to my fist. It was only my force of will and the sudden realisation that I did *not* want to kill this man, that made me change the angle. But it was enough to pin him to the wall, enough to stop his heart and still his breath. It was enough to almost kill him.

Almost.

But not quite, enough.

My heart was in my throat. I could feel the pounding in my head and felt a little dizzy at what I had actually done. At the fact that I'd had no control - well almost no control - and had nearly succeeded in carrying out my original goal for the night, despite my change of heart. I felt bile rise in my throat and choked it back down. I would not lose it now.

I heard a commotion around me, the door slamming back, felt the presence of several vampires enter the room. It was all a haze, I had tears in my eyes and realised they had actually started trailing down my face. I didn't brush them away, I just let them fall, on me, on him. He raised a hand slowly, laboriously towards my cheek and touched a finger to a tear. Just rested his hand there.

I felt a vampire approach from behind, felt the warmth of his hand come out to grasp my shoulder and heard, through a tunnel, Gregor's voice, strained, low, barely audible. "Don't touch her. Stay back."

The vampire stilled, but didn't come further. He didn't move back either.

I looked at Gregor and he smiled, a sad smile, one that

did not suit his handsome, yet slightly arrogant face. “Go, *ma petite chasseuse*. Go while you can.”

I licked my lips, I didn't want to go, I wanted to pull that damn stake right out of his chest, but I knew it could be fatal. Once driven in so far and so close to his heart, it would take precision and a steady hand, not to mention a master vampire's skills, to remove it without inflicting further harm. I may not have killed Gregor right this second, but that didn't mean he wasn't already dead. Dead-dead, that is.

And it would all be my fault.

“I'm sorry,” I whispered. Then let myself drift towards that nothingness, that complete and utter black, that usually comforted me, called to me and sent me back to my body. But now just accused me, condemned me and castigated me.

The last thing I registered before it completely dragged me under was the touch of his hand on my cheek and the overwhelming sense of confusion through my mind.

And then black.

Pitch black.

Nothing more.

Chapter 16
Explanations

It wasn't like the last time I woke from Dream Walking twice in one night. That time it had happened slowly, over a period of a couple of hours, like being in and out of consciousness. Hearing things, then feeling things, then eventually opening my eyes and seeing things. This time I woke with a start, sat bolt upright in bed, gasping for breath and crying.

The sobs coming louder and stronger. My arms circling my stomach, wrapping around my body, trying to hold the tears inside, the pain inside. I couldn't register where I was, who was with me, if I was even alone, just the pain. So true, so pure and so deep.

I had killed him. I knew it. He hadn't survived the removal of the stake. It was all my fault.

That thought just brought on more tears until I was now gulping for air and screaming out one continuous sound. Rocking back and forth and unable to do a thing about it. About any of it.

I didn't register anyone near me. I didn't feel the needle go into my vein and I didn't fight the blackness that came and enveloped me again. This time not judging, not doing anything, but covering me in a heavy blanket and smothering me from the pain.

When I awoke the second time, there was light streaming in the room, sunshine across the foot of my bed. I glanced at my surroundings and recognised the four poster bed I was resting in, the décor of the room. The heavy navy damask drapes on either side of the open windows. The slight sulphur smell in the air. Taupo. I was at Michel's holiday home in Taupo.

I looked around and saw Kathleen reading in a chair, off to the side of my bed. Kathleen is Michel's human servant, she and her husband look after his holiday home in Taupo when he is not there. Their relationship to Michel had always puzzled me. It was more than just master and servant, there was a depth of trust there that I couldn't quite understand.

She hadn't changed since I last saw her, still motherly, a little plump, greying hair, about 60 years old. I liked Kathleen. I didn't understand her, but I liked her.

She looked up at me, sensing I was awake. "Good morning, Lucinda." Her southern English accent was soft, appealing. It always made me think of farms and home. I've never been to England, let alone a farm in Kent, but somehow her accent gave me that feeling. I liked it.

I smiled. "How long have I been out?" My voice wasn't too rough, too dry. I was surprised.

"A little over three days. You woke, but we had to sedate you, as you were...upset."

Oh. It wasn't a dream then.

"Where's Michel? Is he all right?"

She smiled then, as though I had said the most beautiful thing, as though it was what she had been waiting to hear from me. "He is resting in his chamber. You can go to him shortly, if you feel up to it."

She stood then and came over to check the lines connected to me. I hadn't even noticed them. Two stuck in my arms, one up my nose, feeding me, nourishing me, hydrating me. Other lines doing other things in other places, she seemed to know what she was doing. Turning this off, disconnecting that, removing something else.

"You are a nurse?" I asked, surprised.

"I was, long ago. Not any more, but you never forget, do you? It's like riding a bike."

"Is that why Michel brought me here this time?" Last time he'd had me resting in one of his homes in Auckland, in St Helier's Bay. Close to his business, but safe, with a nurse to look over me. He had looked over me too, never leaving my side during the entire week I was out cold. It made me feel a little unsure that he wasn't next to me now.

Kathleen must have seen something on my face, because she seemed to understand. "You needed to hide. And I could not tend to you in his chamber, so we thought it best you stay in your room. He sits with you most of the time, only leaving when he needs his rest too. This room can be light-tight like the rest of the house, but he doesn't get adequate rest here."

OK. So, now I had so many questions it wasn't funny.

"Why not have me in his chamber?"

"There isn't room for all the equipment. His chamber here is purely for resting, it is not large enough for more, not when he can roam the house."

OK.

"Why does he need rest?" He was a level one *Sanguis Vitam* Master Vampire. He didn't need rest in the true sense, just protection from sunlight and a peaceful few hours to relax.

"I think I'll let him answer that."

OK.

"Why do we need to hide?" I was determined to get some sort of answers out of her.

She had finished undoing all the lines, removing them and taping gauze over the incision marks. She switched the heart monitor off, the one I had been connected to, and pushed it further away from the bed. Finally, she turned towards me.

"Gregor is here." Oh God. Oh God. Oh God. I hadn't killed him. "He made contact not long after Michel realised you would not wake that night. I think Michel had thought perhaps you would not be subject to the three days rest required after Dream Walking twice in one night." She smiled at me and added a little conspiratorially, "I think, he thought you were somehow more powerful than that. He was a little disappointed and then very scared. When you didn't wake, he made arrangements for you both to come here, but on leaving Auckland he had word that Gregor was on his way and had requested an audience with him."

My stomach plummeted. Had Gregor met Michel without me in tow? What had been said?

"The master sent Bruno to greet the *Iunctio's* representative in his stead and continued on here with you."

The *Iunctio's* representative? "Hang on. You mean Gregor is here on official business?"

"Yes. And now let's see if you can sit up and shower, then you can get the answers you seek from our master."

"He's not my master." It was reflex, I'd said it before I even thought of it.

Kathleen just smiled, a little of that knowing and indulgent smile Michel does so well. "Of course, my mistake."

As it happens I could stand, only slightly dizzy from so much bed rest. I felt tired, exhausted even, but my desire to get to Michel was almost frantic. So I sucked it up and showered quickly with Kathleen's help. Then dressed in a lightweight pale pink shimmery dress, just above my knees. A 1950's style with short capped sleeves and a low neckline. Not my usual garb by any stretch of the imagination, but I think Kathleen was trying to make me more presentable for Michel. I didn't have the heart to argue, it's only clothes, I had to see Michel now.

She brushed my hair. I felt a little silly having someone fuss over me, but she had that look about her that did not allow for interruptions. Finally, she deemed me fit to face the *master* and led me towards his chamber. I'd never seen Michel's chamber here before. The last time I was here, we weren't intimate, so he had crept off to his resting place and I hadn't bothered to see where it was. Now, I realised it was underground, down near his cellar, full of fantastic wines and champagnes collected over many, many years.

The house upstairs was airy, so light and open. There was glass everywhere. At night it takes in the night time scene towards the township of Taupo, with lovely little glittery orange lights reflected on the lake. During the day, the blue of the lake is blinding, reflecting the sky back towards us through every available portal to the outside. It made the light honey streaked wooden floors upstairs shine brightly.

Downstairs, by the cellar and Michel's chamber, the wood was dark, rich and luxuriant. I hadn't thought two different types and shades of wood would work so well together in the same house, but it was as if upstairs and downstairs were two totally different zones, houses even. This was Michel's domain, upstairs was Kathleen's and

Matthew's.

Kathleen indicated which door was Michel's and simply turned and walked away. I watched her leave and took a deep breath in. I wanted to see Michel so badly, but I was scared. Scared of why he needed rest. Scared of what I would see. Scared that he knew how connected I was to Gregor. Scared that Gregor had already exacted his revenge for what I had done.

I hadn't even raised my hand to knock on the door when it swung open and there was Michel standing before me. He was dressed in his black silk boxers, a matching silk robe over the top, open and showing a line of his deep cream skin from neck to boxers and further. His hair was loose. The dark brown, almost black, shining in the lights of the room. His eyes were deep swirls of blue, mesmerizing. He looked perfect, unharmed, at ease.

He held a hand out to me and I almost collapsed into him as I took it, forcing myself to breathe and not start crying. He smoothed my hair and whispered in French against my neck. Soothing words that didn't make sense, but made me feel so much better anyway.

We stood there holding each other for a few moments and then he carefully pulled me into the room and closed the door behind us with the flick of his hand.

"*Mon dieu*, what is the matter, *ma douce*? Why such sorrow.?"

I shook my head, I couldn't talk, I couldn't say a word. I was sorry for the mess we were in. I knew that Gregor being here would not be good and that it was all my fault. I also felt sorry for letting Michel down, for not killing Gregor when I had set out to do so. And then I felt sorry, for almost killing Gregor when I had decided I wasn't going to, ever. I was so full of sorrow it actually made me laugh. Just a little and it wasn't pretty.

"Lucinda. Talk to me."

He'd pulled me over to his bed and sat us both down. I hadn't even had a chance to take in the room, my head was bent, against his chest, my arms wrapped tightly around his waist. He didn't try to get out of my grasp, just allowed me to hold on fiercely, to feel that closeness to him. He must have understood I had a need. He waited patiently for me to get myself under control, just stroking my head, my back, breathing against my ear, softly, steadily, comfortingly.

Finally I found my voice. "I thought you were hurt." It was small, but at least I had found it.

"What would make you think that?" His was even, cautious.

"Kathleen said you needed rest, but wouldn't tell me why."

I felt him take a breath in. Great, I had probably just dropped Kathleen in it. I could always tell when Michel didn't like hearing something and I was guessing he didn't like hearing that Kathleen had scared me.

Stuff it. I couldn't protect everyone and right now I was needing my full attention just to stay breathing, to stop from falling completely into a blubbering mess.

"I am not hurt, *ma douce*, merely conserving energy." Before I could raise a question he went on. "I am exerting a little power right now to protect us, to hide us and to lay a few false trails. They need to be perfect, they require my full attention and therefore my need for more frequent rest."

"Is it because of Gregor being here?"

He did sigh out loud this time. "Just how much has Kathleen told you?"

"Don't blame her, I was persistent. I like that she answered most of my questions. She always seems so loyal to you, fiercely protective, but I felt like she also wants to please me too now."

"She is my servant, not yours and she has disobeyed me."

"Michel, please. Don't make an issue of this, we don't have time."

He didn't say anything for a while, probably planning out what dastardly things he would do to his disobedient *servant*. Finally, he said, "You are right, there is much to discuss."

I wasn't sure that he had dropped the issue of Kathleen's supposed disobedience. I could only hope we were too distracted by more important things for him to act on it. But, vampires can be very determined when they need to, somehow I knew poor Kathleen would not hear the end of this.

"So, Gregor is here and you're hiding us. For how long? And what does he want?"

"The hiding is merely a delay tactic, until you were well. We must meet with Gregor. We cannot afford to refuse the *Iunctio's* request for an audience with their formal representative. As to what he wants, I cannot be sure. We only spoke briefly on the phone after his arrival. To acknowledge his presence in our land and the request of the *Iunctio* for a meeting. He would not divulge more."

"He didn't tell you what happened when I Dream

Walked?"

He pulled away at that and held me by my shoulders, lowering his face to stare at mine. The look he gave me was not reassuring at all. "You met with him? I thought you would have merely returned to your body as soon as you realised I was not there. That you wouldn't have placed yourself in such a dangerous position without me to aid you. I thought you would not be so stupid, *ma douce*. *What* were you thinking?"

Obviously not what he had been thinking any way.

I cleared my throat. "I couldn't waste the opportunity. I knew I wouldn't get another chance to surprise him and the thought of having to be out cold for three days and not have anything to show for it just didn't sit well with me." Even to my ears that sounded lame.

"And how did it go for you, my dear? Success?" His voice was dripping with sarcasm, his face not at all pleasant.

I smiled up at him then. It was a little crooked, but it was the best I could manage.

"In a manner of speaking."

He blinked. A look of utter surprise flashing across his face.

"What?" Not his most eloquent sentence, that was for sure.

"Well, I kind of staked him. In the end."

"Why...How...*What* did you do?" Oh hell, Michel was practically having a mental breakdown. He never lost control to this extent, where he couldn't even form a coherent sentence. It would have been laughable, if he didn't looked so shocked.

Where to start?

"I went there with the intention of staking him." When Michel went to say something I held up my hand to stop him and continued. "I ended up changing my mind. He's not evil, he has a lot of Light in him, I just couldn't do it. To top it off, he wouldn't fight me, he refused to protect himself. It was as though he wanted me to end it all for him. I couldn't, not like that."

I had expected Michel to have been angry with me, because I hadn't followed through when so close, taking the opportunity when it was presented to me. But what I saw was not anger, not by a long shot. It was sadness and an understanding, but somehow I didn't think it was an understanding of what I had done, or not done. Not an understanding of the final decision I had made to not kill Gregor.

He didn't say anything for a while, just let my words sink in, then he cocked his head and said, "You said you staked him. In the end. Did you change your mind? Again?"

I sighed, the truth, or as close to it as I could manage. "He wanted compensation for being inconvenienced. My *unscheduled* visit had interrupted a meeting." I'd get to Alessandra in due course. "He said, I owed him compensation."

"What form did this compensation take?" I didn't like his tone. It was even, low, a little scary.

You know how vampires can get. There's a threatening menace to their voices sometimes. They don't have to try hard, it's fairly close to the surface for them. It also manages to send a shiver down your spine. Not the pleasant kind of shiver, more like the someone-walked-over-your-grave kind of shiver. Not nice.

I took a deep breath in and let it out slowly. "I can't be sure, because I staked him before he had a chance, but I think his intentions were carnal in nature."

Michel didn't say anything immediately, his face remained calm, his usual mask, non-committal, non-anything. He used that face sometimes while negotiating or dealing with other vampires. Lately, I'd seen it a bit more than I liked.

And then he smiled. Followed by a laugh, almost a huff of breath and then another, until he was laughing quite steadily and I wanted to laugh with him, but wasn't sure if the joke was for me or because of me, so I didn't.

Finally he exhausted himself and lay back on the bed staring up at the ceiling.

"So, you staked him because he was about to make an advance on your virtue, but somehow you *didn't* kill him?" He laughed again. "Two things, *ma douce*. One, you are a vampire hunter and vampire hunters don't miss their target. And two, you staked him." That last was said in awe almost, with a hint of disbelief. "No wonder he is pissed off," he added with another huff of a laugh.

"Great. I'm glad you find it amusing."

He laughed even harder at that. "Gregor has never had his advances turned down, *ma douce.* And not only did you do that, but you staked him for it. You can't imagine the hit to his ego."

He suddenly reached up and pulled me down on top of him, wrapping his arms around me and planting a kiss on my mouth. It was a quick touch of the lips. He was still laughing, but he didn't let me pull away. Instead he began stroking my hair, nestling me in against him.

He whispered against my ear, “I should never have doubted you.”

“You like that I staked him for coming on to me?”

“I *love* that you staked him for coming on to you. Perhaps the lothario has met his match after all.”

I didn't know what to say to that. Had Gregor met his match? Part of me, that big, huge, defiant part, wanted to insist he had; the other part of me, that small, but not so silent, drawn to Gregor part, disagreed.

I wasn't sure which part I liked better.

That didn't bode well.

That didn't bode well at all.

Chapter 17
Rendezvous

Part of the reason we had come to Taupo was to hide. Hide from Gregor and his entourage. It was possible he had more vampires in the country than those he had turned up with in Auckland. And that they were, even now as we speak, searching for us, trying to find us and do whatever the hell it is Gregor wanted done. Another part of the reason was that Gregor had been offered Michel's house in St Helier's Bay, a suburb of Auckland. The same house he'd had me resting in the last time I Dream Walked twice in one night. St Helier's Bay is close enough to the CBD for Gregor to be able to meet with us, but far enough away from *Sensations* to allow Michel's base of power to remain untainted by the *Iunctio's* visiting party.

The first meeting was to be held at the St Helier's Bay house, almost like neutral territory. I think Michel was trying to protect *Sensations* for as long as he could. It was probably futile, Gregor being the *Iunctio* could go anywhere in our land without invitation. It was only required that he give us 24 hours notice of an impending visit and he had issued that as soon as I had left him. I'm not altogether sure if *he* had issued that, with the stake still embedded in his chest, or if one of his flunkie's had. It didn't matter, he hadn't broken any rules in turning up when he did. If anything Michel had by not greeting him in person, but even the *Iunctio* would allow some leeway when a vampire's kindred Nosferatin was injured. Kindred joinings are sacred to vampires, the *Iunctio* cherishes them too.

Gregor had been here two whole days already. Despite

issuing the notice of his impending arrival, he had not arrived until 48 hours after it had been given. I'm picking he hadn't been in any fit state to travel. Vampires heal quickly, super fast, but a silver stake to the chest, within millimetres of his heart, would have required an enormous amount of *Sanguis Vitam* to fix.

Michel, Bruno and I were travelling in one of Michel's black tinted vehicles, a huge four by four, *Land Rover Discovery 4.* Michel didn't go for American vehicles, European or British all the way. We were silent on the short trip from *Sensations* to St Helier's Bay, all of us consumed by our own dark thoughts. The lights of small watercraft along Tamaki Drive reflected in the still waters of the Hauraki Gulf, sparkling and dancing to a tune I couldn't hear.

I didn't feel very musical. Music is for when you are happy, I wasn't happy.

I sighed, a little louder than I had intended. Michel's hand came out and touched my own. He and I were sitting in the rear of the vehicle, Bruno was driving. Why weren't we bringing more of our vampires to the meeting? We were trying for unconcerned. Michel's vampires would be surrounding the property and throughout the area, right back to *Sensations.* We wouldn't be alone, but the appearance of only a small greeting party was hopefully going to tone down any shenanigans from Gregor. Well, that's what we hoped any way.

"What are you thinking, *ma douce*?"

I turned to look at him in the dim light of passing street lamps. His hair was clipped back at the base of his neck, his face a serene mask of casual interest, but his eyes sparkled with amethyst and violet flecks. A sure indication that Michel was not as relaxed as he was trying to convey. He was dressed in his usual business attire; a beautifully made-to-measure Armani suit of dark, dark grey, almost black, with ever so small pin stripes in a slightly lighter shade of grey. You couldn't quite see them unless you really tried to focus on the material up close. His shirt was a Pierre Cardin in crisp white, his tie the deepest blue with a shining relief of something smaller, again not noticeable unless you looked closely. Everything Michel did was subtle. The blue of the tie brought out the darker shade of blue in his eyes. The combination was striking.

I reached up and ran my hand down his tie, feeling the embossed design ever so slightly under my finger tips. I traced the outline of one of the images, huh, dancing dragon. I almost wanted to ask, but we were already passing through Mission Bay, St Helier's wasn't too much further. I didn't have time right now.

"Why would he be here on official business? What would the *Iunctio* want with us?" I asked instead.

We'd discussed many outcomes from his being here over the past few hours, but never really touched on the why. I guess we'd all assumed he'd found a reason to come calling because of the challenge. But to be on official *Iunctio* business, would mean the *Iunctio* had approved the visit. This could not have all been for personal gain. What would it mean for us though?

Michel's hand tightened on mine, just slightly, a reassuring grip, his thumb tracing circles over the back of my hand. "There could be any number of reasons. Sometimes the *Iunctio* will simply visit a city to see how the Master is operating. They like to keep abreast of power struggles, of where certain Masters are flaunting their rules. We have been behaving ourselves, my dear, that will not be why they are here, but....I have recently started a base in Wellington, two cities in one country is not unheard of, but a country the size of New Zealand *and* one Master holding both, not so much. To be allowed to hold two cities when there are so many Master vampyres, is unusual."

Michel had been forced to start a base in Wellington for two reasons. One, his line had practically doubled when those of Jock's were accepted into the fold. Auckland was not set up for that amount of vampires, so Michel decided to spread the load a little over two cities, not one. But the main reason for setting a base up in Wellington, was because there had been some unexpected and unexplained vampire killings by humans, Norms. The need to get on top of that was paramount. We couldn't afford the *Iunctio* getting involved.

"Why the Enforcer? Wouldn't they send someone else for such a task?" Gregor's job title was explanation enough of what his job description was. If the Enforcer was here, he was here to enforce something.

Michel shrugged, that delicate shift of his shoulders that he somehow managed to make so elegant. "I do not know."

Neither of us said anything for a while, but it was too late to discuss it further, we had arrived in St Helier's Bay. Michel's house was visible as we came to the end of the point and the road rose steeply to a cliff. The lights were blazing from every window, making the big house stand out like a Christmas Tree, all golden squares of light, twinkling in the night time darkness. The windows were enormous, allowing for spectacular views of the Gulf and smattering of Islands. Vampires like big windows, hiding from the sun in closed rooms during the day, made them feeling like opening up in the dark.

Bruno parked the car in the paved driveway and turned the engine off. He exited and came round to open my door. Before I stepped out, I took a deep breath in, closed my eyes and centred myself, allowing my mind to shift to that black nothingness before Dream Walking, but stopping myself before I got too far down that path. I then sent my senses out, the new Blood Life Seeking senses, into the night. I wanted to get a feeling for how many vampires were here. They could hide their *Sanguis Vitam* from me under normal circumstances, but not when I was *seeking* them.

Several vampires were in the house, five in the main living area, six upstairs and perhaps another half dozen in and around the immediate house. All of them foreign to me. So, Gregor had brought a large entourage then? I sent my sense out further and found our vampires in the area, maybe twenty. I didn't bother to count, I wasn't going for accuracy, just an indication. Some of Gregor's vampires had streaks of evil in them and lots of Dark. None of them doing anything untoward just yet, but the threat was there. This could get ugly if we weren't careful.

I fell away from that realm and opened my eyes. Bruno was still standing tall by the open door and Michel was staring intently at me.

"What did you sense, *ma douce*?"

I took a deep breath in. "Four with Gregor downstairs,

six upstairs and another six in and around the house. All of them tightly wound and reeking Darkness." I didn't say evil, I couldn't bring myself to acknowledge that just yet. For some reason a part of me kept hoping Gregor wasn't going to walk down that path, that he simply wasn't capable of it. Ignorance is bliss.

Michel looked a little surprised. "Not quite what I had sensed. He has brought lower level vampyres then, only four are Masters." Michel being the Master of the City, can sense when powerful vampires enter his territory. Obviously lower level vampires are not immediate threats, so his *awareness* does not acknowledge them.

He reschooled his features. "Shall we then?"

Suddenly I found my heart in my throat, beating a staccato rhythm across my chest. Nervous, me? Hell yes. Was I going to throw myself at Gregor, in front of Michel? Would I feel that undeniable pull to him and embarrass myself? Would I fall all over my feet in an eager rush to be close to my *Sigillum*? I so did not need this.

I had come to stand next to Bruno, having held his hand to exit the car. Michel came up behind me and took hold of my shoulders, bending his head to my neck, as though he was going to mark me. In my head he sent his thoughts, *It is all right, ma douce, you will feel attracted to him. Your Sigillum will call to you, as his calls to him.*

Great. That's all I needed. Michel to know how hard this was. I pulled away from him, took a deep breath in, centred myself on my heartbeat and made it slow. I. Would. Not. Show. Fear.

Michel didn't try to touch me again, but swept past and headed up the stairs to the front door. It stood open with a short vampire holding it ajar. He had piercing black eyes, with a slight red ring to them. Vampires tended to only show that creepy redness when extending power, but I felt none rolling off this guy, just an eerie sort of Darkness. As though he had spent too long in an evil state of mind, that he simply couldn't switch it off entirely any more.

He was dressed casually, black jeans and a loose dress shirt, a deep plum colour that didn't quite match the red rim of his eyes, the two colours just not complementing in the slightest. He nodded to Michel, but stared right past me to Bruno, the obvious threat. He should have known better, despite my small physique, I can pack a punch *and* I was carrying concealed two silver stakes and a long silver knife. Stupid.

I felt his presence at our backs as we headed down the entry corridor and turned into the main living area of the house. One full wall was all glass, showing the watery scene out towards Rangitoto Island and the dots of green and red lights marking the main shipping channel. The room was understated elegance; modern furniture, soft furnishings, light and airy. So *not* what you would expect a vampire's house to be. It always surprised me when we came to visit here.

There were only three other vampires in the room we entered, one had vanished since I last sent my senses out. I didn't like that thought and resisted the urge to look over my shoulder as we came through the door. I made a concerted effort to ignore Gregor, instead taking in the other two vampires to the side, by the windows, feigning interest in the view. It wasn't that spectacular, so I knew they were bluffing.

One was tall, almost as tall as Michel, but short an inch or so. He had white blonde hair, past his shoulders, loose and fly away. It was snow white and made his pale features pasty. His eyes were a deep green, forest green almost. Green is not a common colour amongst vampires, don't ask me why, just isn't. I had met one other vampire with green eyes before and he was nasty, pure and simple. He was called Max. I think I've mentioned him before. This one didn't have too much Darkness rolling through him, just a sense of menace, as though he was trying to fit the bill of bodyguard but failing miserably.

The other vampire was slightly shorter, about 5'9" and had long auburn hair tied back in two plaits. Most vampires either go loose with their hair or clip it back snugly at the nape of their necks, like Michel and Gregor do, but this one had formed an intricate design with his tresses, as though it was his signature. I kind of liked it. His eyes were a pale blue, distant sky blue, they weren't his most striking feature. No, that would be the hair.

Both were dressed suavely; dress trousers encasing their long legs, dark dress shirts, slightly open at the neck. Both wore gold jewellery. Something I was not used to seeing on a male vampire. Watches yes, usually *Omega* or *Longines*, the top brand names only, but not Italian Mafioso style gold chains and thick gold bracelets. They weren't feminine, just a bit gaudy, that's all.

This perusal had taken mere seconds. I can scan a room in a heartbeat, ascertain threats, take in the scenery. I don't think it's an acquired skill, I think it's part of who or what I am. Nosferatins are always on the look out for danger and anything that would help them in an attack. I'd sized the vampires up, knew what they looked like, what their outfits said about their personalities and sensed what their power levels were. Aside from Red Eyes at the door, these vampires both had clout. Not the same level as Gregor, by no means, but enough to make the hairs stand up on my arms under my black denim jacket. I resisted the urge to rub them.

Finally, I did what I had been avoiding all along, I looked at Gregor. He was standing by the fireplace, which wasn't lit. Auckland is warm almost year round. Now in Spring, it was extremely pleasant, a fireplace is a luxury most houses don't have this far North in the country. I'd prepared myself, with that little warm-up of sussing out his flunkies, so I didn't catch my breath or feel my heartbeat rise, I simply entered that place you go to when you shut down a little. The vampires do their preternatural calm, we humans do that blank void. Steel ourselves, our minds away and face the bogeyman.

This bogeyman though was gorgeous. I may not have have let myself respond on a basic level to the sexual attraction, or *Sigillum* induced attraction that I had to him, but I did allow myself a small shake of the head and a slight smile on my lips. He'd dressed to impress. His black hair was neatly pulled back making the curve of his lips and the high cheek bones on his his face more prominent. His scar standing out against the pale of his skin, not ugly, just part of him and his silver grey eyes in stark relief against his dark suit. I'm betting Armani too, these vamps tend to follow trend. He had a silver grey shirt on, that did make him appear slightly more modern than Michel's white, it also did wonders for his eyes. No tie, but then the collar on the shirt seemed to not warrant one, it was a statement all on its own. Simple, but closed, higher on the neckline than a normal shirt would be, almost a Chinese collar, but not quite.

My gaze went back to his eyes and my *Sigillum*, even I can't resist that pull indefinitely. I briefly flashed on the thought that Michel would know now what form my *Sigillum* takes, but didn't dare glance at him and give away my thoughts. He's a big boy, he could handle it. My mark was even more obvious in person. When I'd seen it Dream Walking it had been breath taking, beautiful in a subtle shining way, now it almost seemed blinding. I wondered if that was because I was nearby and it noticed my presence.

Tension built in the air for a moment. Not too long had passed since we had walked in, but enough for there to now be a small edge of awkwardness to the room. Who would speak first?

I'm a sucker for silence. Tension doesn't get me, but silence, that's the killer every time.

"So, you managed to get the stake out?" I asked casually.

I felt his *Sanguis Vitam* come out and wrap around me, pulling me towards him, stroking my arms, touching my cheek, his mark, grabbing my hand. I even lifted my foot to take a step towards him, then clamped down my shields with a resounding clang in my head. The clang was probably more for my benefit than any one else's, I'd be the only one to hear it. I shook my head and frowned at him.

"Ah, ah Gregor. Play nice."

Michel obviously hadn't sensed Gregor's power floating across the room to me, because I felt rather than saw him stiffen slightly and turn his head towards me questioningly. He didn't bother to send me a thought, he probably knew I was battling something he couldn't see and needed my concentration.

"You can't blame me, little Hunter. You are a sight for sore eyes. Any man would find it hard to resist your allure." His eyes held hints of mischief and a whole lot of desire. The bastard wasn't even trying to hide it.

Of course his voice coated me in warmth, swirled around my stomach making butterflies dance across my skin. I shuddered, I hadn't meant to, but it was either that or cover my body with my arms and start rubbing against my skin. I thought the shudder was the less of two evils.

Michel decided he'd had enough of the show and stepped forward. Not in front of me, but enough to make Gregor's gaze shift to him. Michel was the Master of the City, Gregor should have acknowledged him as soon as he entered the room. Tut tut.

"Gregor, *mon ami*, it has been a long time. Welcome to my city." So, Michel was going for the *old friend* line, I silently wished him luck on that one.

Gregor smiled slowly at Michel, a languid smile, one I would have thought he'd reserve for a more intimate setting. Maybe he was trying to play at Michel's heartstrings, I was quite sure he'd fail. Well, fairly sure.

He said something in French I didn't understand. Michel answered, something along the lines of *you had your chance* but I couldn't be sure. My French is rudimentary and theirs was fast and fluent. I was going to have to practise more.

"English boys. Don't you know it's rude to carry a

conversation in a language others don't comprehend?"

Both sets of eyes turned towards me, their combined intensity was almost enough to make me stagger. I stood firm and met their gazes, cocked my head slightly and raised an eyebrow.

It was Gregor who spoke first.

"Did you think you would keep her all to yourself, Michel?"

"I was never one to share, Gregor, you know that."

"Then it must be very disappointing that she came to me."

OK. I *so* did not come to him, but I'd let this conversation play out a little more before I truly lost my rag. The night was still young after all.

"You have made your point, now what do you want?" Michel's tone was flat, but demanding.

Oh, so Michel wasn't playing patient then, just me. Good to know.

"I thought that was obvious when I marked her."

All right, so I was starting to get a little pissed off with all this talking as though I wasn't even here, but I didn't get a chance to enter the fray, Michel was winding up.

"She is my kindred Nosferatin, we are joined and Bonded, do you really think you even have a chance?"

Gregor just laughed at that, a rich, deep full bodied laugh that did make me wrap my arms around myself and rub my sides. His eyes fell on me and he pulled the laugh back slightly, only allowing a slight warmth to wrap me up and stroke my cheek. I resisted the urge to push my cheek further into that warmth.

"You have already lost her, Michel. Be a man and let

her go." His voice was soft, sure, confident.

Who the hell did he think he was?

"You have underestimated her, Gregor. It is a surprisingly common fault, one that usually ends disastrously for those who are not prepared."

Gregor hadn't bothered to look at Michel as he spoke, his eyes were all for me. I tried not to squirm under his hot stare, but I did shift slightly. He noticed of course, they always do. A small smile curved his lower lips. I couldn't let this go on, it had to stop now.

"You're wasting your time, Gregor, you might as well pack up and head back to Rome, there's nothing for you here."

I thought I sounded pretty convincing, I mean I really meant it. I was joined to Michel and we had Bonded. Not just your average Bond either, but an intense early Bonding that reflected the physical and emotional relationship we shared. We were meant to be together. *No one could pull us apart. Our Bond would not allow it.*

"Are you so sure, little Hunter? Being Bonded does not mean exclusivity. You are still free to roam. It is merely a choice you can make. I would be happy to help you make the right one."

I think I had stopped breathing then. Michel had never indicated that that was the case. Even Nero had acted like it was a foregone conclusion and I was no longer available. When he had found out I was Bonded to Michel, Nero had seemed momentarily disappointed and since then, if I look back on it now, he had toned down his flirting and always tried to keep things professional between us. Sure, occasionally he got carried away, but that was just proximity and heightened emotions when battling side by side. I was sure the Bond was final, I'd only been fighting it because that's the kind of girl I am. I do not like being backed into a corner. But a part of me had accepted it as a *fait accompli*, I just hadn't let the rest of me catch up yet.

I turned slowly to look at Michel. I don't know what I thought I'd see on his face. Defiance? Anger? A shake of his head to disagree?

What I saw left me reeling, set adrift on an iceberg at sea.

Pain. The pain of someone who had been caught out hiding the truth and knew that this would have ever lasting consequences.

Michel?

Now he shook his head.

Too late.

Chapter 18
Vampire Politics

Gregor didn't laugh, like I expected him to. I think he realised I was shaken to the core, that any joke he made of the situation would hurt me, alienate me, push me from him. I hated him for his diplomacy. I wanted someone to rage against and I wanted it to be him. He had brought this out into the open, he had upset my apple cart. Oh I know, I should have been angry at Michel and I was, don't get me wrong, I was furious with Michel, but I didn't want Gregor. I didn't want to want him and giving in to that fury at Michel would only throw me towards Gregor.

I took a step away from both of them, which brought me closer to the other two vampires in the room. Not a wise move, but right then I didn't care. I already had my hand resting on the stake inside my jacket. A comfort measure, to ground me and stop me floating away for real. If it came down to it, I'd slay the whole fucking lot of them. I was so sick of all this shit.

Michel could sense my emotions and by the look on his face it was crushing him. Bruno had even taken a step closer to his master, a movement so protective that I shot him a look. He gazed back blankly at me. He was about the only vampire in the room managing to maintain that blank mask of nothingness they prized so much.

Old Snow White and Pipi Longstockings were watching avidly, devouring every feature on my face. I think they relished the idea of their master winning the prize. And Gregor, well he just looked patient and confident, don't forget the confidence, he was swimming in it.

I took a deep breath in, if no one else was going to end this nightmare, I'd have to take charge myself. Familiar territory.

"Why has the *Iunctio* chosen to visit our lands?" I directed the question at Gregor, lifting my chin and glaring at him in the process.

A brief flash of surprise crossed his features, followed by respect, then quickly reschooled into a pleasant mask.

"We are interested to see how the newest joined vampire is progressing. Michel's increase in power has not gone unnoticed, we would like to ensure it is remaining in check and not compromising our kind."

Michel didn't seem capable of comment, he was still staring at me with a slight look of pain on his face. He needed to suck it up and get on with this.

"Do you see him as a threat?" I asked, returning my attention to the main threat in the room.

"Define threat, Hunter."

"Something that would do you, the *Iunctio*, damage?"

"Define damage."

I sighed. "Are you always this difficult or just tonight?"

He smiled. "Only when negotiating with a worthy opponent." I think he was trying to compliment me, it didn't work.

I stared at him for a moment, no one else was offering up anything. Michel's face was back to its normal mask, but for some reason he did not wish to participate. I was beginning to worry that the fight may have been extinguished in him. That was way scarier than it sounds.

"Are you afraid? And don't tell me to define afraid, you

know damn well what afraid means."

His smile broadened. "The *Iunctio* is afraid of nothing and no one, my little Hunter. It merely wishes to determine Michel's control of his powers, to ensure our kind's safety. Is that succinct enough for you?"

I nodded. Short and sweet.

"How do you plan to determine Michel's power then?"

"By observation, the occasional task or challenge."

OK, so now we were getting somewhere, the occasional task or challenge. I didn't like the sound of that.

"What sort of task or challenge?" My voice had gone a little quieter, I mentally chided myself for giving away too much.

"Now that would ruin the surprise, would it not? And only those challenges with the element of surprise are truly worth their salt."

"And if Michel fails the tasks or challenges?"

"Are you *afraid* he will?"

"I didn't say that, Gregor. I'd just like to know where the *Iunctio* is going with all of this."

Michel stiffened slightly, oh great, he was paying attention, but why the reaction?

Gregor took a few steps closer, still some distance from me, but the movement alone was a threat, exactly as he had intended it to be. "No one questions the *Iunctio,* Lucinda, not even you."

I sighed, not the reaction he was looking for I'm guessing, by the slow blink of those glowing silver and platinum eyes. The funny thing is, Gregor represented the *Iunctio*, the big bad powerful vampires that controlled all of them. I should have been afraid, but for whatever reason

Gregor didn't scare me any more.

Huh. Strange, but true.

"I intend the *Iunctio* no offence. You are their Enforcer, you're here to enforce. What does that entail, Gregor, or is that meant to be part of the surprise too?"

He studied me for a moment, as though he would be able to answer all of life's most difficult questions merely by looking into my eyes.

"You're not scared of me. You should be. I am the *Iunctio* here. I could end it all for you and your kindred vampire. One judgement from me and you would be sentenced to the final death. Does that not warrant your fear, Hunter?"

Michel began to say something, finally entering into the fray, but he was silenced by one flick of Gregor's hand. No power came with the motion, but a movement and look that said it all. "Let her answer Michel, it is the Hunter who has garnered my response."

Fantastic. Now I'd pissed him off.

"I didn't mean to ruffle your feathers, Gregor. You do run a little hot and cold, don't you?"

He was in front of me in an instant. Not touching, but looming over me, threatening in his stance. What the hell?

"You need to remember, Lucinda, that my official business here is not to be confused with my personal pursuits. As the *Iunctio's* representative, there are certain formalities to be obeyed, even you are subject to them. We are discussing *Iunctio* business, therefore you address me as Enforcer and you show some respect."

The last, show some respect, was said very slowly, clearly, precisely. If he was looking for another apology or a whimper or even a cower he was sorely mistaken. I'd long ago realised that the only thing to do in the presence of a threatening vampire was to show no fear.

I stood straight in front of him, didn't move away, didn't cringe, just met his gaze and held it for a good few long seconds.

"Is the lesson over?" Yeah, that's me, all mouth no brains sometimes.

He slowly shook his head. "How do you put up with her?" The question was for Michel, but his eyes hadn't left me.

"Lucinda is not familiar with *all* of our rules Enforcer. She is a young Nosferatin."

Oh well done Michel, if I was furious with you before, now I was just livid.

Gregor smiled then, he must have seen something flash in my eyes, he *was* studying me rather closely.

"I shall take great delight in teaching her then."

Super. You do that. Just warn me about the mood swings next time.

He let a little laugh out, just a huff, but he was smiling a little more, his shoulders now relaxed. The light dancing around his eyes, calling to me. Sometimes reading my mind could come in handy, at least the tension in the room had dissipated. On to more pressing matters.

"How long do you intend on staying?"

"That depends on you."

"On me?" I couldn't keep the sarcasm out of my voice.

He flashed me a sparkling grin, no fang, just teeth and a whole lot of attitude. We'd definitely switched back to his alter ego, the one he uses when not enforcing.

"On how long you resist my advances."

And there goes the voice again. He'd been reining it in, taking the questions as they were meant, a professional conversation, even while he lost his temper earlier. But now he let me feel the full force of his desire, his need, his intentions and I couldn't stop the gasp from slipping through my lips.

Michel was in front of me, blocking Gregor in an instant, a low growl escaping his lips. I couldn't see his face, but I saw the look of amusement on Gregor's. He looked passed Michel to me and said, "I'm picking the *Iunctio* will have their answer before I have mine. They wont object however, if I stay on a little longer to pursue my own interests."

He was goading Michel and I had to unfortunately concede, succeeding. Michel had for some reason been thrown off his game tonight. This was not the evenly tempered and tightly controlled vampire I was used to. He was acting like a school boy, reacting to a territorial threat display. He was bigger than this, older than this. He was the consummate politician. What the hell was happening to him?

I wanted to reach out and touch his shoulder, but I also didn't want to lend weight to the obvious lack of control he was displaying. The only thing I could think of doing to end this abysmal evening, was to get us out of here.

"OK. Well if we're all finished here then, welcome, enjoy the sights. If you need anything just send us a message. I'm sure old Snow White and Pipi Longstockings here could make a good message delivery service when needed."

Bruno stifled a snigger, not altogether successfully and both Snow White and Pipi took menacing steps forward, eyes glowing red, fangs on display and *Sanguis Vitam* pouring off in waves of pure evil. Oh goody a reason to draw my stake.

I didn't pull it right out, just enough to reflect the light in the room and to get the vampires' attention..

"Boys, please. Stand down if you know what's good for you."

Gregor was laughing quietly, taking the scene all in. His voice was soft but firm. "*Lasciare il comando.*" The two vampires immediately pulled back at his command and reschooled their features into just menace with a hint of evil.

"I'm guessing Gregor, sorry *Enforcer*, I don't need to tell you the rules. But I will any way, it's just the kind of hunter I am. If any of your vampires let that evil that their holding onto out on my people while they're here in my city, I will hunt them down and stake them."

"Evil, *ma cherie*?"

"They're leaking it all over the place. Evil. Darkness. Call it what you will, but it's strong and rotting right through to their innards."

"You paint such a pretty picture, my dear. They will of course behave themselves while they are here. You have my word."

I wasn't entirely sure if his word was good enough, but I'd pushed my luck too far this evening and really, I just wanted out of here. Michel and I had a lot of talking to do.

I nodded and turned to leave, Michel falling into step beside me, Bruno coming up the rear. We hadn't made it more than couple of steps when Gregor's voice reached out and ran a finger down my spine.

"There is one more thing."

Oh boy.

"Part of the challenges I must set are for you, Nosferatin. Your challenge will begin tomorrow."

I turned slowly, making sure my face was a pleasant mask. I wanted to say bring it on, but I held my tongue and just looked blankly at him, expecting him to elaborate further.

"I will call for you at sunset, *ma petite chasseuse*. All will be revealed then." He smiled wickedly at me and then turned his attention to Michel. "And for you, *mon ami*, so you do not feel left out tomorrow evening when I am *occupying* your kindred, I have a gift."

Oh, I did not like where this was going. I think we had all taken a short sharp breath in and were holding it.

From behind Gregor, through a door to another room that had been well concealed, swayed the sultry steps of a long legged female. Dressed in a tight fitting blood red satin floor length dress, with a split up the side showing her leg right up to her hip. Alessandra's blonde curls bounced around her pretty little face lighting up the room as she curled her arms around Gregor's shoulders and looked hungrily at Michel.

Oh damn. I knew there was something I had forgotten to tell my kindred Nosferatu.

Chapter 19
Surprise!

If Michel was surprised he didn't show it. He had his game face back on and was wearing it well.

"Alessandra. A pleasure, as always." He bowed slowly, arm across his chest, bending at the waist. It was the formal greeting vampires reserved for those they respected. Somehow I was getting the impression that Michel's was all an act this time. I could feel through the Bond how tightly coiled he was and it wasn't pretty.

"*Mio caro*, it is good to be back." She was, of course, talking to Michel, but her eyes were on me. No doubt looking for a response. She didn't get one. How stupid did she think I was?

Gregor was watching Michel, almost hungrily. As though he thought this surprise would elicit the reaction the *Iunctio* was after. Luckily, Michel was back on form and as much as Alessandra being with Gregor was a shock to him, and I'm betting it definitely was, he was that consummate politician again. Never let them see anything.

There was a brief silence hanging between us in the room, not so much tension, but just the quiet you get before a storm. You can tell something is building, you can feel it in the air, but when exactly that first thunder clap and lightning bolt will strike, is still a little mystery. I forced myself to keep breathing evenly. I'd leave this one up to Michel, it was aimed at him, not me.

"I look forward to our evening together, *dolce*." He bowed again, then put his arm out for me to take. I didn't hesitate, I *really* wanted out of here now, so I placed my arm in his, his other hand taking hold of mine on top of his arm and we swept out of the house. Bruno flashed past us in a blur and by the time we came to the bottom of the steps at the front of the property he was already holding the door to the car open for us.

I could feel the proximity of Michel's vampires, they had closed in and although not visible, their *Sanguis Vitam* filled the air. Michel had obviously been closer to the edge than I had realised, to have called his vampires in like this.

He let me get in the car first and I scooted over to the other side, so he could follow. Bruno shut the door behind him and was in the driver's seat before I had taken a breath. He wanted out of here too it seemed.

Nothing was said until we were a few hundred metres down the road and making steady progress away from the house. I figured I'd have to confess to knowing Alessandra was with Gregor. I didn't like secrets and I most certainly didn't like having secrets from my boyfriend. I'm old fashioned like that. If he's good enough to sleep with, he's good enough to deserve honesty.

"Michel. I'm sorry, I forgot to mention Alessandra was with Gregor when I last Dream Walked." I had turned slightly in my seat to look at him. He was sitting vampire still, not looking at anything in particular, pulled in on himself, thinking, protecting, doing God knows what it is that they actually do when they *disappear* like that.

He didn't answer me straight away, just let me sit there watching him do nothing. Not the most pleasant of experiences.

"A rather interesting piece of information." That's all, no inflection in his voice, just words.

I took a breath in, just a small one, nothing too

obvious. I wasn't scared yet, he wasn't flashing magenta in his eyes, his *Sanguis Vitam* was in check. Nothing to raise goose bumps along my skin, just an unnatural calm, that didn't feel quite right.

I broke first. “Say something. What are you thinking?”

He turned his head slowly to look at me, his eyes were a flat blue. A dark pit of blue, the darkness becoming stronger, deeper, more obvious the longer he looked at me. OK. So, maybe I was starting to feel a little scared.

“What else have you failed to tell me?”

I thought about that for a second. “Nothing.”

“You don't seem so sure.”

“I am.”

He just watched me with those dark, deep blue eyes, blank of all expression, unnatural, otherworldly, not right.

For the life of me I didn't know how to reach out to him. It should have been easy. He was my kindred vampire, I'm joined to him, Bonded, but it was like there was a wall between us. Not just separating us, but shielding me from all those connections to him. I'm not sure if it was Michel who had put up that wall, intentionally maybe, either to protect himself or keep me out from what he was feeling. It didn't matter who or what had put it up, or even why, it did what it was meant to do. It dulled my feelings towards him and made it impossible for me to take the final step and pull him back towards the Light.

My little internal monologue chose that moment to pop up. It's the voice of reason inside my head. Some might say I'm losing it, listening to a voice inside my head, but it's never let me down before. It's made me run, when I needed to run; fight, when I needed to fight; hide, when I needed to hide. It was like a guardian angel on my shoulder, always watching and only interfering when things got really bad. I guess we'd entered the *really bad* territory tonight.

This isn't right, it said. *Do something.* Usually I listen to it. I may not like what it has to say, but I listen. Tonight, I just brushed it aside as though it was a nuisance, an annoying little fly buzzing around my head.

Michel just continued to stare at me, but it was like he was looking through me, not really seeing me. He didn't say anything else and neither did I.

The next thing I realised was we had pulled up outside my apartment. The surprise of that jolted me out of the stupor that had enveloped me and I blinked a few times to clear my head. I had expected us to go back to *Sensations*, to discuss this further. There was so much to talk about, to prepare for. Michel was about to be challenged and tested and I was, it seemed too. We needed to have a united front, to work on this together. Did he want to have this talk here, at my home? Privacy maybe?

Bruno had my door open, so I stepped out and turned to make sure Michel was following. He wasn't, just sitting in his seat staring forward, at nothing again.

"Aren't you coming?" My heart was in my throat. I think I knew the answer, before I had even asked it.

He kept staring forward, didn't look at me, just said, "No." Nothing more.

"We need to talk about this. We need to prepare."

"I think you are more than prepared, my dear. You do not need me."

"What does that mean, Michel?" I was staring to feel the beginnings of anger. Good. Anger I could use, despair, not so much.

He looked at me then and let me see the magenta bleed slowly into the blue of his eyes. I refused to show fear, to show anything. What was his problem? I should be the one pissed off here, or had he forgotten that little bit of misleading information about our Bonding and it not necessarily being an irreversible truth.

That thought alone was enough to tip the scale and I felt my anger turn into something more. It morphed from a fury, to a rage, to a deep seated desire to strike out. I stood back from the doorway to the car I had been leaning into to look at Michel, took a deep breath in and let my anger, frustration, rage and fury build. Until I could contain it no more and thrust it out towards him, into the car, letting it swirl around the cabin of the vehicle and bounce along his skin.

Michel blanched, the first sign of true emotion on his face. The magenta in his eyes stilled, faded slightly and then he gasped as my emotions ran through him. I had hurt Michel once before with my emotions and I had sworn I would never do that again. He's not as accomplished as humans at controlling and dealing with strong emotions. Vampires have a limited range, that's why it's so hard to pull them back towards the Light. If you can't feel emotions such as empathy, compassion, sympathy and love, how can you feel Light? Most vampires are full of only the negative emotions, allowing only the Dark to prevail. My job as a Nosferatin is to turn them towards the Light. Let them relearn to have emotions that fill you with warmth. Somehow I'm guessing my ancestors hadn't picked my using this talent I had, to instil rage.

I didn't feel any guilt. I didn't care. That alone was a little strange.

I turned from the car without another word and slipped my key in the lock of my door. Opened it, walked through and closed it, without a second glance. I knew my emotions would still be playing over and over in his mind, I hadn't stopped projecting them yet. I vaguely realised they had snapped back to me, when I heard the Land Rover squeal tires out of my building complex's drive as Bruno took Michel away from the threat at high speed.

I leaned my back against the door and closed my eyes. With Michel not close I was starting to lose the rage, starting to realise a Darkness had settled over me and was only now lifting as I found peace in my small flat. I always did feel safe and at peace here. I shook my head as the last vestiges of Darkness left and the full realisation of what had happened sunk in.

"Shit." Nero had warned that I would be closer to the Dark now, that I would have to battle it too. Not good.

I wanted to run to Michel, but I didn't think he'd see me. I wanted to pick the phone up and call him on his mobile. That thought made me glance at my own land line in the kitchen. It was blinking a red light, someone had left a message. Could I even face that right now?

I took a steadying breath in. So, Michel was pissed off at me. Because why? I had forgotten to tell him about Alessandra? I shook my head. I didn't think that was it. Maybe the straw that had broken the camel's back, but it was more than that. There was more going on, but the harder I tried to figure it out, the further away an answer seemed to be.

OK. So, *I* was mad he hadn't told me about the Bond not being exclusive. I had a right to be angry. He had led me to believe we were destined to be in each other's beds, not just each other's lives. I don't like being backed into a corner and this was an enormous corner if I had ever seen one. But, I loved him, didn't I? Was that love because of our joining and Bond, or did it develop before then? The sixty-four thousand dollar question. One I didn't have an answer for right now, despite it being the question I had played over and over in my mind for weeks now. Maybe I would never have the answer I sought.

I banged the back of my head against the door, not too hard, but enough to make me wince slightly. Pain is my friend. It cleared my mind enough for me to concentrate on the here and now. No point getting all philosophical, there were more pressing matters. How to prepare for Gregor's challenge. How indeed.

Arghh!

This was getting me nowhere. My gaze rested back on the blinking light on the phone across the room. May as well deal with that, at least it was something to do with myself.

The first message was from Jerome, the Alpha of Rick's Hapū. He was back in the country and suggested we meet. Great. I'd add it to the To Do List, along with fighting off Gregor's advances, passing whatever challenges the *Iunctio* had planned and getting back on better terms with my kindred Nosferatu.

Fucking great.

The second was a surprise.

"Lucinda, it's Pete. We need to talk. I'm at the bar all

night. See you soon."

Pete was never one to waste energy on small talk, short and sweet and to the point, although there was no point in the message he had left. Pete was my eyes and ears in the city. He's a ghoul and ghouls are very good at finding things out for you. If there's a rumour, they probably started it, or at the very least, were there when it began. Every Nosferatin needs a good network of information, mine just happens to be headed by a ghoul.

But, Pete had never voluntarily offered up information before. It was always, always, me who went to him. I didn't even known he knew my phone number. But then again, Pete could find out anything if he wanted to. The problem was, to a ghoul information was their currency and nothing was for free. If Pete was going to tell me something, he would expect something in return and it needed to be good. I didn't want to tell him about Gregor, but if I didn't have something good to give him, I'd owe him. And owing a ghoul was never a good thing.

I sighed and picked up the phone to call a taxi. Pete's bar was across town, in Newmarket, a bit too far to walk.

Guts and Glory was doing a right roaring trade this evening. It's possibly one of the most popular sports bars in the district. Clean as a whistle, well maintained and swimming in a relaxed Kiwi kind of way. We Kiwi's love our sports and our bars come to think of it.

There were a couple of ghouls in the corner. They never seemed to be the same ones, but they were always there. I gathered they were Pete's henchmen, but I couldn't be sure. Pete was behind the bar, he's always behind the bar. Cleaning glasses, pouring beers, making the customers feel welcomed. Friendly, but not in your face, that's Pete's motto.

I slipped into a tall bar stool at the counter and waited for him to finish serving the big brick out-house of a guy at the other end, no doubt a former rugby player, a forward I'm guessing. He looked right at home here, that's for sure.

Pete had already seen me, so as soon as he was done he came over and poured me my usual. Another ghoul slipped in behind the bar and took over serving the rowdy crowd. Pete slid the lager towards me and indicted a booth to the rear with the nod of his head. I followed, drink in hand. I figured I'd need this one to help swallow down whatever had got Pete so riled. Because he was riled, I could tell.

I slid into the booth on one side of the table and he took the other. I sipped my cold beer, let the feel of it flow down my throat and chill my body ever so slightly.

"So, what's up, Pete?"

He scratched his short beard. Pete's a big guy with curly light brown hair and a short, trimmed beard. For a ghoul, he's really well presented. Most humans wouldn't even pick up that he wasn't one of them. Just because his diet preference is raw, doesn't mean he can't blend in. Ghouls in Auckland City tend to behave themselves, mix with the locals, just like the vamps.

"I heard something on the grapevine I thought you should know."

"Is this one on the house?" It always pays to negotiate your terms with a ghoul before you accept any information. They operate by strict rules, you have to play by them if you want to be a part of their world. I couldn't afford to piss Pete off, he was too valuable as a source of otherworldly info.

He laughed. "Nothing for free, Luce. You know that. But you can owe me. You're good for it."

"Thanks for the vote of confidence, but I don't like not paying my debts."

"Then what you got?"

"You first, then I'll see whether mine warrants it or not."

He smiled an appreciative smile. He always did like his contacts to have a bit of a backbone. Never give in too easily, but readily play the game. I'd known Pete a while now and although I couldn't play him, I certainly knew how to play the game.

"There's been a bloke asking about you. Not here, but some of the other haunts." The other haunts were supernaturally owned bars. Michel and Pete weren't the only Supernaturals to own real estate in Auckland. If you had a hint of sensitivity to the supernatural world, then you knew which bars to frequent, or not. Depending on your persuasion.

"What does he want with me?"

"Don't know. Just asking for the local Nosferatin. Bold as brass. Where you hunt, who you hang with, how good you are. That sort of thing."

OK. So, people: vampires, ghouls, shifters and magic users, they knew who I was and occasionally one would come looking for me. To kill me, to hurt me, to get to Michel. Sometimes, just to meet me. This was nothing new.

"So, what's got your knickers in a twist, Pete? This all sounds fairly mundane so far."

Pete sat back and looked at me a moment. Nothing too

scary, Pete doesn't have that effect on me, just assessing me I think, trying to see something in my face.

"This one's different, Luce. There's nothing obvious about it. I can't be sure he means you harm and even if he does, you can take care of yourself."

"Then what is it, Pete?"

"He says he's family. Your family. He says he's another Nosferatin."

Now that's a turn up for the books.

Chapter 20
Lonely

I took a slow sip of my drink. I don't have a Nosferatin family. Or at least one I know. My parents died when I was a baby and I was raised by my non-Nosferatin Aunt and Uncle. I call them my Mum and Dad. I never knew my biological parents, my Aunt and Uncle are the only parents I've ever known.

I did know my father had a brother, but my parents, that's my Aunt and Uncle, broke off contact with them not long after they adopted me. So, I guess a part of me has always been aware that there was another side to the family tree, but they'd never tried to get in touch with me, not once while I was growing up. And they knew where I was, they had to have. My parents' farm has been in the family for generations, they have never lived anywhere else.

Well, this was interesting news. Pete had allowed me a little notice. If this Nosferatin relative had just turned up on my doorstep, I would have been undoubtedly on the back foot. Now I was prepared at least. What this guy wanted, who could say. Re-establish old family ties? If Pete really thought that, then why the urgency? Why the serious look on his face now?

"You don't think this is a friendly visit, do you?"

He shrugged. I guess I'd got all the info I was going to get out of him tonight. So, do I pay up?

I sighed. "The *Iunctio's* in town."

"Tell me something I don't know."

Bugger.

"They've sent their Enforcer."

"Already know."

Shit.

"He's here to check up on Michel's new powers."

"They want to make sure he's not a threat to their kind. Heard it already."

Ah dammit. I so did not want to share this.

"His name's Gregor and he and I have a challenge in motion."

That got a raised eyebrow. He nodded for me to continue though. Obviously not enough to cover the debt yet.

How do I put this? "He wants to seduce me away from Michel." There said it. Now if that doesn't come back to bite me in the arse, I'll eat my stake.

"Really? Now that is news, Luce."

"He won't succeed."

"Are you saying that to convince me or yourself?"

Damn. I forgot how perceptive Pete could be sometimes.

"He won't. I'm Bonded to Michel, he's wasting his time." Of course I knew otherwise now. The Bond was not the be-all and end-all of our relationship. I only hoped Pete didn't know that yet.

He smiled. "Well, this will be entertaining. Be sure to let me know how it goes. Or is he likely to take out a full page ad in the *New Zealand Herald* when he wins your heart?"

"Ha ha. Very funny, Pete."

His smile dimmed. "Your debt is paid, this one's for free. Take care, Luce. Not just because of this *Iunctio* vamp, but I got a bad feeling about this Nosferatin. Nothing solid, just all gut."

He stood then and stretched his huge bulk. Pete's not fat, just big.

"Enjoy the atmosphere. The drink's on the house." He walked off back towards the bar. Pete never gave free drinks. Occasionally free advice, if I'd been good and given him something that really tickled his fancy, but never free drinks. He really was worried about me then. Funny, I couldn't muster the energy to worry myself. Another thing to add to the List.

The night was surprisingly warm when I emerged from the bar. I like spring, I used to love it on the farm; flowers, baby lambs, a bit more sunshine. Tonight the city smelt amazingly fresh, not the usually foul stench of car exhaust fumes and too many people. Spring had reached Auckland too it seemed.

I let my senses spread out in a circle around me; no vamps, or at least none reeking evil. I didn't bother with my new seeking abilities. They required a certain amount of concentration and right then a cab had pulled up to the curb to let some late night pub crawlers out, so I took the opportunity and grabbed it.

Where did I want to go? Normally, I'd head to *Sensations* to spend what was left of the dark with vampire friends, if not Michel. But I knew I wouldn't be well received there tonight. I suddenly felt very alone. Not only did I not have my kindred Nosferatin to go to, but my best friend had all but cast me aside, threatening to kill me. And Nero was probably still pissed off at me going after Gregor, right after he had risked himself to Dream Walk twice in one night to be by my side.

I must really suck as a friend right now, no one wanted

to have anything to do with me. *Gregor does,* my little internal monologue piped up. *Go to hell,* I spat right back.

I told the Taxi driver to take me home. I wasn't tired, but what else was there to do? It rankled with me that I couldn't just be happy to be in my own company tonight. Normally, it wouldn't worry me. I'd take a long bath, watch a DVD, eat a carton of ice cream. You know, the normal night at home ritual, but tonight I just felt lonely and being on my own did not improve that mood.

My flat was eerily quiet, as though it sensed my despair. I switched the TV on, but set the volume low, so it was a just a soft background noise, enough to cover the white static of emptiness that had settled in my head. I went to the kitchen and primed my coffee machine. Caffeine at night is usually a no-no for most people, not me. I love my coffee and can drink any time of the day and night, as long as it's full-bodied and has a kick. I don't do decaf.

The smell of freshly ground and brewed beans filled the small space and I settled in at the dining table to sip my cup of Java. Just the smell alone had a soothing affect on me, let alone the slightly bitter, thick, rich taste of Arabica beans. So, I didn't jump when the phone rang, I'd actually managed to find a happy place after all. That didn't last long though.

"My sources tell me you are home alone, little Hunter."

I sighed, why didn't it surprise me that Gregor would be watching every move I made? It's just something he would do I guess.

"Are you offering to come keep me company?"

"I'd be glad to, but it would break the rules. We have a date set for tomorrow, it would be an infringement to meet with you tonight." Good to know, at least he wouldn't be knocking on my door any time soon.

"Your sources manage to get on my property?"

He laughed and even over the phone it managed to wrap around my body and snuggle in close. I closed my eyes, at least he couldn't see me. "Your protection wards are strong, *ma petite chasseuse*, but not strong enough for me. Never forget that."

I didn't say anything, *he'd* phoned me, he could carry the conversation. I should have of course, just hang up, but I was lonely. Even the enemy sounded better than my own thoughts alone tonight.

"Your business at thc ghoul's seemed serious. Is there trouble? Can I help?"

I laughed then. "I'm not sure I'd want your help, Gregor."

"You said want, not need. Do you need it?"

"No. I'm quite capable of looking after myself, thanks."

"I don't doubt it at all." This time his voice curled around my neck and ran a finger down his marks. I forced myself not to breath too heavily. That's all I needed, me heavy breathing down the line to Gregor.

"Behave yourself, vampire. You're not playing fair."

"I've already told you, I never said I'd play fair." His voice had gone soft, barely a whisper over the line. I swallowed as quietly as I could manage.

"You took my breath away," he purred, "when you walked in this house tonight. Do you have any idea how hard it was not to simply go to you? You are stunning, Lucinda, so much more so than I could ever have imagined."

"Anticipation always sweetens the result. Don't take it too seriously, Gregor, you don't know me well enough to get besotted."

"Too late."

Hmm. "Why are you doing this? You can't really want me, it's just a game to you, isn't it? Or revenge. Revenge on Michel for whatever ancient grievance you seem to have."

"If I wanted revenge on Michel I could achieve it in much more practical ways. My interest in you was only piqued when you first Dream Walked to me. The fact that you are Michel's kindred Nosferatin is incidental, unfortunate, but incidental all the same."

I didn't believe him, but I wasn't going to argue the point either.

"So, what's the plan for tomorrow?"

"Let's not talk about that. Why waste breath on work, when there are much better things to discuss, like....have you changed for bed, my dear?"

"We are *not* doing this, Gregor. You are not going to try to seduce me over the phone."

"You're no fun, my little Hunter. I merely wished to know if you had entered your boudoir."

I got a little creepy feeling between my shoulder blades then. I quickly sent my senses out, but there was no evidence of residual *Sanguis Vitam* in the apartment. But, that didn't stop my stomach from knotting. I tip-toed towards my bedroom, my phone is cordless, I'd only been staying standing in the kitchen by its base unit to keep from getting too comfortable anywhere else.

I paused before I reached my bedroom doorway and braced myself, then took the step further to see inside.

Sitting on the bed was a medium sized white box with a silver bow on top. One of those boxes you simply lifted the lid off and inside would be tissue paper containing some sort of exquisite gift. I wasn't sure I wanted to know what Gregor thought was an appropriate gift. I hesitate on the threshold of the room.

"Aren't you going to open it?"

I glanced around. The curtains hadn't been drawn, I hadn't even thought of it until then, too wrapped up in my own misery to contemplate privacy. Yet another thing to shut out people and feel more alone. I quickly went around the apartment and closed all the blinds.

His laugh just trickled down the line, curling against the soft skin on my cheek.

"Feel better? Do you really think curtains will keep me out?"

OK, so that was definitely creepy. "You're creeping me out a little, Gregor. This won't win you any favours."

He ignored me. "Just open the box."

Ah damn. "Then will you go away?"

"Maybe. Maybe not."

Creepy and frustrating.

I stomped over to the box and flicked the lid off in a quick no-nonsense manner, it went flying across the room and landed on the floor with a soft thud. Sometimes, I forget my own strength. There was tissue paper inside, wads of it. I had to hold the phone to my ear using my shoulder, so I could use both hands to pry the paper apart and see what was inside.

Part of me expected slinky lingerie, similar to what he had first seen, well *felt*, me in when I found him down that alley sucking on that Italian Nosferatin. Maybe even a naughty underwear set, I'm sure he'd envisaged me in such. But, I wasn't prepared for this. I picked up a shortie PJ set; short shorts and close fitting T-Shirt in a soft cotton, all my exact size. The T-Shirt had a picture of *Sylvester the Cat* licking his lips and writing underneath his image said *Okay mouse I'll fight you, but I aint fightin' no dames*. It didn't make any sense, but it still managed to make me laugh.

"You like?"

I didn't want to say yes, but how could I not now? He'd heard my reaction.

"Very good, Gregor. How did you know I like *Sylvester*?"

"I didn't, *ma cherie*, but he is a favourite of mine. Wicked with a determined frame of mind. Sound familiar?"

Yeah, just a little.

"Will you wear it? For me?" he added.

"I don't think so." I was already folding it back up and covering it with the tissue paper.

"Ah come now, *ma petite chasseuse*, it is merely a gift. It means nothing and I think the lady could do with a little more smiling this evening. It makes you smile, does it not?"

This was wrong. I was not going to wear this.

"It doesn't matter if it makes me smile, Gregor. I'm not wearing your gift."

"You disappoint me, *ma cherie*. I did not take you for one to be swayed by convention. Just because your current lover would object, does not mean you should not have your own desires rewarded. Do it for yourself, Lucinda, regardless of the consequences."

"No, Gregor."

"You don't like my gift?" Again with the soft voice, creeping lower down my body.

"You're pushing, Gregor and let's not forget the fact that you entered my home and left it here, uninvited I might add."

"I do not need an invitation, we share *Sigillum*."

What?

"The sharing of *Sigillum*, little Hunter, allows for a close relationship. One would not give their *Sigillum* unless one wanted to extend an invitation of sorts."

"But I can't remove the *Sigillum*, an invitation should be able to be rescinded."

He laughed, obviously someone was finding it amusing. Great.

"Most people don't give their *Sigillum* unless they truly mean it, Lucinda. To share *Sigillum* is practically to propose."

"Why did you do it then?"

There was silence for a brief moment, not long, but enough to make me realise he was reluctant to answer.

"Would you believe you stole my heart?"

My turn to laugh now. "No, not at all."

"Ah, you are harsh, *ma petite chasseuse*. I see I have my work cut out for me. To convince you of my noble intentions shall be my one and only goal from this day forward."

"I don't think you have noble intentions, Gregor. I don't think you are capable of them."

"They are pure of heart. Can they not be called noble too?"

"It's only words." It's only ever words as far as vampires are concerned.

"So cynical for one so young."

"Yeah, that's me. Vampire hunter for only two years and I've lost all hope of romance in this life."

"That saddens me, Lucinda. No one should give up on romance."

"Hadn't you? You'd given up on life after all."

Now the pause was longer. I didn't say anything, it was the truth.

"Perhaps, I shall share with you my reasons one day, but despite what you may think, I am a romantic at heart. Especially where you are concerned." His voice was quiet, not broken, but slightly fragile.

I had sat down on my bed when I opened the gift box and hadn't moved since. Just perched on the edge while we continued the conversation. I lay back down and closed my eyes now. I wasn't meant to feel anything for this guy, not even sympathy, but he had a way about him, that made you think there was more to him than meets the eye. I almost wished I'd met him under different circumstances. But, I hadn't and I was Michel's now, even if part of me was furious at him and the Bond didn't mean what I thought it meant, I had given my heart, my body to Michel. I'm not a fickle person, I don't go back on my word easily.

It's just a shame that Michel wasn't playing the same game right now.

"Your breath has quickened, my little Hunter. What are you thinking?"

"Can you not read my mind?"

"Oh, if it were only that easy, but alas no. I think you

have worked out when your mind is open to me, you play it well now. What are you thinking that has made your breath hitch so?"

"Too many thoughts to mention. I have to get some sleep, Gregor." I paused, stuff it, I'd say it. "Thanks for keeping me company."

I could almost see his smile from here. "Now, if only you would wear my gift my night would be complete."

"Somehow, I don't think you need me to complete your night."

"Please. Just consider it, Lucinda. If not for me, then for yourself."

"Good night, Gregor."

"*Bonne nuit, ma cherie*."

The line went dead but I didn't disconnect straight away, just listened to that tone. Finally I returned the handset to its cradle and walked back into my bedroom.

Consider it he had said. I looked at the open box on the bed and did just that.

Then stripped and got into an old baggy T-Shirt and climbed between the sheets.

I left the box on the bed next to me though, open, but not too far away.

Chapter 21
Broken

I wish I could say I slept well, but I didn't. No one visited my dreams, no one pulled me into a Dream Walk, but I did dream. Just normal ones, human ones, and they weren't pretty. Mixed pictures, flashes of images, confusing messages, words and faces and Darkness and Light. I woke with the feeling that I had run a marathon, that I had run from something or someone, I couldn't tell what. But that I had run and run and run and run all night long. I was exhausted, but hey, what else was new?

Even my morning ritual of strong, strong coffee didn't seem to lift the fog that had descended. I was due back at work too. It was my choice to keep working my day job, Michel had made it clear that I didn't need to, he would take care of me. But I'm a modern-day girl and besides, after nights like last night, it's nice to know I have a bank account with a regular salary going in and I'm accountable to no one. It's not like the *Iunctio* pays vampire hunters a retainer.

So I donned my uniform and set out early for work. Normally I'd jog there, then shower at the branch, but today my body screamed *take it easy* and I hadn't even been in a fight. What was wrong with me?

My day did improve, just being amongst humans can have that effect on you. None of the vampire politics that was consuming the rest of my world, just deposits and withdrawals and the occasional friendly customer chat. I've always said my job grounds me, being the business banking teller at the BNZ Bank in Queen Street had its perks. Lots of customers and not much time to mull things over. The day whizzed by and I hadn't even spared a thought for the *date* tonight and exactly what the *Iunctio* wanted from Michel. I hadn't even thought about Taniwhas and homicidal ex-best friends. Or about Nosferatin trainers and their high moral standards. And I most certainly hadn't had time to think about extended family reunions and just what that might mean.

All in all a good day really.

I toyed with the idea of heading out to the Hapū's settlement out at Whenuapai to talk to Jerome, but truthfully, the Taniwhas were the least of my problems right now. One thing at a time. I knew Michel wouldn't really want to see me, but one of us had to be the adult. You'd think a 500 year old vampire could play grown-up a little better, but there you go. So, I headed up to *Sensations* straight from work. I was still in uniform, so nowhere to put my stake, but I did make sure it was easy to access in the front zip pocket of my backpack. I slung my backpack over just my left shoulder, so I could reach across my front and grab my stake with my right hand without too much fumbling. Not that I planned to stake anyone at *Sensations*, but you never knew. Always be prepared.

The bar was already open, it opened early on a Friday for Happy Hour. No vampire groupies in tow, it was too early for the creatures of the night, so the clientèle and staff were all humans. The staff knew me and I even got a few waves from the daytime barman and bus-boy, but mostly I was just left to my own devices.

I'd figured out the code to access Michel's private quarters not so long ago, but it did briefly cross my mind that he may have changed it just to lock me out. I held my breath, but it flashed green and I heard the door softly click open. The sounds of the after work drinking crowd disappeared instantly as the door closed and locked behind me. Michel wasn't in his office, I hadn't expected him to be, so I just made my way towards his chamber at the back.

I'd come this far, so I wasn't going to pause and have second thoughts on the threshold of his room. I didn't waste any time rapping on his big thick door. The sound echoed slightly in the hallway. Michel would have known I was there, he would have sensed me, maybe even recognised my scent, even through the closed door, so the time it took to answer was unnecessary, but not unexpected.

Finally it swung open and I took a step inside. He was sitting in the corner on a comfy couch, he'd been reading from his tablet computer. He read a lot during the day, what else do you do? He's not that into TV, so he reads. Newspapers, eZines, eBooks, anything electronic, he's on it. He hadn't bothered to get up and greet me, so still angry then. I walked straight over to him and stood a few feet away.

I took a breath in. It was a mistake. I could smell fresh wild flowers and clean cut grass, ocean breezes and storm washed gardens. I shook my head. It didn't matter if he didn't want me, I'd always want him.

He stood then and came to me, he was dressed in casual black trousers and a loose blue shirt, buttoned half way up, exposing a nice V shape of deep cream flesh at his neck and down his chest. He moved his hand up slowly to my cheek and brushed the backs of his fingers along my skin. I'd reached up and taken a hold of his hand before I even realised what I was doing, turning my head into his palm to kiss it.

He sighed and pulled me to him, wrapping his arms around my shoulders and resting his head against mine.

"I am sorry, *ma douce*. I have been cruel." His voice was soft, warm and so familiar, like a favourite blanket you'd reach for in the night.

I pulled back and looked at his face. His eyes, one of my favourite parts of his body, were a mix of blues; from Arctic ocean to Mediterranean Sea, a stunning combination of shades.

"Why do we do this to each other, Michel?"

He shook his head and leaned in to kiss my forehead.

"I have a theory," he said against my skin. "The more you love something the easier it is to hurt." I wasn't sure if he meant hurt the thing you love, or be hurt yourself. Both worked in this case I think.

"We shouldn't be doing this, not now. What's going to happen tonight?"

"So practical, *ma douce*." He was smiling, but it was a little sad.

"What would you have me do, Michel? Ignore that the *Iunctio* is here to test you, to test us both? One of us needs to be practical."

His eyes flashed then, just briefly and too fast for me to get a handle on the colour. I was just hoping it wasn't magenta.

"Were you being practical last night, my dear? When you spoke for so long to Gregor on the telephone."

What?

He saw the look on my face, surprise and his smile just turned a little bitter.

"Tell me, did you wear it?"

Oh hell.

"I'm not answering that." I pulled away from him and wrapped my arms around my body. He just stood there, watching me, not saying anything, just waiting, like he knew I couldn't help but fill the silence and give myself away.

Well, he was partly right, but there was nothing to give away.

"You have my home watched now? Or maybe you're bugging my phone? Which is it, Michel? Do you not trust me, is that it?"

"You have yet to behave in a manner that would warrant my trust."

"That is so not true!"

"Are you sure? You return from a Dream Walk marked and having marked him. You refuse to end this when given the chance and now... now you seem to be settling in to a relaxed relationship, speaking for hours on the phone with your curtains closed."

"Oh for God's sake, Michel. This is ridiculous. Not that I need to defend myself or justify my actions, but I did not ask to be pulled into that first Dream Walk. I had no idea what exchanging the marks actually meant. I can't kill just because someone has pissed me off, excuse me for having a conscience. And *he* phoned me!" My voice had risen at the end, I wasn't trying to hold it in, Michel was really pushing me to my limit.

But that thought alone was enough to make me calm, just a little.

"You know, this is what he wants, don't you, Michel?

To unsettle us, to push us apart."

I thought he'd agree, it made complete sense. If he loved me, he would have agreed, but all I could see was anger and maybe just a little resentment, or it could have been regret. Regret that he'd joined with me at all, I'm thinking.

I refused to let the tears I had building show, so I turned away and took a deep breath in, centring myself, forcing the tears back down. He didn't come to comfort me, he just sat back down and picked his tablet computer back up as though I wasn't even there.

If I had felt alone last night, then I felt lost in an abyss right now. Nothing to hold on to, nothing to keep me from floating away. I turned to look at him, but he wouldn't acknowledge me. What was he hoping to accomplish by this? Hurt me. Obviously. But why?

I took a step towards the door and stopped. I didn't want us to part like this, but what choice was he giving me? I stood there for a good few minutes just shaking my head, trying to figure out what to do to make this better. I wanted to ask, what he wanted me to do? What would make things the way they were? But I do have my pride.

He didn't want me here, so I would go.

I straightened my shoulders and walked through the door. I say walked, but it was closer to a run, even though I was using every piece of my strength to *not* flee.

Despite being in my work uniform and not my training gear and sneakers, I ran all the way home. No doubt my feet would suffer for it later, but what's a little more pain when you're breaking up inside any way?

It wasn't until I was in the shower, alone, that I allowed

myself to cry. To really cry. Sometimes I hated my life. Sometimes, just sometimes, I wished I'd never come to Auckland and found out I was a Nosferatin. And then joined with a vampire before one month past my 25th Birthday. Sometimes, I wished I'd just gone the same way as so many of my ancestors before me and denied the vampires my powers and my strength.

I think I must have lost track of time, because the water turned cold and I only noticed when I began to shiver. I'd never used the whole hot water cylinder before, it surprised me enough to make me want to move.

The sun was starting to set, I knew Gregor would be here as soon as true dark closed in. I had no idea what lay in store for me tonight, but I was determined to be prepared. Hunter prepared that is. So I dressed in my usual garb; black short mini skirt, black tight fitting T-Shirt, tights and black boots. And my new best friend, my custom made black denim jacket. I slipped the stakes in their hidey holes, the silver knife in its pocket and just for good measure, slipped another knife down the inside of my boot. I had no idea if I would need them, use them, or lose them, but they made me feel better. They made me feel safe.

I went and sat on the couch and waited. What else was there to do? Pace? I don't think so.

I felt it when true darkness came. Dating a vampire, you kind of got in tune with that time of day. It's not the same time every day. But the feeling of it is always the same. When you're around vampires, they seem to just perk up a bit, breathe a little easier, take a lighter step. As though the weight of the day has been lifted off their shoulders. I don't feel any lighter, I sense the dark as though it's a tangible enemy, something to battle. But I do recognise the moment that it arrives.

I took a breath in and waited for the knock.

The phone rang and I almost jumped out of my skin in fright.

Nervous, me? Nah.

"Miss Monk?" I didn't get a chance to say hello, before the low male voice asked that question. Which was probably good because I was a little breathless, but still not perfect, because I had to answer.

"Yes." I think it sounded OK.

"My name is Luxor. My master has sent me to pick you up."

I'd managed to get my breathing under control enough to form full sentences.

"Who is your master?"

"Gregor the Enforcer."

OK. "I don't know you, Luxor."

"We have not been formally introduced, but I believe you know me as... Pipi Longstockings." The last was said rather slowly, as though he had difficulty getting the words out.

"Oh, OK."

"I cannot come to your door, Miss Monk. Your wards are too strong. Would you be so kind to meet me at the gate?"

"All right then." What choice did I have?

I hung up and rubbed my palms against my skirt to get rid of the light film of sweat that had coated them. One last look around the flat, then I really couldn't delay it any longer. I locked the door behind me, waved to my neighbour Mrs Cumberland as she sat on her couch watching TV, visible through the open ranch-slider door. And then walked towards the vampire at the end of my drive in front of the obligatory bad guy tinted black van.

He was dressed much the same as last night. His hair in one long braid down the back, being the only noticeable change. Pipi Longstockings always had two, I'd have to think of another nickname. He smiled openly and friendly, a definite improvement on last night and looked relaxed in the early evening light.

“Good evening, Miss Monk. My master awaits.” He turned and opened the sliding back door to the van. There was no internal light inside, just a black void of darkness.

I hesitated. Call me cautious, I'm a vampire hunter, I can't help it.

“Where is the Enforcer?”

“He has been detained, but I will take you to him.”

“Can't I sit in the front with you?”

He smiled more brightly. “A lady should travel in style, the front has not been cleaned since a companion spilled his evening meal last night.” I so did not want to know what his evening meal had consisted of and so I blame my squeamishness for what happened next.

I nodded and went to get in the rear of the van. He was only a blur in my peripheral vision, a flash of light and colour and long, long hair. And then he had one arm around my shoulders and the other holding a cloth to my mouth and nose.

I fought not to inhale, I struggled as best as I could, but he was prepared for all of that and he simply bent my head over and went in to bite my neck. I felt his fangs on my skin, felt my skin give as they slid in and I screamed.

Of course to scream, you have to take a breath in and that's all it took for me to watch the world turn blurry and the colours all fade to black.

Chapter 22
Bound

I woke with excruciating pain in my neck. Not where the vampire had bit me, but at the back. And I realised it was because I was sitting up in a chair and my head had been hanging forward on my chest. The next thing I realised, was that my arms were tied behind the back of the chair and my feet to each of the front two legs. I was friggin' tied to a chair. At least I wasn't gagged and blindfolded.

I moved my head up from my chest, resisting the urge to groan at the stiffness in the movement and rolled my head from side to side to loosen up a bit. The room was fully enclosed, no windows, but lit by two overhead lights hanging from the ceiling. Both shaded with a rudimentary cone shade above a naked bulb. Classy.

It was a large room, I didn't know what was behind me, but I wasn't backed on to a wall. In front, however, was a kitchenette off to one side, complete with fridge and a dining table with four chairs on the other side. A door was between the two, closed. Sitting at the table playing a relaxed game of cards were old Pipi Longstockings and Snow White. Great.

My mouth was dry and there was a nasty after-taste of something not altogether sweet, a little bitter, but furry at the same time. Yum. I swallowed twice before I attempted to talk.

"You know, you didn't need to drug me, I was getting in the van." My voice was husky, it probably would have sounded sexy even, given different circumstances.

Luxor/Longstockings looked up and smiled. Still

pleasant, still friendly. "Then you would know where we are. Can't have you communicating telepathically with your kindred vampire."

Oh, I got it, this was all part of *the test.* See what Michel did when he came to save me. I almost laughed out loud at that.

"It won't work you know."

"What makes you think that?" Luxor again, old Snow White was just leering. Probably something to do with the fact that my jacket was off and my T-Shirt was stretched rather tightly and thinly over my protruding chest. Not to mention my short mini skirt had ridden up my thighs and he was no doubt getting a good flash right now.

"He won't come for me. He won't do what you think he will."

"You're his kindred Nosferatin, of course he'll come for you." That was Snow White, he did have a voice after all.

I smiled, it wasn't at all sweet. "Not all kindred joinings are created equal."

He stared at me blankly. OK, he can talk, the lights are on, but nobody's home.

They didn't say anything, just kept looking at me, watching me, almost studying me. Eeew.

"Where's Gregor?"

"The *Enforcer* is on his way." Oh that's right, we were in the zone of *Iunctio* business, I couldn't call him Gregor.

"Can I get out of this, or do I have to stay tied up like a criminal?"

Luxor's smile widened, always a sign I was betting, that he's about to play a trick or do something nasty. I hadn't known this guy long, but he just fit that bill.

"You kill vampires, is that not a crime, Nosferatin?"

I sighed. "Don't tell me, you're on the bandwagon for free vampire rights. Let the Nosferatu take over the night, the way it's suppose to be. Good in theory, not so good when you exhaust your food source."

"We are at the top of the food chain, we do not need a half-human to tell us what to do." This time Snow White. All he really needed to complete the picture was a small *Swastika* sewn onto his sleeve.

"Can I at least get a glass of water? That drug tastes disgusting."

"We wouldn't want you to suffer, as our master did when you staked him and ran." Luxor - and no he wasn't smiling any more. Yippee. He walked to the kitchen and then glided towards me with the glass full of water. Tap water, nothing bottled or chilled. I was betting the glide was to emphasise the difference between him and me. He, heap big vampire; me, half-human tied to a chair.

He held the glass to my lips and let me drink it, then leaned in close, his own lips brushing where his fangs had struck, his breath a hot line down my skin. I didn't shiver, it didn't have that kind of affect.

"You know you taste different from others, so light and full of honey. Tasty. I think I could go for some more."

His fangs flashed down in the light of the room and he pulled his lips back slowly. It wasn't the usual grimace some vampires seem to have before they feed, this one was for pure show. Maybe, it was because he was hamming it up, that I didn't believe he was actually going to do it. Maybe it was because I sensed Gregor nearby and I suddenly felt safe, but all I could do was laugh at him. And it felt good.

He wasn't impressed. His staged grimace turned into a real one and he hissed, a low nasty, hiss. I blinked. I don't think I'd ever heard a vampire hiss before, growl yeah, but hiss? Are you kidding me?

He didn't get to do much more because Gregor had arrived. Luxor pulled back and stepped aside as Gregor strode in the room. He stopped inside the door and took the scene in. His eyes running over me, taking in Luxor and the glass of water and then turning to survey the rest of the room, including Snow White.

"Have my children been looking after you, Hunter?"

I glanced quickly at Luxor, he didn't make eye contact with me, just stared straight ahead. He was still, not vampire still, but waiting. Ah hell, I had goaded the guy.

"Yeah, just peachy. Thanks for the water, Luxor." He did glance at me then, a strange look in his eyes and then the mask was back in place. He nodded and walked back to the kitchen.

Gregor smiled. I didn't think I'd fooled him, but he didn't raise the issue further. He came and sat in a chair by the table, turning it to face me, crossing his legs as he sat. He was dressed in a fine suit tonight, silver grey, like his eyes. The lapels a darker colour, making the line of the jacket stand out even more. His shirt, again high collared and grey, complementary to the suit. He was just spiffy, wasn't he?

"What has amused you, Hunter." What no *little* Hunter tonight, we *were* on formal ground then.

"Your suit, Enforcer, it's lovely."

He laughed, that rich, deep, melodious laugh. I felt it

run up my bare arms and tickle me at my neck. I did move my head a little to try to rub my neck against my shoulder, but then who wouldn't?

His smile broadened. “Do you know why you are here?”

“I'm guessing, because you said so.”

His smile dimmed slightly. “Now, now, Lucinda, I'm sure you can play the game a little better than that.” His voice had gone flat. “Why do you think you are here?”

“You want Michel to come for me.”

“Yes.” Soft, intimate. Bastard. “Do you think he will?”

“Do you?”

“I am no longer so sure. You seemed somewhat upset when you returned to your apartment this evening. A lovers quarrel?”

“You'd like that, wouldn't you?”

“I do not wish for your pain, Lucinda, but perhaps it is for the best that you see your kindred as he truly is.”

OK, I'd bite. “And what's that, Enforcer?”

He shrugged and it didn't escape me that he made shrugs look just as elegant as Michel can. Man, did these guys go to the same vampire training school, or what?

“A manipulator, a user. Someone who will do anything to advance their own power base.” Well, if you want to rub it in, thanks.

“You don't like him much do you, Gr...Enforcer.”

“Not really.”

“But you *were* friends once, weren't you?”

“A long time ago. Did he tell you why he left?”

I paused, did I really want to give him more ammunition when he was in this persona? Curiosity did kill the cat, they say. Meow.

"No."

His smile twisted slightly. "He heard a rumour, that it had been foretold, that the strongest Nosferatin in all our time would be discovered in the New Land."

"You mean New Zealand?"

"Yes. That is what our kind called your country."

"And you think he came here to find them? You think I'm that Nosferatin?" My voice was surprisingly level, neutral even.

"It remains to be seen, but he gave away much for his pursuit. Why?"

I knew the answer to this one. Easy. "Power."

He cocked his head at that. "You are not surprised?"

My turn to shrug, I doubt it was as suave. "I know what Michel craves."

"That does surprise me." He leaned forward in his seat, elbow resting on his crossed knee and placed his hand up to his mouth, loosely fisted, thumb to lips. A bit like that famous sculpture *The Thinker*. "It does not worry you, as a Nosferatin, that you have fed this hunger for power in one of my kind?"

I thought about that for a second. I knew what he was asking. Nosferatins have for so long denied the vampires our powers. We've hidden and died for that belief, why not me?

"I wasn't raised by Nosferatin parents, I never knew what I was until I came to Auckland, until I met Michel. I grew up on a farm, in the fresh air, surrounded by lambs and nature and life. My Aunt and Uncle loved me, showered me with their love, gave me everything I could have ever wanted. They instilled in me a love of life, a love of people, of nature, of what this world can be." All the vampires had stopped moving and were watching me avidly, devouring every word. You'd think they'd never heard a person's life story before. Jeez. "It wasn't a conscious decision. I mean, I knew what I was doing when I joined with him, but it wasn't for him, or for your kind, or for mine. It was for me. I didn't want to die Gregor, I wanted to live."

I knew I'd used his name, not his title, but I was trying to make a point. I held my breath to see if he'd bite.

He sat still, as still as the other two vampires in the room and didn't say anything for a long time. Finally he sat back in his chair and just looked at me.

"You are a mystery, Nosferatin. Not many of your kind would have divulged so much, not to the *Iunctio* and you know by now that I am the *Iunctio* here. Are you not afraid we will use this information against you? Get to you through your love of your family? Through your very honourable outlook on life?"

"Are you threatening me, Enforcer?"

"It would be my prerogative if I were. Answer the question."

What did he want to hear? What would stop this madness and make the *Iunctio* go away? I've never been good at second guessing psychology tests. You know those ones that ask *would you prefer to party with a group of friends or walk alone on a beach at sunset?* What the hell did they want to know? So, I chose honesty. It is the best policy I've heard.

"Yes. I'm afraid."

He blinked slowly, then smiled. "Good. Then you are learning."

I let a little breath out, one I'd been reluctant to let go.

"But why tell me, Nosferatin? If you are afraid we will use this information against you, why tell me?"

"Because if one of us - and I mean either the Nosferatu or the Nosferatin - doesn't take that leap of faith, then no one will."

He laughed, a short huff. "You are an idealist. Perhaps you do not understand our world at all."

"No. You're wrong. I understand better than you."

He stood then and came towards me, a stalk, not a glide. He didn't need to impress, only intimidate. When he came within a foot of me, he crouched down, smoothly, sleekly even and stayed crouched in front of me, his eyes now level with mine. I was momentarily stunned by their sheen, silver platinum with flecks of lustrous grey, my *Sigillum* making the colours stand out even more. Like they were dancing under one of those multifaceted glass disco balls, sparkles of other colours glinting at the edge of your vision, making the silver or grey seem so much more than it really was. I felt myself leaning out from my chair to get closer, the only thing stopping me was the tight binds at my wrist behind the back. I even yanked against them.

He smiled and that did wonders for my pulse.

"What is it you understand better than me?" His voice was low, a whisper, running along my arms, down my chest and spreading out over my legs. The thought that he would try to affect me when acting as the *Iunctio's* henchman brought me back from the edge. I slowed my breathing down and met his gaze.

"I am the Light to the Dark, Enforcer. You call to me, as I call to you. I will always hold you dear. You know what I am, why fight it?"

I have no idea where that came from. Just popped into my head and out my mouth and whoa! What the fuck?

He pulled back, a slight look of shock on his face. Then abruptly stood and said in a low growl, "Leave us." I'm guessing that wasn't for me, because I kind of couldn't move a muscle. The other two vampires didn't question him, just turned and left, closing the door behind them in a blur.

He didn't move from where he was standing, looming over me, his head though was turned to the side, looking at the floor. Finally, he turned his gaze back to me and there was fire in his eyes, no other word for it. Just pure flames of orange fire.

"What's with your eyes?" I asked mesmerized.

He closed them and kept them shut for a good minute then opened them to look back at me. Gone, no licking flames of hot light.

"The *Iunctio* fears you, Lucinda." His voice was strained, whisper quiet, as though he didn't want anyone else to hear. "I had not thought their concerns were justified until now. You are indeed the *Sanguis Vitam Cupitor,* but you are in fact more." He paused, considering his words with care. "I am not only the Enforcer for the *Iunctio,* I am also their Scout. It is my job to investigate, shall we say, any indication of the Prophecy's commencement. I was sent here to see if you were merely a cog in the wheel, or the whole machine."

I swallowed. "What do you think I am?"

"Honestly? I do not know. You are the *Sanguis Vitam Cupitor,* but you are more. I fear for you that this *more* is what the *Iunctio* seeks. And if it is, they will kill you. They will not hesitate, there is no negotiation, no leap of faith."

"What will you tell them?"

He turned away from me then. I could tell he was still breathing, actually it looked like he was having trouble getting enough air in, from the rise and fall of his shoulders.

His voice when it did come was even more strained than before. "I am bound to them until I leave. I can leave, but it would appear unusual to do so right now, during an investigation." He paused and did take a deep breath in. "But I am bound to you through the *Sigillum*, I cannot betray you even if I wanted to."

"*That's* a conflict of interest. Why would they have sent you to investigate me?"

He turned back to me and gave me one of his boyish smiles. "They do not know we have shared marks. They are not aware of the conflict of interest."

Naughty boy. "How will you hide it from them?"

"I may not be able to eventually, any way, but for now only those of my line are aware and I control them."

"Michel knows, he could use it against you."

"To do so would be to endanger you and therefore his position of power, his life. I do not think Michel would see it as a worthy tool for revenge."

How convenient.

"So what now?" I asked.

"Now. We wait for Michel. If he can come for you, find you and save you without causing too much trouble, then I can leave and tell the *Iunctio* something they will believe."

"You can't just let me go and make a story up, can you?"

He shook his head. "It would be a lie."

"But, it would be a lie telling them I am nothing more than the *Sanguis Vitam Cupitor*."

"Oh, I will be telling them you are more than that, just not what they think."

"What then?"

"I will tell them you are the strongest Nosferatin I have seen, more than just the *Sanguis Vitam Cupitor,* but not enough to rule the Prophesy alone. It is close enough to the truth for them to believe it, I almost do myself. They may decide to keep a close eye on you, but they won't sign a death warrant on that. Despite their fear of the Prophesy, they fear the loss of a Nosferatin more, they fear the loss of their power base. Since you joined with Michel the *Iunctio* has grown stronger."

"What do you mean? Because of my powers?"

"Yes. Every joined Nosferatin adds to the *Iunctio's* power, as they add to the collective power of all Nosferatu. It has been centuries since they had received a gift as powerful as yours. They crave you Lucinda, yet they fear you. It is a fine line, but one you will have to tread."

I didn't know what to say to that. I did know that my arms had now gone to sleep and I had pins and needles in my toes, slowly working their way up my legs. I shifted slightly in the chair to get more comfortable, but failed. Gregor came over immediately and began to loosen the ties.

"You don't complain much, do you, little Hunter? Most

would have demanded release by now."

"I didn't want to interrupt."

He laughed, making a few strands of his hair come loose from the clip and slide down the side of my face as he leant over me to untie my arms. I could smell the shampoo he uses, strawberries or raspberries, I couldn't quite tell. They went nicely with the chocolate coated ice cream. I inhaled deeply and sighed.

He pulled back and cocked his head at me, raised his eyebrows. "What?"

I licked my lips, what the hell. "You smell of chocolate covered ice cream and raspberries, or maybe strawberries, I'm not sure which."

He stilled with a small smile playing on his lips. "Maybe I have been too hasty removing your ties. There could be possibilities here." And he raised his hands to place them on either side of the chair back, by my shoulders and slowly leaned in. His eyes never leaving mine, my eyes transfixed by the silver flashing in his. I didn't fight him, when his lips met mine. I should have, but I didn't. I wanted him to kiss me, like I'd never wanted anything else before. I wanted to see if he tasted as good as he smelled, if I could lick him and taste the chocolate or strawberries. If I could nibble and feel like I was having a decadent dessert. And I wasn't let down. He was all of those things and more. And I wanted it, all of it.

But thank God for small miracles, because right then Michel barged through the door in a swirl of iridescent light.

Chapter 23
Oops!

Of course, it didn't look good, did it? I was tied to a chair and flushed, Gregor had been standing over me, taking advantage of my position. What was Michel supposed to think?

He came towards us like a raging tornado, lost in the swirl of colours, just a funnel of power churning the air before him. He hit Gregor, more than he hit me, but it was enough to tip my chair back with such force that I felt, as well as heard, the loud crack as my forearm broke on my left side. I screamed, but the sound was lost in the battle that raged before me.

I'd landed sideways to the room, on my arm, but facing back towards the kitchen and dining area, right where Michel and Gregor fought. Any attempt to reposition myself, off my broken arm, was excruciating and impossible. I had to contend myself with lying perfectly still and taking short, small breaths in that didn't make me move my shoulders. You've no idea how much of your body moves when you breath, especially when your heart is in your mouth and your breathing is ragged from fear and pain.

All my concentration was on not moving my shoulders, remaining still and taking small breaths, so several minutes had passed before I was able to think coherently and realised that Michel was going to kill Gregor. Gregor was holding his own, I don't think you become the Enforcer for the *Iunctio* without learning a few tricks. And I'm guessing, some of that power the *Iunctio* has from my joining and the joining of others like me, was being channelled into Gregor right now, because he shouldn't have been able to fight Michel the way he was.

Michel is perhaps the most powerful vampire alive. If I am the strongest Nosferatin in centuries, which I don't quite yet subscribe to, but it is a little hard to deny, then his power boost on joining with me was the biggest any kindred vampire had ever received. I knew it at the time. The joining with me had more than doubled his original power base, something that hadn't happened before then. Michel had been strong before, now he was a force to be reckoned with.

But, Gregor was holding him off. This was perhaps the most beautiful and yet so frightening thing I had ever seen in my life. Gregor didn't spin like Michel, I think that is peculiar to those kindred vampires who have joined. When Michel fought Max a few weeks ago, they both spun in a dance of twin tornadoes. Splendid in the magnificent light display, dancing a devilish tango. Now Michel spun, sending flashes and spikes of light in a multitude of colours around the room, but Gregor was simply a blur.

Wherever Michel spun to next, Gregor simply vanished. He stayed one step ahead of the storm by a mere fraction of a second. So fast, even with my enhanced vision, I was unable to keep up with the movement. One second he was there, the next gone and reappearing for a flash of split second somewhere else. To only disappear again and then repeat the action over and over and over again. They would never tire of this, I thought and yet neither of them was landing a blow, was succeeding in hurting the other. It would have been laughable if only I could have breathed in enough to do it.

I'd managed to settle my breathing. There was nothing I could do for my heartbeat though, it was on its own. So I just worked on ignoring it pounding in my chest, reverberating around my body and centred myself on each slow, shallow breath in and each slow, shallow breath out, until I could think clearly.

Michel. Stop. I threw the thought at him.

Nothing, just a swirl of chroma glowing in the room.

Michel listen to me, it's a test, a trap. They want you to lose control, so they have an excuse to kill you. To kill us. Please stop.

Still nothing, not even a blip on the colour wheel turning before me. No pause, no hesitation, just continuous strobes of colour dancing before my eyes.

Michel please! Listen to me! Stop! Don't do this, you're killing us!

I noticed it then, a small hesitation, not enough for Gregor to take advantage of, but enough for me to realise Michel had heard. I wasn't at all sure if Gregor was getting my thoughts, I was throwing them at Michel, but I was also shouting them in my head. Theoretically, Gregor should have been able to hear them. I was hoping he could.

Michel slow down and Gregor will stop too!

OK. The moment of truth. I talked before of someone taking that leap of faith, of either a Nosferatu or Nosferatin taking that first step towards trusting, towards a chance to work together for peace. I had meant me. I was quite prepared for that first treacherous step, but I wasn't prepared for anyone else to take it with me. I just didn't think that was possible, but here I was asking Michel to take that step and hoping Gregor would too. Idealistic, me?

Bloody oath.

I do not trust him, ma douce.

I let my breath out in a rush and gasped at the pain down my arm, then cringed at the pain the gasp had caused. A few precious seconds passed before I could think.

Trust me.

How ironic. He had only hours before said he didn't trust me. I had no idea at all if he could again and would now. But what else was there to do?

The swirls of colour continued to dance, the blur of Gregor flashing before my eyes, making dots of white appear behind my eyelids each time I blinked. I was starting to feel nauseous and it wasn't from the pain in my arm. Although now that I think about it, that was doing strange things to my equilibrium too. Still, Michel did not stop.

I felt a weight centre in my heart. He didn't trust me.

Why won't you listen to me, you've listened before?

No hesitation, still a determined swirling pursuit across the room.

You have been tricked, ma douce. You do not know what you are saying. This is the trap. You are the trap.

Oh dear God. He was going to keep doing this until he had killed Gregor. Not so long ago, I would have cheered from the sidelines, but now? Now, a part of me screamed at the thought of Gregor dying. Did I love him? No, I didn't think so. Could I? Yes. But, that was irrelevant. What mattered to me was he did not deserve to die. Even now there was Light amongst the Darkness before me. Both in the swirls of brightly lit colour from Michel and in the flashes of brightness as Gregor moved across the room out of his reach.

They had both moved a little further towards the Light because of me, neither deserved to die. But how to stop this now?

Please Michel. Stop! For me?

Je suis désolé, ma douce.

No.

No reply, just a ramp up in speed of the tornado tower in front of me. Gregor faulted, his speed still unfathomable, but not enough and Michel went in for the kill.

I don't really know what happened next, I was blinded by the lights and colours in the room. And by the pain in my chest, so heavy, so crushing, so frightening in its intensity. I felt my world fall away from me, not just the room and its technicoloured splendour, but my life as I knew it. Michel didn't trust me. Did that mean he no longer cared? Gregor was about to die. Did that mean I failed as a Nosferatin and didn't bring him to the Light?

The thought of Light is probably what did it, but it certainly wasn't conscious. It simply began to build in me, slowly at first and when my body responded to it's internal glow, more quickly. Until I felt it brimming and pouring over the top of me, still contained within my body, but as though it was filling me up so full, that waves were splashing over the side of my shields, my mental walls, like a cup being filled too high with water. But this water was bright, shining, glowing, burning, sparkling, streaming around my mind and body until I could hold it no more and didn't want to. Why should I be only one to bask in its glory?

I thrust it out into the room and let it wash all over

them. I had never thought I was more powerful than Michel, that was just not simply possible. He is a very old vampire, Master of the City, joined to the most powerful kindred Nosferatin in centuries. He had strength and power before I gave him mine, so it was unbelievable that I should be more powerful than him. But, as it happens, I am.

My Light burst through, stopping them both in their tracks. I did what neither vampire was capable of, I landed the first blow. Michel was no longer a swirling stream of colours, Gregor no longer a blur of speed. They were both immobile in a wash of brightness that had stilled their hearts and stopped their breath. It wasn't as though the whole room had immobilised, hung in suspension in the air. I could still hear the fridge whirring in the corner, still see a small drop of water drip from the faucet above the sink, but the vampires were dead still. Not vampire still, Nosferatin still. I held them both in the cusp of my hand, metaphorically speaking. It was more like a simple thought could have crushed them. But I had no intention of crushing them, I just wanted them to damn well listen to me.

"Now, both of you will stop for just a minute and listen to me!"

I didn't like talking to their backs, so I turned them towards me so they could look me in the face. It was a bit awkward, I was lying on my side, if I'd had the energy, I would have used my Light to right the chair, but I was tiring. This Nosferatin Light thing was hard work.

"I will not lose either of you tonight." I looked at Michel. "Michel, I love you, but sometimes you think you know more than me and quite frankly, that's starting to piss me off just a little. I am not who you think I am. I don't quite know what I am yet, but it's more than that and whatever it is, there are things I know, so deep down inside me, I think they have been there before time itself began. Trust me, like you once did." I flicked my eyes to Gregor. "Gregor, I wish I'd met you before all of this, there is more to you than you let people see. I see it, I don't quite know what exactly it is yet, but it's worth fighting for, worth living for. I will not let you die, but you have to meet me half way. You know what you have to do Gregor, I want you to trust me too."

OK. So, they couldn't answer me. Gregor can't even speak in my mind and Michel couldn't, because I'd frozen his, only allowing my words to penetrate the Light I had them suspended in. So, now was the moment of truth, again, but this time so much more was hanging on its outcome. I couldn't hold them much longer, I was sweating profusely and a small tremor had started down my body, making my arm spasm and the fracture hurt like a bitch. That alone was causing my concentration to waver.

"I'm going to let you go. Please don't let me down."

I lowered them gently to the floor. Yeah, they'd been hanging, suspended in mid air, I hadn't even realised until that moment - wow - and pulled my Light back towards me. It washed over me, easing the pain slightly and rejuvenating my energy, enough to stop the trembling and allow me to relax, just a bit, just enough. I had closed my eyes when it came flooding back in. It's intense, rather like an orgasm, but not quite as intimate. When I opened my eyes and saw the looks on both vampire's faces, I realised it probably *was* that intimate for them. Oops.

Both had collapsed to the floor, breathing heavily, their pulses in their necks thundering along, faces flushed - a neat trick for a vampire - and eyes glazed in the afterglow of my power. They looked a little funny from my angle, still on my side on the floor, which made me realise I really wanted off my arm now.

"Can someone get me out of this, please? I'm really sore."

Both heads sprung up in unison and blazing eyes of indigo and violet, and silver and platinum took my predicament in. I bit my lip and waited.

Michel was the first to try to get to his feet, but only managed a half rise from the floor and then collapsed again. Shit. What had I done to them? Gregor actually reached out to stop his fall, Michel grabbing his hand automatically. Both of them ending up leaning against each other for support. I smiled, only moments ago they had been prepared to kill each other, now they seemed to be holding on to each other for grim death.

"Maybe if you crawl, stay close to the ground or something, but one of you has to move me, I think I might pass out soon."

They looked at each other and actually rolled their eyes in unison.

"What's wrong with you guys?"

"*Ma douce*, it has been a long time since I have shared anything remotely like that with Gregor. Allow us our moment of shared memories."

What the hell?

Gregor laughed. I'm not sure if it was at me or because of what Michel had just said, or maybe at the memories they shared. I was starting to realise these two had been more than just friends once. Huh. I glared at them both, which is no mean feat considering my position on the floor and the pain in my arm.

"OK. OK. *Ma douce*, we are coming."

They both crawl-glided over to me. At least they were getting a bit more of their otherworldliness back and made the movement seductive and beautiful. I didn't complain, I wanted something of my old world back right then, the ground had somehow shifted a little in the last few minutes.

They started untying my restraints, neither bothering to avoid touching my skin. Stroking here, a light touch there, a shot of warmth and heat shooting up my body.

"Stop it," I breathed, the words coming out in a whisper.

"Stop what, *ma cherie*? Untying you?" Gregor had that wicked gleam back in his eyes. He was definitely enjoying himself again.

"You know what I mean. I can't breath through the sensations you're making me feel without hurting my arm."

"*Ma douce*, it is difficult for us to contain them right now. You have done something to us, none other has ever before, but we will try to behave."

Michel glanced at Gregor then and something passed between them; a shared knowledge, old memories, an understanding that only the closest of friends - no maybe lovers - could share. I shuddered and gasped, but they had untied the last of the restraints in a flash of vampire speed and Michel was already lifting me into his lap, cradling my arm.

Pain had shot down my shoulder from moving the arm

forward, not just because of the break in the bone, but because it had been so long in the one position. Blood flooding back into muscle and tissue in sharp stabbing waves.

I tried not to let the tears fall down my cheeks, but I was tired and sore and hurt and overwhelmed by everything that had just happened. This was worse than my body's reaction to terrible fights in the past.

"Lower your shields, *ma douce*. This must be repaired before permanent damage sets in."

I didn't argue, I wasn't sure if I could hold my shields together much longer. There was a fog descending, not dark, but white light, threatening to block out all vision and smother all sound and touch. As soon as my shields dropped I felt his healing touch, but also his thoughts and feelings. He was having a hard time controlling anything right now.

Ma douce, ma douce, ma precieux douce. Je t'aime plus que la vie elle-même. Je ferai n'importe quoi pour tous. Je t'aime. Je t'aime. Je t'aime.

I didn't understand it all, but I knew he still loved me. I let that thought wrap around me, blanket me, comfort me, as I felt myself sink deeper into the white light bliss and drifted away.

Chapter 24
Trois

I woke up on a white leather couch, a soft white blanket over the top of me. I glanced around and recognised the large expanse of glass, the night time view of the Hauraki Gulf. I was in the lounge at Michel's house in St Helier's Bay. Michel and Gregor were talking quietly in the far corner, sitting in armchairs close together, but not touching. They were intense, talking quickly in French to each other, but they weren't threatening, weren't about to rip each other's throats out. It was more of a serious conversation, than a deadly one.

I listened to them for a while. They hadn't sensed I was awake, which was surprising, but then not. They were too wrapped up in what they were discussing. I couldn't understand a word, however, their voices too low, the words too quick. I let them all roll over me for a while then sighed.

"English. I can't keep up."

They both turned to me and smiled, it was Michel who spoke first.

"Perhaps we do not wish for you to, *ma douce*." He was still smiling, teasing I think.

"If you both keep this up, I'll be forced to take French lessons, you know."

Michel stood and came over to me, settling down on the couch by my side. I could feel his warmth through the blanket. His hand reached out and stroked my hair back from my face. "I have long wanted you to learn my native tongue, *ma douce*. I would gladly teach you."

Gregor was watching us closely, his head slightly on an

angle, a look of understanding on his face. I don't think he had seen Michel and I interacting like this before. I think he wasn't so much as surprised, but maybe enlightened would be the right word.

I turned back to look at Michel. "What were you two talking about just now?"

Michel glanced at Gregor and Gregor rose to come and sit closer to me, in another armchair just off to the side.

"I have been called back to the *Iunctio*, they wish to know why I used some of their power earlier tonight."

I had been right then. "You used some of their power to stay ahead of Michel?" I turned the statement into a question.

"Yes. It was either that or perish." He smiled slightly at the look on my face. "I did not wish to perish." His voice was softer as he said that last, he'd seen my surprise. A few nights ago, he may have let Michel kill him off, end it all, but not now. We were making progress then.

Michel brushed my cheek and rose. "Forgive me, *ma douce*. I must attend something briefly, I will return shortly."

He nodded to Gregor and left. I was sure he didn't really have anything to attend that he couldn't do telepathically with his vampires, but he was giving us a moment alone. That did surprise me.

I sighed and looked at Gregor. He was just watching me, his face neutral, his eyes however, keen.

"You two kiss and make up?" I asked to ease the tension I had started to feel at his avid gaze.

He did that laugh he does; a little huff, as though he's trying to hold it in but can't. I kind of liked it, it was one of the more natural things I'd ever seen a vampire do before. It was endearing.

"Of a fashion, *ma cherie*. The wounds are still deep, but...I think we understand each other better now."

I smiled up at him and he moved to kneel before me at the edge of the couch, taking one of my hands in both of his. He didn't try to wash me with his *Sanguis Vitam*. He didn't try to make his words engulf me with desire. He just held them and looked at me with a kind of awe on his face, an openness that was almost raw.

"I am yours, whichever way you desire me. Tell me and I will come." His words were barely a whisper.

I wasn't sure what he was asking me, so I just shook my head.

Maybe if I stick to the obvious. "You know I love Michel, don't you?"

He nodded.

"What do you want me to say?"

"Say you will have me too."

I shook my head. I am so *not* that kind of girl. You're barking up the wrong tree, buddy.

He smiled. "I can hear your thoughts. I am not asking for a *ménage a trois* in the modern day sense. I am happy to wait for you to decide. But I am asking that you let me stay. I cannot bear the thought of being apart from you. I must be near."

Oh boy. I had a trillion thoughts pour through my head at what he had just suggested. I couldn't possibly contemplate being with someone else other than Michel, I loved Michel. I knew this, even though I sometimes fought it and even though he sometimes abused it. Whether it would stay that way, I wasn't one hundred percent sure, but the thought of having someone waiting in the wings for me to make that decision was wrong. Just so wrong. But then, I couldn't stand the thought of Gregor leaving for good either. I'm not sure if it was the exchange of *Sigillum* that made me feel that way, but I was sure that I was attracted to him in some way I couldn't fight.

Oh bugger. Why oh *why*, was my life so damn complicated?

"Does Michel know you are asking me this?"

He nodded. Damn.

"Does he mind?"

He hesitated briefly, then shook his head. "No, he does not."

Double damn.

"I still don't know what to say." I really didn't, I was at a loss for words.

He reached out and placed his hand against my chest, above my heart.

"What does your heart say, *ma cherie*?"

What did it say? It said I loved Michel, but Michel was also hurting me right now and when I looked closer, it also said I might just love Gregor too. Aw damn. Confused much?

"You'll give up your position in the *Iunctio*?"

"Yes. I have already made that decision."

"Regardless of my answer?"

"Yes."

"Are you so sure of my answer?"

He smiled again. "No. I am so sure of what I feel."

I sat up on the couch then, I needed to be at his height

to confront this. He still held on to my hand and I let him. It was a comfort that I hadn't realised I craved. I looked down at our hands now clasped together.

"Is what I feel because of the exchange of marks?" I asked a little uncertainly.

"Yes and no." I sighed, I hated ambiguous answers, but he continued before I had a chance to complain. "I only mean, that the exchange works rather like a Bond. It brings you together, it wishes for you to be close, but that final step, that final commitment, is all yours and yours alone."

Like the Bond. The Bond I had with Michel. The Bond Michel had made me think was exclusive. But it wasn't, he had lied. It pulled us together, but did not mean we were meant to share a bed. Ah, crap.

So, I now had two men in my life I couldn't cast out. Both equally attractive to me, both equally as dangerous to me. But because of who I am, I could only ever choose one to take to my bed.

Or neither, my little internal monologue whispered. I didn't tell it to shut up.

In fact, I sat there and thought about it a bit more. *Are you sure?* I asked it. *Could you do it?* it replied. OK. So, now I was feeling a little more than just crazy. It's one thing to hear voices and occasionally yell at them in my head, it was a whole other to carry a perfectly normal conversation out with them though, wasn't it?

"What are thinking, *ma petite chasseuse*, please tell me?"

It was my turn to huff a laugh out and shake my head. "I think you'll both make me crazy."

"Is that an agreement that we can *both* be in your life?"

He looked hopeful, but still cautious.

Part of me wanted to ask Michel about this, about what he really thought, but Michel had made my life hard lately, a little too hard. So I'd make this decision on my own, for me, for the better good. For whatever reason I could think of that would make it all OK.

I nodded. I couldn't risk talking right then, but Gregor accepted my action as the consent he was seeking and he pulled me into his arms, laying a kiss on my forehead.

"*Merci, ma cherie, merci beaucoup.*"

I let him hold me tightly for a moment. His hands stroking my head and back, his face buried in my neck, inhaling me, devouring me with each breath. It wasn't erotic, just lovely. Just right.

I sensed Michel approaching, he wasn't trying to hide, he was giving me fair warning. How was it he was playing so fair?

I didn't pull back from Gregor. If he was going to be a part of my life, I wouldn't hide how I felt. I detest lies and secrets. My honesty is probably what gets me in trouble the most in my life.

Michel came into the room on silent feet and stopped just inside the door, watching us. I lifted my eyes to his and held their gaze.

He did look a little sad, but not angry, as I had expected, maybe resigned. Possibly a little shattered. But that emotion playing across his face, if it had been there at all, was gone in a flash.

"You have decided, *ma douce*." His voice was even, but soft.

Gregor stiffened slightly and went to withdraw from

my embrace. I held him tightly for a second longer, letting him know it was OK, then let him pull back and face Michel. Both men glanced at each other, but turned their attention immediately back to me.

This was a little more uncomfortable than I had even believed it would be.

I swallowed. "There has to be some rules."

Michel glided closer and came to sit on the couch beside me, slinking down into the cushions with practised ease.

"Go on," he said. I think Gregor was just holding his breath.

"I truly don't want to lose either of you."

"You won't." Michel again.

"But I am confused, very confused." Understatement of the year.

Michel sighed quietly and sat still. Gregor hadn't moved an inch.

"You both have manipulated me into this position. Don't think I don't know this." Michel stiffened now too. "I would have joined with you regardless Michel, but now I truly don't know if what I feel is real or the Bond." He nodded his head slowly. I turned to Gregor. "I had no idea what I was doing when I marked you Gregor and let you mark me, but here we are. Now though, I don't know if what I feel for *you* is real or because of the exchange of *Sigillum*." Gregor nodded slowly too. "So, this is how we're going to do this for now." I took a deep breath in, this really didn't sound right in my mind, but it's all I could think of to say. "Give me space. I need to sort this out in my head. Please don't push me. Let me find my way."

Maybe I could do the *neither in my bed* as my internal monologue had suggested. Yeah ri-ight.

Both men sat so still, not vampire still, they were with me, but waiting, expecting me to say more. *Sorry, to disappoint guys, but that's all I've got right now, I just don't know any more.* I didn't project that thought, I didn't shout it, so I'm quite sure they didn't *hear* it, but you never know.

"So be it." Michel was the first to break their silence.

"So be it," Gregor echoed.

Why is it that vampires have the habit of turning even a few small words into something more formal, more ritual in nature? Like it has so much more meaning or weight than it actually should.

I decided I *really* needed to be alone after all of that, so I got Bruno to drive me back to my apartment. Gregor was heading to the airport immediately, to fly out on the *Iunctio's* private jet to Paris. And Michel, well, I couldn't quite face Michel right now. Guilt? Probably. But it didn't change the fact that I couldn't face him right now, did it? I guess I'm just a coward sometimes, so sue me.

My apartment was the same as it had always been. Some part of me thought it should have changed too. *A bigger bed maybe?* my little internal monologue said. *Fuck you!* I replied.

I switched the coffee machine on - when in a mental or emotional quandary, have coffee, it not only clears the mind, but soothes the nerves. A universal tonic for all internal dilemmas. I was just settling in to sip my brew when there was a soft knock on the door. I glanced at the clock on the wall. Nearly two in the morning, not the usual time for a friendly visit.

I checked my pockets to make sure I was armed and went to look through the peep hole. I've got glass and a peep hole on my front door. The frosted glass just lets me see the shape and size of what's on the other side, the peep hole, who it actually is.

He looked medium build, not too bulky, but maybe he worked out, it was hard to tell, but I didn't recognise the man on the other side of the door. He was human, about my age, maybe slightly younger and a total stranger. I came down off my tippy toes and had a think.

Hmm. Late night caller, human and at my door. Well, I'm not too scared of humans any more, I can kind of hold my own, but the hour of the visit was strange. Then again, maybe his car had broken down and mine was the only light on in the building and he needed to borrow a phone. Then again, we're in Auckland and petrol stations abound and who the hell doesn't have a cell phone any more?

Ah hell. I opened the door, but kept it on the little dinky chain. Anyone could probably rush it and snap the thing, but it would give me time to draw a knife.

"Yes?" My voice was even, non threatening, calm.

"Hello. I'm sorry to call so late, I've been waiting for you to come home. I hadn't realised it would be in the middle of the night, but I'm here now so I thought I'd just knock. I've been waiting so long to meet you, I simply couldn't wait any longer."

I looked at him through the gap in the door. He was slightly taller than me, maybe 5'8" high. He had dark brown, short, thick hair, matching dark brown eyes and a tan over well toned muscular arms and no doubt the rest of him. But he was wearing loose fitting jeans and a loose fitting T-Shirt, so I could only make out his bare arms, not the rest. He seemed harmless, in a casual sort of way, and was kind of good looking. But why was he here?

"Um. Who are you?" I asked.

"Oh sorry, sorry. I got so excited to finally meet you, I haven't even introduced myself, have I? I'm Tim, um, Timothy Baxter."

Baxter. That was my father's name.

"You're my cousin, aren't you?"

He nodded vigorously. "Yeah, we're cousins. Your father was my uncle."

"Do you carry the gene?" The Nosferatin Gene.

"No. My father is your father's younger brother. The third born is free of the gene."

Yeah, that's right. The first born is the Nosferatin, or vampire hunter. That would be my older uncle, whom I have never met or know anything about. The second born carries the gene and passes it on. That's my father and I'm the Nosferatin he passed the gene on to. Had my parents had another child after me, that child would have been the carrier of the gene. The third born, or any others after that, are free from the curse/gift.

"But you know all about it?" I guessed.

He nodded again, more slowly this time. "I know it's late, but can I come in?"

"It's not just late, Tim, it's damn near morning and I've got to work tomorrow and I've kind of had a shit of a day."

He looked like he might cry, he seemed really young in that moment. Ah shit.

"How about we meet for lunch tomorrow? You hanging around for a bit?"

“Yes, yes. I came to meet you. I'd really like to meet for lunch.”

His head was bobbing up and down like one of those toy dogs on the back seat of a car.

“OK, I work at the BNZ on Queen Street, meet me there at 12.30, I'll take you to lunch.”

“OK, OK, that's great, thank you, Lucinda, I'll meet you then.”

His face beamed at me as he waved goodbye and turned to run back down the drive towards the street. For someone who had scared Pete into telling me to be careful, he seemed pretty damn near harmless, if not a little mouse.

Just what was Timothy really?

I guess I'd find out soon enough.

Chapter 25
Heartache

I didn't think I'd ever fall asleep, but around 3am I somehow managed to, knowing I'd be getting up again in little over four hours time. It felt like I had only just drifted off when the dream coalesced around me. My parents' farm. Before it even finished fully forming I was turning to scan the surroundings.

"You may as well show yourself, Michel, I know this is your doing."

"Was it the location or the dress, *ma douce*?" He walked out of the nearby trees, sauntering in his lovely black outfit, hands in pockets, beguiling smile on lips.

I glanced down at what I was wearing; a long softly flowing apricot coloured dress, low neckline, full skirt, with bare feet. I wasn't sure apricot was my colour, but Michel had a tendency to pick colours well. This choice was either for my benefit, I love orange and in any shade, or I actually could get away with wearing it.

"Nice, but the location did it," I replied.

"I shall have to branch out a bit more in future then."

"Why are you here, you know I said don't push?"

"You said a lot of things, *ma douce* and then you ran."

I sighed. "So, this is your answer, trap me?"

He spread his hands out in a semi shrug, semi signal of peace.

"You can leave any time you wish," he answered.

I turned away from him and took in the view. The lambs were always only a week or two old in my dreams. I'm sure Michel knew they would grow bigger before actual slaughter, but he never let them get to that point here. He somehow knew how much I loved them at this age; tail still long, waggling their last few times before docking.

He came to stand beside me, but didn't look at the view, his eyes were all for me. I let him stare, he called this dream, I'd let him have his moment. I think he needed it and truthfully, I was feeling guilty.

“Are you angry with me?” My voice was soft. I had actually started looking at the ground just in front of me, as though I was starting to pull myself in tight. I forced my chin up and gazed again at the the distant lambs.

“No, not at all. You were right. I did plan for you to be in my bed, not just by my side, but I will not apologise for it, *ma douce*. I wanted you like I have never wanted another. I still do.” His voice was like velvet, it coated me in ways I didn't think his power ever could. I felt tears sting my eyes and my breath catch in my throat.

“You're making this hard.” My voice did hitch a bit there, but I no longer cared. He could see what he was doing to me already.

“I am glad, it should be hard. It should not be easy to walk away from someone you love.”

I turned to look at him then and that was definitely a mistake. I had to force myself not to go to him. I'd always had trouble here, in my dreams. He had always seemed so much more to me, his call to me stronger, his effect on me so much deeper.

He was only a couple of feet away, but I felt myself swaying towards him. He didn't move in response, just watched me with steady eyes of deep blue and indigo swirls.

"How do I know that it's real?" It was a plea, no two ways about it. And I guess, that it's also the crux of it all right there. I could be pulled to him, drawn to him, want him as much as I liked, but was it real?

He sighed and closed his eyes. "Only you can answer that, *ma douce*. Only you."

I shook my head and felt the tears fall. *No. I didn't want to feel this confusion, I wanted it back how it was. I wanted him, I wanted to love him and I wanted him to love me back.*

"Is that not your answer, *ma belle*?" His eyes were open again and looking at me, I just kept shaking my head.

"I can't do this right right now, I just can't. Too much has happened, too much *is* happening. I just can't do this Michel. Please. Leave. Just leave." I think I did sob the last out. It wasn't too audible, but I think he got the message. He looked pained, sad, desperate even. I sobbed a little harder at that.

Finally he nodded. "As you wish, *ma douce*." And vanished, the dream disappeared and I woke up in bed crying and couldn't stop.

I bawled, for I don't know how long, but eventually there were no more tears, just sounds. And after even longer they went away, to be replaced with a numbness so complete I think I truly felt I no longer existed at all.

Facing work was a challenge and a relief. I stumbled out of bed, showered and grabbed a coffee to go. Walking briskly to the branch, sipping fortifying caffeine and stomping away my worries. The morning was slower than usual, which didn't help. My mind playing over last night, from what Gregor had told me when I was still tied to that chair, to the battle they fought, to the proposition on the couch at St Helier's, to the dream. Bouncing around from one to the next, to the next, to the next. My concentration was shot, my customers frustrated, my boss a little annoyed and my co-workers perplexed. I was normally much more orderly and in control than this, they all knew something was wrong.

I didn't get into trouble, but my boss did hover. She even asked if I was all right, but what could I say? *No, the vampire head honcho wants me dead, two vampires are fighting over my affections and I don't know which one to choose and my heart is breaking into a million pieces.* Somehow I didn't think that would help my cause. At around noon I received a call, luckily my boss was out the back and I didn't have any customers, because it was personal and today just wasn't a take-a-personal-call kind of day.

"Hey, Lucinda, it's Jerome, sorry to get you at work, but we need to talk."

Ah shit, I thought at least this could sit on the back burner for a little longer. He heard my sigh.

"Is it a bad time?"

"Would it matter?" A bit rude, I know and Jerome didn't really deserve it, but I was stretched pretty thin right now, so I didn't apologise.

"I wish it would, you know that, but we need to talk."

I glanced around the branch, everyone was occupied. I grabbed some slips out of my drawer and pretended to be checking them whilst holding the phone to my ear with my shoulder.

"All right, Jerome, what's up?"

"Rick has made a challenge for Hapū leader."

I dropped the phone and it took me a couple of seconds to get it back up to my ear. The deposit slips disregarded for now.

"What does that mean, Jerome?"

"It means he will fight me for the position and only one of us will remain alive to take it." So matter of fact, so unemotional.

Oh no. Oh no. Oh no. This could not be happening. Not now, not when my life was so much a fucked up mess, not the Taniwhas, not them too. I was panting, I didn't think I had any tears left to shed, but I was in a panic, like I had never been in before in my life. This just seemed to be the last thing my mind could handle, the last straw, so they say. I felt the world tilt slightly and then slid down the drawers behind my counter, out of sight of the customers, but garnering a concerned look from one of my colleagues just off to the side.

"Lucinda. You still there?"

"Ah huh." I couldn't manage any more.

"I'm sorry if I've scared you," he went on in his low, gruff voice. "But you have to know. I can't refuse his challenge and even though I'm quite sure I could win, I won't kill him. He's like a son to me, so I guess, what I'm saying is, I'm going to let him win and when he does, Lucinda, you need to be prepared. He has it in his head that we should be fighting for the night, taking it back from the vamps. He plans to make it the Hapū's sole focus and he sees you as standing in his way."

Oh dear God.

"When?" My voice was barely a whisper.

"Two week's time. Friday night after next; the *Rākaunui*. All challenges must be met on the night of the Full Moon."

"Is there no way to stop this?"

"No." And that one word was weighted with so much pain, so much heartache, so much fear and pride and love and strength. So much Taniwha, I couldn't breathe.

"I'm sorry, Lucinda, I tried to talk to him, to make him see sense. I have failed our alliance, I have dishonoured our treaty. I beg your forgiveness."

I started crying then. Who knew I had more tears in me? "No, Jerome, you have nothing to apologise for, this isn't your fault. There has to be something we can do, something I can do. I'll go to him, I'll make him see."

"No! You mustn't. He will kill you, Lucinda. Please promise me, you'll stay away. On the *Rākaunui* too. Once the Hapū witnesses the fight, they will not be able to stop the change. They would tear you apart. Just let this happen, there's nothing to be done for it now. Just tell your vamps and get prepared. Please."

I was shaking my head. My supervisor; my boss, was crouching down next to me, trying to get my attention, trying to pat my shoulder. I couldn't stop the tears, I couldn't stop the pain. I couldn't stop Rick from making the biggest mistake of his life and killing his mentor, his idol, his kin.

"OK," I whispered.

"*Kia kaha, Kaitiaki, kia kaha.*" He rang off with those words; Maori for *be strong* and *Kaitiaki,* the name he called my kind.

My boss bundled me up and pushed me towards the

staff room. I couldn't tell her what was wrong. She offered to call someone for me, to come and get me and take me home, I was in no fit state to work. I shook my head. Who could she call? All the vampires in my life were tucked up in bed, all the Taniwhas were preparing for a leadership challenge and the humans, well parents, lived over two hours away by car. There was no one else.

As I was sitting there trying to get myself under control, one of my co-workers came in and said my cousin was waiting for me out the front. I'd forgotten all about Tim. My boss took this as a sign from on high, someone to care for me and it was family to boot. I didn't even get the chance to stop her, before she raced out and escorted him to the staff room. Great. My cousin, who I didn't even know, sees me in a tear streaked mess. Bloody great.

Tim just jumped in as though he'd known me all his life. Promising to take good care of me, telling them he'd drive me home, that I'd be all right. He put his arm around my shoulder, like he'd done it a thousand times before while we were growing up and he cuddled me out the door. For the life of me, I couldn't resist and he was family after all. He was silent on the short drive to my flat, he parked in a spare car park on the property and came round and opened my door, cuddling my shoulder again as he led me to my apartment. I managed to get my key in the door and he placed me on the sofa while he went and familiarised himself with the coffee machine. He had to get the instruction manual out, its got so many bells and whistles even a qualified barista would have had to read the instructions first.

Finally he sat next to me with a near perfect fluffy

coffee, a little cinnamon scattered on top. My life began to settle on the first sip.

"Bad day, huh?" he said quietly, sipping his own coffee.

"Thanks for the lift home. For the coffee." My voice was scratchy from too much crying. I really didn't think it would ever recover after the past 24 hours.

"No worries. That's what family is for." He smiled broadly, I didn't smile back.

"We don't even know each other, Tim, we're hardly family."

"But, we're blood, Lucinda. We come from the same ancestors. You may be the Nosferatin of our generation, but I have Nosferatin blood in me. I don't carry the gene, but what flows through my veins, can't be that different from yours."

I cocked my head at him and tried to get a handle on this guy.

"Is that why you're here? You have a fantasy about what we are? Do you want to hunt vampires too?"

He laughed and it was a young boy laugh, all innocent and carefree. This guy had probably never even met a creature of the night.

"Nah, but I'd like to know more about what we are, where we've come from. My parents keep pretty hush, hush about it all, actually. I only found out because of some hidden stuff in a box in our attic. I don't even think my father knows that it's there. I think it was my uncle's, you know *our* uncle's, Uncle Jeff. Our fathers' older brother, the Nosferatin."

"What happened to him?" I think I knew the answer,

but I wasn't really prepared to hear it.

"He died when he was 25."

One month past his 25th birthday I was betting.

"Same age as me."

Tim nodded and took another sip of his drink.

"Are you expecting me to die too, Tim?" I don't know why I asked that, gut instinct, I don't know, but I still couldn't get a handle on this boy, no, man. He was a man, just young and naïve.

He wouldn't look me in the eyes, just kept staring into his half empty coffee mug. Finally, he said in a quiet voice, "Will you?"

"Why do you think he died?"

"Because he didn't join with a kindred vampire."

How much did this guy know?

"Do you know what a joining means?"

"You live forever. You gain powers and your kindred vampire gains powers too. And without a joining you die."

There was no hint of what he really believed in his voice, it was empty, even. Too even. Like he was scared to show his true feelings. Let's see how he'd handle this?

"Do you think the vampires should have our powers?

He didn't hesitate, but it made me feel like he had been prepared for that particular question, had rehearsed his answer well. Maybe I was just too cynical, maybe I'd just had a bad day and couldn't see the best of people, but I didn't trust Tim right now, for whatever reason.

"Yes, of course they should. It's why we exist."

If there had been a text book on How to be a Good Nosferatin, I think that would have been lesson #1. *It's why we exist.*

"Have you ever met a vampire, Tim?"

He shook his head and went back to looking in his coffee mug.

"They can be evil, you know? Cruel. They take what they want without pause. Some even think they should take over the night completely." I was watching him closely, trying to see if he would react. He was either a good actor, or he really was scared of what I was saying. Or, oh hell, I'm just making something out of nothing and this young man found a box of old journals in his attic and wants to know if it's real.

I sat back on the couch, my coffee finished and mug on the coffee table. I didn't know what to make of Tim. He seemed OK, but Pete's warning kept blaring in my head. And to be honest, I didn't think my judgement of people had been too hot lately. Should I give the guy a chance?

"How long are you in town for?"

"I've been here a week, I'm on leave. I gotta go back to work next Monday. I'll head back over the weekend."

"What do you do?"

"I'm a carpenter's apprentice, down in Wellington. I just started earlier in the year. It's cool, I'm learning heaps."

"But it's not vampire hunting?"

He smiled. "It's not exciting, no."

"Vampire hunting's not always exciting, Tim, sometimes it can be heartbreaking too."

He looked at me then. "Is that why you were so upset at work?"

I laughed, could I tell him there were shape shifters too? Nah, the guy was bug eyed enough as it was.

"No actually, a friend is about to die. A close friend."

Close enough to the truth, Tim hadn't yet earned my no lies, no secrets policy.

"I'm sorry. That's sad, no wonder you were upset."

Yeah. No wonder.

"What have you got planned for the rest of your stay?" I asked, to turn the conversation to more unemotional territory.

"Well, I'm really stoked to have found you, that was my goal and it took me all week. You're not listed in the white pages."

No, too many vampires know how to read.

I shook my head. "It's good to be anonymous."

"It's Friday, so I think I'll just head out on the town, see what the night life in the Big Smoke has to offer. What about you? You feel like coming out with your cousin and showing him the ropes?"

I'd have actually quite liked to do that. I may not fully understand Tim yet, but he was pretty easy to talk to and I haven't had a human friend to talk to for ages. Rick was as close to that as I ever had and now he was gone. But, at that moment I felt Michel call. Nothing frantic, just ringing the doorbell kind of thing in my head. It was the middle of the afternoon, so it was unusual. There must have been a reason for it, so I couldn't ignore the call.

"That would have been nice, but I've got something on this afternoon, it'll probably go well into the night. But hey, thanks for looking me up, it was nice to meet a relative."

"You gonna be OK? You know, after what happened at work?"

I sighed. Was I ever going to be OK again? No, I didn't think so, but instead I gave Tim an only slightly awkward hug at the door and said, "She'll be right, mate."

Just like any good Kiwi girl would say.

Chapter 26
Coming Home

I sent Michel a thought, that I was on my way soon and jumped in the shower. I needed to freshen up and it was *not* because I was going to go see Michel, but because I wear a little make-up to work and I looked a fright. Mascara does run when you cry like a baby, don't let anyone tell you otherwise.

I decided to jog up to *Sensations.* I know it sounded silly after just having taken a shower, but I'd been slack lately and I could no longer go to the gym where Rick worked to keep fit. I'd even been walking to work and not running, so a jog was well overdue. I packed my backpack with my evening hunter gear, so I could change up there. Even though Michel and I weren't technically seeing each other intimately right now, I was sure he'd let me use his shower. I could always steal Bruno's.

It took me fifteen minutes to make it to the bar, so only about half an hour since Michel *called.* The door was locked, but the day crew let me in and said the master was in his office. I don't know why that upset me. It shouldn't have. There was no real reason for him to meet me in his chamber. I just had never seen him bother to be in the office during daylight hours. Was he conducting our meeting there on purpose? Neutral territory? Ah damn. I'd asked for this, I was just going to have to get used to it, I supposed.

I entered the code in the door to his private quarters and walked the plush carpet to his office. The door was open, so I just walked in. Why is it when you decide not to see someone romantically that they continue to take your breath away by just by existing? I didn't want him to have this effect on me. I couldn't trust that it was real, so I didn't want it to keep happening. But it was. Dream or no dream, Michel took my breath away simply by being there. It was just not fair.

"What is the matter, *ma douce*? I feel your sadness."

I was just standing inside the door to his office. I'd taken the step inside, but when I'd seen him behind his desk, I had simply stopped breathing, I'd also stopped walking too. I must have looked like an idiot. I wrapped my arms around my body to stop myself from fidgeting and I took a deep breath in through my mouth. I was damned if I was going to smell how fresh and clean his scent was and crumble further into the pit of embarrassment and despair.

"I've had a bad day." It came out small, even for me. God, I could do better than this.

Michel came around the desk and stood in front of me, he hesitated before he took me in his arms, his eyebrows raised in a question. I didn't shake my head, so he continued to fold me into his chest. I allowed myself a small inhale of his scent and almost whimpered. Damn this was hard.

"*Ma douce, ma douce*. Why are you doing this to yourself? It does not have to be this hard. Not everything needs to be black and white, Lucinda. There can be grey. Grey is good."

I didn't think he realised what grey meant to me, otherwise he wouldn't have used it in his attempt to make me give an inch. Grey is the colour of Gregor's eyes. Granite sometimes, silver mainly, platinum if you're lucky. It's all grey, just varying shades is all.

I pulled away from his arms and went and sat in one of his comfy chairs in front of his desk.

He sighed and walked back around to his side.

"Why did you call?" Great, my voice was back to normal. Normal is good. Not grey, normal.

"I've heard from Gregor. Our presence has been requested by the *Iunctio.* We must leave for Paris tonight."

"Wow. You don't beat around the bush, do you?" He just smiled his knowing smile back at me. "Gregor must have only just landed, he can't have been there long."

"Yes, but his report was given on the way. The *Iunctio* has already deliberated and passed their verdict."

"Their verdict?"

"Well, not the sentence, but the fact that they don't entirely believe him. They want to assess us themselves."

Oh shit. It hadn't worked. Gregor hadn't been able to convince them I wasn't a threat. That Michel could contain his powers and not give the Nosferatu away.

"Anything else he could tell us?"

"He was very cautious on the phone, I believe he feared he was being watched."

Oh fuck. This just kept getting better and better.

"What do we do?" I asked.

"We go to them, to refuse would be unwise." I'm guessing *unwise* was a euphemism for deadly.

"This isn't good, is it, Michel?" I'd started to wring my hands in my lap, it's a nervous thing, I can't help it. I'm working on it though, dead give-away to anyone watching.

Michel sighed again, he was doing a lot of that lately. "Please, *ma douce.* Let me come to you, let me soothe you. I can't stand seeing you suffer and not be able to help."

I stopped wringing my hands and sat up straighter in the chair. “I'm fine. I'm OK.”

“Damn it Lucinda! Why are you fighting this? Why are you pushing me away?” I didn't think I had ever heard Michel swear before. Me, I do it all the time, but Michel? He always seemed too refined for that.

“I...I...” I didn't get to say anything else because Michel was around the desk and pulling me to my feet.

“Tell me you do not feel anything for me?” His voice was low, not a growl, but close to it.

I shook my head. It wasn't that I didn't feel anything, it was that I felt too much and I had no idea if it was me or the Bond. Why didn't he understand this?

He cried out in frustration and I thought that he might try to kiss me, pull me in and lavish me with his mouth, his tongue, his lips. But he spun around and walked away across the room and just stood there. I felt abandoned and disappointed and frustrated to hell.

“Until you ask me to again, I will not kiss you, *ma douce*. I will not force myself on a woman who does not accept my advances. I am, after all, a gentleman.”

OK. So, I knew where I stood, wasn't this what I had been asking for? Then why did I feel sad?

I let a huff of breath out. Michel turned and looked at me, small flashes of violet mingling with the indigo in his eyes.

He shook his head slightly, a small smile playing on his lips. I think he wanted to say something, I think he wanted to ask me to ask him, but he didn't. It's one of the things I admire about Michel the most. His self control, his resolve, his ability to maintain his façade. I just never thought he'd have to use those skills on me.

I loved him. I kept telling myself this, so why was I refusing to accept him? I took a step towards him. I don't think I really meant to, it was just natural and that scared me. Everything I do around Michel feels natural, but I still can't help thinking it's because of the Bond. His eyebrows rose slightly at my advance, but he didn't move just waited for me.

I'd had a shit of a day. A really awful, absolutely foul, shit of a day. I needed to feel his arms around me, I needed to feel his support. He's my kindred Nosferatu. Despite the Bond, despite my confused emotional state of mind, being with him is meant to centre me, ground me, revitalise me. Being with him is how I am meant to be.

"I can't promise I won't freak out on you at some stage, but I need you Michel. I don't know if that means more than just physically being with you. I don't even know if we can do that, just be together without it leading to more. I'm scared that's the case. I'm scared that I can't just be near you to feel better without it leading to your bedroom or mine. And I'm *so* scared that's what I actually want."

He was standing very still, as though any movement would frighten me. His eyes dancing all shades of blue and purple imaginable. They were beautiful, just like the rest of him; mesmerizing, enchanting, and oh God, I so wanted him right then.

"Say something," I whispered.

He swallowed. "I...I am unsure if I can be near you and not want more too, *ma douce.* In fact, I am fairly certain I can not. I want you, all of you, but only if you are willing to give it."

I closed my eyes. This was it then, a true stalemate. I couldn't have his comfort, unless I took all of him. I couldn't take all of him, because I was scared my wanting him was a falsehood, a by-product of the Bond. Stalemate.

I opened my eyes and he was standing right in front of me. He'd moved while they had been closed and the effect that had was as though he'd popped up out of thin air. Of course, he'd done that to me before, with my eyes open. He was quite capable of disappearing and reappearing at will, but the slowness of the blink and his now close proximity, made me gasp, just a little.

He let out a breath of air at my reaction and the warmth of it brushed my face.

"Kiss me." It was out before I'd even formed the thought.

"Are you sure?" His eyes never left mine.

"It's just a kiss."

"It is never *just* a kiss with us."

"Dammit Michel, kiss me now."

He laughed and it lightened my soul. "As my lady wishes."

His lips met mine tentatively. A warm brush, lip to lip, breath to breath, but I wanted more. I reached up on the tip of my toes and went to place my arms around his neck to pull him close, but he caught my hands and brought them back down to my sides, holding them firmly.

"Let us see if you can handle the kiss first, shall we?" His voice was low, a rumble against my mouth.

I stared into his eyes, his gaze holding mine. His face a wicked smile, then he bent towards my mouth and lightly licked across my bottom lip. Still keeping eye contact, still moving slowly.

I opened my mouth slightly and let a breath, I had been holding, out. His gaze lowered to my mouth, then flicked back up again. The next time he came in, he took my bottom lip into his own, lightly sucking, gently licking, then releasing. Moving back to look into my eyes. I was spellbound.

He smiled. "So far, so good."

Then he lowered his head again and I expected this time to be firmer. He'd been building the pressure up, each effort more intimate, more mouth involved. But he simply lay a delicate kiss on my top lip, followed by another on my bottom lip, then back to looking in my eyes.

I think I may have stopped breathing by this point. Again he came in, still holding my hands by my sides. I'm not sure it was needed any longer, I was dumbfounded, unable to move, but this time his lips met mine and his tongue flicked inside. I whimpered when he pulled away and surprisingly did try to move my hands; I wanted to touch his face, to pull him closer.

"Ah, ah," he whispered as he lightly licked across my mouth, then nibbled on my bottom lip.

"Michel, please." It was also a whisper, as he pulled away.

"I am not finished, *ma douce*." Then he kissed me more deeply, allowing my tongue to roll around his, to flick in his own mouth and then he pulled back.

"Would you like more?" He was breathless, he might have been putting on this display for my benefit, but it wasn't escaping my notice that he was enjoying himself too.

"Yes." I couldn't deny it, he'd got my attention and my body's full attention at that. I was wet with need from a few simple kisses. How did this man do this to me?

"How much more?"

"Michel."

"No, *ma douce*, let there not be any misunderstandings between us. How much more?"

I licked my lips and he immediately kissed them, long and hungry and full of need. He abruptly pulled back and looked a little surprised. I don't think he had intended to show me just how much he wanted me too. He'd slipped.

His desire did it for me though. I'd always known he wanted me, wanted me like only a man could want a woman. But at this moment my need, my desire for him was so great, that it possibly eclipsed even his. And what was wrong with that? Even if the Bond did bring us together, I couldn't blame my sexual need entirely on that, it would be like copping out or something. Not admitting that I wanted this man with my entire body seemed a sacrilegious act. How could I not let him know how much I wanted him too?

"I want all of you," I breathed against his hovering mouth.

He responded immediately and swept me up in his arms. In a blur we were in his chamber down the hall, the door clicking shut behind us. He lowered me onto the bed and crawled slowly on top. A slow sexual movement, covering my body with kisses as he worked his way up my legs. Lifting my T-Shirt and laying a lick of his tongue along my stomach, right up to just under my breasts.

"You are salty," he said raising his head and licking his

lips.

Oh shit, I'd forgotten that I'd run here. Even though I'd had a shower before I came, that small fifteen minute jog had worked up a sweat. Yuck.

"I need a shower, I ran here."

He chuckled. "That can be arranged."

Again he swept me up and carried me into the bathroom. I don't normally go for all the carrying, I'm small and being cradled in someone's arms can make you feel even more tiny, like something that needs protection. I don't need protection. But, I needed Michel today and truthfully, I'm not entirely sure I could have walked right then.

He stood me up on the tiles, holding my hand as he reached into the large shower and turned all the shower heads on. I just watched him and enjoyed every movement he made. Now that I'd made the decision to do this, to keep doing this, I was damn well going to enjoy every second. Michel turned back to me and noticed me watching him. He raised his eyebrows at me and smiled.

"Strip," I said and couldn't help smiling.

He grinned. "As my lady wishes." And began to slowly unbutton his shirt, one button at a time, his eyes locked on mine. Finally he made it to the top of his black shirt and he opened it, centimetre by centimetre, allowing me to take in more and more of his perfect unblemished deep cream skin across his chest. He slid the shirt off his shoulders and let it fall to the floor at his feet. Then ran his hands up over his stomach, pausing at the darker area around his nipples and then returning to the lower curls of hair at his waist, where they disappeared into the top of his pants.

He slowly undid his trouser top button and almost laboriously undid his zip, millimetre by millimetre, still maintaining eye contact, but by then I'd had enough. I pulled him closer by grabbing the top of his trousers and claimed his mouth with mine. His arms went around me and he moulded against me almost moaning with need. He reached down and pulled my T-Shirt off over my head, throwing it against the far wall. Then continued to lay kisses down my cheek, onto my neck and across my collar bone as he undid my bra and tossed that away too.

Finally his mouth found my breast and he took it inside and sucked. I almost bucked against him from the shockwave of desire that poured through me. His arm coming around the back of me to support my body as I arched backwards. His mouth never leaving my nipple, his tongue continuing to roll around its sides. His head came up as he pulled my body upright and he looked me in my eyes.

"More?" he asked innocently.

I just smiled and went down on my knees in front of him to finish undoing his trouser zip and gently peeling them down his legs. He was wearing silk boxers, in a deep blue to match his eyes. The length of him already straining against the fabric, trying to slip out the gap in the front. I looked up at him and almost stopped. The look of utter adoration on his face making me pause for breath. I kept eye contact as I licked the length of him slowly through the material, making it wet against his skin. When I came to the tip of him, I licked around the top, adding to his own wetness, making the material cling to his length like a second skin.

By then he had to close his eyes, no longer able to hold my gaze, throwing his head back ever so slightly. So I returned my full attention to what was in front of me. The room had started to fog up, the shower still streaming water and we hadn't even made it inside yet.

I peeled his boxers off and managed to strip the rest of me, kicking off my shoes and peeling off my leggings and socks while I played with him and stroked him. And then was able to lick him and take him inside my mouth and suck hard. I managed to get several good strokes and licks and sucks in before he pulled away from me, reached down and pulled me up his chest to kiss my mouth. All the while pulling us back into the shower stall behind him. The door closed behind us as the water hit our bodies and fell all over us and we just continued to kiss.

There was no longer any finesse, just raw hunger and desperate need. Even while we devoured each other with our mouths, Michel had grabbed a sponge, lathered it in soap and begun to rub it all over my body in small swirls. Lathering up the suds, making them slide down the length of me and add to the sensations coating my skin. He moved the soapy sponge between my legs, down my inner thighs, my calves and then back up to wash the crease between my legs.

"I am sorry, *ma douce*, but your hair will have to wait." And suddenly he lifted me up off the tiled floor, with both hands on my rear, making my legs spread wide around him. My soaped up body sliding against his chest and stomach as he pushed my back against the cold tiles, making me gasp at the initial coolness against my skin, then cry out as the firm length of him entered in a rush. He didn't waste time, kissing along my cheek, down my neck and pounding inside me in equal need.

I met every thrust with an urgent movement of my own, clawing at his back, gripping his shoulders, laying my own kisses against his face. My hands rushing up to grip his hair and pull his head and lips back to mine, when he'd moved away. He moaned against my mouth and continued to pound against me. I was sure I was going to have bruises tomorrow, but I didn't care. I wanted all of him, every long inch, every bit of his body and soul.

The orgasm came quickly, washing over my body as the water from the shower washed over my skin. And Michel continued to pound against me, taking me further than anyone had ever taken me before. Just as I started to come down from that wave, he lowered his head to my neck and I felt his fangs slide in. The sharp spike of them entering my flesh immediately replaced with such hot desire it burnt as it flowed down inside me. From my neck to my stomach and lower, making me call out his name and beg for more.

His pace faltered slightly, his mind sprang open and suddenly I couldn't tell if it was my words or his that kept repeating in my head: *mine, mine, please, mine, please.*

I felt my Light build up inside me in a rush that raced the heat and I flung it out the open door of my mind directly to Michel, bathing him in it. In all it's brilliance. And then felt him release inside me and call out in triumph against my neck.

We both slid down the tiled wall. Michel on his knees, me still straddling him, his length still inside but softening, slowly. And our breath and heartbeats in sync as the warm water washed over us and out the floor below.

And all I could think, was that I was home.

Chapter 27
Unexpected Visit

OK. So, I was one confused and messed up little puppy. I can't tell if what I was feeling for Michel was because of the Bond, so I pushed him away, only to run back into his arms and bed (read shower here), when I'd had a shit of a day. But, I do know this, I absolutely and unequivocally *loved* having sex with Michel. I just had to separate that from all the rest of the mess and emotions and I'd be all right. Men do it, why couldn't I?

Yeah, ri-ight!

"What are you thinking, *ma douce*?"

We were still on the floor of the shower. Hadn't moved, hadn't switched the water off. I guess Michel's hot water cylinder was bigger than mine, it was still beautiful and warm, still covering us in its blanket of water, still holding us in it's embrace like we were holding each other. My heart had slowed a little and my breathing was back under tighter control, but my body couldn't move to save itself. I'm guessing Michel was the same, because he hadn't budged a muscle either. Something about my Light when shared left both parties more than just sated.

"I was thinking how screwed up I am." I said the words into his shoulder, where my face had been buried. I'm surprised he could hear me over the sound of the water, but then, he was a vampire.

"Please do not regret this. Do not make this into something other than what it is."

"What is it?"

"Beautiful. A gift. Ours."

"You make everything sound easy, Michel." I pulled

away from his shoulder to look him in the eyes, watching the swirl of violet in amongst the azure. "I don't work, *think*, like you do."

He laughed and reached up to cup my face. "That you do not. But promise me, *ma douce*, just this once. Try to enjoy and not condemn your actions. Just this once, love me as you have a right to do."

I looked at him, really looked at him. Taking in the beauty of his eyes, the curve of his lips, the shape of his face. He was so easy to love. Even after all this time - and I know it's not been that long that I've been admitting I love him, but so much has happened it feels like centuries have passed and then, none at all - that I still lose my breath when I look at him. That I still can't believe he is mine.

"You're mine." I sounded surprised and I'd meant to just think it, but the words just found their way to my lips and my lips betrayed me.

His face lit up in a glow that I had not truly seen before, something of him being held back all this time. "Yes." He ran his finger along my lips, his eyes following that movement and all of a sudden I felt him harden inside me, lengthen and swell. Still inside me, still a part of me.

He shifted slightly beneath me and my body responded. My lips found his and his hand clasped the back of my head, pulling me closer. Kissing me, eating me, trying to get inside my mouth and further inside my body than he already was. It didn't take long for the heat to overwhelm us and our bodies to take on a rhythm of their own, but it was slower, more luxuriant, more exploratory than demanding. As though we had all the time in the world to please, to pleasure, to take what we needed and give it back in spades.

The water continued to fall all around us. Still fast and furious little droplets of wet, but everything seemed to slow down as we took our time to find release again and held each other dear.

I'm not sure if it was the slowness of making love this time, or the feeling that we had all the time in the world to love one another, but for some reason, I felt something click into place inside me. Something permanent, something sure, and it felt right. It was as though we had just sealed ourselves together, which sounds strange, considering we have *joined* and Bonded. And you can't get more connected than that, but yet we could, because we were, right now sealing our fates.

No matter what happened in the future, our bodies would always recognize each other, call to each other, want and need each other. There was really no other way to describe it. But I knew in that instant, Michel and I could not fight this attraction, this basic of needs. A hunger for the flesh of the other. And I could tell he felt it too. He'd probably think that what he felt in my emotions, was me giving myself over to the thought of us, that final part of me that I had been holding back, but it wasn't conscious. It wasn't something that I had just this second recognised and formed a coherent thought around. It was more basic than that, more animalistic. As though evolution was just doing what it had been doing for millennia before and I was just along for the ride.

He sighed and hugged me tighter. I didn't try to explain what I was feeling, it wouldn't have made any difference. He wanted me to want him without reservation, did it matter *how* I had come to that conclusion?

Somehow we did manage to use the shower for what it was intended and I finally found myself wrapped up in a fluffy white towelling robe - one Michel had purchased just for me as I just can't get the same satisfaction from a silky one - lying on the bed, trying to get my body to move and get going. And my mind to think clearly about what lay ahead. Michel watched me from the corner of the room where he was dressing. How was it that he had more energy than me and could get on with things? All I wanted to do was sleep.

He smiled. "Have you had much sleep lately, *ma douce*?"

I thought about that for a moment and realised I hadn't. From kidnappings, to meetings in bars, to family reunions and shape shifter power struggles, to dreams that lead to crying half the night away, I hadn't had a full night's sleep in days. No wonder I was tired. A combination of stress, heightened emotions, lack of sleep and amazing sex can take it out of a girl.

I shook my head at him, suddenly unable to form sentences and only managing to yawn.

He glanced at his watch. "There is still time before we must leave for the airport, why don't you get under the covers and sleep? I have a few things I must attend with Bruno before we go."

He came over and helped me under the covers, slipping the robe off and letting me slide between the sheets nude. Usually, I'd wear something, but right now I was too tired to worry about my nakedness and Michel didn't make any moves to make me regret it.

"I need to pack," I said, already closing my eyes.

I felt his lips on my forehead and he whispered, "Leave that to me." And then he was gone.

Part of me worried about what Michel would choose for appropriate wear in front of the *Iunctio* and in the fashion capital of the world, Paris. But the other part just curled up in a ball by an imaginary fire and purred.

I heard his low laughter rumble through the room as he slipped out the door.

I don't know how long he let me sleep, but I wasn't disturbed, by supernatural dreams or human ones. I just slept in blissful peace, safe and warm and content. It had been days since I had felt so good upon wakening. Alive, healthy, whole. I had always known how important staying in touch - and I mean literally *in touch* - with your kindred was. For those like Nero and Nafrini, who also share a Bond, but one more of sibling love than sexual, the need to touch is still as strong, still as important. When you see them together, you know it's not lustful, but the slide of fingers against fingers as they pass, the touch of a hand to a shoulder at the table, the brief stroke of arm against arm as they walked side by side. More intimate than human siblings, but also so natural that it doesn't make you blush.

For Michel and me, I don't think we'd ever have that platonic need for touch, ours was definitely in the realm of sensual.

For some reason that no longer bothered me.

I was just contemplating getting up and getting dressed, ready to face the rest of the day - and had even sat up, the sheet falling away to my waist - when a flickering light appeared in the centre of the room and before I had a chance to comprehend it's significance, Nero materialised. The look on his face said it all: one, he'd caught a glimpse of my naked upper body and two, he had *not* expected to.

His face flushed a deep crimson and he spun away from me uttering apologies in both Arabic and then English. I grabbed the sheet and covered myself instantly, feeling an equal brightness wash my cheeks. Well, this was unexpected.

"What are you doing here?" My voice was high, slightly panicked. "If Michel finds you in here he'll kill you."

"I am so sorry, Kiwi." His back was still to me. "I had not realised. You were no longer with your kindred. For some time now you had been alone. I thought it safe to Walk to you. I am truly sorry. I will leave."

"Why are you here?" There had to be a reason, the last time we had seen each other I thought it would be the end of him Dream Walking to me. He was so disappointed in me, angry even, I thought I had lost Nero too.

He turned slowly, raising his eyes to me, ready to look away if necessary, but I was covered, if not in clothes, at least in material. But somehow he managed to make that seem too sparse, his eyes looking through the thin sheet as though it wasn't even there.

"Hey!" I said, stiffening slightly.

He looked away again, blushed even more. "My apologies, but I am only male. Please, if you wish me to stay, put something on." And he turned his back to me again.

I hesitated, then jumped out of bed grabbing my robe and fastening it about me, knotting the cord twice. If

Michel came in, it was better I looked bundled up for the depths of the Antarctic than not.

"OK. You can turn around."

He did and his smile said enough. I was covered, but his imagination was still filling in the gaps. Men!

"Come on, we might as well sit down." I led the way to the cluster of comfy chairs in the corner, where Michel usual read from his tablet computer. It was still sitting on the low table waiting for him. "You might as well tell me why you are here." And truth be told, I had missed him, I didn't want him to go away.

He sat down with his usual grace. Nero may be part-human like me, but he's been around about 500 years longer. You pick up ways to make your body move in its best possible light over that period of time. I didn't think it was a conscious thing, just something that has become second nature for him. I wondered in that second just what effect he had on other women in his life, the ones who were free to return his favours.

His eyes flashed their gold flecks, in amongst the coffee and cinnamon swirls at that instant. I shook my head in puzzlement. Sometimes his eyes flashed with emotion at the oddest moments.

"So, why are you here?" I asked.

"I wanted to make sure you were OK."

"It's been almost a week since I left to kill Gregor, you could have called." It sounded a little childish. I mean I could have called too, but he was the one who had been angry and practically stormed off. Not that you can storm off in a Dream Walk, but he did have the last word. I don't normally let anyone else but me have the last word, so I was still smarting just a little.

"I heard you had not killed him, but that he had come to New Zealand. I wanted to make sure you were not in trouble."

"Trouble." I said it in a huff.

"You *are* in trouble, Kiwi?" He had reached out his hand to touch me, but hesitated in mid air, then pulled it back with something like a look of pain on his face. His features quickly reschooled into their usual intense Nero look.

I ignored it, what could I do? Sometimes Nero just did weird things. "I'm neck deep in trouble, Nero."

"Tell me." It never sounded like a command from Nero, more a slightly abrupt request, but never a command.

"Gregor was sent here to assess us. To see if Michel could contain his new powers and not give the Nosferatu away and to discover if I was more than just the *Sanguis Vitam Cupitor*."

Nero stilled. "What did he find?"

"That Michel can't control himself when my safety is concerned and I am *more* than just the *Sanguis Vitam Cupitor*."

"Shit." Nero had blanched, the deep crimson of before replaced with a paler version of his normally dark skinned self. To top it off, if hearing Michel swear had been unusual, hearing Nero was downright astonishing. I was having a bad influence on the men in my life.

"This is not good, Kiwi. What have the *Iunctio* decided?"

"They have requested an audience with us. We fly out to Paris tonight."

His head snapped up and he looked at me, sitting forward in his seat. "I will return to Cairo and organise a flight to Paris immediately. You cannot go alone."

"No!" Even to my ears it sounded harsh, but dammit, I was *not* going to lose Nero too.

His eyes flashed again, that beautiful coppery-gold, inside the swirls of coffee and cinnamon. "You are too important to the Prophesy to not protect, Kiwi. You are the key that opens the door, without you there can be no fulfilment of the Prophesy. No further Nosferatin called to the duty of the Light."

"I don't believe that," I replied a little sullenly.

"How can you not?" He looked utterly stunned.

"I don't see the Prophesy as being final. Prophesies in their nature are self fulfilling. Just because I fit the bill right now, does not mean that if I die, another won't come along and take my place. Filling that role, *the key,* you call it."

He shook his head vigorously. "The Prophesy was about *you.* A Nosferatin born in *this* time, in the New Land. It is specific to you. It was written millennia ago. To replace you now would mean a completely new prophesy would have to be written and if that were even possible, which I do not for a moment consider so, then how long before *it* could be fulfilled? It would simply be too late to help us now."

I shook my head back at him, he just didn't get it. "Just because I die, doesn't mean another Nosferatin can't be born now, in this time in New Zealand. I have a Nosferatin family Nero, I met my cousin. Even if he doesn't hold the gene, I can't believe the New Zealand Nosferatins have died out with my father's death."

He paused, giving the words the weight they deserved. He did reach over and take my hand at that. "You have found your family, Kiwi." His voice was soft. Nero had always understood the gaping whole in my heart for the family I had lost before I could walk and craved from the moment I knew they existed.

Then his face reschooled itself and he pulled his hand away. "I still do not believe the Prophesy would be so accommodating." He paused again, his eyes lowering. "Besides, it is not only the thought of the Prophesy losing you, that stills my heart."

I didn't know what to say to that. He was my friend, I knew he cared and I'd feel the same way about him, but the tone of his voice conveyed more than the words and I felt momentarily confused.

"I will leave you now. Your kindred may return at any moment, but I *will* meet you in Paris."

He stood then and took a step away from the chair. I was in front of him in a flash, my hands resting on his chest, to stop his progress any further. I vaguely acknowledged I'd been a blur, more of a blur than I had ever seen Nero be. My speed just kept getting faster and faster didn't it?

Nero looked as surprised as I was, but regained his composure and his hands came up to rest on mine, on his chest, gentling rubbing. As though he didn't even realise he was doing it at all.

"No," I said. "I will not lose you too. It may not come to that, but if it does, you need to stay safe. You are the Herald and if the Prophesy does re-build itself upon my death, you would make it happen faster by staying alive.

Can't you see that? Please, Nero, just trust me on this."

He looked at me for a long moment, his face so serious, so intense. I almost felt like squirming, but Nero had always been a bit like this, I was kind of getting used to it. Kind of.

"You are the *Sanguis Vitam Cupitor* and you are more." Everyone seemed to be saying that lately, I still didn't know what it actually meant. "You are the Light to the Dark. You call to me, as I call to you. You will always hold the Dark dear."

Huh. Wasn't that something like what I had said to Gregor just before he flipped out and said I was more than just the *Sanguis Vitam Cupitor*?

"What does *that* mean, Nero?"

"It means, you are the Prophesy, Kiwi. I am not quite sure how much of the Prophesy, but you are more than what we had at first thought."

"That's scary, isn't it? I mean being the *Sanguis Vitam Cupitor* was bad enough, what else is in store for me?

He shook his head and reached up to brush my cheek. "I do not know, but I do know that I must respect your wishes on this. I will not come to Paris, I will await your call should you change your mind."

I was glad he had decided to stay safe, but why? "Why? Why are you doing what I ask now?"

He laughed and his eyes sparkled their mesmerizing combination of autumnal browns and glinting golds. "If you do not know the answer to that, my little Kiwi, then you are not meant to, yet."

And with that cryptic answer he brushed his lips against my forehead, his now almost routine farewell when he Dream Walked to me and flickered out of sight.

Confused, me? Nah.

Chapter 28
Lutetia

The flight to Paris was long, but comfortable. It's not like we had to share a 747 with hundreds of other people, crammed into economy class or even first. We had a *Gulfstream G650 Jet* all to ourselves, Michel's personal aeroplane.

I'd been on his plane before, when we flew to Cairo to help out Nafrini and Nero. So, I knew all about the comforts on board. There was a personal bathroom to rival the *Ritz* and in the main cabin, where we were sitting now, cream and gold plush carpet, with intricately designed dancing dragons throughout. Beautifully hand stitched cream leather couches and arm chairs, 52 inch plasma flat screen TV and every electronic toy you could desire to keep you occupied on a journey to the other side of the world. It was stunning, with excellent kitchen facilities and Michel's own little manservant to bring me nibbles and whatever else I desired. But it was still only so big, could still only travel so far and we had to make two stops on the flight over, making a 15 hour direct flight, turn into more than a full day.

It made me realise that whatever Gregor had flown on, whatever type of jet the *Iunctio* had, it was bigger, stronger and faster than Michel's. That comparison only made me shudder with a little fear. Everything about the *Iunctio* seemed bigger, stronger and faster than us. How on Earth were we going to convince them we were safe, no threat and stay alive?

We were met at Charles de Gaulle Airport by an *Iunctio* flunky and two big, burly vampire bodyguards to escort us to their complex. It didn't escape my notice that the bodyguards treated us as their charges the moment we exited the plane. I felt like an extradited criminal returning to face murder charges in front of members of my own kind. Not too many words were shared on the trip towards the city centre. The vehicle was a long sleek limousine with pitch black tinted windows, but it was still true dark outside, so they were not essential and instead made it difficult to see the views of the never sleeping city as we sped through the streets. Not that I would have taken too much in anyway, my nerves were a jangled mess, but I was trying my best to shield them from the vampires nearby and seemed to be winning.

Michel sat vampire still next me, which only made me even more fearful. He only ever shut down like this when normal shielding was beyond him and clearly tonight was one of those occasions. I decided to ignore his presence, or lack thereof and concentrated on sending my new *seeking* abilities out into the night. I can be ruthlessly practical when required. It's the vampire hunter in me. This may not have been a hunt, but I was entering foreign territory and I was definitely on the back foot. If this wasn't a hunt, it was still a deadly game and I do not like walking into the ring unprepared.

I centred myself on my heartbeat, despite it being slightly elevated. I've learned to ignore the speed and use the simple regularity of the beat to calm myself down, allowing my mind to enter that black nothingness before Dream Walking, in order to send my senses out and *seek*. There were no vampires around us, we were still too far out of the city centre, but I could sense them, en masse, near the city proper. And in numbers that were staggering. I had been keeping tabs on where all the vampires were throughout the world. Paris has always been that much busier, partly due to the *Iunctio* being here and partly due to the number of magical Ley Lines the city boasts, but the number evident today had more than tripled. Ironic really, that there were so many vampires harbouring such Dark in the *City of Light*.

Why so many more than usual, though? *Why are there so many more vampires here than last time I sought?*

I wasn't sure if Michel would hear me, he was still, so still. But he *was* paying attention, perhaps more than I had given him credit for, because he answered my mind-question straight away.

They come for you, ma douce. They come to see the Sanguis Vitam Cupitor.

Oh, I didn't like that. Just what were these vamps thinking? Yippee, she's here! I doubted it somehow. What did I represent for the majority of vampires? I could seek them out, tell how much Darkness lurked within *and* Dream Walk to them to possibly kill them. I stifled an hysterical laugh. If I was a vampire, I'd want me dead.

I knew that the *Iunctio* was based as near to the centre of Paris as it could get. All vampires, from the beginning of time, have ensconced themselves in the centre of humanity. Be that a village or town or city. They need the numbers of humans around them to survive and a city the size of Paris offers up a wonderfully easy buffet of transiently populated central suburbs. The *Iunctio's* headquarters, for want of a better word, had been based in Paris in the same building since the 5th Century A.D, but it is rumoured they have had a presence there since 52 A.D. It had been called *Lutetia* and is still called that today by most vampires, only humans call it the *Île de la Cité*.

Lutetia shares its island with the famous catholic cathedral *Notre Dame*, but the *Notre Dame* only came along in the 10th Century and was built at the request of the then Champion, or head of the *Iunctio*. Apparently he thought it a lark to pick off the odd parishioner after their Sunday morning Mass.

Vampires are strange, in some ways they cling to tradition with utter ferocity and in others they embrace modern ways in an effort to blend in. All the titles of members of the *Iunctio* have both Latin and English translations, but they only go by their English versions. It is considered *déclassé* to refer to them in their older language. Yet Nosferatins hold onto those Latin names with an equal measure of ferocity. The only exception to the rule, is the Herald. I am the Blood Life Seeker, but any Nosferatin you meet will only call me the *Sanguis Vitam Cupitor*. Go figure. Nosferatins are a little more traditional in this regard, than the Nosferatu.

So, Michel had only referred to the Champion by her English title. I still didn't know what the Latin translation of that would be. He had prepared me, as much as he could, for what to expect when we met her. Practically the entire flight over was in discussion of the various roles within the *Iunctio* and those vampires who held them. I felt I knew as much about the *Iunctio* as I would ever know and it did *not* calm my nerves one little bit.

It took over an hour to reach the *Pont Neuf*, the bridge across the river Seine to *Lutetia.* The traffic from the airport had been light, but Paris is big. The closer we came to the *Palais*, the *Iunctio's* headquarters, the tighter the knot in my stomach. But Michel was fairly sure that we would not be expected to meet with the Champion on our arrival, that it would no doubt be tomorrow evening that we would be called to her. I glanced at Michel's watch, I don't wear one, as the sturdy limestone walls of the *Pont Neuf* sailed passed the dimmed windows. It was only 11.30 at night, that seemed way too early to relax. Besides, from what Michel had said, the *Iunctio* never slept and the *Palais* was well equipped to accommodate vampire light-sensitive needs.

The first view of the *Palais* was from the side. Large imposing stone walls, that appeared pitted and greying with age and decay, consumed the view from my window as we slid past on the roughly uneven cobbled road. I've been around old buildings before, not in New Zealand, we're an extremely young country, but in Cairo, in the suburb called *Old Coptic.* The buildings or walls there, at least, went back to Roman times. But this, this was ancient. How it was still standing, I have no idea, but I could sense the wards and they were off the scale.

I don't know why I was surprised by that. This was the centre for all vampire hierarchy, it would of course be well protected, but what I sensed now was a mixture of magic. Spells overlaying each other, some so deeply entrenched they would have existed for centuries, others newer but stronger and still more pulling on Nosferatu or Nosferatin powers. I'd only recently been able to tell the difference between a ward placed by a vampire and a ward placed by a Nosferatin. They were subtle in their differences, but their objectives were much the same. I knew that the *Iunctio* was powered by both Nosferatu and Nosferatin power, but for some reason it felt wrong that Nosferatin power would ward their building. It just did. These guys were still the bad guys, or at the very least, could turn bad in a heartbeat.

We came around the corner of the building and finally I got a glimpse of its front façade. It wasn't pretty like the Gothic *Notre Dame* or the majestic *Palais de la Justice;* home of the Paris Police. Or the even more fairytale *Conciergerie,* part of a hotel. They all shared this island, but the *Iunctio's Palais* was blocky and straightforward, as though whoever designed it made it for strength and strategical defence purposes, not to enhance the locale like its prettier neighbouring buildings. That saddened me a little. Vampires on a whole are fashionable people, they usually dress in the height of fashion and we were in Paris. It seemed such a shame that their central government building was nothing more than a fort. It brought the mind back to the basic desires of a vampire. Survival at all cost. You'd never forget your enemies strengths when faced with a building this ugly.

We drove into the courtyard, passing the multitude of external wards like passing under a waterfall. I felt my skin awash with a cold tingling, that left me shivering and unable to stop. Michel placed his arms about me and pulled me close. He didn't seem affected by it, but was aware of its effect on me. He quickly rubbed his hands up and down my arms, trying to bring the warmth back to them, but still I shivered. Nothing he could do could stop the shaking or the chattering of my teeth. Some greeting.

The limousine stopped by the main stairs up to the

front doors, even from my seat in the car I could see how oppressive it all looked. Two vampires were manning the huge wooden doors at the top of the stairs. They didn't come down them to open ours, the vampire bodyguards with us did that. We followed our guards inside, past the intricately carved doors, which on closer inspection displayed vampires in various forms of battle. A nice secondary reminder of their strength. Michel had let go of me by then. It wouldn't have looked good having to cuddle me on the way in. A show of our own strength and confidence was required, so I had to battle the shivering myself. Why wasn't it stopping?

The guards led us to a moderate sized room, not far off the entrance hall, which had been covered in cold stone floors and starkly bare stone walls, not a decoration to be seen. From the intricacies of the carvings on the front door, I had expected more displays of vampire strength and prowess inside, but then it occurred to me that starkness said more than opulence or fearful images ever could. It said *we are what we are and if you don't know us by now, you've already lost.*

That didn't help my shivering any.

The guards left us, probably to man the only door, which we had just come through, from the outside. Nothing was said, I almost began to think they may have been mute. The room held several smaller tables and chairs, nothing comfortable, nothing calling out for you to lounge upon, everything was so utilitarian and bare. I really did feel sorry for them all, working in this stark and bleak environment.

Be sure to speak in my mind and not aloud, ma douce.

They will be listening and watching our every move.

I turned to face him, still shivering, still chattering and wanted to curve myself against his chest, wrap myself up in his arms, but knew he was right. They were watching. So I nodded and just walked around the room, trying to get some warmth into me, trying to stop the damned shivering. I was dressed in my usual hunter garb. Michel had packed my suitcase, but I hadn't seen what he had packed yet. He hadn't said a word when he found me in my black short skirt, tights and Tee, with another of my custom made black jackets - this one fitted, not denim, a step up from my absolute casual best - when returning to his chamber. He either wanted me to feel comfortable, or he thought it was appropriate. I was also armed. He had said that I may be disarmed upon meeting the Champion, but not necessarily. It was considered a Nosferatin right to be armed in the presence of vampires and those of the *Iunctio* would be well out of my class.

At least my hunter outfit travelled well. I had freshened up on the plane, which makes a huge difference psychologically, the outfit itself just didn't crease at all. I looked as fresh now as I did when I boarded, just shivering.

How long will they leave us here waiting?

Michel did his elegant shrug. He was sitting reclining in one of the upright wooden chairs, making it look way more comfortable than it possibly could have been, watching me pace the room. He seemed relaxed, unfazed, well into his consummate act as a politician. The only evidence of any heightened emotional upset, was a small smattering of indigo in his deep blue eyes. He'd played this game before, he was probably in his element. I kind of disliked him a fraction right then.

They have no reason to leave us here, other than to unsettle us, do not give them the satisfaction. Our rooms will be already waiting, we were well expected. This is just a game.

I may have mentioned before, that patience is not my greatest virtue and that would be true. But I had been working on it lately, so I bit my lip and kept walking my well travelled path around the room, to keep from wringing my hands and in a vane attempt to stop the shivering. It had progressed to abrupt spasms now, involving my entire body, almost like I was epileptic, having a seizure as I walked. Or perhaps more like the ticking of muscles Tourette's Syndrome patients have. At least I wasn't having phonic ticks, I could hold my tongue well.

It had reached a ridiculous length of time, maybe two hours, maybe more. I was tired, I'd walked the length of a marathon in this now seemingly tiny room and my body was simply starting to shut down with all the shivering. Michel's flecks of indigo had increased as his concern for my wellbeing heightened. I finally came to the conclusion that they were waiting for something. Certainly a reaction, but from Michel or me? And that their patience would undoubtedly last longer than mine. I knew I couldn't continue pacing and if I sat down now, my body would give over to the shivers completely and I may well have a full blown tonic-clonic seizure in the end.

So, as I normally do, when backed into a corner, I thought to hell with this and I lay myself down on the floor, in the middle of the room, on my back. Stretched out completely flat, hands clasped together over my waist, my hair spread out around my face, no doubt in stark relief to the light grey of the stone floor.

What are doing, ma douce? Michel whispered in my mind. His voice very even.

Giving them what they want. I fought to control the shivering in this more relaxed pose. It was a catch 22. I needed to relax, but letting go would let the shivers take over completely, distracting me from my task. I had been unable to *seek* since the shivering had got worse, unable to concentrate on more than just throwing the odd thought to Michel and pacing. I had no idea if I could do this, but I had to try.

What would that be, pray tell? Michel still sounded very even in my mind, but I could tell he was becoming a little concerned. Just a sensation down the link we shared, nothing else.

Just keep an eye out on my body, I'll try to time this right.

At that Michel stood up abruptly. He didn't come near me, but his whole body screamed the tension I had begun to sense in his mind-voice.

Is this wise, ma douce?

Don't know, don't care. Someone has to take that first leap of faith.

With that I shielded him out and allowed myself to fall into the blackness of nothing faster than I have ever tried before. Racing the shivers, stretching my abilities to the extreme, in order to cross the line first.

I found myself outside the room, standing in front of the guards, on either side of the door. The Dream Walk had coalesced quickly, faster than usual, maybe because I had allowed myself to fall into it quickly too. They couldn't see me or sense me, of course. That allowed me an illusion of calm. Had they been evil bastards, I could have staked them. Probably wouldn't have, considering my current predicament, but the thought was a balm to my ragged nerves anyway.

I looked around, no one was coming running. I put my senses out, now being free of the shivers and able to concentrate on my powers, first to the room Michel was in, to make sure no one had entered through a secret door. No, it was empty aside from Michel and no one approached from any secret passage way. Then I sent my *seeking* abilities further afield. I found them all. All the vampires in the building, every single one of them. I knew where they were, how to get to them, how many were in each place, how much Darkness they had within. It didn't scare me, like I thought it would. There were a lot, but my earlier *seeking* had prepared me and I just washed over them all, feeling, *seeking*, sensing.

I had several options open to me. Simply stand here and wait for them to come, once they noticed my body had gone still, no more shivers now I wasn't in residence. I'd begun to put it together, about an hour into being in the room. It had taken me another three quarters of an hour to come to the final conclusion, shivers can be distracting, but I realised eventually, that the shivers had been placed on me purposely. This was the first test. A good one too, subtle, appearing a consequence of the heavy wards, enough to make me dysfunctional and Michel panic. But Michel had held it together longer than even I had thought he could and I had managed to think through it.

So now, wait for them to come, or go to them? I knew where the Champion was, she wasn't alone, but she also only had two others with her. They were watching, I couldn't tell this from my *seeking* talent, but I just knew. Gut instinct, Nosferatin know-how, I'm stuffed if I can label it, but it's true. I knew she was watching and waiting.

Part of me wanted to go to her, to scare her just a little. Turn up in her chamber with a stake in my hand, but I am not stupid, contrary to popular belief in some quarters, I would not walk from one trap into another. But, she was expecting something and it's not that I wanted to show off - well maybe just a little - but I also wanted to end this torture. I'd had enough shivers to last a lifetime and although I could Dream Walk for hours, Michel *was* cracking.

So, option three. I gathered all my Light inside me, this time letting it build to such a height, such a depth, such a density, I had never attempted to contain before. A small part of me, momentarily thought, perhaps this was a bad idea, showing my cards, before the hand had really been played, but right now, I was at the end of my patience. Any longer and I would well and truly crumble. Crumble in front of the enemy; show that fear? Or give the best offence I can muster?

What do you think I chose?

I'm a vampire hunter. We don't show fear.

I let my Light flow out from me, touching every vampire in its path, which I decided would be a very round-about way to its target, to ensure the maximum effect. Why touch two or three vampires, when you can touch 120? So, it took a few minutes to reach her. Surprisingly, it was as strong as it had been when next to me touching our guards at the door beside where I stood in the Dream Walk, when it did finally arrive.

I wrapped it around her two companions first, allowing her to sense it and see what effect it had on them. They, like all the other vampires in the building, collapsed to their knees, not in pain, but in safety and warmth and love and happiness. I made sure not to make it any more than that. Vampires may like to spread desire like butter on toast, I'm a little more reserved. And then I let it engulf her. She tried to shield, she tried to push it away, she even almost succeeded. And I admit, I even almost let her. Would it have been good to let her think she was stronger than me? Safe from my attack? Probably. But I was also a tad pissed off. She had kept me waiting, after all.

So, I gently, slowly, slid passed her walls and lay a kiss against her skin. I tried something then, that I had never attempted before. I had no idea if it would work, but it felt right and if there is anything I have noticed in the past with my new skills, it is if the feel is right, it usually works. I whispered in her ear, *With respect Champion, greetings from New Zealand.*

I withdrew my power, letting it caress down her arms and pulling it back to where I stood. I did stagger slightly, not a good sign. It had been a mammoth undertaking, on top of a strained and exhausting 24 hours. Before the weariness could fully envelope me, I fled back to my body, through the comforting blankness of nothing and woke up with Michel holding me in his arms.

It took me a moment to focus on those swirling pools of indigo and violet, with hints of magenta around the edges and before I could smile up at that beautiful sight, he said aloud,

"What have you done?"

Chapter 29
The Champion

“She's coming.” Michel's voice was flat, neutral, well contained. His *Sanguis Vitam* was not. *She* was obviously the Champion and he didn't need to tell me she was on the way, I could feel her too.

“You need to rein your *Sanguis* in, it's leaking everywhere,” I offered.

“I can *not* imagine why.” Ah, now a little inflection to the voice. Michel's trademark sarcasm.

I sat up and pushed away from him. He was still kneeling on the floor, I was sitting on my rear, legs straight out in front. I glared at him.

“It's not like she didn't know I could Dream Walk and get away from the spell she had cast. It's not like she didn't know I could *seek* her out. She knew all of this, Michel, it won't be a surprise.”

He looked like he was about to blow a gasket, I don't think I had ever seen him so riled, yet so desperately trying to hold onto control. If Michel got this angry, he'd normally just give in to it. Why contain the emotion when you can use it to demonstrate your strength to those of your line?

“And I suppose your Light touching her wasn't a surprise either?” he gritted out between clenched teeth.

He knew the answer, he was just being facetious. She may have had an idea of what I could do, but seeing it, feeling it, was way more impressive than just believing it. I suddenly had little desire to tell him I had whispered in her ear.

He suddenly stood, in that puppet-on-a-string kind of way the older vampires have, a fluid motion that no normal human could ever master unless harnessed to a stunt wire and hauled to their feet using pulleys. I just scampered to my feet in the usual human way, with a little bit of Lucinda-lack-of-grace thrown in for good measure and dusted myself off.

I could feel Michel pulling his *Sanguis Vitam* back in, tightly wrapping it around himself, containing it, controlling it. I could tell though, that this conversation was not over. Not by a long shot. I was hoping he'd get the opportunity to tell me off later. Strange, but true. The Champion was not shielding her anger as she streamed towards us, so the jury was still out on that one.

The shivers had returned with a vengeance, as soon as I had entered my body and now I was having trouble standing without toppling over. I grasped the nearest chair and gritted my teeth. Michel was streaming a string of thoughts at me; angry, ugly, frustrated thoughts, with flashes of images of what the Champion could actually do to us because of my *attack* on her body. I hadn't even realised he could project images, I didn't think he had either, both of us too angry right now to acknowledge how cool that really was.

I could feel the Champion getting closer, but still Michel was ranting in my head. He was pacing backwards and forwards, not really looking at me, just being in his little manic moment. Finally I'd had enough. I had ended up on the floor again, the shivering now so uncontrolled I couldn't support my own weight. Or the Champion was having an effect on me, the closer she got.

If you've finished lecturing, a little help wouldn't go astray right now. Please?

Michel turned in a blur to look at me for the first time since he started ranting and raving in my head. He immediately cut off his mental tirade and came across to look down at me. He sighed and shook his head, reaching down to lift me to my feet, pulling me into the warmth of his arms and holding me close.

As soon as his body engulfed me I let my shields down, without him even asking and he came tumbling in, in a healing rush. Washing away the shivers and coating my body in heat, not quite enough to start a flame, but enough to focus on and warm the coolness the shivers had set deep inside my soul. I took a big deep breath in, smelling the freshness of him, the salty sea spray and clean cut grass of the meadows back home on the farm; centring me, grounding me, bringing me back from the edge.

What am I to do with you, ma douce?

Then he stiffened and turned me in his arms to face the door, still holding me against his chest, in front of him. His arms casually wrapped around me, not shielding me from what was about to come through the door, but supporting me, backing me.

She's here. His words, just a whisper in my mind.

She glided through the doors as though she was a few centimetres above the ground, floating. Her aura flashed around her in angry colours; the red of fire ants, the orange of an open flame, the yellow of a glowing hot poker tip. She slashed her anger out at the room making me double over, falling to the floor from Michel's arms at the force of it, but he hadn't feared better. He landed next to me, one hand on my back. Just touching, keeping the connection there, helping each other to battle her rage.

I vaguely thought, through the stabs of pain darting down my body, that she really needed to go to anger management classes or maybe take a chill pill, because, come on! It wasn't that bad.

"Wasn't that bad?" Her voice, a hint of a French accent, was like thousands of tiny icicles dancing against my face, freezing cold and sharp as a pin, stabbing over and over and over again. I brushed my hand against my cheek and checked to see if it came away with blood. I wouldn't have been surprised if it had, the pain felt real, but there was no blood and even that thought didn't help me. No shields I could muster could stop her metaphysical pursuit for revenge.

I couldn't lift my head from the floor to look at her, my forehead now resting against the stone, not even registering the feel of it. I had no idea if she was beautiful, ordinary or scary as hell. And right at that moment looking at her face seemed like a really bad, bad idea. I did know that abasing myself at her feet was right, even though this movement was not voluntary, it felt right. I was in my rightful place, beneath her, begging for forgiveness. I almost opened my mouth to say I'm sorry, to tell her I had made a terrible mistake, I deserved to be punished, I welcomed her rage, it was because of me she was angry and I had to pay.

But I didn't and she just got madder.

And the madder she got, the calmer I did. And I felt the Light settle within me. *I am the Light to Your Dark. You call to me as I call to you. I will always hold you dear. I am the Light to Your Dark. You call to me as I call to you. I will always hold you dear. I am the Light to Your Dark. You call to me as I call to you. I will always hold you dear. I am the Light to Your Dark. You call to me as I call to you. I will always hold you dear.*

It took me a while to even register the words in my head. It was as though I was reciting a prayer, a mantra, something you might repeat to yourself at the end, when you face the final hurdle, when you need the courage to take that last step. It wasn't about monsters, it wasn't about Darkness, it was about taking that last step and the courage needed to make it so.

Whether it was the words, or the fact that I wasn't scared, or the fact I wanted to take that last step, but her anger receded and the pressure to be flat on my face at her feet lifted. I could breathe, I could think and now I wanted to see her face, because nothing could be as scary as what she just did and I had survived that.

Michel helped me stand, of course he'd got to his feet first, swiftly, smoothly, elegantly, but with his aid I didn't do too badly. I dusted myself off, a nervous gesture usually reserved for post hunting dust downs, but it's a ritual I can live with. I took a deep breath in and raised my eyes to hers.

She was short. That was the first thing I noticed. About my height, but I didn't think we'd be bonding over it somehow. Then it was as though there was too much to comprehend at once, because it took me several seconds to get the picture straight in my head, to be able to acknowledge that what I was seeing made sense.

Her aura had toned down, but she looked like she was a projection, she wasn't even here. A ghost, or a shadow of herself. She was translucent, but at the same time glowed with an inner light, not my Light, this was darker, but lighter too. Hard to explain, which is why I was having trouble getting my head around it. It was as if you tilted your head one way, she'd be more solid and shining a white light, but if you looked at her from your peripheral vision, she was see-through and surrounded in black. She was both Light and Dark, both solid and clear. Was she real or just an image projected here, to protect her own body lying somewhere else? Not really here at all.

"What do you see, Hunter?" Her voice no longer stung like needles, but it did scald, like a flash burn; there one second, gone the next.

I shook my head, I didn't understand the question.

"When you look at me, what is it you see?"

I really wanted to answer, not because looking dumb was not one of my favourite pastimes, but because the less she spoke, the less painful it would be. I didn't want her to have to rephrase the question again.

"You are both Light and Dark, clear and solid, here and not here." I was glad my voice was steady, a miracle under the circumstances, but Michel was holding my hand and I could feel his *Sanguis Vitam* pouring through the Bond. Not something that had happened before. My shields were in place, so he shouldn't have been able to help me. But then, the Bond chose what help I needed and sometimes just took without permission. Maybe he didn't even know he was helping me right now.

"Interesting."

I don't get it. I threw the thought at Michel.

I think he would have answered, but the Champion can read minds, apparently. No need to throw the thought, no need to shout it in your head, no need for a Bond, she can simply hear every thought in anyone's head. Damn.

"How I am perceived is a clue to who *you* are. You see *Light and Dark*, because that is what you were made for. You see *clear and solid*, because you only partially understand what I am and what I can do. You see me *here and not here*, because you both want me here to face me and also do not. Interesting."

I had managed to get a better look at her while she was talking, never waste an opportunity to assess your enemy. She was still all of those things, but because I had sorted out what I was seeing in my head, I could now look past it to her. She was dressed in a period dress; floor length lustrous material, hooped skirt, tightly boned bodice. She was petite and looked a little like a china doll. Her skin so pale, when it could be seen, unblemished and perfect, not only in hue and tone, but in her finely honed features; delicately cupid mouth, arched eyebrows and piercingly blue, blue eyes, like the Mediterranean Sea. An azure I didn't see often in Michel, but occasionally was blessed with. Her dark lashes were long and curled and her hair a mass of dark, dark hair - black I think, but it was hard to tell with the here and not here - in a mass of curls piled high on her head. She was stunning, but I also wondered just how old she was when she had been turned.

She was more of a child than I was, but she was over 1000 years old. The weight of her *Sanguis Vitam* flowing over me as I thought of her age, showing me clearly how long she had been here. It wasn't painful, it was more a curtsey you could say. I thought the question, she answered it. She just hadn't answered it the way I had asked. I still didn't know how old she was when she had been turned.

"Why are you not shivering?" She cocked her head delicately to the side as she asked that question.

So far, her attention had been entirely on me, Michel was merely an attachment. But, she turned her head slowly, like a predator following its prey; methodical, quiet, unseen, until she was looking at him. I wondered what he saw when he looked at her.

Her mouth curved into a knowing smile, she'd heard my thought and knew the answer and it looked like she liked what it was he saw, but held her tongue. Such control.

"Let go of her hand, Michel."

He did what she asked without hesitation. He had been well trained. The moment his touch left me I convulsed with a shiver, then another and another, until I was on the floor gasping for breath and unable to do a thing to stop it.

Her laugh echoed around the room and finally she'd found something to make her think of desire - always a fall-back for any decent vampire - because I was suddenly gasping with more than just shivers, but a need so raw. I found myself crawling across the stone floor towards Michel, painfully, but determined to satisfy my lust.

I was no longer shivering, it was as though one spell had been replaced with another, but I couldn't stand. The thought to stand just wasn't there, the need to touch him though was and the quickest way to do that was to crawl along the floor directly to him. I needed him, I wanted him, I had to touch him.

I looked up into his face from a few feet away on the floor, still crawling, he had his hand out to me in a stop motion. *Don't, ma douce, do not touch me*, he whispered in my mind. I hesitated, but then saw the hunger in his eyes.

He wanted me too, but was fighting the spell. The look alone was enough to cloud my thought processes and I pounced.

My hand touched his shining leather shoes, smoothing up over the top of them, over his sock until I felt his warm skin. As soon as my fingers touched his body, unhindered by materials, he collapsed on the floor next to me. Grabbing my arms at my shoulders, fingers digging into flesh and pulling me towards him.

We were both now kneeling, facing each other, body to body. His arms went around me, mine around him and we kissed. It wasn't like our usual kisses. It wasn't sweet and slow and full of love and desire, there was desire there, but it was laced with a hunger I had never felt before. It was more than just a hunger for his touch, or his attention. I smelt him and I tasted him and I wanted more. I could hear his pulse beating under his skin, his heart hammering away and the desire to taste more of him was overwhelming. I wanted to taste his blood. To free that pulse, to let it loose and let it flow through my mouth and down my throat.

There was nothing right now that I wanted to do more. My desire for his touch and body had morphed into a vampiric need for food, a blood lust I couldn't control. Part of my brain was telling me it wasn't my lust, it was Michel's I was feeling, but I couldn't stop it. I couldn't break away from it, it was in me, a part of me, it was what I wanted too.

I'm strong, really strong for a human, I can hold my own with pretty much any vampire that crosses my path, if I'm lucky and things go as planned. They can still get the drop on me, if I make a mistake, or I'm tired, but I am strong. It's just that right now I was under a spell and I was tired and this was Michel. The strongest vampire I have ever met. Part of his strength is mine and the Nosferatin in me can call to it, but right then all my body wanted was his blood. And I was working so hard to get to his neck, to get to his artery pulsing just under his beautifully creamy skin, that all other thought had fled me.

It's not a move I've practised much before. I've trained in martial arts, in street fighting techniques, I run to keep fit, but I don't practice controlling a combating body. Manoeuvring the head and neck, so I can place my lips upon flesh and bite down into the delicious flow of blood. It's just not something I've done before, so I wasn't that good at it.

Michel, on the other hand, is. Even though I was fighting him to get to his neck, I wasn't fighting *him*. I wasn't stopping him from getting to mine, but it was still enough for us to have ended up on the floor. Almost chasing each other in circles. Me going for his neck on one side, him following my movements to go for my neck on the other. Our limbs were entwined, our arms around each other, linked with each other's arms, our legs tangled beneath us, our bodies pressed against the length of the other. It wasn't a beautiful melding, but frantic movements, roiling motions, swirling actions. One thing following the other in rapid speed, that to those watching us, we were probably just a blur.

When his fangs finally found purchase I had a moment of clarity, enough clearness in my head to think that I was glad it had been him to win. That brief sting of fang to flesh was enough to douse the burning blood lust, for me to realise that I *really* wouldn't have wanted to sink my teeth into his flesh and swallow blood. But for him, it was heaven. And I could feel that now.

His body hummed like a tuning fork against me. I could feel the effect my blood was having on all of him; how it animated him, filled him, stretching his skin smooth, made his heart beat and his beautiful blood circulate his body. His skin grow warm and fill out with a soft plumpness, so subtle, but so necessary to stay alive and look alive and not just be a walking corpse. Then I felt the effect my blood had on his emotions, usually so contained and controlled. Blood allowed a vampire to feel more than they usually were capable of. Hunger, lust, they're just basic vampiric needs, but my blood filling his mouth, coating his throat, spreading through his body filled him with more than just lust and satisfying a hunger. It filled him with a love of my body, my blood, me. It told him how precious I was to him, how important I was to him, how central to his existence I was to him.

I felt it all and I think he did too, because he hesitated. The sucking slowed, almost to nothing, almost, but not quite, as though he couldn't quite find the strength to stop that last desire to taste. I am quite sure he would have found the strength to pull away, he was fighting his desire, he was battling it. Trying to stay clear-headed, trying to cling to the feeling of loving me, not just for my blood, but for me. But, whether the Champion was still very angry, or she just thought this was a handy way to kill us both without going to trial or passing an official judgement. *Oops, our guests killed each other, how unfortunate, but there you go.* But, for whatever reason, she amped the desire up a notch. Maybe, she wasn't all Darkness, because she threw a little bone out to me too. She made me want Michel to drain me. Want it so badly, I clasped my hands to his head and pulled him against my neck, not allowing him to release, even if he could. But he couldn't, not now, because he wanted it too.

I could hear my heartbeat in my head; so strong, yet so frantic. And I heard when it missed a beat and then another and then another. I heard when it paused, for a second, then beat once, then paused for three seconds. I heard it slowing, but not just slowing; faulting, missing, dying. The heart doesn't just slow down, it's not smooth and even, it's frantic and scared and panicked, it doesn't want the beats to stop. Adrenaline had shot through me, fighting to keep the heart pumping, fighting for its survival, but there just wasn't enough blood. If there's no blood, there's nothing to pump. If there's nothing to pump, the heart gets confused, it falters and eventually it dies.

I knew I was dying and I didn't care. I didn't hear my internal monologue shouting at me. I didn't hear what answer I might have given. I didn't see my Light trying to build inside me. I didn't try to help it against the sluggish response of my body and mind. I felt when my heart beat it's last beat.

And I just let it.

Chapter 30
Home

Being dead is unusual. I'm a Christian, I believe in the afterlife. Despite my hobby of killing the undead, I do try to live within certain rules. God says, *Thou shalt not kill, Exodus 20:13.* It's the sixth commandment, isn't it? It is perhaps the one commandment I have the biggest challenge with. I mean, I kill. I just kill things that are already dead.

Part of me believes God would understand. That the creatures of the night are evil and undead, not human. And I'm sure that he meant *Thou shalt not kill human beings,* but then it's also what I want to believe. So, I don't really know. I have thought about it a lot though. What would happen when I die? Will Saint Peter let me in the gates to Heaven? Will he unlock them when I come? Or slam them in my face?

I don't know.

So, I wasn't sure I was dead, but then I knew I wasn't alive either. There was no pearly gates, no Saint Peter, well none that I could see, but there was light. So bright, so everywhere, so beautiful. How could I not be in Heaven, with such beauty washing over me, such light dancing around me, hugging me, welcoming me, loving me? I was filled with such a sense of being home, of being safe, it made me cry. I had come home.

I became aware of noises. Musical laughter, children playing, the sounds of a school playground, laughter, singing, shouting. It was beautiful, it made me smile. Even though I couldn't see it, it felt so happy, so light, so innocent. Who can't smile at children having fun?

I turned from where I was standing, trying to follow

that delightfully happy sound, trying to see through the bright white light that surrounded me, but there was nothing to see. Just light, bright white with edges of a rainbow here and there. No forms or shapes within, just light.

Time didn't seem to matter here. I wasn't aware of how long I had been standing there, of how long I had been listening to that happy, happy sound, I was just there, enjoying it, loving it. I wasn't thinking of anything else, just smiling and enjoying and being happy. So happy.

So, I got a fright when she spoke to me. I couldn't see her, just glimpses of a face through the light. Of long, long black hair; wavy, but not curls. Of a dark skinned face with high cheek bones and fine thin lips, that didn't look too small for the face, but spread across it; owning it, centring it, making it alive. Her eyes were big round molten pools of lava; gold, no other word to describe that beautiful colour. They shone a bright, bright gold. But all of this, was only caught in glimpses, here and there, in and out of the white bright light.

"Child, it is not your time." Her words were everywhere. In my head, around me, above me, under me, through me. She spoke them, but I felt them inside me too. Deep, deep inside. They were light and musical and if words could be pretty, then these most definitely were. I loved her voice, I wanted her to speak again, but I couldn't think of a thing to say.

"You must return and finish what we have started." She faded slightly, but I so did not want her to go, to leave me, to send me away. I wanted to stay with her, be with her. She was my home, my haven, my safe place on a stormy night.

"Never fear, Lucinda. The Light will always be with you. You are the Light."

I felt a brush across my cheek, as though she had touched me, stroked me. An intimate caress between mother and child. I felt my tears fall silently, unhindered down my cheek, not washing away her touch, but sealing it underneath the warm moisture.

"Do not forget, you are a Child of Nut. A Child of the Light. Do not forget."

The last was just a whisper, barely heard or felt, just a faint noise on a distant breeze. There one second and gone the next. You almost believed you didn't hear it, but then maybe you just did.

And then the light faded and my heart felt crushed. Pain rushed in, my chest was so tight, so sore. A sharp stabbing pain right where my heart was, a deep wrenching ache right where my lungs were. I felt the coldness of stone beneath my body, heard the sounds of raised voices off to the side and realised I could breathe. And when I did, the pain in my heart subsided slightly and my lungs filled up with air, chasing away the ache and filling me up with life.

I raised my head up off the floor and waited for my eyes to come into focus. I was on the ground in the waiting room, still at the *Iunctio's* headquarters. The Champion was in a heated argument with the two vampires, all of it in French, none of it making a damn bit of sense. I turned my head slowly, scared that it would hurt, but it didn't and the world didn't swim, like I thought it would. The guards were just inside the room, a startled look on their faces, but their stances told me, they were ready to intervene, protect the Champion if she needed it. They had that bodyguard readiness about them, despite their larger than usual eyes.

Well, I didn't hurt anywhere any more and I didn't feel dizzy, so things were looking up. I reached up to my neck, to feel where Michel had bitten me. There were small bite marks, two little lumps, but no blood, no wetness and it didn't hurt, at all. I moved my head around in a circle on my neck. All OK. So, could I stand? I didn't fancy being on the floor when the Champion noticed I was conscious. I felt an overwhelming desire to face her eye to eye. So, I gingerly sat up, then just as gingerly got to my feet.

I held on to a nearby table, just for security more than anything. I didn't really think I needed to, it was just there. And then I was at full height, stretching out my body, freeing up my muscles, making sure it all worked.

I noticed the silence first. It had been so full of angry words. Angry words are angry words in any language, even delightfully romantic sounding French. But there was no French now, no angry words, just silence. A silence that made you want to curl up into a little ball and disappear.

I turned to look at the Champion and she looked different than before. Not angry, but surprised, but that wasn't what I noticed initially. She was still both light and dark, but no longer looked clear, translucent. She was solid. What did that mean? Had she changed, or had my perception of her? In her more solid form, she was even more stunning. The shadow or ghost like essence she'd had before had hidden her true beauty. Now it shone with a strength of purpose, with the weight of solidity to back it up. I almost stopped breathing at how extraordinary she was.

I flicked a glance at her two companions. Both male,

both vampires of course, both tall. As tall as Michel. One was dressed in, what I guess you'd call, a frock coat. It was black and long, like a suit jacket but all the way down to just below his knees. The cut was perfect, fitting against the shape of his shoulders, moulding to the line of his body, but the style screamed old. His trousers weren't the same colour, but a lighter grey and he wore polished black leather shoes on his feet. I let my eyes travel back up the length of him, past the lapels of his coat where a strange looking brooch sat pinned to his left breast and then gazed on to his face. He had an aristocratic look to him, it was more to do with the way he held his head than his features; stiff necked, chin up, looking down his nose at you. He was austere but handsome, despite the harshness of his posture. His eyes shone a liquid brown, his hair a sleek dark brown, brushed tightly against his scalp and tied back closely to the nape of his neck.

The other vampire was more relaxed, giving you the sense that he was younger than the frock coat vampire, but the *Sanguis Vitam* signature told otherwise. They were both about 500 years old, Frock Coat a little older. The younger looking one was dressed in a suit; dark grey, with a pale mauve shirt on underneath and grey tie, Windsor knot at his neck.

Number two vampire had a pleasant face, not handsome, but not unattractive either, just a softness to the edges. His mouth a little small, his chin not quite as strong, but his eyes a lovely shade of blue, almost blueberry blue, intense and deep, as though something could be hidden in them. He smiled at me, making his eyes sparkle and his face suddenly seem very handsome indeed.

His hair was loose, down round his shoulders. Light brown with stripes of blonde, not highlights, but actual stripes, as though someone had died it that way, methodically, on purpose and with much effort. His hair had a soft wave to it, that made it fan around his shoulders and shift as though alive when he moved his head. Like his eyes, his hair was mesmerizing.

There was one thing to be said, none of the *Iunctio* so far appeared to be lacking in the beauty department.

That thought must have got through to the Champion, because she shut her open mouth and stood a little taller, staring me down.

"You were dead." A statement, not a question, so I didn't answer. What would I have said anyway? "Michel was dying."

Michel. Oh shit, I hadn't even checked him. I did a stupid thing then and turned my back on the vampires. Stupid, reckless and *so* not a vampire hunter move. Amateur. So, I stopped myself and turned back slowly, instead allowing my senses to flow down that metaphysical line that connected us, the Bond, and sensing he was still in there, just hidden away, shut down, but alive. I poked him down the line, but didn't get an answer.

But, I had more pressing things right now to deal with, so I breathed a little Light towards him and kept my eye on the Champion.

"How are you alive?" she asked. Regaining some of her composure, no longer quite so stunned.

OK. So, she'd asked a question now and I was guessing she wanted an answer, just a shame I didn't have one to give.

"I'm not sure how." Well, it was the truth. I knew I'd been somewhere close to death, to Heaven if you want to call it that. But I also knew it wasn't me that brought me back. It had nothing to do with anything I did.

"You were drained, we all felt it. Your life force vanished, we felt the loss of your power." She stopped then and cocked her head to the side, as though she was trying to hear something the rest of us could not. "It's back, your power has come back to us and it's....stronger, more." She straightened her head and looked at me, her face a picture of pretty puzzlement. She really was perplexed. "I demand you tell me how."

Her voice had gone lower, not a growl, but a definite threat. She wanted me to tell her, but I had no idea what to say. She'd sense a lie, a falsehood, but then the truth? Would she believe me? Could she accept it?

I sighed. She frowned. "I honestly don't know how, Champion. I thought I was dead, I thought I was in Heaven and then she sent me back."

"She?"

"My mother." As soon as I said the words I knew they weren't entirely true, but they also felt right. Had that woman I heard and saw in glimpses, been my mum? My biological mum? But, that didn't quite sit right either. I've seen photos of my mum and she didn't have black hair, but brown. And she didn't look like that face, hers was rounder, softer, smaller. So, if it wasn't my mum, but it felt like I was her child, then...

"Nut. It was Nut"

The Champion actually collapsed then. Frock Coat sweeping a chair out of nowhere to catch her fall, placing her perfectly on her bustled rump in the centre of the hard backed wooden seat.

"This is not possible, but I smell the truth on you."

I knew then, that she was scared. I sensed it, I smelt it, but I also just knew it, like someone had whispered it in my ear. She wasn't scared that I was a Child of Nut. That Nut existed even. She had accepted that long ago. She was scared that if she really wanted me dead again, she wouldn't be able to achieve it. Nut would intervene and bring me back. Shit.

I sunk down into a chair too. No one sweeping it under me, just damn luck it happened to be there.

"You understand. But why you?" Her voice was soft, no vampire mood tricks, just genuine amazement.

"I don't know." The Prophesy maybe, I thought.

She shook her head. "It doesn't work like that. The Prophesy has started, we knew this. We now know that you are the *Sanguis Vitam Cupitor*, you are the key, but *I* can not kill you. I should be able to, so there is a reason for that."

I didn't understand what she was saying. If Nut had saved me now from death, then surely she'd do it again, regardless of who tried to kill me.

"No," the Champion said looking at me and for the first time it didn't hold anger, or hatred. For the first time it looked like she was truly seeing me, almost assessing me. I got a creepy feeling she was sizing me up. Trying to decide how she could use this new information, this new thing she had discovered. She couldn't kill me, there had be a reason why, so what good was I to her? What purpose was I to fill?

"I can see a connection between you and this Hunter." Old Frock Coat could talk and I realised I recognised his voice from those arguing before, he had been the most vehement.

I looked at him, but he only had eyes for the Champion. He was *really* concentrating on seeing her, or around her, something like that.

"There is a reason you are connected, but I cannot determine what it is?"

"How can you see we are connected?" I couldn't see a connection, how could he?

He turned to look at me and it wasn't exactly unpleasant, just neutral, austere. "I am the Diviner. I can sense how people are connected. I can see your Bond to your kindred, its strength, its unyielding connection. I have never seen one before so enduring. I can see you have a connection to another, but until I see you both together, I cannot tell to whom or how. But, I can see you are now connected to the Champion. It isn't weak, but it isn't strong. It just is and I cannot see why."

He'd turned back to look at the Champion, who actually looked a little pale, maybe a little sick. I didn't think she liked the idea of being connected to a Nosferatin. She may be power hungry, but she was not willing to share her own power to get it. She got all the power she needed by heading up the *Iunctio* and being able to tap into its deep pockets of stored Nosferatin powers. She didn't want me this close, but then, neither did I.

Her facial features changed then. It was like watching someone flick a switch. She'd come to a decision and she was ready to move forward with it, regardless of how uncomfortable she had been moments before.

"I cannot kill you, yet you pose a danger to my kind. Until we can discover what your threat is to me through this connection, you will remain here, in the *Palais*."

The Diviner looked like he was going to say something, even the other vampire who had not yet spoken, came forward. Whether they were objecting to keeping us in the *Palais* or just objecting to the fact that we still existed, I couldn't tell, but they were both unhappy. Unhappy and scared. I didn't think I had ever seen vampires of their *Sanguis Vitam* level, so scared.

The Champion waved them both aside and stood to leave. "You will be escorted to your chamber and tomorrow evening when Michel has recovered we will dine and then we will see."

She floated out of the room. Both the Diviner and the younger looking vampire paused to look at me, then followed on behind her like loyal little lap dogs.

I was left sitting there with my heart in my throat and my mind spinning out of control. I glanced at the two bodyguards, but they had turned their back to me and were standing in front of the open doors, blocking. I wasn't sure what, it wasn't like I could run and leave Michel here and escape on my own, so maybe they were blocking anyone else from getting to us. Not a nice thought.

I slid off the chair next to Michel and touched his shoulder. I could sense him there, but he felt so far away.

"Michel?" Nothing. He wasn't breathing, which isn't saying much, vampires don't need to breathe to survive. He didn't move.

"Michel, wake up!" Still nothing.

I hadn't reached the spot where I'd normally start wringing my hands yet, I was concerned, but not worried. I could feel Michel there, I just had to think of a way to reach him.

Michel. Come back to me. Still nothing, no hint he had heard me in his mind. No hint he had felt me, nothing.

"Shit."

"Your language has always been the most endearing feature of your character, little Hunter."

I spun around and there was Gregor. My breath caught in my throat at the sight of him; tall, handsome, beautiful. His eyes flashing splashes of silver in amongst deeper greys, with the odd fleck of platinum. His smile beguiling. I don't think I even noticed the scar any more, hidden by his natural beauty and the sparkle of my *Sigillum.*

I found myself on my feet and in his arms before I even realised what I was doing. His laugh rumbling around the room as he spun me.

He gently placed me back on my feet in front of him and bent his head to my ear to whisper, "I do not think the *Iunctio* would be used to the Enforcer being greeted thus."

I pulled back and whispered, "Oops."

His eyes flashed, but his smile was wicked.

"I am here to escort you to your chamber."

I let a breath out and glanced over my shoulder at Michel, still on the floor.

I guess we'd be unpacking after all.

Chapter 31
Compromising Position

"I can't wake him."

Gregor and I had been in our chamber for about twenty minutes and I had done everything I could think of to reach Michel. I tried to talk to him, plead with him, shout at him. I'd sent thoughts and attempted to send images. I pulled on the connection we shared, tugged it, yanked it, shook it. I'd even gathered my Light and thrust it at him, against his shields, over the top of his walls. I thought that last would work, but all it did was bathe Gregor in it's afterglow and make him slump to the floor off the chair he had been sitting on. I didn't think he was complaining.

"He just won't wake."

"Maybe, it's a time thing. Maybe you will have to let him rest and he will come to you when ready." Gregor hadn't moved from the floor, his foot resting against my calf, where I was kneeling next to the bed.

The chamber was, in fact, more like a hotel suite and nothing like the utilitarian waiting room we had just come from. It consisted of a large lounge with luxurious furnishings and every amenity you could desire, a kitchenette, a bathroom and a large bedroom with equally large bed. We were in the bedroom, Gregor had Michel placed there. I was at his side and Gregor had been watching my attempts from a chair in the corner.

I sat back down on the floor and faced him. Maybe he was right, I'd tried everything I could think of, but although I could still sense Michel there, I just couldn't get him to come out.

"So, now what?"

"Be patient, *ma petite chasseuse*. You can sense him there, no?"

I nodded. He stood then, with that otherworldly grace and reached his hand down to me. I looked at it briefly and placed my hand in his, letting him pull me to my feet. He didn't try to pull too hard, to bring me against his chest. A part of me was disappointed and another part just thought how tacky that would have been right next to Michel lying unconscious in bed.

Gregor went to lead me out of the bedroom, but I pulled against his hold.

"I need to stay near him, watch him." I couldn't think of leaving Michel.

"It's all right, Lucinda. We will watch him from in the lounge, but you are tired, you need rest and food, I think."

He was right, I was feeling exhausted all of a sudden. He led me by my hand to the couch and sat me down, then disappeared into the kitchenette, returning a few minutes later with a plate with cheese and crackers and fresh fruit displayed on it. And a large glass of chilled water.

"It's not much, *ma cherie.* I am afraid my skills lie elsewhere. However, I would be more than happy to show you some time." His face had taken on that slightly wicked look, eyebrows raised, crooked smile.

"Not now, Gregor." There was just too much to think about right now, but I was smiling. Somehow Gregor always managed to make me smile.

He didn't argue, just sat down next to me on the couch and settled in to watch me eat. I got a strange sense of deja vu then, Michel liked to watch me eat too. I shook my head.

"So, you bathed the entire *Iunctio* in your Light and angered the Champion enough to see you dead, yet here you are. You are an enigma, my little Hunter. A beautiful, captivating enigma."

I smiled. "That about sums it up."

"I have one question for you."

"Shoot."

He smiled again. "Your Light was different from that which you have bathed myself and Michel in, how is that?"

I hadn't really thought about it before. When I'd shared my Light with both Michel and Gregor it had been instinctive, natural, it came from somewhere deep within me. But when I sent my Light out through the building, touching on every vampire in its path, I had controlled it, thought about how I wanted it to be received. I hadn't let it get out of hand, I suppose, kept it as a safety and a warmth and a love and a happiness, nothing more.

I blushed slightly as I realised that for both Michel and Gregor it had been much more intimate and I hadn't even been aware that was what I had sent out. I had thought that was just the way my Light appeared.

"I guess I'm learning control." It was the only thing I could think of to say.

He laughed, that little huff of a laugh he does. "Please, don't feel the need to control anything when you are around me."

I blushed further. "You didn't like my Light from earlier?"

He leaned forward and placed his hand gently on my cheek, letting it trace down the side of my face, until his fingers were cupping my chin. "It was wonderful, but I have tasted more and I hunger now for only that."

His eyes were intense; swirls of silver in deep grey. They held me captive, stilling my breath, but making my heartbeat flutter like a butterfly caught in a jar.

I sensed Michel then, just a slight stir towards consciousness. My head swivelled towards the bedroom and Gregor let go of my chin. Sitting back against the pillows at his end of the couch.

"He's waking." I couldn't hide my joy, my relief at knowing he was going to be OK.

"You love him very much." It was a statement, but I felt he deserved an answer anyway.

"Yes, I do, but he frustrates me." I laughed slightly, then took a breath in. "He challenges me and sometimes, I think, he believes he owns me."

Gregor laughed at that. "You cannot blame him, *ma cherie*, you are a prize any man would wish to possess."

"But I am not a possession, Gregor, you'd do well to remember that too."

He nodded, a slow nod. "Still, we are vampyre." I hadn't heard him use the old pronunciation before. Michel did, all the time, but Gregor had more of a modern turn of phrase, most of the time, occasionally he sounded old fashioned. "It is in our nature to amass power and you are power, *ma petite chasseuse.* You are an awful lot of power."

Huh. "Is that all I am to him, to *you*?" I was looking at him closely, hoping to tell if he lied, to see a hint of something, but Gregor isn't a member of the *Iunctio* without having picked up a few diplomatic skills. He could hide his feelings just as well as the next.

His face was a pleasant smile, his eyes sparkling just a hint. He didn't answer straight away, just leaned forward and picked the tray of crackers and fruit off the couch, which had been sitting between us, and placed it on a low table to the side, then moved closer. I suddenly felt like a possum caught in the headlights of an on-coming car. I couldn't move or breath, but I knew I should stop him, I just didn't know how.

He ran a hand down my cheek, brushing my hair back from my face, his other hand taking one of my own and running small circles on my palm. I wasn't sure how he could do the two actions at the same time and not be jerky. You know, like when you rub a circle on your tummy and pat up and down on your head at the same time, it's harder than it sounds. But somehow he made each movement perfect, as though all of his attention was on that and not on my face, my mouth, my lips.

“Perhaps I should just show you, what it is you mean to me.”

And with that, he closed the gap between us, his hand at my face slipping behind my head, to rest at the base of my neck, so warm against the skin there, and pulled me towards him. His other hand, which had been holding mine, now slipping behind the small of my back and pulling me against his chest and his lips claiming me in a soft, eager, hungry pursuit.

I didn't stop him and I should have. I didn't push him away and I should have. I found my hands going up around his neck, into his hair, removing the clip at the base of his head and spreading my fingers through the strands. And then I kissed him back.

He tasted divine. Hints of chocolate and ice cream, I could smell strawberries and raspberries and I wanted more. God help me, but I wanted more. I was practically in his lap. He'd pulled me so tightly against his chest, but we were still sitting up on the couch, so the angle was all wrong, my back bending backwards, curving the wrong way, just to stay close to his body. He realised it would have been uncomfortable, but rather than releasing me, he simply lay back down on his back, on the couch, pulling me up his chest, so I was lying on the full length of him.

His tongue devouring me, his hands covering every inch of my back, up into my hair and down to my rear. Everywhere he touched felt wonderful, alive, calling for more. I could feel just how happy he was to have me there too, his hardness pressing against me, almost perfectly placed and I think that managed to break through a bit of the fog. I hesitated, stopped kissing him back, but he simply moved his hips against me, making my body respond all on its own.

My legs slid out to either side of him, so I was straddling him, almost kneeling over him, but still pressed firmly against every part of him. And he groaned as he moved against me, making me tight and wet, wanting more and more than I should ever have wanted from this man.

He didn't try to take it further, yet I wanted him to. He didn't try to get my clothes off, yet I was struggling to undo his shirt, slip my hand inside and feel his skin. It wasn't me that pulled back, but Gregor. And I whimpered in frustration and need.

Breathlessly, against my mouth, he said, “I would die for you, Lucinda. I would cast away everything I possess to be near you. I would take anything you willingly give and no more. *This* is what you mean to me."

My mind was spinning, my heart thumping against the confines of my chest. *Then don't stop.* I managed to throw the thought to him.

He shuddered against me and crushed his lips to mine and just as I thought he was about to take it further, rip my clothes off and satisfy that hunger and need we both felt, I sensed Michel. Awake and aware.

I must have done something, or thought something, because Gregor stopped. We both lay there still. Me a wanton mess on the top of an extremely turned on vampire and said vampire's hands up under my skirt, holding the edge of my underwear, brushing against bare skin.

"I see you have been taking care of my kindred, Gregor."

Oh shit. Big, big, big shit.

"I could not have said it better, *ma douce*."

I raised my head up from Gregor and looked Michel directly in the eyes. They were calm pools of deep, deep blue, only the small flecks of violet and indigo in the mix gave anything away.

I had absolutely no idea what to say to him, but even if I did, I couldn't say it lying on top of Gregor. I sat up away from Gregor's chest, but that only left me straddling his waist, not much of an improvement then. I don't have the otherworldly grace and puppet-on-a-string moves the vampires have, so getting myself off of Gregor's groin was never going to be pretty. But somehow whilst trying to lift the leg against the couch back over his body, I got caught against his thigh and ended up toppled over on my back on the floor, banging into the low table in the process and making the tray of crackers fall off the other side in a loud crash.

I lay there stunned for a moment and then heard a low laughter coming from Michel. I glanced over at him standing in the doorway of the bedroom, with his fingers to the bridge of his nose, shaking his head.

"Only you could make such a move, *ma douce* and yet still be adorable."

Huh, well at least I was still adorable and not dumped on my arse outside the door with a packed suitcase. I sat up slowly to find Gregor leaning over the side of the couch watching me calmly, a slight curve to his lips.

"Why are you so calm about this?" I was looking at Michel again as I asked that.

He came further into the room and sat down on an armchair just to the side of the couch, with a clear view of me on the floor. Crossed his legs and looked down at me. Gregor hadn't moved.

"Oh, I am not calm, *ma douce*, merely practical. I will not share you lightly, but.... I do believe I broke the treaty first, so it is only fair that Gregor has had his chance."

Gregor sat up at that and turned to look at Michel, his head cocked to the side. "You broke the treaty?" His voice was low, even, the kind of voice vamps get when they're working to stay in control.

"What treaty?" That was me, still on the floor.

"Our agreement, *ma douce*. Have you forgotten it already?"

"What agreement?" Still confused, not quite on the same page.

"The agreement you made Gregor and myself subject to. To... now what were your exact words? *Give me space. I need to sort this out in my head. Please don't push me. Let me find my way.* That agreement. I do believe your intention was *not* to get pushed into a compromising position with either of us for a while. Would that be correct?"

Huh. That agreement. "Yeah."

"Yeah," he repeated. It sounded funny coming from him. "I merely assume you are levelling the battlefield with our dear Gregor here.

Levelling the what?

Michel sighed and rubbed the bridge of his nose again, I suddenly realised he was probably not 100% after what had happened with the Champion. Man, did that make me feel worse.

"Lucinda. I took advantage of your fragility when you came to me upon hearing of the trouble with the Taniwhas. Gregor has only done the same now, after your confrontation with the Champion. It is in our natures. We find it hard to resist an opportunity when so presented."

I just wasn't getting it. Yes, I had been upset when I came to Michel after hearing from Jerome, but he had done everything in his power to give me control of that moment, refusing to even kiss me until I asked him to. I was the one that had taken it the step further. I was the one that had lowered my hastily built walls and let him back in. So, why was he saying he had taken advantage of me? I needed him, he gave me what I wanted only when I asked.

And then I got it. He wasn't saying this for Gregor's benefit, or because of any stupid treaty or agreement that we have made. He was saying this to remind me. To remind me of what we shared and how it hadn't been. He had not taken advantage of me, he had let me come to him, but Gregor, right now, that was a different thing altogether.

I was both upset and exhausted from confronting the Champion, nearly dying and losing Michel. Gregor had pushed me, maybe even taken advantage of me, I'm not sure, but he certainly hadn't stopped me from making a mistake when I was *so* not my normal self. But this knowledge only made me angry with Michel. Angry that he was proving a point like this, in this way. For making me feel used by Gregor now and dirty for doing it, all under the pretence of it being OK. Acceptable. Just what vampires are. But really, to make me recognise, that Michel was the good guy and Gregor was the bad. I've never liked round about ways of saying something. If you've got something to say, don't beat around the bush, just say it.

His eyes hadn't left me as I'd processed all of this. There was a slight coldness there, a calculating intelligence. Oh Michel, if this wasn't manipulation, then what was?

But what I said was, “OK. Battlefield levelled. I'm taking a shower.”

And I walked out of the room.

Chapter 32
Dinner

I managed to find some more of my regular hunting outfits in my suitcase after I had showered. In amongst pretty dresses and sparkling evening wear, which I reluctantly hung up in the wardrobe. How Michel expected me to wear long dresses around so many vampires who want me dead, I did not know. But he had put in some black gear and thankfully, some short skirts and tight tops. My comfortable, easy-to-move-in hunter gear. Yippee.

So, dressed in familiar near Gothic-look ensemble, including two stakes and a silver knife inside my black jacket - I know, what did I think I needed those for in the *Palais*, but a hunter is always a hunter - I felt able to face whatever waited for me out in the lounge. When I came out of the bedroom however, Gregor was gone and Michel was reclining on the couch, eyes closed, hand still to the bridge of his nose. Ah damn, he never looked like this. He must have been suffering.

He opened his eyes and looked at me. I didn't move, just held his gaze, trying not to sink into those beautiful blue pools of sparkling light. I was still angry with him and definitely uncomfortable about how he had found me and Gregor, I so didn't want to crumble under that gaze. He just smiled slowly, he knew how hard I found it to resist.

"Come sit with me, *ma douce*." He held a hand out for me to take.

I hesitated.

"Please, *ma douce*, I need you close."

That did it. I could not deny him my strength when he looked so tired, so *not* him. I slipped onto the sofa next to him and let him wrap me in his arms. My head resting on his chest, my feet both up on the seat, under my legs. I was almost curled in a little ball next to him. I guess part of that may have been to protect me, from what he might say, but I didn't care what message it sent, I felt a little fragile myself.

He kissed the top of my head, leaving his nose in my hair. I knew he'd be inhaling my scent, taking me all in. It's just a vampire thing, they can't help it. Scent is important to them. I found it a little strange, when I first met Michel. Even before I really got to know him, he'd find ways to get close to me, to smell my hair, or when he kissed the back of my hand formally, he'd linger there. It didn't take long for me to realise he was smelling me and I admit at first I thought it weird, but once you start to understand a creature, it's easier to accept what they do as normal. Hell, even I enjoy people's scent more now than I used to.

"Where's Gregor?" I don't know why I said it, it just came out. Stupid foot in mouth moment. I wasn't even thinking of him as I said it, I was thinking about Michel holding me in his arms, so why, oh why, did I mention *the other man?*

Michel stiffened, just slightly. I think it was a reaction he couldn't control, one he then tried to hide, but failed miserably.

"Why do you ask?" His voice was even, neutral. I knew better.

"Just wondering."

"Just wondering. Mm-hmm."

Oh dear, this was not going well.

"Should I be apologising?" It came out a bit harshly.

I really don't know what was wrong with me, I could

have been handling this so much better. Michel had been sitting here waiting to cuddle me, prepared, no doubt, to sweep everything aside and just comfort me in his arms. So why was *I* so angry? Angry at him. But I was, I realised, I was so, so angry at him. For putting me in this position, for acting like he owned me, for degrading me in front of Gregor. For even coming to me that first day we met, when he walked into the bank in broad daylight and I knew my life as I had known it was over. For making me what I am today. Damn him. Damn him to hell.

"Do you have something you wish to say to me, Lucinda?"

Oh, and there you have it, we'd made it to Lucinda, bypassed *my dear* and got right to the end mark. This was really not going well, was it?

"I don't like the way you made your point before." Perhaps honesty was the ticket here.

"And I do not like finding my kindred Nosferatin on top of a rival vampyre while I have been compromised so."

I pulled away from him. It's hard to continue to cuddle into someone when they're angry and you're angry and everyone's just so damn angry.

"Do you think I hadn't looked after you?" I demanded.

"You tell me. I was out cold. The first thing I hear is you telling Gregor to *don't stop.*"

Oh bugger. He'd heard that thought.

"I don't always have control over how I react around Gregor, you know that. And besides, hadn't we *all* decided Gregor could be a part of our lives. All so bohemian."

He stood up abruptly then, so quickly I couldn't even appreciate the grace and walked away from me, turning when he reached the far wall and just glaring. The deep blue of his eyes had lightened and flashes of indigo and violet were swirling in their midsts.

"It was not *my* desire to have Gregor so close and... perhaps you should learn some control."

"What? You acted as if it was OK, as if it was par for the course, unavoidable. And control huh? *Perhaps* I don't want to learn control." OK. So, now I think I was just saying anything to get a reaction, to hurt, because I was hurting. But that was so not what I had meant to say. *So* not.

"Is that what you wish?" He'd gone so still.

No. I wanted to say. No dammit. I really wanted to say: I want you and only you, but you keep doing things that aren't fair, that make me feel small and used and just something you want to possess. You keep shifting the goal posts and I don't know what's right or wrong or out of my control. Or something I should be able to just say no to anymore. But what I said was, "Maybe." Jeez, could I possibly be putting my foot any further in my mouth here?

I think he'd stopped breathing. There was definitely no blinking, he was shutting down, he was shutting me out. I wanted to go to him and tell him I was sorry. Tell him I didn't mean it, but a small part of me kept saying, you have a right to be angry, you have been used and manipulated and you are *not* a possession.

So, I just sat there and watched him. So still, so unmoving, waiting for *him* to say he understood, to say he was sorry, but he's a vampire and a vampire is as a vampire does.

"I need to feed." It was so not what I thought he'd say, I

just blinked and looked at him.

"I am weak. Whatever happened with the Champion, I have not fully recovered. And we must face them again tomorrow night. I need to feed."

"You don't want to discuss this any more?" Was he just giving up, ignoring it, trying to piss me off some more?

"Lucinda!" That made me jump. His voice bounced around the room, I had a brief moment to duck before the lamp next to me on a side table shattered, shards of china from its base flying out in all directions, scraping along my hands as they covered my head. Luckily I had my jacket on, but my hands bloody hurt.

He was upon me in the next instant, lifting me up off the couch by my arms, his fingers digging into my flesh, through the jacket, shaking me, like a rag doll. Shaking me, like he thought he could shake some sense into me.

"We do not have time for this! Do you not understand the danger we are still in?" He'd stopped shaking me, just held me off the ground by his hands at this stage. I couldn't reach the floor, so I tried to get my feet under me on the couch at least, but he simply took a step backward, away from that last hope of support and kept me dangling in the air. It wasn't nice, it hurt like hell and made me feel small. Again.

"So, what? You want to ignore the whole Gregor issue?" I asked, face blank.

"You are the one obsessed with Gregor. Not me." His voice was low, a definite threat.

Was I? I thought we needed to get this sorted. I just about had sex with another man, shouldn't this be something we discussed? Come to an understanding on, decide where to from here? Hell I don't know, but ignoring it, that just seemed wrong.

"Lucinda. I need to feed." It was almost desperate this time, pleading.

"Well, you're not getting any from me." And with that, I knew I'd just done the most irreparable damage I could have possibly achieved to our relationship. He actually looked stunned. Then quickly recovered himself and placed me gently on the ground. He didn't push me, he didn't throw me, he just gently placed me on my feet.

"I shall order in take out then." His voice so hollow, so not Michel.

He turned and went to the phone, hanging on the wall by the door. He spoke briefly in French into the mouthpiece, then hung up and rounded to look at me. A small amount of magenta now edging the violet and blue of his eyes.

"So, now they know. You will not feed me. They know we have a weakness."

"Is that all that matters to you, Michel? That we appear weak in front of our enemies?"

"When at war, that is all there is, Lucinda."

"No. It's not."

We stood staring at each other for a long time, long enough for the *take out* to be delivered. The knock on the door making us both startle a little. I didn't want to see who it was. Male or female. Young or old. Black or white. There's just some things, you can't make yourself confront no matter how tough a vampire hunter you are.

Michel didn't answer the door straight away, just looked at the discomfort on my face. Then he simply walked across to the bedroom and said, "Show them in, would you? I will freshen up and await my meal in here." Shutting the door to the bedroom behind him.

Bastard. The door reverberated with another louder knock. I could have ignored it, just gone into the kitchen and Michel could have starved. The *meal* leaving when no one answered the door. I could have, you know, I was angry enough. They knocked again, more demanding, but still not quite bringing down the house. I sighed. Michel was lashing out, part of me acknowledging that he may have just cause *and* he was weak. Could I just go to him and bare my neck and say, *here slip your fangs in*? I shook my head. Another knock, not quite so certain, on the door.

That's what he wanted of course, for me to capitulate. My staunch opposition to him ever feeding from any one else, making me go to him now and offering my vein. He should have known me better than that. I do not like being backed into a corner.

I went to the door and swung it wide open. A young female human stood across the threshold. She blinked, recognising immediately that I wasn't a vampire. She glanced quickly at the number of our chamber at the side of the door, then back to me and frowned.

Of course, she was pretty, in a French casual chic kind of way. Long auburn hair, down past her shoulders, wrapping around her neck, no doubt to hide any recent fang marks. Not that Michel always took from the neck, there were other more intimate, larger veins that did just as well. *Oh hell, Lucinda! Stop it!*

She had large hazel eyes, with thick lashes, a shapely body, contained in casual dress trousers and a black blouse with tiny embroidered flowers all over it. And she was, of course, taller than me.

"You must be dinner." So, I was pissed off and feeling small, sue me.

"*Excusez-moi?*"

Great, no English.

"*Vampire, dans la.*" I pointed to the bedroom and she smiled, waltzed past me, with her hips swaying and her beautifully curvy body moving to some music I couldn't hear.

She knocked on the bedroom door and I suddenly did not want to be there when Michel opened it and saw what his dinner would entail. So I slipped out of the front door to our chamber and firmly closed it behind me, sinking to the floor on my butt, legs pulled up tight, arms around them, holding them close and face hiding between my knees.

I didn't want to think about what Michel was doing. Unless in a battle, feeding is a very intimate, personal thing. The bite can be painful, it can be made excruciating, but most vampires when they feed on willing donors, make it pleasurable. Pleasure to a vampire is desire, sex, the loss of inhibitions. Donors like our tall and auburn-haired French pretty, could become addicted to it. Why wasn't I? Michel and I shared a Bond, feeding was intimate because we made it so, but only because I allowed it be. I could have switched that part of me off, just like I shield from his *Sanguis Vitam.* Regular humans can not.

French Pretty would be enjoying herself very soon and I was sitting outside the chamber door like some love sick puppy cast aside. I hadn't planned on crying, I even considered just getting up and walking away, that's what a strong vampire hunter would have done. But I was so hurt, I felt so small and even the anger I had felt at Michel was numbed by the sheer injustice of it all. By the fact that *my* vampire was about to place his lips against that perfectly smooth, young flesh of a willing female donor and make her feel things that only I should be feeling.

Well, you got yourself into this position, you've only got yourself to blame, my internal monologue piped up. I just sobbed harder into my knees.

It hadn't escaped me that I'd had my lips on someone else's flesh, other than my kindred vampire's, but it' just no consolation when it happens to you, is it? And, he had made me so angry. He had done this on purpose. Everything Michel does is planned. Don't worry about how we get there, just do whatever is needed to win, to survive.

I hated him right then, with such a bitter hatred it made me cry even harder, but these were no longer tears of loss, of pain. They were tears of frustration and anger. Frustration of having him make me feel all of these awful emotions when all I really wanted was him to help me out of this mess.

I don't know how long I'd been sitting there, not long enough for French Pretty to come out of the room though. And if Michel had fed like he normally does, it should have only taken a minute, maybe two, considering how weak he was feeling, but not the many I felt it had been. No, he was either taking his sweet friggin' time about it, or progressed to more pleasurable pursuits than just feeding.

I balled my fists and slammed them into the carpeted floor by my sides.

"Is there a reason you are beating up the floor, little

Hunter?"

I lifted my tear stained face to Gregor. His teasing smile faltered slightly and he slowly sat himself down next to me, back against the same door.

"I take it, things did not go well after I left?"

I humphed a sound, quite unattractive I might add, but didn't elaborate further.

He's friggin' feeding. He's friggin' feeding. It seemed to be all I could think.

"Ah," Gregor said. I didn't even worry that he'd heard my thoughts.

He stood then, that beautiful magical swish from floor to standing in a smooth motion and held his hand out to me.

I just looked at it, not comprehending.

"Come, little Hunter. Let me show you *Paris*." He said *Paris*, like the French do, not pronouncing the s and rolling the r, so it's kind of like Parree, but prettier.

I shook my head.

"Do you really wish to be here when the donor comes out bathed in the afterglow of a feeding?" He said it gently, softly. He wasn't trying to hurt.

I gulped in a breath of air. *No friggin' way!*

"That's my girl. The night is still young and there is so much to see in this fair city."

I attempted a smile, it was small and probably pathetic, but it did make me feel better and took his hand, allowing him to pull me to my feet. His arm went around my shoulders and before I could protest, he whispered in my ear, "This is how the French do it, *ma petite chasseuse.* Let us do as the locals do, *non*?"

Yeah ri-ight. But I didn't make him pull away.

Chapter 33
Champs-Elysées

I don't remember how we got to the *Champs-Elysées*. We travelled in an *Iunctio* car; black, long and with tinted windows, driven by a vampire driver. I vaguely remember the driver saying something to Gregor when he'd flashed a look on me and Gregor's *Sanguis Vitam* pouring over me towards the other vampire. But I don't know what was said or what it all meant. Gregor simply bundled me into the back of the limousine and sat next to me, not touching, but watching.

My mind was elsewhere, on thoughts I really shouldn't have been indulging. They were dangerous and painful and didn't do a thing to help me slow my breathing or still my rapidly beating heart. Or take away the ache that had settled in my chest, threatening to consume me.

The world was suddenly darker than the night alone should have made it. The only thing stopping me from falling completely into that darkness was the lights of the *Avenue des Champs-Elysées.* They sparkled. Not just from the lights of the traffic, which were plenty; both diamonds and rubies, jewels shining in the night, but the glittering decorations of the trees that lined the eight lane road on either side. Like Christmas trees in December. Bright dots of dancing white, splashes of yellow and gold, hints of diamonds and crystals, glowing and warming the night. At the end of all that splendour was the majestic *Arc de Triomphe* also lit up like a centrepiece, sitting proud at the end of all that magical light. No wonder they called this city the *City of Light*.

"Do you like it, my little Hunter?" The first words

Gregor had uttered since we got in the car.

"It's beautiful. The lights." I didn't know what else to say, they took my breath away, but in a wondrous, most happy way. They had the ability to lift my soul, when I had only moments before thought that an impossibility, lost to me forever.

"I could not think of another place in *Paris* that would help you more."

I turned to look at him, trying to see what he meant. Had he known the lights would help? Had he chosen this on purpose? Did he know me better than I knew myself?

"Thank you," was all I could think of to say. I turned back to the lights.

Gregor leaned forward and said something in French to the driver. I didn't pay attention, I just let the lights wash over me and felt a small shadow of warmth seep in, chasing away the chill of before.

The car pulled to the side of the road, negotiating the hordes of vehicles, like the parting of the Red Sea. They simply moved out of the driver's way, almost a dance-like movement, as though it had been rehearsed and practised for years. We stopped next to the curb and some brightly lit shops and cafés, all of which seemed to be open, even though we must have been well into the wee hours of the morning by now. Clearly this city never slept.

The driver came to open my door and I took his offered hand. There is no elegant way to exit a car in a short skirt, you take every advantage offered to you, otherwise you could end up flashing the world. I did not particularly wish to flash the Parisians on the pavement, somehow their own sophisticated demeanour making me want to improve my own casual and less than graceful ways. The driver's hand was cold, he hadn't fed recently, unusual. Vampires were normally more careful than this. A human touching that hand might have been alarmed. I just looked at him as his gaze met mine and tried not to blink as hunger filled his eyes and they shifted to my neck.

In a flash Gregor was gripping his hand, another wave of *Sanguis Vitam* flowing out towards the driver. He uttered a few short words in French, quietly, so as not to arouse the attention of the many people sauntering along the wide footpath arm in arm. I understood him this time, *go feed, before you expose us all*. It was a command. So, was this one of Gregor's own vampires, or was he simply able to command him because of who Gregor was? Could he command an *Iunctio* flunky like one of his own line? I didn't know and I also didn't want to know. The thought that this leech could belong to Gregor was not happy, neither was the thought that Gregor had the power to influence others who weren't part of his line. I decided it might be best to remain ignorant on this one.

The driver bowed, not too low as to get looks from passers-by, but enough to show respect and returned to his side of the vehicle. Gregor turned to me and flashed a smile, letting a little sparkle enter his eyes and my *Sigillum* shine a little brighter. Seeing the *Sigillum* come alive was enough to make me reach for for him, even before he'd begun to offer his arm. He cocked his head slightly, then the smile lit up even further. That wonderful display of beguiling innocence, laced with a hint of more wicked things to come.

"Shall we walk, *ma petite chasseuse*?"

I nodded and snuggled in next to his arm, for some reason unable to keep a respectable distance between us. What was wrong with me? He shifted his arm to around my shoulders, pulling the length of my body against his firm side. Making me mould into him and making me wrap my own arm around his waist and feel his warmth. It sent tingles down my body and made me catch me breath. Damn it, what was wrong with me tonight?

I took a deep breath to clear my head and felt marginally better. I could still feel him, it still felt good, but I could think a little now too.

"Why are all the shops still open, it's late?" Surely, even Paris had to sleep.

"The *Champs-Elysées* is very important to the vampires. Did you know *Champs-Elysées* is French for Elysian Fields?"

I shook my head. "What is the Elysian Fields?"

"*Elysium* is the place of the blessed dead. It is the afterlife for those related to the gods. Elysian Fields is considered the garden of *Elysium*, where we can come to play before returning to that realm. It exists solely because of the vampyre and therefore its hours are made to suit our needs."

"You feed here?" Feeding was a vampire need. I was a little shocked they'd feed openly here. Vampires nowadays, usually fed in private, off the streets, away from discovery, using only those donors aware and willing. Those that feed on the street are usually rogue, full of evil and what I am made to hunt.

"Among other things. *Paris* is different from the rest of the world, *ma cherie*. It is the home of the *Iunctio*, the seat of all our power and as such, certain liberties are available to us."

Oh that was so wrong. "Have you fed tonight? Or are you planning on picking up a little something along the way?"

He laughed, my temper not having a blind bit of effect on him. "*Ma cherie*, I have fed already this night, you need not worry, however should you be offering..." He let the sentence hang in the air.

Not in this lifetime, I thought.

He just laughed harder, pulling me tighter to him, making me feel the rumble go through his body and then into mine. I took another deep breath in and failed to hold on to my anger.

"Have you eaten, little Hunter? You hardly touched your plate of food in your chamber, I am guessing you have not eaten anything else since?"

As soon as he said it, my stomach rumbled, as though on cue. He manoeuvred us towards a brightly lit café, which had a red awning over the gold framed glass windows, simply saying *Fouquet's*. We were greeted at the door by a doorman, who seemed to recognise Gregor and rushed to seat us at a window seat, shooing away a waiter in the process and taking it upon himself to be our personal maître d'. The plush red and black, with gold trim seats, were both facing the street, making Gregor close to me and nothing between us as we sat. His leg brushed mine and my heart skipped a beat. I shook my head in disbelief. Everything he seemed to be doing tonight had a far greater effect on me than usual. It just didn't make any sense at all.

The maître d' handed me a menu, he didn't bother to

hand one to Gregor, simply leaving us for the time being. It surprised me, that he had known Gregor would not eat. I was not used to humans being so aware of the creatures of the night.

"Does he know what you are?" I whispered.

"Of course. This is the *Champs-Elysées*." He didn't elaborate further, he seemed to think the answer alone was sufficient. I guess it was. He'd said the *Champs-Elysées* was there because of the vampires, I guess he had meant it.

I studied the menu, just for something to do. I was hungry, but not really seeing the words in front of me. Traditional French cuisine, but for the life of me, I couldn't decipher one word from the other.

Gregor reached over and took the menu form my hands, placing it on the table next to him. He took my hand in his and ran circles around my palm. The movement calming me immediately, helping me to focus on his eyes; flashing silver, with hints of grey.

I just stared at him, unable to pull my gaze away. He didn't shift under my scrutiny, just ate me up with his look, devouring every inch of my face.

"You have no idea how much I have wanted to have you here in *Paris* with me," he whispered, still devouring me with his eyes.

"I thought Rome was your home."

"Rome is my work, *Paris* is where I play."

I didn't miss the innuendo, instead I leaned in a little closer, completely unable to stop myself. His hand went up to my face, cupping it, stroking along my jaw. My lips parted, again all of their own accord and my eyes kept tracing the line of his mouth, the curve of his own lips.

Making me want more than anything to bridge the small gap that remained and taste him, lick him, consume him. All of him.

"You have bewitched me, *ma cherie*. I can't seem to stop wanting you more and more. What would you have of me? I am yours." His voice was slightly husky, low, barely a whisper, but I heard every one.

Before I could even think of a response, the words were out of mouth. "Kiss me." Part of me yelling, *what the fuck?* Another part wanting, needing, pleading for this to happen.

His eyes flashed platinum, making me blink mine to stop from being blinded and he pulled me against his chest as he whispered, "Yes."

The touch of his lips at first so soft, but as soon as skin met skin, I felt a jolt of liquid heat rush through me, straight to him and he made a small inarticulate sound and pulled me closer. His tongue devouring mine, his mouth smothering mine, his need just as strong as mine. I gave as good as I got, attempting to suck his very soul out of his mouth. I think we had both forgotten where we were, still very public, sitting in a café on the *Champs-Elysées* with other customers all around.

We only pulled apart from one another when I started to feel faint from lack of air and it was only then that I noticed the waiters had quietly surrounded our table with screens, providing us privacy from the people in the restaurant, but unable to stop anyone from glancing in the windows. I had to convince myself that no one had bothered to look, but I had no proof, it was a hollow thought, and even then it didn't seem to matter.

While I tried to catch my breath and Gregor continued to gaze at me with utter desire written across his face, I kept thinking, what has got into me? What on Earth has got into me? Only moments before I had been upset at Michel, but still wanting him with every fibre of my body. But right now all I wanted was Gregor and to hell with Michel. What the..?

The thought was gone as soon as it came, with the feel of Gregor's hand on my own, stroking softly, sending more and more shivers down my body. The maître d' came and Gregor said something in French, eyes only for me.

Moments later we had still not moved. Stuff the view from our window, I couldn't have told you if people even existed on the street outside. Then the maître d' came back with a frothy coffee and a slice of delightfully looking cake. It looked like a chocolate cake, layered with sponge in between the sheets of dark rich looking chocolate. I smelled the coffee and almonds before I'd even tasted it and my mouth watered in anticipation.

Gregor laughed; a low chuckle that wrapped around me and stroked down my cheek. "Eat, *ma cherie.* The Opera Gateau waits for no one."

He didn't need to tell me twice, suddenly tasting what was in front of me was irresistible. It did taste as good as it looked too and with the rich creamy coffee, I was in Heaven. Gregor sat back and watched me, his smile wide on his face, his eyes flashing the occasional silver streak.

"Do you miss it? Eating I mean?" I asked between delicious mouthfuls.

"Yes and no. I could taste it also, if I were to kiss you now. I would most definitely taste it, if I were to drink you now. There are ways to taste food, that does not require my eating it."

I laughed. *I bet you just want to taste me right now.*

"More than you can imagine, *ma cherie*."

I flicked him a look, that said *whatever*, but I couldn't stop smiling.

He continued to watch me as though I was a performance, put on especially for him. His own personal opera; every move I made, followed, every bite I took, devoured with his eyes. By the time I finished the cake I was almost beside myself with lust for him. I had no idea how bad it was for Gregor, I could only imagine from the look in his eyes that he was barely containing himself.

He stood up swiftly and reached for my hand, said something to the maître d' then practically pulled me out the front door and down the street.

"Shouldn't we have paid him?" I asked breathlessly.

"He's put it on my tab." OK. So, Gregor had a tab at a restaurant. A top French restaurant on the *Champs-Elysées*. A restaurant where he could not eat the food. Why did that not seem to worry me? Huh.

I followed dutifully behind him for a few metres, then he disappeared down a side alley, pulling me against his body and then crushing me to the brick wall behind my back. It was darker here, we were just out of the light spilling from the pavement of the avenue, in shadow, but I didn't care. His body moulded to the length of mine as his lips traced a trail up my neck, over my jaw and across my cheek. He kissed every inch he could find, tasting, teasing, licking. I knew where he wanted to be, but still he took his sweet time getting there. I wasn't sure if the slow path was for my benefit or his, making the final destination that much sweeter, that much more desirable.

His face buried in my hair, my own hands already tangled in his. I couldn't kiss him back, just had to accept what little pleasure I could get from touching him where I could, his mouth not going anywhere near my lips, but every now and then, so close, so close, that I thought this was it, the wait was over, only to be denied again when he moved away. He hovered over my pulse at the base of my neck, I could feel the tension in him as he struggled to fight the need to bite. He could have tasted what I had eaten through a kiss, but he had denied himself my lips for too long and now he found himself hovering over the sweet smell of my blood, the pulse jumping beneath my skin, no doubt calling to him, enticing him. He groaned, but didn't draw his fangs. It was me who pushed my pulse against his lips, it was me who rubbed my body against the length of him. It was my leg that wrapped around his side and my hand that pushed his head against my skin, forcing his mouth open.

He groaned as his fangs came down and scraped the side of my neck and all I could say was, "Yes."

The sting of the bite was bitter sweet, a sharp stab that didn't so much as hurt, but made me want more pain, more pleasure. The anticipation of his *Sanguis Vitam* about to come flooding in electrifying. He didn't disappoint, his power washing over me in beautiful rushes of desire, hot waves of pleasure and promises of so much more. My body tightened, the heat flowing down through the centre of me and settling between my legs. He gripped my rear and lifted me off the ground, my other leg wrapping around him, so I was pressed against his groin and could feel the full weight of his desire, rock hard against my sensitive place, only making me want more and more.

He pushed against me, rubbing in a slow circular motion with his hips, making me gasp and dig my nails in through his jacket, making me wet with my need. The circular motion changing to a more rhythmic pumping, a rubbing through the material of his trousers and the thin material of my underwear. My skirt long ago hiked up around my waist like a belt, my legs crushing against him, my body moving with each of his thrusts.

I felt his hands against the skin of my upper thighs, under my underwear against my rear, kneading, pulling, moving again in a circular motion. Which only managed to pull the more intimate places of my body, which were being hammered by the hard length of him, in ways that just sent me groaning and panting and pleading for more.

I felt one of his hands move to the front of his trousers, making his body pull away from mine slightly, while he somehow managed to undo his pants. Lowering them enough for his hard length to escape and then coming back to rub against my underwear. No longer hindered by his clothes, but still not able to make steps any closer to being inside me.

I didn't fight him, I wanted him. And that alone should have made me wake up from the fog which had descended. Even when his hand came back between us, and I felt him simply move my knickers aside, still on me, but out of the way, and then the hard wet tip of him rest against my entrance, eager but waiting for me to object.

He withdrew his fangs and licked the spot he had

bitten, bringing his face to look me in the eye. His breath was uneven, his face flushed with more than just my blood and he asked, “Is this what you want?”

I already knew my answer, I had it formed in my head and I opened my mouth to demand it, when I felt it. Stronger than I had ever felt before. Evil-lurks-in-my-city, the Pull that calls to me above all else. And it was shouting.

“Stop,” I breathed.

He looked momentarily disappointed, then embarrassed and then slightly angry. The emotions playing across his features, one after the other, like a movie on a big screen. He recovered himself and pulled away slightly, his erection no longer pressing against my wet folds. I felt bereft, but clear headed, more so than I had ever felt all evening. But, evil was lurking and I couldn't even consider smoothing his ruffled feelings. Someone was about to be hurt and from the level of evil, I had no doubt that it would be fatal.

Gregor lowered me gently to the ground, thank God the wall was behind me, because I don't think I could have stood on my own when his hands left me to quickly make himself presentable again. He ran a hand through his hair as I pulled my underwear back in line and my skirt back down my legs. His eyes unable to meet mine. Aw damn.

“Gregor.”

“I am sorry, Lucinda, I got carried away. I told you once that Nosferatin blood has an effect on me. It seems yours, more so than most. I apologise if I have placed you in a compromising position, it had not been my intention. I swear.”

I took a step away from the wall and didn't collapse, go

me! I came around and stood in front of him, placing my hands on his hunched shoulders. He flinched slightly. I didn't have time for this, but I couldn't just leave him to think it had all been him. That I hadn't wanted him as much as he wanted me. I couldn't believe I let it get to that point, let it get so far, but I had, willingly. And I would not let him take the fall for this.

"Gregor. Look at me. Please." His eyes slowly rose up my body to my face. There was pain in them, such pain it almost made me blanch, but I would not show him my fear. My fear for what he was feeling. I took a breath in. "I wanted you just as much as you wanted me. I still do. I don't know if it's the right thing to do, to want you, but right then, I would not have stopped you for the world, but something is happening. Something I can't ignore."

He looked puzzled, but his hands had come back up to hold my arms, gently, almost tentatively. "What's wrong?"

There's one thing to be said for master vampires, they are very quick to pick up on a threat. I could feel his body tensing already, preparing for a battle. And I knew it wasn't a battle with me he was gearing up for. He had already sensed I was talking about something else, a threat to both of us.

"I can feel an evil pull, my hunter instincts have kicked in. I can sense where they are and what they are about to do. I have to go help whoever is about to be hurt."

He relaxed, just a little, not completely. "Leave it to the local Nosferatin, Lucinda. They will take care of it, you are not here to hunt."

"How many Nosferatins have you got here in Paris?"

"Two or three within the *Boulevard Peripherique*." The

Boulevard Peripherique was the road around central Paris which marked the enormous area all Parisian based vampires were allowed to roam. All vampires stick to the centre of a city, vampire central we call it, its central hub. Paris' zone just happened to be that much bigger than most other cities, due to the number of vampires drawn here by the *Iunctio*'s presence.

"Well, they're probably busy. I can sense four or five groups of evil about to attack. Like a coordinated effort or something."

Gregor straightened up at that and cocked his head to the side, a look of concentration on his face. "The *Iunctio* is not aware of it. You say groups, is it more than one vampire in each location?"

"Yes." I started to pull him towards the end of the alley, but he simply stood his ground. There's nothing you can do to move a vampire who does not wish to be moved. It's like they turn to stone or something, you simply can not budge them at all.

"You cannot hunt, Lucinda."

It might have been the way he said it, but I knew instantly, that I shouldn't have been out of the *Palais*. That Gregor was breaking the rules by having me outside of the *Iunctio's* building right now.

"I'm not meant to be free on the streets, am I?"

He smiled, a little bit cockily, but not unattractive. He still looked good enough to eat. "There are some benefits to being the Enforcer."

I just shook my head and then felt the evil getting ready to strike. I gasped at the strength of that pull. I had never denied myself a chase, a hunt, before for this much length of time. Maybe the pull got stronger, the longer I delayed in responding to its call.

"It doesn't matter, Gregor, I have to go to them. I can't resist the urge any longer."

His fingers tightened on my shoulders and he pulled me closer towards him, as though he was afraid I'd slip away.

"I can't let you." He didn't sound sorry when he said, it was just a matter of fact.

My stake was out and against his chest in the next instant. Just enough room between us to allow for the action. Any closer and I wouldn't have been able to hold it at the right angle.

"I've staked you before, Gregor, I don't want to do it again, but we both know I can and not kill you, just immobilise you. So what's it going to be? I *am* going to hunt this evil. Are you coming with me to keep an eye on me, or are you waiting here for your vampires to come and remove another stake from your chest?"

His eyes had bled all grey and were now a maelstrom of silver and platinum, so not human looking. So beautiful. He just stared at me for a few seconds, anger and frustration pouring off him in waves, mixed with a little excitement. Huh. The threat of a stake in the chest still did for him, I guess. Good to know.

Finally he removed a hand from my arm, where he had been gripping me tightly and ran it through his hair. "Arghhh! All right then, lead on Hunter."

I smiled up at him. "You *are* cute when you're angry, aren't you?"

"Isn't that my line?" he whispered into the silence of

the darkened alley. His last grip on my arm changing to a soft stroke then released altogether.

I laughed and tried not to smile back. It was hard and I don't think I managed to completely pull it off, but hey. I'd tried.

Then I turned towards the lights of the *Champs-Elysées* and headed towards that Pull.

Chapter 34
Arc de Triomphe

I knew immediately where they were, down by the *Arc de Triomphe*. Luckily, we weren't that far away, just a couple of blocks, one of them rather long. But I'm fast and there's no denying that Gregor can move with speed when required. I slowed as I came to *Place Charles de Gaulle*, the lights shining on the monument like a beacon calling me in.

"How many are there?" Gregor asked, not even puffed.

I was a little, so I took a few deep breaths in before I answered. "Five."

He turned to look at me, surprise evident on his face. Vampires don't normally hunt together, they are solitary things. Recently, the *Iunctio* had issued a warning, suggesting that vampires hunt in pairs, in case I managed to *seek* them out and Dream Walk to them, but the order had been removed, when I struck the deal with Gregor. Man, that felt like months ago, was it only weeks, days even?

"So many," he said and his tone told me this was news to him too.

"Yeah, and they've got a group of humans with them. Somehow they've lured them on to the top of the *Arc de Triomphe*." Gregor's gaze went to the top of the monument as soon as I had said that, no doubt scanning for movement.

The *Arc de Triomphe* is bigger than it looks in pictures. Up close you feel dwarfed by its sheer size, it's huge. Maybe 50 metres high and just as wide across. Napoleon couldn't have made a more grander statement than commissioning this monument, that was for sure. It was possible to climb the stairs to the roof and the view from the top is said to be impressive, but it was not open to the public tonight. I was glad of that.

"Come on then, let's find the back door." I took a step towards the behemoth.

"Do you have a plan, Hunter?"

"Not really, we'll just see how the chips fall."

Gregor followed my steps, keeping pace easily, his legs striding out to full length, so his was simply walking, yet I was kind of jogging. I did hate that sometimes, when you ran with a taller person and they made everything look so easy and graceful and you were running full tilt.

"Are you always so *laissez faire*?" he asked almost casually. Like we were sitting down to coffee and not running hard out to face rogue vampires on the hunt.

I thought about that for a second. I guess I did kind of follow my gut more than think about my actions, when on a hunt. It was almost like a deeper, more instinctive or intuitive part of me took over when I hunted and I was just along for the ride.

"Yeah, I guess so. So far it's worked."

"Has it worked against five vampires at once before?"

"Are you trying to make me doubt myself, Gregor?" I didn't say it angrily, there was a smile to my voice. He could say what he liked, this was my territory. It was as easy as breathing air, as natural as the beat of my heart, as necessary as water.

He shook his head and laughed quietly, almost under his breath. "You seem so sure of yourself, so....certain. Like nothing could stop you now. Not even a rampaging pack of rogue vampires. It's....extraordinary."

"Yeah, that's me. Unafraid." OK, so that was a little

sarcastic, but Gregor either didn't pick up on my tone, or chose to ignore it.

"Sometimes frighteningly so."

I just shook my head at him, but we'd found the door, so my hand slipped in my jacket and retrieved the stake I had threatened Gregor with just before, from its hiding place, my other hand rested on the door itself. I'd popped the stake back in its pocket as soon as we had left the alley. It's so much easier to run with your hands free, don't ask me why, balance or something. Or the lack of having to hide a nasty looking weapon from the general public. But, I wanted it out and ready now, you never knew where the bogeyman would spring from.

Although, I did have one advantage up my sleeve. I sent my senses out, locating all the vampires and making sure none were hiding behind the door, waiting to ambush us on the narrow stairs inside. They were all on the roof, but I was also no longer naïve. Humans could have been helping them, so the stake stayed out.

"Ready?" I asked over my shoulder.

Gregor just huffed an indignant sound at me, as if to say *I was born ready, get on with it.*

I fought a smile and opened the door slowly. No surprises hidden in the shadows within, so I let me eyes adjust to the dim interior and when I could make out the shape of the stairs inside, slipped in. Gregor following behind, closing the door quietly. We heard a scream from up the stairs then and I almost started running at full speed, heedless of any further obstacles that may have been in my path, my only desire to get to the human whose cry that had come from. It was full of terror and a realisation that things were so, so very bad. Whatever the evil bastards were doing, they weren't expending any energy to make it seem pleasurable for the humans involved.

I did manage to stop myself tearing off up the stairs in a stupid burst of speed though, even before Gregor's hand came down on my shoulder. He released his grip, as soon as he realised I had got myself under control and wasn't about to run head on into a trap blindly. I took the treads more slowly, one at a time, head cocked to the side trying to listen for sounds of life around each corner. I even realised I had started using my nose, to sniff the air, like a dog, or more accurately a vampire. Trying to smell an emotion on the air in front of me, or more basic smells, like sweat and dirty skin. Nothing seemed to be waiting. Even though my body kept telling me to be cautious, my mind had already come to the conclusion that these guys didn't want the battle inside, on the stairs, they wanted whatever Nosferatin came to them, to find them on the roof. Why?

Surely an ambush on the stairs would have been better, easier, quicker. They would have had the higher ground, the upper hand. And I knew this was an ambush. These vampires were hunting in the open, flaunting the rules, reeking evil in a purposeful way, they *wanted* to be caught. But why?

I didn't have the answers right now, those would be found on the roof, so I picked my speed up and Gregor didn't try to stop me, so he must have come to the same conclusions too.

It was a long way to the top and I mean a looooong way. I am fit, don't get me wrong, but stairs have always been a challenge for me. My legs are short. You wouldn't think that would matter, but for some reason the height of each step here was just a little too much for my comfort. I have trained on stairs before and lots of them, but I was still struggling with the size of these steps. My speed had buttoned off and my legs were starting to ache, almost shaking with each step I took. I think I was still going fast though, faster than a human, but the screams had become more desperate from the roof top and my thoughts were giving me away.

Gregor didn't even ask. He simply picked me up in his arms and flew. I have been held in vampire arms before when they fly, it's freaky. That's Freaky with a capital F. I try not to do it too often and I think most vamps who know me, know it's not something I would normally accept. But, he'd read my mind, he'd heard the frustration in my thoughts, the desperation and defeat that I had begun to feel. So, I didn't argue, just used the moment to slow my breathing and centre myself for what was to come.

He stopped just before the last bend in the stairs and placed me back on my feet. I rested my hand against his chest to get my balance. He wasn't even breathless, his chest barely rising and falling, the small movements almost an afterthought. And it probably was. More a reflex action brought on by centuries of attempting to blend in with humans. Unnecessary to live, but necessary to survive.

I glanced up at his face, he wore an eager expression. Vampires like confrontation, they do not shy away like most humans do. He was ready and almost enthusiastic for what lay beyond the next bend. I suddenly had an insight into why he was the *Iunctio's* Enforcer, he was no doubt going to be very good at this.

I pushed that thought aside and silently crept around the corner, not hesitating when I came to the door at the top and pulling it open.

If the vampires on the roof had been surprised they certainly didn't show it when I stepped out with a stake in hand. However, a brief flash of fear did cross their features when Gregor followed behind me, coming into full view a second after they had seen me. It didn't do much for my confidence, but then I've never really needed my enemy to think me a great challenge, to be able to hold my head up high. The more they thought Gregor the greater danger, the easier my job would be.

I took the scene in with one quick glance. All the vampires were spaced out evenly, on the opposite side of where the door came out, some 5 -10 metres away. There was none behind us that I could sense, but I shouted in my head to Gregor to check for humans behind where we were. He must have heard, and must of done it, because he whispered, "None."

My eyes hadn't left the group of evil in front of me. Each vampire was dressed in fighting black. Well presented, nice attire and well groomed hair. These were not your average rogue vampires, wasting away, crazed with blood lust, unable to function in normal society any more. These were well kept little vamps, which made me think, they were following a command. Why else would they be acting out like this? The thought didn't make me feel any better.

Each vampire was holding a human, all of them had been fed on. So, you could bet each of of these evil creatures was at full strength, full of fresh human blood, ready to face whatever came their way. They were all up against the railing at the side. It's quite high, no doubt for safety reasons, so I didn't think it would pose a threat unless they decided to jump up on it and over the side. Some of the humans looked unconscious, others had eyes so wide, all you could see was white.

"So, what's up?" No one had spoken, so I thought it was time to get this ball rolling. Unfortunately, they weren't entirely used to my Kiwi accent and colloquial turn of phrase, so they only looked puzzled, not scary, for a split second. But the scary returned.

"Can you not hunt alone, Nosferatin? Do you need the Enforcer to hold your hand?" This from a vampire off to the side. I hadn't picked him as the leader, but he was the only one to speak, so he got my attention. My peripheral vision not leaving the rest, but my head turning slightly to look him in the eyes.

He'd recognised Gregor, but Gregor hadn't responded. I had no idea what he was showing them on his face, but he was leaving this up to me. I was the hunter, this was my hunt. He might be the *Iunctio's* Enforcer, but even he wouldn't have been called in for this under normal circumstances, this was entirely my show.

"Actually, he's here to make sure I don't do too much damage. I tend to get carried away on a hunt. I'm currently under investigation for going *above* and *beyond* the call of duty." It was all a lie, but vamp boy didn't know it.

He flicked a look at Gregor, must have seen something that made him believe what I had said and then returned his now slightly uncertain gaze back to me. I just smiled sweetly.

"You are not French. You should not be hunting here."

"International Hunting Exchange. It's new. You probably haven't heard of it."

"Enough!" This time from a vampire in the centre. So, we'd found the leader finally. I pulled my attention slowly away from the first vampire and took in the one right across from me on the roof. Now this one I could believe was the guy in charge.

He was tall and dressed the same as the others, with long blonde hair tied back at the nape of his neck. It wasn't so much how he dressed, or the fact that he was undoubtedly handsome in that vampire kind of way they all had, but the way he held himself, that led you to believe he was in charge. I should have picked up on it sooner, but it had been a long night.

"You think this is a game? We have five humans here, all of which we intend to kill. What say you, Nosferatin?"

"You don't seem to be like your average rogue vampire. What's got your knickers in a twist to be making such a scene?"

I know it was childish of me, but I did love vampires cringing at my language. Sometimes they just didn't get me and took themselves *way* too seriously. Even vampire hunters have to have pet hobbies.

"We are not rogue." He spat the word rogue out as though it tasted bitter. "We are the answer to your prayers."

I laughed out loud, this guy really was a card. "How do you know what I pray for, vampire?"

It was his turn to laugh and it was scary, like the rest of him. It didn't run over my arms and cause me pain, it slipped into my mind, bypassing my multitude of shields and whispered, I *can see your heart's desire. You want her dead, so do I.*

I shuddered as the whisper caressed my mind and withdrew slowly. I felt, more than saw, Gregor stand a little closer to me. I don't think he'd had his mind raped, like me, but he'd either heard the words inside my head, or picked up on my discomfort. Either way, his body was now screaming tension.

"Who are you?" And somehow I managed to keep my voice level, no fear. Must be years of practice.

"It doesn't matter who I am. But, if you stop us tonight, you will not have your prayers answered. You want free of her, let us go about our plans unhindered."

You'd think I'd be tempted. He was of course talking about the Champion. If I could have her killed off by someone other than myself, then maybe, just maybe, the *Iunctio* would stop gunning for my death. But, I'm not stupid, I may have wanted to believe that, but I knew better. There are twelve members of the *Iunctio's* High Council and I've only met four, including Gregor. The two vampires with the Champion earlier tonight, were undoubtedly council members. The Diviner, I now knew, but the other one, I didn't even have his name yet and there was still so many more to meet. Somehow, I didn't think the death of the Champion was necessarily going to make the others less threatened by me remaining alive. At least right now the Champion couldn't rightly kill me, or pass an order to have me killed. Nut would make sure she didn't succeed.

So, scary monster here didn't have a convincing argument for the lives of five human beings.

He must have seen something on my face, I was

slipping, getting tired and not controlling my facial features as well as I usually do. It was not a good sign. But he tensed slightly, looked surprised and then simply threw the human he was holding up and over the side of the railing.

It all happened in slow motion. The unconscious body floating up through the air, like a loose limbed manikin; arms flailing, legs spreading wide out of control, head lolling back and then it was out of sight. I screamed and ran towards the vampire, shouting in my head for Gregor to catch the body before it hit the ground.

He hesitated, not wanting to leave me, but felt my panic at the loss of a human life and so flew. He was out of sight over the side of the *Arc* in a blink and I was already on the vampire in front of me.

Of course, it was what he had planned. Get rid of Gregor and then it's five to one. The one being me, one stake in my hand, one Nosferatin and five master vampires. The others dropped their dinners, not throwing them over the side, simply dropping them at their feet on the roof. Where they lay perfectly still, even those conscious, not daring to move.

I managed to get my stake across the leader's chest, ripping his shirt and laying a gash in his flesh, before he flung me backwards. I think he was surprised, perhaps none of the French Nosferatin have been joined, or perhaps my strength and speed is much more now, that he hadn't expected it. I'm guessing he did his homework and knew what to expect when he entered the city, but he hadn't expected me.

I spun in the air as I flew backwards from his thrust and landed a direct hit on an approaching vampire before hitting the ground. Dust swelled around me like a blizzard. The other vampires paused. This was so not what they had expected. I centred myself quickly, gathering my strength and pushing out to the side as a vampire regained composure and rushed me from the left. I pushed off to the right in a spin through the air, away from his claws and teeth. My feet leaving the roof top, my body suspended in mid air, my arms in tight against my chest, as the world spun around me.

It's a nifty trick, one Nero can do with ease, but has taken me a little longer to perfect. Sometimes it works, other times it doesn't, but when it does, boy, do the vamps go crazy. I have to admit, the first time I watched Nero do this spin thing, my mouth was open and I was frozen to the spot in utter disbelief. I had no idea we were capable of such a beautiful move and judging by the expressions of the vampires around me, neither did they.

I sensed, rather than saw, Gregor land on the rooftop to the left of me. I could almost feel the weight of his eyes on my body, but distractions are bad, when spin fighting, so I blocked him out and thrust out my right hand, the one holding the stake, as I passed a vampire, connecting with his chest and dancing in the air again a split second later, before he'd even burst into dust. It was as if I hadn't even paused for a breath.

By this time the other vampires had woken from their shocked state and started to round on me. Gregor grabbed the one that had come up to me on my left before I did my spin routine and simply twisted his head right off. That'll do it every time. Either a silver stake to the heart, or decapitation. Both work. I'm more of a traditionalist though, so I avoid the head off the shoulders thing. I'm not even sure I have the strength, but truthfully, I've never tried, so I can't be sure. But with that one swift motion, the vampire Gregor had parted from his head, burst into dust, followed shortly thereafter by the head itself.

So, three down, two to go. My next vampire just happened to be the leader and he was ready. He'd had time to adjust to the sight of me spinning, to gauge me speed and trajectory and he simply flung a hand out at the right moment, connecting with my arm and making me lose the grip on my stake. The momentum causing it to spin across the roof top to the corner and the force of his strike making me crash to the ground in a heap. Gregor of course, was busy with the other vampire, who seemed to be better at hand to hand combat than the others and was keeping Gregor's attention away from me.

That just left me and leader vamp. And I was on the ground. Not the best place to be, trust me. He flew at me and I mean literally flew, like superman, horizontal to the rooftop floor. I braced myself, as best I could, but the weight of his body still threw me off balance and sent me flying out beneath him, crashing my head against the concrete parapet, making stars appear before my eyes and a wave of nausea flush up my body. I gasped, but couldn't see straight, everything blurring and on a tilt. It didn't matter, I knew what was going to happen next, I'd seen this movie. Been there, done that, got the T-Shirt to prove it too.

Leader Vamp picked me up like I weighed as much as a bag of potato crisps. One handed too, just to rub it in some more. His free hand going to my head, pulling it sideways by my hair. Why do they always grab the hair? Sadistic bastards. Serves me right, I should cut it, or at least tie it back, but I can't. If you want to threaten me with something, don't make it my death, make it the chopping of my hair. That'll work every time. His fangs slid out in a menacing flick and he smiled at the look in my face.

"I don't know what you are, Nosferatin, but you are no more."

If he had just gone in for the bite, I may have remained in shock and not fought him, but the snide comment was like a mental slap to the face and my own smart-ass personality rose to the bait, like a hungry little fish.

"Right back at you, vampire."

I raised my hand to his face, covering his nose and mouth and almost his eyes. My hands are small, his face a bit bigger, so I couldn't cover it all, but it would do. It would do nicely. I centred myself, while he laughed and slowly pushed against my hand, his fangs pricking my palm. But, he wasn't even bothering to seek blood, he wanted the neck and thought he could have it despite my hand in his face. And then, I gathered all my Light towards me, holding it close. This time when I sent it out, it wasn't with lust, or desire, or a sexual need. It wasn't even a safety, or a warmth, or a love, or a happiness. This vampire had only Darkness in him, the Light took over and I was no longer in control. It responded to his Darkness with a Light just as bright and crashed through his shields to get to him.

I'm not sure I would have killed, not like this. With a stake, for sure, but with my Light? No. I didn't want to use it that way again. I have before, twice, both times as my absolute last line of defence, rather like now. But, I had sworn that I would never place myself in that same position again, never cause the death of another simply with my Light. It was wrong. The Light to me meant everything good in this world, good things don't kill. But, it was as if I was no longer in the driver's seat and the Light just whispered through my mind, *You tried little one, now let me do this last.*

I think I screamed *No!* I think I tried to remove my hand, tried to push the vampire away for real this time, using both arms and my legs, but it was too late. The Light had already left me, it had already done what it had set out to do. The vampire shone an iridescent rainbow of colours and simply burst apart, floating down around me as dust.

I heard myself saying, “No. No. No. No. No.” Over and over again softly, under my breath as I frantically tried to gather the vampire's dust together in my hands, as if that would bring him back to life.

Gregor was beside me calling my name, trying to grab my hands out of the pile of dust in front of me, but I kept pushing him away, kept trying to get to all the dust. Trying to mould it back together like you would *Play Doh*, but it wasn't working. Nothing would.

“It's not meant to kill. It's not meant to kill. It's good, not bad. It's not meant to kill.” I almost groaned the words out.

Gregor had managed to get my arms under control and had pulled me into his lap, rocking me, soothing me, kissing my cheek and neck, whispering, “It's OK. It's OK. It's OK.” Over and over, trying to drown out my words, making me hear his and bringing me back to reality.

I stopped saying useless words, stopped crying wasted tears and just sunk into his arms in defeat. For the first time since I had found my Light, I didn't like it much.

For the first time, I really wished I was dead.

Chapter 35
Apparitions

Gregor handled the clean-up. Getting a few from his line to tend to the humans, to get them to hospital, so we could escape without the *Iunctio* knowing I was out of the *Palais*. He carried me down the stairs and got me settled in the back of the car, the one with the same driver, who didn't look at me, who pretended I didn't exist at all. Maybe if he didn't look at me it would be easier to lie when faced with an *Iunctio* council member trying to find the truth. Whatever, I didn't care. I didn't care about much really.

Warm arms wrapped around me on the back seat of the car pulling me close. I couldn't fight, nor did I want to, being held sounded about OK. I was finding it difficult to feel much of anything though. I could feel his warmth, his breath against my head, but I couldn't feel enough to care, or not to care.

I heard Gregor tell the driver to just drive, anywhere, but keep driving. He didn't want to take me back to the *Palais* like this. I understood. I vaguely acknowledged I needed to pull myself together. I just didn't know how. I didn't even know where to begin.

He softly lifted me up in his arms, sitting me across his lap, kind of like a child, but I couldn't even get angry about that. It just was. His hands pushing my hair out of my eyes, touching my face, stroking my now dry cheeks. I couldn't even get upset enough to cry.

"Are you in there, Lucinda?"

I just nodded.

"I don't believe you. Come back to me."

I didn't say or do anything, just sat on his lap and

breathed. I thought that was pretty clever actually. Breathing.

He sighed and said softly, "Forgive me, *ma cherie*."

Then his lips met mine, softly at first, a little hesitantly, then more demanding, more hungry, more forceful. I vaguely thought, *how nice* and then shut the door on that feeling too. It was too strong, I didn't want to feel. To feel would be to remember what I had just done and I didn't want that. That would be bad.

But Gregor is nothing if not persistent and he slipped my jacket off my shoulders letting it fall to the footwell between the seats and ran his hands up my arms, into my hair and back down again. All the while devouring me with his soft mouth and warm tongue. When I didn't respond he lay me down on the long seat, pressing his body on top of mine, biting gently on my neck. No fangs, just teeth, not breaking flesh, just marking gently, trying to get a response. I didn't fight him, I didn't want him to stop, but I also wasn't participating. Just existing right now was OK.

He groaned in frustration. "Come on, Lucinda. Don't make me take this further. Fight back."

I just looked at him, not taking him in, just seeing him, but not seeing him, if you know what I mean. He lowered his head against my chest for a moment breathing hard, then lifted it to see the driver flicking a glance in the rear view mirror. His hand came down on the button that made the divider rise up and block his view of us, and he turned to me with liquid silver swirling in his eyes.

"I am not complaining, little Hunter, but usually you are slightly more of a challenge than this. I like challenges, I like them a lot. So, why don't you come out and play, for me. Make me work for this, Lucinda, don't just hand it to me on a platter. Make me want to take you. Make it worth my while."

His eyes flashed and I felt something stir inside me, just a little swirl of desire, just a hint of something more than nothing. He smiled and slowly removed my T-Shirt, up over my head, throwing it away in the corner on the other seat.

His eyes travelled down from mine, taking in my bare skin, across my clavicle, down between my breasts, over my stomach, my arms and back up to my eyes. His held a challenge. Part of me knew what he was asking, but I wasn't there yet, I couldn't open my mouth, let alone form the words. So, he slid his hand behind my back and undid my bra, slowly, so slowly, sliding the fabric away, to bare me completely from the hips up. He sucked in a breath at the sight of me, platinum now swirling in with the silver.

"Stop me, Lucinda. Stop me." It was whispered, not convincingly, he didn't really want to stop, but I still couldn't find the energy to fight. His head came down between my breasts. His lips lightly touching my skin, tongue lashing out in a wet streak, hot breath sending shivers across the path his tongue had left and I realised I *was* feeling. And it was better than OK, it was good. And it wasn't making me remember, it was filling me with other thoughts and other images, all mine, all OK, if not a little naughty, but perfectly good, in a healthy have-a-sexy-vampire-lavishing-attention-on-me kind of way.

I let a breath of air out. "Gregor."

His head came up and his eyes met mine. "Do you wish for me to stop?"

And that's a doozy of a question right there, because (1) I so did not want him to stop, but (2) This was wrong, I was with Michel and sure he had just fed off another woman, but I had kind of forced him into it, so I said, "Yes." And immediately wanted to take it back.

"That, *ma petite chasseuse*, is more like it." He wasn't angry, he was perhaps a little disappointed, but I think also relieved. And part of me realised, he didn't want to just take from me, he wanted me to offer it willingly, on my terms.

I thought a lot better of him in that instant.

He turned away from me and handed me my T-Shirt and bra. I quickly got myself in order and sat back on my side of the seat. He turned back, sensing I was presentable again, a small smile playing on his lips.

"You had me worried there."

I let a little huff out, a semi laugh. I must be doing better. "What, you didn't want to lose your virtue so easily?"

His smile widened. "I have pictured the moment many times and in all of them, you were doing more than just lying there. Trust me, the reality just now did not fit the fantasy. I want the fantasy."

His eyes bore into mine. I licked my lips. Damn. But he didn't miss it.

"Would you like to reconsider your answer?" His voice was husky and low.

Yes. No. Hell I don't know.

He laughed, a full body laugh, making his shoulders shake and his eyes shine.

"Don't laugh at me and stop reading my mind!"

He just laughed more.

I crossed my arms under my breasts, but I was also having trouble keeping the smile off my face. His hand came out and took one of my arms, slowly untangling it, and letting my hand fall into his. His fingers lacing with mine. It was such an intimate thing to do, but so simple. How many people do you lace your fingers with? Normally only your lover, Gregor was not mine. He'd almost been, on a couple of occasions, but he wasn't really. Just because I wanted him and lusted after him, didn't make it so. Or right. But, I didn't pull away, I held his hand back, I enjoyed the sensations of his fingers in mine.

"Dawn is approaching, *ma cherie*. We must return to the *Palais*."

I didn't want to go back, I didn't want to face Michel. Part of me thought that the donor would still be there, but the other part of me just scoffed, *don't be silly, it's been at least two hours since you left, he's probably worried sick.* That made me feel better, but it also made me think about what he was doing right now. Pacing the chamber, sounding an alarm and letting the *Iunctio* know I was missing, presumed kidnapped.

The thought of what he might be doing right this instant made something happen, something that had never happened before. I don't know if it was the Bond, it certainly hadn't done anything like this before, but all of a sudden I could see him. Like a movie in my mind, but I knew instantly that this was live, this was a window through space and over distance, directly to my kindred vampire. And I momentarily got excited, because it's Michel and I can't help it, he does it to me every time.

So, it took me a moment to get the picture straight in

my head, because he was naked. I recognised the bed in the chamber, the duvet; a rich forest green, was on the floor at the foot of the bed. The white sheets all twisted and down passed his hips, showing bare skin from his face to his thigh. His eyes were closed, like he was sleeping, his skin still slightly flushed, as though he had just fed, or done something that made his blood pump. And that's when I noticed he wasn't alone.

I wanted to pull back from the image then, I wanted to stop seeing what it was I was seeing, I didn't want to look, I didn't want to see, but I couldn't stop it. My eyes moved of their own accord and there she was. Naked too. All her curves and soft pale perfect skin, one arm holding his as it draped over her chest, his leg draped over hers. And when my eyes trailed down the length of his body, so familiar, so mine, I couldn't help noticing the two little marks at the crease at the top of her right leg, in close to that perfect little triangle of auburn hair. Two slow moving lines of blood flowing away from the site and I knew. I knew he had chosen to feed from her femoral artery, the most intimate of places, and I knew he had done more than just that.

But my heart didn't break, it turned to stone. So heavy in my chest.

Somehow he felt me, or sensed me, because his eyes opened and it was as though he *could* see me, as though he was looking right at me. The shock on his face didn't touch me, the sudden look of despair, didn't even come close. I just pushed away from that image, but before it completely disappeared I heard him whisper, “Lucinda. No.”

I came back to the long seat in the limousine, Gregor

watching me closely. I have no idea if he saw in my mind what I did. Whether his ability to read my thoughts extended to the pictures too, but he didn't give me sympathy, he didn't ask, he just opened his arms with a look of understanding and I went straight to him.

"You can stay with me for the day, Lucinda." He was very careful not to use a pet name, not to touch me too much, just arms around me, making me safe. He didn't kiss me, he didn't try to smell my hair, he just sat there, holding me, while silent tears streamed down my face and I cursed everything I ever loved about Michel to Hell and beyond.

We entered through a back door, servants entrance I think. I was walking, I didn't really need his support, but I was clinging to him all the same. He let me, not saying a word and simply steered me down the various small corridors. Down a flight of stairs, quickly across another larger, wider and brighter corridor, then through more mazes, until we finally reached wherever the hell we were going and hadn't seen a soul.

He unlocked the door to his chamber and led me inside. The lights came on automatically, showing a tastefully decorated room, not too dissimilar to the one I had Dream Walked to him in Rome. His taste obviously trending towards fine antiques and soft colours. Artwork adorned the walls, all beautiful, all no doubt originals, but I just stood there, unsure of what to do next.

Gregor took his jacket off and laid it across the back of a couch. The layout of his chambers was pretty much the same as the one Michel was in. Bedroom to the side, kitchenette at the back, bathroom off the bedroom and large comfortable lounge. He came and stood in front of me.

“You are tired, you need to sleep. I'll stay out here, you take the bed.”

I just nodded. He followed me into the bedroom, rifled through a chest of drawers and brought out a large T-Shirt. He placed it on the end of the bed and then slipped out the door, closing it softly behind him. Nothing said, no quick glance my way, just privacy, respect. I didn't know he had it in him.

I picked up the T-Shirt and had to smile. Amazing, I know, but it had a picture of *Sylvester the Cat* on it. It looked like he was dancing, a look of happiness across his feline face. No saying or phrase, just the picture. It said everything that words could and more.

I slipped out of my clothes, leaving my knickers on and pulled the T-Shirt on over my head. It was so big, it was like a nightdress, down to mid thigh. I folded my clothes and placed them in the corner on a chair, then climbed in under the sheets and blankets. I lay there for quite a while, maybe half an hour, unable to get the images of Michel and French Pretty out of my head. My mind wandering to dangerous thoughts. What had they done? How had it happened? How could he have done it at all?

I know, I thought about how close I had come with Gregor, how easy it would have been and then I thought, well now it doesn't matter, does it? That last little bit of me, I'd been holding in check, no longer existed. There was no reason for me to fight what I felt for Gregor any more. Michel had made it quite clear how he felt. What I meant to him. I denied him one meal, turned him away to another's vein and he cast me aside completely.

Yes, I was hurting, I acknowledged that, but I was also

relieved. Relieved that it had been him first who had made that move, not me. Relieved because now it was so much easier for me. I'd been fighting my attraction to Gregor for some time, telling myself it was wrong. But it wasn't wrong any more, was it? I was free.

I sat up in bed, unable to sleep, my heart thumping in my chest, my breath a little rapid. The thought of being able to follow my desire for Gregor to completion sending a wave of heat through me. There was a soft knock at the door, I just about jumped out of my skin. Nervous, me? Yep.

Gregor opened the door slowly and peeked his head inside.

"Are you all right? I can hear your heartbeat from out here. It's motoring."

I concentrated on my breathing for a moment, trying to settle myself. Finally I managed a quiet, "No."

He came into the room and walked towards me. His shirt was undone, I think he had removed his belt and shoes, but he was still in his trousers, still dressed. But I could see a line of his skin, between the open sides of his shirt and my pulse skipped a beat. He stopped, mid way across the floor and just looked at me.

"Lucinda?"

I just shook my head.

"Do you want me to leave?"

I shook my head again.

He slowly walked closer, stopping at the edge of the bed, looking down at me. I didn't raise my head, just kept staring at the bedspread, gripping the covers between my fingers. He knelt down next to me and hesitantly reached out a hand. It hovered slightly for a second and then he touched my skin on my arm and the moment he did just that simple motion, lust burned through me uncontrolled.

He quickly pulled his hand away and gasped. "What the hell was that?"

I looked at him then and I don't know what he saw, because he paled, just slightly and then licked his lips.

"What do you want me to do?" he whispered a little breathlessly.

"Touch me." It was barely a whisper, but I knew he'd heard. He was shaking his head, back and forth.

"No. Not like this, not when you're angry at him"

"Please."

"No." More firmly this time. He even shifted to get up and stand, but I reached out and grabbed his hand, my hot skin against his, slightly cooler. He collapsed back to his knees.

"What *is* that?" he asked, almost in pain.

"I don't know," I whispered.

"Something is not right. This is not right." He didn't sound too convinced on that, I was still holding his hand. I moved my thumb softly over his palm and he stilled. My eyes locked with his, platinum shooting through the silver and I pulled him slowly towards me.

He actually looked scared. Startled even. This was not going how I had imagined it. Why was he fighting me? I finally had his body hard up against the side of the bed, still holding his hand. I got up to my knees and faced him, pushing my body against his chest. I was taller than him in this position and it didn't feel right, so I slid one leg off the bed on one side of him and then the other to the other side, so I was back sitting on the edge of the bed, my legs on either side of his hips. He looked like he was drowning.

I wrapped my hands around his neck, snuggling my lower body in against his waist, wrapping my legs around his hips. Making the T-Shirt ride up my thighs and yet he was still just kneeling there, stiff, breathing too quickly.

"Touch me." It was more a command than a request.

His hands immediately came up to my thighs, running along the bare length of them, sliding up under my T-Shirt. Better, much better. Slowly working their way up my sides, until they rested either side of my naked breasts and he shuddered against me. I pulled his head towards me, his eyes still a slightly startled silver, but his mouth already open, waiting, wanting what was about to happen. Our lips brushed together, so softly, then I went back for a small nibble, taking his bottom lip between my teeth and biting down, just gently, just enough so that if he pulled back it would hurt.

He groaned against my mouth, his hot breath almost scalding me.

"I want you," I whispered against him. "Make love to me."

He whimpered. A strangled sound I never thought I'd hear from his lips, but he pushed me back against the bed, climbing on top of me, his legs between mine, mine wrapping back around him again, so that I could feel the full hardness of him against me.

"You want me too," I said.

"Yes." It was just a breath, husky, raw with need.

And suddenly we were kissing like before, like the alleyway. Like we wanted to get right inside each other, to get closer and closer, to climb inside each other's mouths and devour every inch. His hand had found my breast, gripping tightly, almost too tightly, moving and rubbing and squeezing. It was rougher than I had ever felt before and I wanted it, I wanted it so badly. I wanted rough, I wanted to feel. I wanted him and it had nothing to do with what Michel had just done and everything to with a fierce need I felt only he could satisfy.

I pulled the oversized T-Shirt off over my head and his mouth found my breast, where he had only seconds before been fondling. His teeth scraping along the already taut nipple, making me gasp and writhe beneath him.

"Oh God." I heard him say, voice strained, his mouth no longer sucking on my nipple. I didn't stop moving, wanting to feel that hard length against me, deep, deep inside me. This was going too slowly, not fast enough, I needed him right now. I wanted him right now, but he had stopped, stilled above me. No longer moving his hands and fingers over my flesh, no longer kissing, licking and biting his way across my chest. His eyes were closed, his face looked pained.

"Stop moving!" It was a growl and it did make me pause. A vampire growl can be very intimidating.

He opened his eyes and I almost drowned in all that delicious silver and grey. I felt like I was being pulled towards them, into them, down to depths of him. And I felt something, vaguely, against my shields in my mind, but I didn't pay it too much attention, I wanted to drown in those eyes. So when I felt it again against my shields, I didn't fight it, I just lowered them and his *Sanguis Vitam* came rushing in.

The last thing I remember before blissful, safe and comforting sleep washed over me, was Gregor in my mind whispering, *je suis désolé, ma cherie.*

And then sweet blissful sleep.

Chapter 36
No Goodbyes

Whatever Gregor had done to my mind must have been powerful, but then I had lowered all of my defences for him, so it may not have been too hard. I have a natural repelling power to most vampire mind control, but some are able to have a small and short lasting effect on me. I think Gregor has had this effect on me in the past, but I can normally shake it off quite quickly. Last night, or more precisely, this morning, he had bespelled me a beauty, because I didn't wake until very late in the afternoon, having slept the entire day away.

Of course, I probably needed it, it had been a hell of a day, even by my standards. Not only having flown half way across the planet, I'd faced off against the Champion, doing some amazing bespelling of my own, nearly died, met my metaphysical mother, watched Michel nearly die, then fought a group of well mannered rogue vampires, witnessed my kindred's infidelity and fought with Gregor to have sex. So, yeah, all in all one of my more productive nights, that's for sure.

So, was it at all surprising that the clock next to the bed when I woke said 4:45pm?

Sunset was still a couple of hours away, I could feel it approaching though, like a breath of fresh air and an anticipation through the building of the joys of the night to come. I don't think I had ever been so in tune with vampires en masse before. Maybe it had something to do with being near the *Iunctio* and all the power they possess, or maybe it was just me. I felt different after my little visit with Nut, not quite the same any more. I was also very cautious of my powers, more so than I have ever been since coming into them.

My Light actually scared me now and I didn't know how to deal with that.

One thing at a time.

I got up and went straight into the shower, dressing back in my hunter gear. I would have liked a complete change of clothes, but they were of course back in the chamber where Michel was. I knew I would have to face him before sunset, before we were due at the dinner with the council, but I just didn't know if I had the strength for that. Confrontation has never been my strongest suit. I'd far prefer, right now, the idea of a full on battle, stake in hand, than a sit down conversation with my kindred.

I hesitated before I opened the bedroom door to the lounge. I hadn't forgotten last night, every little detail was emblazoned on my mind. From the addictive and delicious feel of Gregor's touch, to the outright kill-me-now-if-I-don't-have-you desire I had felt. To the fact that he had stopped it before it got too far. He at least deserved my thanks for that one.

Would I have regretted it if we had gone all the way last night? I think so, I think I really don't want to be unfaithful to Michel, despite everything that has happened. Call me a sucker for punishment, but I can't stop thinking that Michel is still mine and even if he has cast me aside, I am still his. That may change, I may get my head around our new living arrangements eventually, but right now, I still loved him, I still wanted him. It sucked. But it was true.

So, yes. Gregor deserved my thanks.

I opened the door slowly. Sometimes fast is good, sometimes slow is better and sometimes you just do what comes naturally and go with the flow. Slow, was definitely the order of the day.

He was sitting on the couch in different clothes from last night, so he must have come in the bedroom at some point and even showered by the look of him. I hadn't even stirred. He could have done anything to me and I wouldn't have known. I blushed slightly at the thought, but pushed it aside. If he hadn't taken the opportunity when I offered it to him so readily last night, he wouldn't have done a damn thing with me out cold. That was for sure.

He looked up and smiled. It was cautious, it didn't quite reach his eyes. If I hadn't known better, I'd have said he was holding his breath, waiting for the hammer to drop. I guess I was the hammer.

"Hi." Well, that was pathetic, but my mouth was suddenly dry and saying anything more than a one syllable word seemed damn near impossible all of a sudden.

His smile widened slightly and this time it did reach his eyes. I can't decide yet if his eyes are the best part of him or the curve of his soft lips.

"Good evening. I trust you slept well?"

"Like a log. What did you do to me?" I had meant it as a joke, but somehow it held more weight than it should have. His eyes flashed, but it was so quick I didn't get to register what colour.

"You were under a spell, Lucinda, I had no choice. I am sorry, but I had to override whatever was controlling you, making you act the way you were. It required a little more force than I had expected."

What the hell? Under a spell? Impossible.

"Not impossible, true." He was looking at me intently, almost waiting for me to start acting strange again, I suppose. So, what happened last night was because of a spell, but what spell and to what end?

I came and sat down on an armchair across from him, I noticed he relaxed slightly. What had he thought I would do? Jump his bones as soon as I walked through the door? He laughed, that huff of a laugh he does when he's trying to stop it from spilling out altogether.

I glared at him. "Get out of my head, Gregor."

"I am sorry, little Hunter. I seem to be having some trouble blocking you right now, or maybe you are just projecting too hard."

"I'm not projecting."

"Are you so sure?"

I thought about it for a minute, tested my shields, the ones I used to contain my thoughts, they all seemed intact. So, no, not projecting.

"Then it is me. I am sorry. I will try a little harder to block you."

"Are you hearing *every* thought in my head?"

"And more," he whispered. Did I want to know what *more* meant?

"Probably not," he answered.

"Hell, Gregor! Try harder."

"OK. OK. You are right. Sorry." His head ducked and he crossed his legs, fidgeting in his seat. So *not* him.

I sighed. This was insane. Could my life be any weirder?

OK. So, I'd just have to ignore the reading my darkest

thoughts part and concentrate on what I had intended to say to him when I first came out here.

"Thanks for last night. You know, for not letting it get out of hand." Well, any more out of hand than it had already got, thanks to me.

"You are welcome. Somehow, I do not think you would have been happy with me or yourself today, had I not."

Yeah. He was right. So, why did I feel like crap about it all? Aw shit. This sucked and the night hadn't even begun yet.

"I have to go back to my chamber," I said rather pathetically.

"Yes."

"I don't want to." More of that same pathetic-ness.

"I can tell."

"From reading my thoughts?" He wasn't trying hard to block me, was he?

"No. From knowing you and knowing how hard this would be for you. You don't like personal confrontations, Lucinda. You run from them if you can."

Really? He didn't answer my thought, maybe he was just biting his tongue.

"I shall escort you to your door. Unfortunately, I can't allow you to go on your own and I would not trust another to get you there safely." He stood then and picked his jacket up off a chair, slipping into it with practised ease. I hadn't meant to watch his every move so closely. To notice how his shoulders flexed as he stretched to put an arm in a sleeve, the movement making me remember the feel of his muscles under my hands. I swallowed and he stilled, mid motion and turned to look at me.

"It is a strong spell." He sounded choked.

"Are you under it too?" My voice was low, a little husky. Shit.

He looked pained, almost sad, but just shook his head at me.

"No," he said, voice controlled, even. "But I can feel your desire for me, your hunger and it is not yours, Lucinda."

"How do you know it's not mine?" I whispered, my eyes never leaving his.

He swallowed and slowly blinked his eyes. "Because I know your desire, I have felt it before. And it is always laced with guilt, confusion and frustration, never an unadulterated need such as this."

Oh damn. How could I even trust what I was feeling then?

"You can't." I didn't even tell him off for reading my thoughts, they were loud inside my head, I could hardly blame him. "You must only remember that they are not yours, not right now anyway and try to act accordingly."

Easy for you to say. He didn't answer, just finished getting his jacket on and doing up the buttons. I tried to look away.

He went straight to the door and opened it. He didn't come to me and offer a hand up, as he would normally do. He was trying to keep a distance. I shook my head. He was afraid of me.

"Not afraid of you," he said from the door. "Afraid of what I will do, if I get too close to you right now."

I stood to look at him, but he had his back to me, holding the door open, refusing to make eye contact.

Damn, this sucked big time. But, what was there left to do? I walked out the door, giving him a wide berth, it was the least I could do for him. We walked in silence down the corridors. I don't think he was too worried about us being seen together. We looked so solemn, that anyone witnessing it would have assumed the Enforcer had just been questioning me, all official business, no hanky panky going on here folks.

Finally we came to the door of Michel's chamber and I couldn't help the panic that flooded through me. Gregor turned to look at me, sympathy in his eyes.

"He is your kindred Nosferatu, Lucinda. No matter what happens now, he will always be that."

Way to go Gregor. Way to make me feel better about all of this.

He sighed and ran a hand through his hair. "If I could do this for you, I would, *ma cherie*, but only you can walk this road."

I nodded, he was right. There was no avoiding it. Michel and I were tied to each other for eternity, or until one of us dies and the other goes along for the ride.

"Ask him about the Nemesis. He will understand," Gregor added, apropos of nothing.

"Understand what?"

"Just ask him, Lucinda." And with that, he turned and walked away. No goodbye touch, no brush of his lips against my skin, nothing. I wanted to cry. But crying wasn't going to help me now, so I took a deep breath, put my hand on the door and didn't hesitate.

It seemed this time, fast was good.

Chapter 37
No Hellos

Michel was standing right in the centre of the room, facing the door. As if he had expected me to open it that instant. Or maybe he had just sensed me approaching, sensed me on the other side of the door and had just stood and gone to that position, but part of me felt like he had been standing there for a while. For a very long while.

I shut the door behind me and leaned against it, looking at him. It was harder than I had imagined. It hurt more than I could have guessed. Neither of us spoke.

The silence stretched out between us like a giant canyon, all full of shadows and unseen things.

I wasn't the first to break, not that that had been my intention. It just happened that way.

"You came back."

I nodded, still not trusting myself to speak.

"I did not think you would."

How could I have not come back? He was still my kindred vampire. I was still joined to him, Bonded to him. How could I have not come back?

"I am sorry."

And there, he had said it. And it wasn't what I wanted to hear. Despite having seen it with my own eyes, or at least in my own mind, a part of me had wanted him to say *it wasn't how it looked, nothing happened, I didn't turn to another and cast you aside.* But he'd said it now. He'd apologised. That meant it was true. He had done it and there was nothing I could do now to change that. I slid down the door and sat on the floor in an undignified pile.

No tears. I wouldn't give him the satisfaction, but my

legs could no longer hold me and I was too far away from a chair to sit down. Stuff it. The floor would do.

He took a step towards me and stopped, hand raised slightly, as though he was reaching for me. It hung in the air between us, not moving, just reaching, as though he would reach for me for eternity and never quite bridge that gap.

"There is no excuse for what I have done, but please let me explain."

I let a breath of air out. I think it was in indignation, but it was short and quiet and didn't have the force behind it, that it should have. I suddenly couldn't breathe.

"I knew what I was doing." A little noise escaped my lips then, but I firmly closed them, tightly, determined to not let more noises betray me further. Michel looked pained. "I knew that I didn't want to do it. I just couldn't remember why. The only thing that broke through the fog was when I sensed you, realising that you could see me...and then I...I woke to where I was, what I must have done. I woke to find her in the bed next to me. I am so sorry, so, so sorry, *ma douce*."

Don't call me ma douce.

He winced. "Lucinda, please. You must hear me, please. I do not know what came over me. I cannot explain. If I could change the past few hours I would, believe me. I would rather die than hurt you."

I let a little laugh out. *You dying would hurt me, you idiot.*

He smiled slightly, tried not to, but failed. He did manage to banish the smile with effort after a few seconds though. Pain tracing familiar patterns across his face again.

"What is the Nemesis?"

He hadn't expected my first words spoken to him to be those. The look of surprise and confusion on his face spoke volumes.

"He is a who, not a what."

"Who is he then?" Somehow it felt easier to talk of something else, something less painful. I knew I was ignoring the big issue here, but there was only so much a girl could bear at once.

"He is an *Iunctio* council member. He is their Force of Will."

"What does that mean?" Short sentences have always been my downfall. When I'm angry, I say less and less, giving myself away to whomever I am talking to. Strangely though, right now I didn't so much feel angry, as hurt. There is a difference, but clearly my ability to carry a more complex conversation didn't differentiate. So, short sentences it was.

"Whenever the *Iunctio* chooses a more nefarious path of retribution, they will engage his skill. They believe his ability to force what is due, is a just punishment. It can take many forms, but usually it involves making people choose a path they would not normally take, making them do something they would regret." He stopped then, obviously comprehending what it was he was saying. "*Mon dieu.*" He quickly sat down on the couch. "The Nemesis has been influencing our decisions. How did you know this?"

"I didn't. Gregor said to *ask you about the Nemesis*. He said you'd understand."

"Then he suspected." He looked up at me then, a strange look on his face I couldn't decipher. "Did you...?" I don't think he wanted to finish that question. Whether or not it was because he didn't truly want to know the answer, or perhaps because he didn't think he had a right to ask. Whatever reason, he couldn't go on.

"Did I do something I would regret with Gregor?" I finished it for him.

He swallowed. "Forgive me, I have no right to ask."

"Yes you do. Just like I have a right to be angry with you now." Strangely though, I still wasn't angry with him, just hurt. Hurt can be a big emotion, sometimes it just smothers everything else.

My voice was a whisper when I finally spoke. "I almost did. If it hadn't been for Gregor, I would have. He stopped us. He broke through my shields and put me to sleep. He said I had been bespelled and he had to use tremendous force to overcome it." At least it was getting easier to speak to Michel. Despite the topic, my sentences were no longer short.

"*Dieu merci!*" The fact that more and more French was seeping into Michel's language was a sure-fire indication of just how close to the edge he was. He normally had much better control than this.

"If he could fight it, why couldn't you?" I hadn't meant to say that out loud, it just popped into my head and blurted out my mouth and I so wish I could have taken it back, because it made me sound weak. It made me sound desperate and I so did not want to be either of those. I am a vampire hunter, for God's sake, I should be stronger than this.

Michel didn't look at me when he answered. "Could you have stopped if not for Gregor's intervention? He was not bespelled, my dear, we both were. I did not have someone with me strong enough to fight a spell."

No. You had someone with you who would have done anything, *anything* at all, that you so desired. A human donor under the influence of a master vampire while he feeds. I felt a little sick and by the look on his face, he did too.

I couldn't help his conscience, I had my own to defend.

Part of me realised that this was an opportunity to forgive Michel. He had been under the influence of an *Iunctio* council member, of the Nemesis, but I just couldn't make that leap of faith, not today, not when it hurt too much still. Don't the vamps always say the punishment lies with the offence? It doesn't matter why you did something, or how it came about. Even if the Nemesis could be punished for what he made Michel do, under vampire law, he wouldn't be. *The punishment lies with the offence*. The punishment was Michel's to bear. I may not be a vampire, but even I am affected by their laws. That didn't stop me from wanting this Nemesis dead.

How many more of the *Iunctio* members would I wish dead before this visit was over?

My backside was getting a little numb sitting on the carpeted floor. It might have been plush, but it was still the floor. I wanted to move to an armchair, to something more comfortable, not to mention more dignified, but I didn't know how to make my body obey my commands. I just sighed and it sounded so defeated, so sad.

Life could be a bitch sometimes, couldn't it? I loved Michel, I still loved him, but he had done something to hurt me, something he couldn't take back. But... he had done it without intent. He may have chosen to feed on another, but that was because I had denied him my blood. It was a practical requirement, he wasn't to know a stunning female donor would turn up at our door. Perhaps the Nemesis had, perhaps he had even arranged that. But the bottom line was Michel had not slept with her because he wished to hurt me. He hadn't even slept with her because he wanted to, at least not consciously. He'd slept with her because someone else made him believe it was right. And if he felt any of what I had been feeling when around Gregor the past few hours, then he would have wanted it, needed it, like a drug addict craves his fix.

Did this make a difference to how I was now feeling?

Yes. No. Maybe.

I hadn't realised he had moved, he was now standing in front of me, his hand stretched out, waiting for me to take it. He was stunning as always, dressed in a black shirt and black trousers, his more casual wear, the one that gets me so hot so easily. I knew he'd chosen it on purpose. It made me a little angry, but only because he knew me so well and could manipulate me with such ease because of it. So, crunch time. Do I take his hand and perhaps move on from this horrible place we were now in? Not erase it, but maybe allow it to move from the centre of our heart, to the side; a manageable but peripheral home, for such negative emotions.

I've always been a practical person. It's who I am, how I was raised. You don't live your formative years on a working farm, surrounded by adorable, lovable lambs and live through their slaughter every summer without becoming practical. I like the taste of lamb, I can't have my cake and eat it too. So I am practical. The lamb is cute while it is in the field, it is food when it walks up the ramp onto the truck destined for the abattoir.

So, how does that apply to this situation? Michel did what he did when influenced by another. Now he was standing in front of me, holding his hand out, asking me to let him back in. We had a long night ahead of us. If the Champion had orchestrated this little episode, had employed the skills of the Nemesis in the hopes of throwing us off balance, thereby making us act inappropriately at the dinner tonight and perhaps making a fatal mistake, she didn't know me well. Actually, she didn't know me at all.

I reached up and took his hand. It felt warm and soft and right, like a piece of me had been missing and that small touch brought it all back, made it all fall into its rightful place. Michel pulled me up to stand in front of him. He looked uncertain, not sure what to do next. I didn't want to make things easier for him, he hadn't made it easy for me, but then I am practical and together we were stronger than apart.

I closed the distance between us and wrapped my arms around his waist, burying my head in his chest, allowing myself to indulge in the smell of him, letting that fresh clean cut grass and salty sea air wash over me. It didn't take away the pain, but it did dull it, replacing that raw hurt with a small amount of home. It might not be enough in the long run, but it was just enough right now, to keep me going.

He hesitated, his hands hovering over me, then sighed and let them run through my hair, over my back, up my arms and onto my neck.

"*Merci, ma douce, merci. Je t'aime tellement, si très beaucoup.*"

We stood like that for perhaps five minutes, both unable to pull away and break the delicate, fragile spell our closeness had woven. I didn't think it mended the break in my heart, but it did manage to cover it. To put it somewhere out of sight, somewhere where it might just be able to heal all on its own. I hoped so, I really did. I loved this man.

Finally Michel spoke first. "We must get ready for the dinner. They will call for us before too much longer."

I nodded against his chest, still unable to let go. I'm not normally a clingy person, but I just couldn't undo my hands, which were clasped at the back of him. Firmly locked together.

He leaned down and kissed the top of my head. "I am not going anywhere, *ma douce*. You can let go."

"I don't want to." I sounded like a frightened child. "What is going to happen tonight? The Champion can make us lose all inhibitions, make us practically crawl all over each other in lust, right in front of everyone. The Nemesis can make us do whatever it is we don't want to do. How can we face them and survive?"

"I do not wish to add to your fears, but there are more on the council who could do us harm, not just the Champion or the Nemesis."

I shuddered against him. This was futile, we were walking into a trap.

"Yes, we are, but what other choice do we have?"

I shook my head, he was right, but there had to be a way to be stronger, to be able to stand against their attacks.

I couldn't give up, not yet.

I was obviously projecting my thoughts, because it was as if Michel could hear every word, just like Gregor could.

"There is a way we could be stronger." His voice was uncertain, soft, tentative. Almost as though he feared what my reaction was going to be.

"Spill it, Michel. Just say it."

"You could mark me, if we both shared *Sigillum* our Bond would be even greater. Greater than any other connection possible. They would have trouble breaching our minds."

Oh hell no. I was not giving *anyone* my *Sigillum* again, unless I *really* wanted to. I would not be manipulated, tricked or otherwise brow-beaten into giving up that part of me ever again.

"We will find another way, *ma douce*. We will be strong without it."

He had heard every thought and for once I was glad not to have to repeat myself aloud.

Chapter 38
The Great Dining Hall

Vampire dinners are not your normal affair. They feed on blood, but the blood must be flowing; warm, alive. Therefore to feed, they must have donors available to feed from. So, setting out the table with plates and knives and forks was just not going to cut it, was it?

They did have a table, of sorts, set up. Just not a standard one, instead it's like a really long version of a wide coffee table. You know, low to the ground so you can see the TV over the top of it, good for magazines and remote controls and all the other junk that gets piled on a coffee table. Well, at least, my coffee table is always covered in junk.

The table in the Great Dining Hall, as it was called, was one big, long and very wide coffee table, nothing set on it, just a plain black table cloth covering it from end to end. On either side were low and comfortable chairs, beside which were small side tables, where carafes of wine and wine glasses sat. The vamps would feed on live donors, but they would discuss politics over a glass of Burgundy, or as the locals here call it, *Vin de Bourgogne*.

The fact that a human was in their presence who would quite like a plate of normal food was irrelevant. This was a vampire stronghold, so only vampire needs would be met at this dinner. I did have wine next to me though, so at least I could just dull the effects of the evening with alcohol. I wondered if drinking alcohol would aid me in blocking out their mind control mojo or make it easier for them to get behind my shields. I guessed easier, so I quietly pushed the red wine away and poured myself a glass of water.

Michel and I had both dressed quickly and quietly, neither one daring to say a word or turn to watch the other dress. It was too painful. For both of us I think. Michel had chosen my dress. I didn't complain, this was his ball game, his turf, he knew what would work and what wouldn't. He had chosen a short dress, which surprised me, so *not* Michel's normal choice, had we been dining alone together. He liked long dresses. He said it was to keep his imagination fresh, never being able to see what he desired openly, but to be teased through the clinging fabric of a dress throughout the meal obviously did it for him. He said he had a very good imagination and I did not doubt him one bit.

The dress was black. I think he might have been humouring me there, black is my favourite colour choice when it comes to clothing, but this dress was bejewelled. Tiny *Swarovski Crystals*, intricately sewn all over the entire dress in a pattern. At first I couldn't recognise the pattern, it was so intricately done, so small, but when I concentrated enough, I realised it was a dancing dragon. The dancing dragon. The one I had spotted on Michel's private jet and in his chamber at *Sensations*. I also noticed the waistcoat he wore under his Tuxedo jacket now, was covered in the dancing dragon too. This time just a relief on black fabric, slightly shinier than the fabric behind, so it stood out, but not too much.

My dress hugged my body, not a gap to spare. I was silently glad I kept fit, it didn't allow for too much imagination at all. I guess Michel wasn't in the mood to think up fantasies over dinner. The neckline was low and had just two thin straps on each shoulder holding it up. It had to have a specially fitted bra sewn into the dress itself, or I would have simply fallen out all over the place. Surprisingly, it wasn't uncomfortable once on. It moved when I moved, it didn't get in my way, it didn't even slip and make me feel like I would fall out of it. It was stretchy, snug and tight and perfect. Except for one thing. I couldn't hide a stake anywhere. Not even a small silver knife in a thigh shield, it was simply too short.

Not being armed was not making me happy. But, it was probably likely that I would have been checked for weapons at the dinner. Because the dress left nothing to the imagination, I was not frisked however, just glared at by the guards at the door. I flashed on the thought that this may have been why Michel had chosen such a revealing outfit for me, so I wouldn't suffer the indignity of a body search when I arrived in the hall. To the vampires, the thought of being armed at the banquet was not considered appropriate. So, I had to swallow my fear and also had to grin and bear it. Funnily enough, it wasn't the slip of a dress that made me feel naked, but the lack of my stake that did.

There were fourteen chairs around the low lying table, all spread out evenly. Michel and I were placed at either end of the length, meaning I didn't even have Michel's proximity to calm my nerves. It was strategic, of course, for more than than just one reason. It separated us and therefore made us more vulnerable, but it also allowed the the twelve council members, six on either side of the long table length, to be able to watch us and study us, without having to strain their necks. We were on show and under the microscope tonight.

Everyone had dressed for the occasion, however I was the most revealing and it didn't escape my notice that those closest to me weren't against undressing me with their eyes. I refused to blush, or squirm, under their gazes. Vampires all over the world are the same. These guys were no different. The council was made up of ten male vampires and only two female. Sexual equality didn't exist back when the *Iunctio* was originally formed. Even though the *Iunctio* had only recently, in the last century or so, come back into its power, with the help of the Nosferatin, it had been around for millennia. Old rules die hard. The fact that the current Champion is a female is just lucky. Oh, and proves just how powerful she actually is.

There was nothing I could do to stop my short dress riding up my thighs, showing off the lacy tops of my thigh high hose and try as I might, probably a glimpse of the matching underwear too, in the low chairs they had provided. Had Michel known I would be so on display? Was this supposed to help us? I *really* didn't want to follow that thought to completion.

The two vampire council members on either side of me had introduced themselves, none of the others had bothered, only watched me with varying degrees of brightness and colour change in their eyes. On my left was the Scribe, he was responsible for keeping records of our time and preserving those of the past. An historian, you might say. I couldn't help feeling this vampire, although a master and undoubtedly a powerful one to be on the *Iunctio*, didn't really carry much weight. He was old, perhaps 600 years or so, so most of our history he probably knew first hand, but he didn't look older than 35, the age of when he was turned. Definitely a traditionalist, his hair was loose, long and a deep brown, almost lustrous, as though it had been brushed and brushed within an inch of its life. The rest of his appearance had equally been well put together. This vampire liked to impress. Perhaps it made up for his lack of clout.

His clothes were tailored to fit his trim and tall physique, but modern despite his age and his role as an historian. He would have fitted in anywhere, where a Tux was required. Some of the most successful vampires are those who can blend in with current fashion well. He had startling baby blue eyes, that flecked with paler powder blue. The combination unusual, because of its lack of deep and dark colours. Most vampires eyes have shades of a darker colour within them, becoming more prominent when washed with heightened emotions. It would be interesting to see what happened to the pale blues when he got going. Not that I ever want to encourage a vampire to lose control, but I was still intrigued.

The vampire on my right was the Tempest. The skills he brought to the *Iunctio* were all his own. Should he ever be replaced on the council, his title would no doubt cease to exist. He could manipulate and control the weather. He scared me. Not because of his climatic magic, which Michel had warned was phenomenal, but because he just reeked evil. He was, however, doing his best to rein it in and offer up polite conversation. Michel had told me, he was currently the Champion's mate. Not boyfriend, not partner, not lover, but mate. When I had asked why he used that term, he had simply said it was a vampire thing and shrugged his shoulders in that casual elegant way he has.

Mate, did not make me think of elegance however, just animals. How close to the truth was it?

He had light brown hair, just long enough to tie behind his head. His outfit, although elegant, was not as well put together as the Scribe. It seemed rushed, I even noticed a button on his cuff that had not been done up, or he had simply forgotten to put his cuff links in at all, I couldn't see the other side, he kept that hand out of sight. His eyes were a piercing blue, almost ultramarine, with flecks of turquoise. Most alarming. I had to fight not to look at them. I knew, without a doubt, he would be one of the few vamps who could catch me with their glaze, so I was determined not to let him.

He did try to cover me with his voice though, but it wasn't at all pleasant, it just made me feel uncomfortable, as though his goal was to make me squirm. Vampire tricks can be tedious, I was shielding like hell, but it was taking concentration and strength, neither of which I had in abundance right now. That's probably why he was doing it.

I glanced around the table. The council had all arrived, we had only sat down when the Champion, the last to enter the hall, had sat herself. Fair enough, she was the boss. My gaze flicked over Gregor, I had to force myself not to let it stop and linger there. In the brief glimpse I did allow myself I noticed he was dressed as beautifully as the first night I had seen him, in the alley near the *Trevi Fountain*. He looked stunning. He was talking animatedly to the only other female at the table. She was beautiful, in a timeless way, as though her beauty transcended fashion, or trend, it just was. I gathered she had to be the Pandora. Her aura flashed a blackness that seemed so solid, I had to look twice. Whereas the others around the table had varying degrees of Light within them, Pandora just had Dark. It confused me, I hadn't expected such Dark to exist in the *Iunctio*.

The Champion's voice whispered through my mind, I hadn't realised she could do that. Read my thoughts yes, but speak to me in my head? No.

Why are you surprised? Are we not all Children of the Dark?

The we she referred to was of course the Nosferatu. As I, a Nosferatin, am a Child of the Light, they are Children of the Dark.

The Dark exists in all of you, but where there is Dark, there should always be Light; as where there is Light, there should always be Dark, I answered in my thoughts.

Yet you see no Light in her. Does this worry you?

I couldn't lie to the Champion, she already knew my thoughts. And if you have ever tried not to think of a thought, when it has already blossomed in your mind, then you'd know it's impossible. So I didn't.

I am unsure what my Light would do to her should she come close.

Do you have so little control of your Light?

And here was the big, big, question. The reason why we were sitting around this table pretending to have polite conversation. If the council decided I was a threat to the *Iunctio* or to the Nosferatu as a whole, then I would be disposed of. They wouldn't need the Champion's permission, they wouldn't need her to pass the judgement and therefore fail to kill me because of Nut's protection. They would just do. One of them, without direction, but mutual consent.

You already know the answer to that.

I want you to say it. To admit it. Her words were sharp in my mind.

So you can tell the others?

She didn't answer. She just vanished from my mind. It was as though I could feel her when she was there, like a weight inside my head, but there was just an emptiness when she was gone. I didn't understand why she had left. It didn't make sense.

The two vampires next to me, must have realised I was having an internal conversation and they probably knew it was with the Champion, so had started talking to each other, giving me some space. They didn't know the conversation was over, so I took advantage of their lack of interest in me to scan the rest of the table.

My eyes fell on the Diviner. He was studying Gregor. But Gregor hadn't noticed his interest and was just talking to the Pandora as he had been from when we first sat. I had seen that look in the Diviner's eyes before though, when he had noticed the Champion had a connection to me. As soon as that thought was completed in my head, the Diviner's eyes flicked to me and held my gaze. He knew Gregor and I had a connection and he would know it was an exchange of *Sigillum*. He smiled and it was a wicked smile. Oh shit.

He held my gaze, but must have somehow spoken to the Champion. Probably just projected his thoughts, because her gaze slowly shifted back to me. Like a snake spotting its prey.

You have been naughty, Hunter. He is ours and you have stolen him.

Oh double shit.

She stood then and it was all I could do not to run from that room.

The vampires around the table went to stand with her, but she simply waved her hand at them, indicating they should all remain seated. Silence filled the space, as though it was tangible, something you could grasp, or should cower from.

"Enforcer. Would you be so kind as to stand." Her voice echoed around the hall, bouncing off the walls, rattling the chandeliers hanging from the ceiling, making the carafes of wine vibrate next to our seats. This was not good.

Gregor stood, smoothly, with that otherworldly motion. He showed no fear, only polite interest.

"You have chosen one here to share your *Sigillum* with."

There was suddenly a tension in the room. My eyes flicked to Michel's, they were neutral, under control, but he did hold my gaze for a moment, before returning his attention to the Champion.

"Lucinda." The Champion didn't look at me as she said my name, but her voice caressed my arms, making goosebumps rise along the length of them. "Please stand." She was being polite, but I didn't doubt that was about to change, her *Sanguis Vitam* had already rolled across the table and hit me like a brick wall.

She knew I would have trouble standing, even leaning forward in my seat was taking a tremendous amount of effort. If the Scribe hadn't have taken pity on me, I would have still been sitting there after dessert, but he simply reached out and touched my hand and I could breathe. The Champion let a low growl out between her red lips, but he didn't remove his touch. I stood, a little shakily and then his hand fell away.

If it was tension I felt in the room before, it was now fear. Every vampire around that table, perhaps apart from Pandora, was radiating fear. But fear of what? The Champion or what she might do? Fear for Gregor? Or was it fear of me?

"What say you, Gregor?" she asked coolly.

"I have found a mate, Champion, would you begrudge me that?

What the fuck?

Do not show your surprise, ma douce.

For Michel to risk talking to me in my head I was obviously failing at remaining neutral to an alarming degree. I reschooled my features into my usual mask, the one I reserve for vampires, especially those I find most chilling and don't want them to see my fear.

"You have complicated things." The Champion did not sound happy. "She now affords your protection and those of yours sworn to you."

All eyes at the table were now on me. I wasn't sure if I completely understood what was happening, but it was definitely having an effect on the vampires in the room. The Champion glared at me, but she was no longer forcing her *Sanguis Vitam* over me, she was no longer using any vampiric mind control at all. It was as if the entire room had stopped messing with my mind. Why?

Because you are his. The Champion's words were bitter in my mind.

I shook my head. I couldn't form the words in my mind to say *I don't understand.*

She laughed and even that didn't have an effect over me and answered my question out loud.

"The Enforcer has chosen a mate. It is forbidden for us to tamper with the mate of a council member. With his protection, none of the Council can touch you, without suffering his wrath." She paused, to smile sweetly at me. "Unless you have broken a law of course, by which all are judged regardless of connections."

Oh. I got it. No more influence, no more mind control games. The Enforcer was their scary monster, even they didn't want to come up against him.

Exactly.

But what of the Prophesy and the threat the *Iunctio* believes I am to them?

Should you be a threat to the Iunctio you will be judged accordingly. The Enforcer's protection does not cover that. However, should you be found guilty on such charges, he will suffer the same judgement as you.

And then she was gone from my mind.

Wow. Had Gregor planned this? I didn't think so, he would have mentioned it. And somehow the whole, *he will suffer the same judgement as you* didn't sound like the sort of thing a vampire would willing get themselves into. So what did this actually mean? There had to be something in it for him to have opened himself up to such possible danger. Surely he knew the *Iunctio* were not going to rule in my favour.

And why were they so scared of him? It reminded me of the reaction Michel had, when I first mentioned Gregor's interest in me. He had been scared too. Had I missed something here? Gregor just didn't make me scared, well not in that way.

The Champion was still standing, so was Gregor and myself. Gregor flicked his gaze to me, but didn't hold it. Just a glance. I think he wanted to make sure I wasn't mad. I couldn't be mad at something I didn't fully understand, but I was beginning to think I might be, once all was revealed.

The Champion sat then, so we did too and then dinner was served.

A stream of scantily clad humans entered the room. It wasn't enough that they were being served up as dinner, they had to be subjected to displaying as much of their body as was possible, without being actually nude. The bodies all climbed onto the table and proceeded to crawl around the edges of it, like a perverted catwalk show.

Every now and then, one of the council members would reach out and grab a human, pulling them into their laps and proceeding to run their hands over their prize, laying a kiss here, murmuring a word there. I so did not want to watch them playing with their food.

Suddenly, Gregor was at my shoulder, his head bent down to whisper in my ear. It was probably a waste of time, all the vampires here could have heard every word, or maybe because I was his *mate* now they blocked it, out of respect, or some warped vampire mating practice or privilege.

"As my human *Sigillum*-shared and as my declared mate, it is appropriate for me to feed from you, should I wish to *not* partake of the offerings here."

I looked up at him. His eyes were still neutral, nothing

to give away what he actually felt.

"I do not wish any on this table. I wish for only you."

Why was he doing this? He obviously didn't need to feed from me, he didn't need to make me feel like food in front of all the council members, so why was he doing this?

I couldn't help it, I had to look at Michel. And just as my eyes met his, so blue, so many flecks of indigo and amethyst dancing in their depths, I watched numbly as he reached forward almost blindly, his eyes still locked with mine, and grabbed a passing human, pulling him into his lap.

What the hell? He wasn't going to stop this? I suddenly did not want to be here, panic rose up my body threatening to cut off my air. Gregor simply pulled me to my feet, up against his body, so I was facing away from the table, and whispered, "Trust me" as he took my seat and pulled me into his lap. I couldn't see what was happening behind me, I could no longer see Michel and his *dinner,* as Gregor had me still facing mainly him, sitting sideways on his lap. And then Gregor's eyes caught mine, a flash of silver washed over them, he simply brushed my hair to the side and pulled my neck towards his mouth.

I didn't see his fangs come down, I didn't have a chance to brace. He made it a swift action, one I couldn't have time to fight. His fangs simply pierced my skin, the sharpness making me gasp, quickly followed by beautiful, longed-for bliss.

The room disappeared around me and all I heard in my mind was, *trust me, ma cherie, please trust me.*

I wasn't quite sure if I could.

Chapter 39
The Challenger

I don't know how long Gregor fed for. Time had ceased to exist. All I wanted was his lips on my skin, his teeth in my flesh and his hands on my body. Feeding for a vampire is an intimate thing. It doesn't need to be, sometimes it can just be food to stay alive, but given the choice, vampires will usually feed from those they are attracted to.

How far they take that attraction will vary. Before Michel fed regularly from me, he would enjoy it, but I am sure he rarely took it further than the action of the feeding alone. I'm also quite sure, he no doubt *did* take it further when it pleased him on occasion, but that would be more an exception to the rule.

So, it should have surprised me, that Gregor was taking this further, but it didn't, because right then I wanted him to. He wasn't just feeding from me, he was damn near undressing me in front of all the *Iunctio* council members. I couldn't tell if they were paying attention, or too busy undressing their own meals too. All of my attention was on Gregor's hands on my skin, under my short dress, pushing it higher than it should ever go in public and at the back of my neck, up in my hair.

Finally, he finished feeding and withdrew his fangs, licking my skin, but the heat he had sent through my body didn't go away and when his eyes met mine, I felt it build even further. I vaguely realised, he was glazing me to a certain extent and this should have set the alarm bells clanging, but instead I simply shifted my position, so I was now straddling him, my legs either side of his body, his chest against my breasts. And I wrapped my arms around his neck and just leaned in to kiss him.

His mouth met mine in a bruising crush. There was no delicate brush of lips, this was all an almost uncontrolled hunger and need. And I wasn't sure who it belonged to, me or him. But we both fell into it with abandon.

My hands ran through his hair, pulling it loose from the clip. His hands were all over me, pulling me closer and closer, making my body ride up his, the movement sending shockwaves through me, making me shudder against his chest. A sound escaped his lips as I felt him harden between my legs and his tongue started darting in so deeply, so quickly, in my mouth. If it was possible to get inside me through my mouth, I think he would have.

I had no intention of stopping him, of stopping this. He could have laid me out on that low table, stripped me bare and had all of me, right then, in front of all of the *Iunctio* council. I wouldn't have cared, I would have cried for more. I don't know if he would have done that, he was certainly very much enjoying the show we were currently putting on and I could feel just how desperately he wanted to take it further. Whether he had forgotten our audience or not, I didn't know, but he was most definitely caught up in the moment.

If it hadn't have been for the Pull, I wouldn't have lifted from the haze of desire he had created in me. I was damn near drowning it and quite happy to go under too. But my evil-lurks-in-the-city Pull slapped me in the face and then tugged me in various directions, so I pushed away from Gregor with a gasp. His arms stiffened around me as my body arched back, stopping me from falling off his lap altogether. Then the world turned black and I sunk into the nothingness that takes me Dream Walking. But I wasn't Dream Walking this time, I was *seeking*. And what I *saw* made me shudder in fear.

There were so many, so many of them. And they were here. Before I fell out of that black void from fear, I forced myself to feel more, to sense more. Why were they here? What did they want?

It was like asking a question, I simply received an answer. They were here to kill the Champion, they were here to take over the *Iunctio*.

I fell out of the black nothingness into bright lights, loud voices and firm hands on my shoulders shaking me.

"Lucinda. Lucinda." Gregor's voice was the loudest of them all, but the council members were aware that something had just happened, something big and they were demanding explanations too.

I scrambled off Gregor's lap and spun to look at the Champion. There must have been some look on my face, because the council all fell quiet. She simply held my gaze, standing straight, making her seem so much taller than she actually was. If I hadn't have already known she was my height, I would have thought she towered over me now.

Guards rushed in to stand between us. They thought I was a threat, but the Champion just cocked her head at me and raised her eyebrows.

What is it, Hunter? What do you see?

My voice was low and a little breathless, but I held her gaze. This was for her.

"There's too many of them. Hundreds. They're almost here."

The vampires in the room stiffened and moved ever so

slightly, perhaps readying themselves for battle. Perhaps uncomfortable with this whole scene. I didn't pay them any attention, I just had eyes for the Champion alone.

"They come for you. They come to challenge and to kill."

Now voices were raised around me and the guards stepped forward with their hands outstretched, no doubt to secure me, to trap me, but it wasn't me they needed to fight. I didn't want the Champion dead, well not right now, but they didn't know that. I had just threatened the Champion though, even if my words were only a warning.

My eyes hadn't left hers. She didn't show fear, but surprise. Was she that sure of herself that no one would ever challenge her?

Before the guards had crossed the distance required to grab me, I said, "These are the rogue vampires who have been plaguing your city. Does the *Iunctio* not wish to defend its honour?"

"Seize her!" It was the Tempest, off to my right.

Gregor pulled me behind him, trying to protect me, but I didn't need protection from the guards. I needed it from the hundreds of rogue vampires who were about to breach the *Palais* and storm this room.

"Champion." My voice was normal, not raised and to a human they wouldn't have heard it over the voices shouting in the room, but I knew she did. "You need me. Without me you will lose."

It's not that I think I'm the biggest, baddest vampire hunter out there or anything, I mean as far as I'm concerned, Nero's that, but I knew in that moment, as if Nut was whispering in my ear, that without my help the

Iunctio would fall tonight. I knew it and because I knew it, so did the Champion. Whether she just read my mind, or whether it was the connection we shared, the one that I now realised Nut had placed there, but the Champion raised her hand, letting her voice carry over all sounds in the hall, flattening them, until it was only her words we could hear.

"Leave her! Prepare for battle and let the *Sanguis Vitam Cupitor* do her job."

The Tempest made a sound, but it was squashed by whatever the Champion was doing to the room. And then we heard the outer walls of the *Palais* explode and the sounds of hundreds of vampires swarming the building.

The council members of the *Iunctio* are all old and experienced warriors. They hadn't got to where they were without having won a battle or two, so they were already fanning out, placing themselves in the best position to face the onslaught that was about to come. Somehow working together to cover the ground and surround the Champion. I don't know why I felt the need to be close to her, she had guards, she had the council members all prepared to fight to the death to protect her, she didn't need a little Nosferatin getting in the way, but my inner monologue piped up and shouted through my mind, *Protect her! Protect her! Protect her!*

I ran towards where she was standing, no one stopped me, they were all on full alert facing the approaching battle sounds. *Iunctio* guards and flunkies were fighting it out, on the other side of these walls, but they would fail, I knew this, and I had to protect the Champion.

I slid to a stop in front of her and spun to face the sounds.

You wish to protect me, Nosferatin? She sounded amused.

Yes.

With what?

She had me there, no stake. Damn. I could do some damage with my bare hands, but kill? I wasn't so sure. Did I really have the strength to rip a vampire's head off it's shoulders? I doubted that, but what other options were available to me? I had to protect her and I think I was prepared to die trying.

I felt her in my mind then, she didn't say anything, but she'd heard my thought and she was surprised. Astounded more like it. Absolutely blown away. She hadn't expected a Nosferatin to throw themselves in front of the leader of the *Iunctio*. She had not expected me, the *Sanguis Vitam Cupitor*, prepared to sacrifice myself for her. Why?

I couldn't explain it, I just knew this was what Nut wanted me to do.

Ma douce!

My eyes flicked up to Michel. I knew exactly where he was in the room, I didn't need to search, the Bond pulled me to him. He was off to the side, standing with more of the council, ready to do battle. He looked at me and reached inside his jacket, pulling a black felt draw string bag from his inner pocket and throwing it to me, through the air. I caught it, a reflex action, as it was flying with some speed and opened the top to peer inside.

The most beautiful sight awaited, glinting in the lights from the chandeliers: my stake. I let a little laugh out and felt my whole body relax. I slipped my hand in and felt the familiar coolness of silver against my skin. Centring me, grounding me, making me feel like I was connected to all the Nosferatin left in the world. I pulled it out and it sparkled in the room, making nearby vampires turn towards me with fear. *It's all right boys, I'm on your side.*

The Champion actually laughed.

I glanced back at Michel and saw it, love. I think it was mine, my love for him, but it may have been his too, I'm not sure. But only Michel would have thought to smuggle my stake into a room full of potentially lethal vampires. Only Michel would have thought to cover my back.

I love you. I sent the thought to him.

He smiled, the smile he reserves for only me. That smile that takes my breath away, that shows me the little boy he once would have been. He doesn't flash that smile often, it makes him vulnerable, so I really appreciate it when he does. It's just so damn precious.

Je t'aime trop, ma douce.

And then they were here.

There's just something about facing evil vampires. Granted, I usually only face one at a time and there were literally hundreds swarming us now, but this was what I was made for. This was what I do. It's as natural as breathing, as essential as water and as basic as existing. It is who I am.

The first wave of vampires were met with the formidable force of the *Iunctio* guards, who were not the closest guards of the Champion without amassing some skills. They were joined by a few of the council. The Scribe was one, who was more than capable of holding his own, which did momentarily surprise me and I recognised the Diviner in amongst the flashes and swirls. And also the vampire who had originally been with the Champion on the first night we arrived. Michel had told me he was the Keeper. Apparently his role was to oversee the *Iunctio's* power, to keep it contained and direct it where it needed to be. I didn't doubt that someone who held that sort of position was important to the *Iunctio*, but it certainly didn't stop him from entering the fray. He was also very powerful and he was loving it, by the look in his sparkling eyes. His striped hair flashing in the lights as he moved, making the blonde stripes look like a tiger's pelt, dancing in the breeze.

Within seconds the sheer number of attacking vampires had breached the first line of defence and had taken to the entire room. None had made it to the Champion, I wasn't the only one landing blows in an effort to protect her. She was well surrounded and lashing out with her own formidable powers as well. Beside me were two of the most powerful and oldest vampires I had ever felt. I knew in an instant who they were, as though they brushed my mind when I noticed their age and power. They knew I had felt them, not just seen them and they both simultaneously whispered in my head.

I am the Ambrosia. I am the giver of eternal life. The second vampire almost whispering over the first. *I am the Nemesis. I force what is due.*

As soon as I heard the Nemesis in my head I slammed my shields down, throwing him out and changed my stance to partially face him. He didn't look at me, just continued to battle several vampires in front of us and smiled. When I say battle, he simply stood there with his hands raised and directed unseen blow after unseen blow on the vampires clambering to get past us. What good Nut thought I could do when vampires simply sent out thoughts as attacks was beyond me. But ours is not to reason why and all of that.

Despite my shields, despite my formidable walls, I still heard his voice inside me. Not in my mind, almost as though he was whispering it over the walls, as though he had found the top of them and wasn't breaching them as such, just standing on the other side and letting his voice carry over them and down to me.

You are stronger than you appear, Nosferatin. I think he would have said more, but then the Ambrosia decided to show his strength too and joined the party in my head.

Leave her, Nemesis, she is no longer yours to influence. I felt the Nemesis leave, but I was certain the Ambrosia was still there, just biding his time. It was an uncomfortable feeling. Not exactly distracting, I seemed to be able to still focus on everything around me, but I felt his presence and knew he was still there and it left me feeling a little cold.

The attacking vampires were taking a hit, but then so were we. Several of the guards had turned to dust and I saw the Scribe fall. He didn't turn to dust straight away, so he was still alive, but he was on the ground and if he didn't move soon, he would be floating away on the air like the rest of the dead-dead. I couldn't leave the Champion, even if I wanted to, my body would not have obeyed my command. I obscurely thought that Nut was going to really piss me off soon if she didn't let me have free will, but I pushed that aside and concentrated on the Scribe. He had helped me, when the Champion had forced her *Sanguis Vitam* at me, he had stood against her, despite her obvious disapproval of his interference. I owed him. And I always like paying my debts.

I gathered my Light inside me and fashioned it into a spear. When a vampire went in for the kill, I threw it with all my might and watched as it sailed through the space between us and pierced him in the heart. It was as good as a stake, he burst into dust; not just the average grey dust they usually make when killed for real, but a multicoloured rainbow of dust, that under different circumstances would have been quite cool. The Scribe came to and leapt to his feet, in time to face the next vampire on his own.

Impressive. The Ambrosia, still in my mind. *You have taught her well, Nut.*

I hadn't even realised she was there, but as she was having some influence over my actions, being unable to leave the Champion's side, it didn't really surprise me. Her voice was like soothing water running over hot skin. I loved it.

Her actions are all her own, my old friend. This one is special.

I had no idea what she meant by that, but the Ambrosia spoke again, cutting into my train of thought.

The weight of our world is on her shoulders. I will assist where I can. I felt his sadness then, it was overwhelming.

Thank you, Father, Nut whispered and then they were both gone. I still didn't want to leave the Champion's side, but my mind was my own and it was reeling.

I didn't have time to digest that conversation further just then, because a second wave of attacking vampires stormed the room and we were well and truly swamped.

I went from one to the other, feeling my stake sink in. I wasn't immune to their strikes, I had scratches on my face and down my sides, bite marks on my forearms where I had thrown a hand in front of my face for protection, my dress was ripped, my hair torn out in chunks and still I kept finding my targets. It was as if none of what they did to me mattered. I'd heard soldiers could behave like that, as though they detached from what physical assault their bodies were receiving and operated from somewhere else. I knew I had Nut with me, so maybe I just thought she was in control, but she wasn't. It was all me. She was barely touching my mind, just watching, just waiting, but for what?

I finally realised we were losing. We'd only lost maybe one council member's life. When he had turned to dust, I felt the collective sigh from the council members and his name wash over me, the Creator. He was the vampire who had replaced Michel when Michel left the *Iunctio*. Despite only one loss of life so far, I knew we couldn't hold them. And I knew the Champion knew this too.

We were losing and I'd told her she would without my help, yet here I was helping and still I couldn't stop this. I felt frustration fill me up and then quickly replaced it with determination. I gritted my teeth and sent a thought to the Champion.

Help me, I need to concentrate.

She didn't ask what I was going to do, she simply sent her *Sanguis Vitam* out to surround me, to shield me, to make me almost disappear. So those vampires approaching couldn't even see me or sense me, couldn't find me to attack.

I used the time she had given me, precious that it was, as it was no doubt leaving her vulnerable, to fall quickly into the black nothingness of my void and seek all the vampires in the room. I separated those of ours, careful to include the dark Darkness of the Pandora and singled out the evil of those attacking. I briefly brushed on the Tempest, recognising his signature fitted with the attacking vampires, but pulled him back to our side. I'd worry about that later.

Then I gathered my Light, said a little prayer to a different God than Nut, and thrust it out of my body. It was rather like a heat seeking missile, except hundreds of them. All individual projectiles propelled from inside me and forcibly thrust out into the room. It took seconds, but within seconds every vampire who was attacking us was dust. Oh. My. God.

The silence that greeted me as I came back to my body was deafening. If silence can be that. All of the *Iunctio* members were staring at me in wonder and fear. And in the case of the Ambrosia, I think pride. I didn't know what to say or do under the weight of all those eyes, so I turned to the Champion, she was the one in charge and waited for her to speak.

Her mouth was slightly open, as though she had moments before formed an O, but she slowly closed it and a small crease appeared between her delicate brows.

It felt like an eternity, but finally she spoke.

"It appears the *Sanguis Vitam Cupitor* is on our side, after all." I felt she was thinking *for now anyway*, but she didn't say it in my mind and she definitely didn't say it aloud.

Michel was beside me in an instant. I hadn't even seen him move. He was dusty and a little tattered, his hair had come loose and he had some marks on his face, but he was beautiful. So beautiful. And his hand as it took mine made all my aches and the pains from my scratches seem inconsequential. He brushed my mind and I automatically lowered my shields, letting his healing power flood in, chasing away the cold and replacing everything with warmth. I don't know if he had meant to do that right then, right now, with the Champion watching so closely. But it didn't matter, it was done, like a reflex action, he couldn't help himself.

The Champion's lips curved in a slight smile and she whispered in my mind, *However will you manage with two of them at your beck and call?*

I had no friggin' idea how to answer that one, so I just smiled.

She turned her attention to the rest of the council and said, "This was not a random attack, it was well planned, someone meant to challenge me."

And then the room went dark, the Champion the only thing I could see, the only thing I wanted to see. She had risen off the floor and was levitating a few feet in the air. Some vampires, powerful master ones, can fly, but levitation is a little different. Actually managing to stay still in the air is quite something, you ask a pilot, planes need to fly forward to have enough upward thrust to maintain altitude, so do vamps. Levitation is only reserved for those vampires with real mojo.

"Who among us, challenges me?" Why she thought it was one of the council members I didn't know, maybe she already knew the answer and she wanted to make them come forward publicly, rather than strike without evidence.

But, she floated there sure of herself and the vampires in the room simply buzzed *Sanguis Vitam.* Contained, but threatening to release. I was betting most of them were outraged, but one, one was angry and I could feel which one that was.

I turned slowly to that pull, so familiar, so like those of the vampires who had just attacked and I looked directly at the Tempest. The Champion and all the other vampires had seen me move, unable to sense what I sensed, but following my gaze. They all looked at the Tempest and I felt their *Sanguis Vitam* climb.

He wasn't going to go down without a fight. He laughed bitterly and I thought he'd just deny it, tell them I was mad, that I was wrong, maybe even that I was the one who had orchestrated all of this, but instead he just flew at me. The air in the room roared like a tornado had hit, dust flew around us, making it impossible to see, impossible to hear. He knew where he was going, but no one could see me or him to intervene.

But, I'd had practice at this game. The number of times I had been caught while invisible and Dream Walking recently had dented my pride, so I instinctively stepped a few paces to the right, away from where I had been standing before the storm blew up and the Tempest jumped, and crouched down low to the ground.

I felt him approach, to my left, towards where I had been. I closed my eyes and concentrated on the feel of him. I couldn't see his aura, but I could sense him. A type of seeking, but I wasn't even in that black nothingness now, just the darkness of the dust. It worked, because I knew exactly where he was, what position his body was in, where his heart beat and how the stake would feel when it entered his chest wall.

I simply moved my weight onto my left foot, twisted my body with my right arm, as it arced in front of me and found his heart through his back. The dust in the air, from the tornado he had created, fell to the ground, as the stake slid home and his dust joined the others on the floor.

I looked up at the Champion, still floating, and sent the thought, *Oops.*

She just smiled, the kind of smile you share with a girlfriend. An intimate understanding between two friends. Not that I ever thought the Champion and I would go shopping together, but still, I think we understood each other in that moment better than we ever had before. Or probably ever would again.

Well done. I was tiring of him anyway.

The lights came back on, the Champion floated back to the ground and suddenly I was in Michel's arms.

And there was no where else I wanted to be.

Epilogue

We didn't stick around to celebrate. Before dawn was even a whisper on the horizon we were at Charles de Gaulle Airport, our luggage already on Michel's plane and us about to board.

The Champion had bid us farewell, but not before decreeing that the *Iunctio* would keep a close eye on my progress, for the welfare of all those concerned. Of course, I knew it was only the welfare of the Nosferatu that she was really concerned with, but as I had just protected the *Iunctio* from destruction, admitted that I would die to protect her and also managed to kill her challenger when all those around her were unable to, I was kind of in the good books for now, so I didn't make a fuss. Just accepted the reprieve and scarpered.

She had dropped one bombshell on us though. Michel as the Master of Auckland City should not also be the Master of Wellington. Even though Michel had set up a base in Wellington for several reasons, part of it had been because of the increased supernatural activity there and as a by product, the increase in human awareness, leading to a few vampire deaths, which he had been unable to explain to the council. They were concerned and felt the fact that he spent most of his time in Auckland, away from the trouble in Wellington, was not acceptable. We had expected this. So, problem solved. Michel would forfeit Wellington and they would appoint a caretaker, someone they could trust to sort the problem out and report back to them.

Of course, neither Michel nor myself had considered who they would put there, so it was difficult to keep the surprise off our faces when she announced, most pleasantly

I might add, that it would be the Enforcer. I don't know if she just wanted to rub Michel's nose in it, or cause as much disruption as she possibly could to my life. Or really because she thought it was the girl-friendly thing to do, to send my *mate* across the seas to at least be in the same country as me, but whatever reason, she had succeeded in unbalancing me. If my world was confusing before and I had hoped it would settle with some distance from Gregor, it was now just about to spin back out of control.

Damn.

But, I pulled myself together, thanked her for her hospitality, even managing to keep a straight face on while I said that and we made our escape.

Just as we were about to board the plane however, a sleek black *Iunctio* car pulled up on the tarmac. Michel knew who it was before he even got out of the back of the vehicle and so he just kissed me on the cheek resignedly and boarded the plane alone, whispering, "Take your time, *ma douce*."

I was left facing Gregor as his tall frame leaned against the car, hands in pockets, legs crossed at his ankles, a picture of casual ease. I sighed and walked toward him.

Gregor's rich voice reached me across the short distance from where he leaned casually against the *Iunctio's* car and I stood, stock still. "Were you just going to leave without saying goodbye, little Hunter?"

"We're in a bit of a hurry to beat the sun," I managed to reply.

He glanced at the horizon, he didn't need to, he'd be able to sense the sun approaching, right down to the second it breached the dark.

"There is time, I think."

"Goodbye then." I really didn't want to do this. I was so confused and having him near was not helping. I desperately wanted to get back to some semblance of normal life. Not like before I moved to Auckland, that type of normality is lost to me forever, but maybe just the normal of having only one man in my life I couldn't bear to be parted from.

He smiled at me, that knowing smile they have. "You would not miss me?"

"Don't do this, Gregor."

"Why not?"

"Because I'm tired and I've had enough games for one night. And I just want to go home."

He just watched me for a while, a long while. It was a little unnerving and time *was* marching on, so I took a breath in and asked the one question I had been stewing over since the dinner in the Great Dining Hall.

"Why did you feed from me?" After everything I had been through, that seemed to be the biggest hurdle I was currently facing in my mind. Not only the fact that Gregor had fed from me, as though it was his right and I was his property to do so from, but the fact that Michel had encouraged it. Or at the very least, done nothing to stop it. As far as manipulation goes, that was the whammy right there. And both of them had used me, had put me in that position to be used as a means to an end. I just couldn't figure out what that end was and whether it was worth being used over.

"We needed to put on a good show."

I actually laughed out loud. "A good show?" Some

show then, having me almost do the nasty with him on the Dining Hall's table.

He smiled slightly, no doubt hearing the thoughts rioting through my head. I wasn't reining it in, I was pretty damn mad actually.

"Simply declaring you were my mate would not have been enough, they needed to see your desire for me too."

"And you just thought biting me and glazing me was the best way to achieve that? No chance of asking me to play along? Or am I only a tool that just gets used when it suits?"

His eyes flashed silver with those dangerous but enthralling flecks of platinum and his smile slipped quickly from his beautiful full lips. He was definitely not amused.

"You are my mate." He said it, like it should have meant something to me.

"That was obviously something you said in the heat of the moment to get us out of a tight spot. Whatever the hell it means, it's nothing, it doesn't matter. The tight spot is over."

"It matters to me. It should matter to you"

"But it doesn't. I didn't ask for it. I have no idea what it means. It's just another one of the ways for you to get what you want. To hell with what I think."

His eyes bore into mine for what seemed like an eternity, the dark grey no longer visible at all in the silver swirling with more and more small specks of platinum. I kept forgetting that there's a lot of Dark in Gregor, but I could feel it now. And it called to me softly, drawing me in. A shiver went down my spine.

"I told you once, Lucinda, that I would die for you. I

would cast away everything I possess to be near you."

"You also said you would take only what I was willing to give and no more."

He smiled. "You remember."

How could I not remember? How could he forget?

"You are my mate, Lucinda, whether you want it or not. I will be with you again in New Zealand and we shall see just how much you are willing to give."

I didn't like the tone of his voice, so sure, so confident, but I also couldn't think of a thing to say in reply. I was simply losing all cognitive thought around Gregor, operating on basic instinct alone. His Darkness had started a chain reaction. It was pulling and I was trying my best to stand my ground, but in the end, I knew who or what would win. He was dangerous, more dangerous than I had ever realised and he still wanted me. I suppressed a shudder, somewhat unsuccessfully and waited for him to say goodbye.

His smiled broadened and he took a step towards me. I wanted to raise my hand and stop him. I wanted to simply turn away, but the look in his eyes captured me and I don't think he was using his glaze.

He came to stand right in front of me, almost touching me with his body, he was so close. I had to strain my head back to look up at him. I felt Michel brush my shields then, letting me know he was there if needed, but if I couldn't handle this moment alone, then I was doomed. I took a deep breath in and put my hand against Gregor's chest to stop him coming closer. He raised an eyebrow at me.

"That's far enough," I whispered.

"Not nearly," he replied and pushed, ever so slightly

against my hand. I took a step back and then another, until there was breathing space between us. He just smiled more.

"Unless you want to get crispy critter, I suggest you get in your car and go," I said woodenly.

He nodded slowly, but the smile was still firmly in place.

"Until we meet again, *ma petite chasseuse*." And he blew me a kiss, which I actually felt against his mark on the side of my neck.

I turned away before he could see the effect he had on me and almost ran up the steps to the plane.

The cabin crew guy, or whatever they are called on a private jet, sealed the door behind me and secured all the shades in place, so when the sun rose Michel would be protected.

He was sitting on the couch, relaxed, half reclined looking at me. If he had been watching out the window, it didn't show. I suddenly felt very awkward. There were other armchairs to sit in, but I had always sat on the couch with Michel when we flew. I didn't quite know what to do with myself. He didn't offer me any help, just sat observing me.

"Excuse me, miss. We're about to taxi onto the runway, you need to be seated now." The manservant/cabin crewman said in a pleasant voice. I just jumped.

Michel smiled.

That did it. He was so sure I'd come sit with him, so I walked over to a chair opposite him and sat down, securing my seatbelt around me. The manservant hesitated, he had expected me to go to Michel too, but he recovered himself and went to sit in his little private kitchen area, out of sight.

The master could handle his own battles.

Michel was still smiling, this time I think he was trying not to laugh. He really wanted me to rise to the bait didn't he? I just glared at him.

"You know, I only find you more adorable than usual when you are angry, *ma douce*."

I didn't say anything, just blinked.

The plane began to move across the tarmac. Michel settled himself more comfortably on the couch. No seatbelt, he wouldn't survive a crash on take off probably, but then again, maybe he would.

The plane launched into the air gracefully and suddenly we were airborne on our way home to Auckland. Still several hours away, practically more than a whole day, but the anticipation, the joy of being home soon consumed me. I only felt the tug of going home and the emotions that evoked washed away any anger that had built, making me smile.

"What are you thinking, *ma douce*?"

"That we'll be home soon and this will all be over."

"For now, yes." He wasn't trying to put a dampener on my mood, I don't think he could have really, he was just stating the obvious. The *Iunctio* would still be watching us and we needed to behave. I didn't mind, I could be a good girl when I tried. We'd keep them happy and maybe, just maybe, our world would go back to how it was.

That made me look at Michel. He had changed quickly after the battle, as had I and was in his more casual black trousers and black shirt, sleeves rolled up, open at the neck, his deep cream skin a wonderful contrast to the black. I shook my head, he was gorgeous. But was that enough?

Sure, I was joined to him, Bonded even. We had a connection closer than most and it was for the rest of our eternal lives, but I had learnt a lot over the past few days, an awful lot. How could it not change how I viewed him, how I felt about him?

I knew I still loved him, wanted him, needed to be near him, but how could I not take into consideration all that had happened? Could I trust him? He was the master of manipulation, the consummate politician. Everything he did was planned and even if I got in the way of those plans, somehow he managed to find a way to use me. To make me fit his grand schemes. I'm not sure I wanted to fit his grand schemes. The confusion I had been feeling since meeting Gregor and having my world turned upside down was also still there and I had absolutely no idea what to do about it. How to fix it, solve it, mend the break that Michel and I now had.

I did know that I couldn't live without Michel. No matter what I decided, he would have to be a part of my life. But could I stand him being just a platonic part, like Nafrini is to Nero? Could I stand to be around him every day and not be able to touch?

The answer was simple. No.

I sighed and undid my seat belt. The plane had levelled out slightly, not quite forcing you back in your seat, like it does when just taken off from the ground, so I was quite sure I could risk undoing my belt.

Michel was still watching me, no longer smiling, more a cautious hopeful look on his face. He wasn't even trying to shield. It was as though we had passed that and he wanted me to see all of him. Damn. He wasn't making this easy, or maybe he was and it was me who was making this so hard.

I got up and walked over to him. His eyes lit up with swirls of indigo, he held out a hand, no smirk, no confident smile, just his hand.

And I took it, letting him pull me into his arms, against his chest, almost sitting on his lap, but just managing to slide in beside him on the couch. His arms wrapped around me, his face buried in my hair and I felt complete for the first time in days. This wasn't the answer to all my problems I was seeking, but it felt so good and so right. Touching him was as necessary as the air that I breathed. In that instant I acknowledged that, I pushed away the doubt, the fear, the confusion, for another day and I dropped my shields, dropped everything that I had built around me and let him back in.

I felt his warm sea breeze wash over me, the smell of meadows in spring surround me, clean cut grass engulf me, as his whisper in my mind caressed me.

There is only you, ma douce, there will only ever be you. I am yours and always will be.

He lifted my face up to his with his fingers on my chin and I was met with most mesmerizing blues, indigos and amethysts, swirling and dancing, drawing me in. His lips when they met mine were so soft, so careful, but warm and smooth, and I melted against their touch, opening myself up and letting him in. He took the hint and began kissing me in earnest. First a little more firmly, then a slip of his tongue, followed by the press of his body as he lay me back on the couch. I gave back everything I had, tasting him, smelling him, trying to get as close as I could to him. It was as though we hadn't touched for weeks, not just days or hours and our bodies craved each other, longed for each other and we were just along for the ride.

Despite every doubt I may have had, every horror of the past few days, Michel was a part of me I couldn't deny, didn't want to deny. I knew reality would, at some point, come knocking on my door, but for now this was all I wanted. All I needed.

The couch disappeared, the plane disappeared, it was just us. With frantic movements and small pleads and soft sounds as we devoured each other with a need so strong it left room for nothing else.

But then there *was* something else.

I tried to ignore it at first. I tried to pretend it wasn't buzzing in the background, trying to stop this moment, trying to force me away from Michel, but it was persistent and got louder and louder and louder, until finally I felt it burst inside me. Like a thousand different flashes of light, so bright, so dazzling, so strong. They burnt for so long and shone so bright, that I couldn't breathe through all of that blinding light. I couldn't do anything but let it wash over me, around me, through me, until finally it all began to dim. Slowly at first, just a bit, then a little more, then I felt a door quietly open up inside my mind.

At first, just a small crack and then wider, further, until it got so far open it just tipped the scale of balance and sprang back that last little bit, to lock wide open against the wall of my mind. I couldn't close it, I couldn't reach it and I knew I needed to, because what was on the other side scared me. It scared me half to death. Scared me more than facing the Champion, scared me more than loosing Michel, scared me more than all the multitudes of problems my life existed on right now.

It scared me so much, that I woke up abruptly, from wherever the hell I had been, with a gasp and reached blindly out for something to anchor me. Thankfully finding Michel, who was looking down at me with concern written all over his face.

"What is it, *ma douce*? What happened?"

I swallowed passed the fear and managed in a strangled whisper, "I think it's another Nosferatin power, but it's strong. So, so strong." I closed my eyes again, to try to calm my ragged nerves.

He didn't say anything, just sat there holding me, stroking my arms, letting me know he was there.

Then I felt them, so many of them, everywhere. They were familiar and yet different. I knew who they were, what they were, how much Dark resided in each and every one. I'd got good at *seeking* them, seeing them, finding them, and now... now they were all looking at me.

"Oh my God, Michel." I shuddered at the vision in my mind. "Oh my God. There's just so many of them."

"Many of what, *ma douce*?" His voice so level, so contained. I could tell he was scared too. Unsure of what had my emotions so raw and full of fear.

I swallowed and forced myself to open my eyes and look at him again.

"Dark vampires. Those that I have *sought* before and always knew where they were, what they were, how Dark they were, but now.... now they know where *I* am too. And they're coming." I let him see the fear I felt inside in my eyes. "My God, Michel, they're coming.

I saw it in his eyes then too, he understood. My shields were still down, my mind still open to him and he slipped inside and saw it all.

"*Mon Dieu,*" he whispered.

Made in the USA
San Bernardino, CA
31 October 2017